FIREFLY

BY PIERS ANTHONY

Xanth
(Books One Through Thirteen)
Adept
(Books One Through Seven)
Incarnations of Immortality
(Books One Through Seven)
Bio of a Space Tyrant
(Books One Through Five)
Cluster
(Books One Through Five)
Orn
(Books One Through Three)
Tarot
Macroscope
Mute
Battle Circle
Rings of Ice
Prostho Plus
Shade of the Tree
Ghost
Anthonology
But What of Earth?
Hasan
Race Against Time
Steppe
Triple Detente
Bio of an Ogre
Balook
Chthon Phthor
Total Recall
Pornucopia

FIREFLY

Piers Anthony

WILLIAM MORROW AND COMPANY, INC.
New York

Recognizing the importance of preserving what has been written, it is the policy of William Morrow and Company, Inc., and its imprints and affiliates to have the books it publishes printed on acid-free paper, and we exert our best efforts to that end.

Library of Congress Cataloging-in-Publication Data

Anthony, Piers.
    Firefly / Piers Anthony.
p. cm.
I. Title.
PS3551.N73F5 1990   813'.54   90-61708
ISBN 0-688-09705-7

Printed in the United States of America

First Edition

1 2 3 4 5 6 7 8 9 10

BOOK DESIGN BY PAUL CHEVANNES

FIREFLY

❖ 1 ❖

SKIN AND BONES, literally. The skin was like parchment, crinkled and collapsed, draped over the skull, limbs, rib cage, backbone, and pelvis within the clothing. It was as if a giant snake had swallowed a man, digested him but not his clothing, and shed its skin, leaving only the bones within it.

Geode shook his head as he gazed at it. This was the same effect he had seen with animals, but on a larger scale. This time the remains were human. The figure lay supine, arms slightly spread, face turned to the side, as if sleeping. The clothing seemed undisturbed, except that the fly of the trousers was open, as if the man had been urinating when abruptly shriveled.

It was recent. The bones might have endured a long time, but the skin should have rotted away soon enough. It overlay the brown bed of pine needles beneath a leaning tree, and a few green blades of grass. On the left wrist was a watch whose time was current. Lying nearby was a modern sport rifle. A hunter, illegal on at least two grounds: this was posted property, and it was out of season.

He stooped to peer more closely at the face. It was grotesque. The skin was almost colorless, hanging in wrinkles over the nasal cavity and the gaunt jawbone and teeth. The eye sockets were glazed over, but no eyeballs remained, just the glaze. It was as if some thin lacquer or fixative had been sprayed over the body just before the contents had been removed, leaving only the shell. What natural process could account for this?

Geode felt a reaction. He was getting an erection. Astonished, he froze in place. Did this macabre sight somehow turn him on? He had heard of this in some men, but had never experienced it himself.

He stood upright and backed away. This body would have to be reported. The unnatural death of a man was always a notable occurrence. But first he would complete his rounds. Perhaps he would be able to spot where the man had come from.

He returned to his bicycle and resumed his ride along the forest path. He was near the northwest corner of the ranch, where a development was approaching. Its lightly tarred dirt roads extended outward like the strands of a spiderweb, terminating abruptly at the fence that marked the boundary of the square mile that was known as the Middle Kingdom, after its reclusive oriental owner. Sometimes illegal hunters drove up to the blank dead-ends, parked, and climbed through the fence to poach deer.

That was one reason Geode was here. His employer regarded the ranch as a wildlife sanctuary, and wanted no intrusions. He was not, as Geode understood it, a wildlife enthusiast; it was just a pretext to maintain privacy. The Middle Kingdom was registered and managed as a 600-acre tree farm, which Geode understood cut its taxes to an eighth of what they might otherwise have been. Since intruders could build fires or damage trees, Geode's job was to patrol the property and to report anything he deemed to be worth reporting. But since his employer did not like to be bothered with trifles, Geode was supposed to do his best to resolve any problems by himself.

In short, he was to treat the ranch as if it were his own. These were his trees and his animals, and he watched constantly over them. This was in effect his kingdom. He liked it that way.

He came to the fence. Sure enough, there was a parked pickup truck. It was empty, and locked. The man had stopped here, squeezed between the strands of the barbed wire, gone on in to poach—and died mysteriously.

Geode had no sympathy for the hunter. His affinity was with the wildlife. But the death was both strange and gruesome, and it made him queasy in the stomach. Coupled with the similar corpse of the rabbit he had seen the week before, it bothered him. He had not reported the rabbit, but this he would have to put on record. He might value a rabbit more than a poacher, but others did not.

He returned to the bike and pedaled on south. In due course he intersected the entry driveway and shifted to top gear on the asphalt, picking up speed. A gopher turtle at the edge of the road gazed at him, pondered, and pulled in its head as he passed. "Hello, friend," he called reassuringly, but he was beyond before the turtle could answer. He felt guilty about that, but there was no help for it, this time. Midday in the heat was the time for turtles, just as dawn and dusk were the times for rabbits. All of them were relatively tame, for they were not molested here. The drive was fenced on either side, but the animals could handle the fences, and claimed to like the open corridor.

He followed the road half a mile down, past young slash pines, old live oaks, mixed magnolias, and reclining palmettos, until it curved up a slight hill to the house. He parked the bike at the lesser entry to the side, and used his key to open the door. As he did so, the steady sound of the security alarm came on. He walked to the keypad set inside the main door and punched in the defuse code: 1206. It was the year that Jenghiz Khan was proclaimed supreme leader of all the Mongols. An awareness of Asian history was helpful here in the Middle Kingdom.

Then he called 800-555-1369 (the accession of Tamerlane) to report to his employer. How many numbers Middleberry had he didn't know, but this one was reserved for calls from this address only.

He got an answering machine. No identity was given; there was only a beep. That was standard. "I found a dead man," Geode said. "Strange circumstance. I need instructions soon." That was all; he was not supposed to waste words. Indeed, he never called unless there was something significant to report. He left routine reports on the local answering machine for Middleberry to pick up at his convenience.

He had no notion where Middleberry was; it could be anywhere in the world, the call transferred to his phone by satellite. It might be a day before he received the callback, or it might be minutes. He would remain at the house until it came; that was part of the deal, when he made such a report. His time was worth nothing, compared to that of his employer.

The phone rang thirty seconds after he had hung up. It was Mid, of course; this line had no other connection. He lifted the receiver. "Geode."

"Detail," the slightly thin voice said.

"Northwest sector, near the development. I conjecture that a hunter

parked at the fence, went inside, and suffered some kind of malady
while taking a piss. He fell on his back, and something dehydrated
him. The body is undisturbed, but nothing remains except clothing,
rifle, watch, skin, and the skeleton. It happened within the past day,
maybe at night. No evidence of violence, no tracks other than his own.
I have not touched the body, and have reported it only to you."

"I will investigate. Hide the body safely. Take the car to an isolated
waterfront and throw the key in the water. Do not be observed."

Geode hesitated. If this was not an illegal procedure, it was bordering on it. Yet if he refused, he would be fired. Mid did not fool with
employees.

"You have a problem, George?" Now the vague oriental accent was
more pronounced, signifying the man's irritation. There was also a
warning: Mid used his given name only when what Mid said was to be
ignored or denied. Geode would do the same, addressing him as
Middleberry only if someone were with him, overhearing the conversation, in that way warning his employer to say nothing private.

But in this case he had to skirt the warning. "Yes, Mid. The authorities may think I killed him. With my record—"

"I will protect you, Geode."

That decided him. He owed everything to his employer, including
blind loyalty; that had been clear from the outset. "I will do it. Do you
want a subsequent report?"

"Only in the event of a new development. Is there anything you
need?"

That was Mid's way of offering a reward, which was in turn his
indication of pleasure in Geode's performance. "No, Mid." What
Geode truly desired, not even Mid could provide.

The connection broke. Mid did not waste time with amenities.

Geode got right on it. He put on a knapsack, donned heavy work
gloves, put in a folding shovel, and went out. He had cooled off in the
intermission in the air conditioning; now he felt the rising heat of the
Florida day. He rode the bike rapidly up the drive and off it at the turn,
shifting to a lower gear and crunching over sand and twigs as fast as he
could. The bicycle had fifteen speeds and wide tires; it was made for
this. Mid would have provided him with a motorcycle or a helicopter
if he had wanted them, but Geode preferred the quiet and efficient
bicycle. It let him be closer to nature, so that he could talk with the
animals without alarming them, and it didn't require trips into town
for gasoline.

He stopped at the body. He found the pocket containing the keys, and carefully worked them out without disturbing the rest. Again he experienced an erection, and he wondered about the skeleton's open fly. *Had* it been urination? Then he looped around to the truck, picking trails that would not show his tires. He hoped no one else had spied the vehicle.

He was in luck; there was no sign of activity. He used the key to unlock the door, then checked the back. There was a canvas bag, such as might be used to haul the stripped carcass of a deer. He took it out, wadded it into his knapsack, and took that over the fence, hiding it in the concealed crotch of a twisting live oak tree.

A squirrel was watching him alertly. "Don't tell it's here," Geode said, and winked. The squirrel nodded and moved on up the branch.

He returned to the truck, put his light bike carefully in the back, got in, fastened the seat belt, and turned the key in the ignition. He wasn't much for powered vehicles, but he did know the rules of their operation. The motor caught immediately; it was a good machine. Better than its owner, he thought with cynical bemusement. It had four-wheel drive and automatic shift. He was used to gearshift, but was able to figure out the principle: R for reverse and D for drive.

He backed it cautiously onto the road and turned. By the time he had maneuvered it to face the other way, he had a reasonable feel for its mechanism. He drove it slowly down the road, marveling at its clutchless shifts.

He took it down-country toward Inverness, then east on Turner Camp Road until it dead-ended at the river. His luck held; there were no other cars there. He pulled the truck off the turning circle, parked it close to the water, got out, locked it, and lifted the bike out of the back. He walked it beside the river, then hurled the key into the murky water. Then he got on and pedaled away.

He was thoroughly sweaty by the time he returned to the ranch, for the day was typically hot and he had expended a lot of energy riding rapidly along back roads. He had taken a circuitous route so that anyone who saw him would not realize where he had come from or where he was going. Cyclists were not uncommon here, and they did prefer the back roads so as not to be endangered by traffic. Chances were that no one would remember his passage, if they noted it at all.

He came to the spot where the truck had been parked. There was still no sign of attention; as far as he knew, it was a clean job. He lifted the bike over the barbed wire, climbed through himself, fetched the knapsack, and rode back toward the body.

It remained undisturbed. He laid the bag on the ground and lifted the boots, putting them in. The body was both light and cohesive, no trouble at all to move. He had to fold it, which was awkward in the bag; he had to haul it out, push it into a crude fetal position, and work that into the opening. Again he found himself getting an erection, and again was repulsed. He was no necrophiliac and no homosexual, and this disgusted him.

Once the body was in, he set the bag aside and rearranged the pine needles, covering the traces. No casual passer would realize that this site had ever been disturbed, and after the next rain it would be just about impossible to tell.

He tied the closed bag to the top of his knapsack and donned the whole. It required some adjustment, but in this manner he was able to carry the bag on his back while riding the bike. All he needed was muscle and endurance, and he had those.

He headed east, winding toward the old limerock mine pit. This was the best place to hide something, for even if a person strayed onto the posted property, he was unlikely to go in there. Geode had explored the pits as a matter of policy and curiosity, wanting to know everything about the land for which he was caretaker. He knew their recesses. Now that knowledge was handy.

He came into the young section of the tree farm. Here there were two-year-old longleaf pine seedlings, still looking much like grass. Longleaf was different from other pines; it did not form a main stem until it was ready to grow rapidly. It gathered mass below the ground, and then shot up quickly. This seemed to help protect it from the ravages of wildfires.

Near the pit was a copse of larger slash pine. Once the full tract had been slash, but the soil and moisture were wrong in this section, and it hadn't done well. Mid had had it taken down and replaced with longleaf, which was expected to do better. He had left some of the slash at the fringe of the mine, where it seemed to have better fortune.

Geode stopped at the brink and dismounted. He leaned the bike against a slash pine and started down. There was a fifty-foot drop-off, but this was readily bypassed where an old mining ramp descended. Everything was overgrown with bushes and small trees now, but it was passable to a man on foot. The tops of grown trees were visible beyond

the thickets at the verge; it had been several decades since the mine had
been worked.

He wound down to the bottom, then around to a cul-de-sac sheltered by a truly formidable thicket; only a really determined intruder
would come in here. He laid the bag within this. There was no need
to cover it, as it would not be visible from above, and there was no
strong odor; even animals would probably leave it alone, as there was
nothing for them to eat. He had brought the shovel, but didn't need it,
which was just as well. The job was done.

He withdrew from the thicket, and his erection finally subsided. He
climbed back to the surface, making sure he had left no obvious traces.
He rode the bicycle around the mine, taking a different route back.
There was no sign of any other human activity.

The chime sounded: eight notes. That meant that someone was at
the main gate, three quarters of a mile distant.

Geode pressed the admittance button, then went out into the afternoon heat to see who arrived. He could have ignored it, pretending
that he wasn't here, but that wasn't his way; he needed to know whatever went on at or near the ranch so that he could guard against
trouble.

Soon a vehicle came into view and rolled up the slight hill to the
house. Geode's stomach tightened when he saw that it was a sheriff's
car. Had they traced the dead man to this property after all?

The driver parked and got out. He was a solid man of about forty,
sweaty in his uniform. He was not the one Geode knew. That might
or might not be bad news.

"Hi!" the man said, approaching and shoving out his hand. "I'm
Frank Tishner, deputy sheriff." He was pale of hair and eye, but
evidently no one to fool with; Geode could read the little signals of
toughness despite the superficially breezy manner. This was someone
who didn't let go readily when crossed.

Geode took the hand; there wasn't much way to avoid it. "George
Demerit, caretaker for the Middle Kingdom."

"So I've heard. Look, I won't keep you long. There's been something going on, and we're trying to run it down. Have you seen
anything unusual recently?"

He knew! But that was fear rather than certainty; how could he
know? "Like what?"

"Well, there've been some bones turning up, animals'. Maybe a voodoo cult, we don't know. You seen anything like that?"

Geode thought quickly, and decided on a compromise. "Yes, I found a rabbit. Bones—and fur. I thought it was an old body, but I hadn't seen it there before."

Tishner nodded. "That's it. Was it where people go?"

"No. I patrol the ranch every day. I saw it beside one of my bike trails. No one else goes there; it's my business to keep them out."

"Could a cultist have sneaked in and left it there?"

Geode shrugged. "Maybe. But I saw no tracks. I don't think anyone was there." Indeed, the rabbit had mystified him; it had seemed like a natural death, yet was so unnatural.

Tishner turned to gaze at the forest ringing the house. "Any domestic animals here?"

"Several burros and ponies who run wild. Why?"

"If this thing spreads to larger animals, we want to know. Can't tell if it's a disease or what."

A disease! That hadn't occurred to him. Mid wouldn't like that on the ranch. Were there any diseases that caused erections? That was disquieting! "I'll let you know."

"Thanks. Here's my card." Tishner produced the card and proffered it. Then he returned to the car, and paused. "Oh, by the way, you seen any hunters around here?"

Geode, relaxing, was caught off guard. "Uh, hunters? No. The property's posted."

"Okay." The deputy sheriff slid into his car.

❖ 2 ❖

FRANK TISHNER STARTED the motor and pulled the car around the paved loop and back up the drive. It was good to get back in the air conditioning; the day was sweltering, especially here by the lake. This was a beautiful forest property, with the drive lined with oaks, pines, and wild magnolias and fenced throughout. Must've cost a fortune just for the paving, and more for that huge house! But the absentee owner was said to have that fortune; indeed, to be rich beyond imagining. Who knew how many such retreats he had scattered around the world, all in readiness just in case he should one day choose to make a call?

That Demerit, the caretaker—funny character. He seemed to live alone, just cruising the property, watching it all the time, and no doubt reporting the fall of every leaf to his boss. Why Middleberry would want to maintain such premises virtually unused, or why Demerit would be satisfied to go it alone like that, was beyond Frank's understanding. But that wasn't his business.

What was his business was this mysterious plague of odd animal deaths—and the disappearance of a hunter. Frank had learned to judge reactions, so he could pretty well tell when a man was speaking the truth and when he wasn't. Demerit had been nervous, but had told the truth about the rabbit. He had lied about the hunter.

Frank stopped at the gate, which had closed after he entered. He rolled down the window and reached out to touch the signal button. In a moment the gate opened, as Demerit gave it the command from the house. One could only envy affluence like this! He pulled on through, and watched the gate swing closed in his rearview mirror. It was a private ranch, sure enough.

It was getting late, and he had paperwork to handle before he quit. He headed for the office down on Cooter Pond.

Frank had known there was something funny about the hunter's absence because he had questioned the woman on Turner Camp Road who had reported the parked pickup. She had sworn that the vehicle hadn't been there overnight. Now it was there, and if it belonged to a hunter, she wanted to know did the hunter have a license, because this was out of season now.

Frank had gone out immediately when that call came, because they already had a missing-person report on a camper from St. Pete. Yeah, sure—camping with no sleeping bag or tent, and a quality rifle. He had checked the truck, and it matched; it was the one. Looked as if the guy had parked at the river and gone hunting along the shore, fallen in, and drowned. A fairly clear-cut case, and probably served him right.

Except for two things. No body—and that woman's claim about the truck. The call about the camper had come in at the crack of dawn; he was supposed to be home by midnight, not staying late. That matched nicely with hunting: best time to do it was dusk, when it was legal to shoot deer—when deer were in season. It also meant the carcass wouldn't be visible in the darkness. So he had been out hunting, and gotten in trouble himself, and his wife had lost her nerve and called. But the pickup truck had come here later in the morning. That meant either that it was a false alarm, and the guy was just running late—or that he was gone, and someone else had driven his truck. Which in turn smelled just a bit like foul play.

If they found a body in the river, they could determine the cause of death, and have the answer about the nature of the mishap. Accident, or murder? How long before? If it turned out to have happened during the night, then they would have to decide who else had driven his truck, and why. But Frank didn't think they would find a body in the river, because why should it be there—if the truck had been driven from somewhere else after he died? He must've died at that other place, and the river was just a false lead.

Frank doubted that the demise would turn out to be natural. More likely it was an accident or a killing. In either case, the involvement of another party was suspicious. Frank felt challenged by such mysteries. They excited him. Maybe it was compensation for the dullness of his home life.

Meanwhile, there was the other matter. Dead animals, mostly small, but getting larger, turning up as bags of bones, no flesh remaining. Animals could be killed, sure, but how had these been so thoroughly defleshed? Ants could pick bones clean, but they didn't leave the skin intact. It happened fast too; he now knew that from life to bonebag occurred in less than twenty-four hours. Perhaps a lot less.

He had picked up on this about three months ago, soon after he transferred to this region. He had noted it as an anomaly, and been intrigued, and started collecting information on it, in the course of his regular duties. Data was spotty, but there seemed to be a pattern of such deaths starting several months before in neighboring Marion County and proceeding here to Citrus County. The rabbit which Demerit had admitted to was confirmation that it had arrived here. Whatever it was. Frank wished he had a pretext to drop everything else and follow it up.

But he couldn't. He was in effect on probation here, and if he messed up, he would be out of a job and perhaps out of law enforcement entirely. His hands tightened on the wheel as he thought about it; he had never been able to abolish the anger. But he had a wife to support, and he couldn't handle another major disruption. He had to tide through this one, no matter how angry it made him. So he did his job and kept his eyes open, and if he was lucky, maybe in time he'd be vindicated and have his curiosity satisfied too.

His thought was interrupted by a 25: a fire. It was in his territory. "Ten twenty-six," he said, acknowledging, and headed for it. As he did so, he smiled briefly, remembering the half-humor that crept into this efficient numerical system of classification and response. Ten forty-two was "Out of Service at Home," so naturally when a deputy's wife was taking his time it was ten forty-two and a half. Frank never had need of that designation; his wife had no interest or involvement in his business.

Several days later Frank got another clue.

The matter of the missing hunter remained unsolved; they had been unable to locate either the man or his body. Such things occurred distressingly often, though it was not gladly bruited about; the body could be anywhere, awaiting some chance discovery by kids on a picnic or a girl picking wild berries. By that time it would be impossible to track down the murderer. It could be a local property owner who didn't like hunters, so took one out and moved his truck somewhere else to divert suspicion. Or it could be a marijuana farmer: if the hunter had stumbled into his devastatingly booby-trapped little plantation in the state forest, there might have been nothing for it but to bury the body. The illicit proprietors of such enterprises were known to use guns connected to trip-wires, or covered pits filled with punji sticks. Veterans who learned their business in the Orient during war didn't fool around. Frank had done what he could on the case, insufficient as that was, and made his report.

But his private quest got abruptly warmer. It happened unexpectedly. He went out on a routine call and struck a kind of paydirt. That was sometimes the serendipitous way of these things.

The call was from one Jade Brown, evidently a country housewife. Neighbors had played some sort of prank on her, only she wasn't laughing. They had flung a dead raccoon in her yard. Or something; she wasn't sure exactly what it was, but she was upset.

It took him forever to locate the isolated address. Asphalt degenerated into packed dirt, and thence into loose dirt. He hoped it wouldn't become sugar sand; he didn't have four-wheel drive, and that stuff could mire an ordinary vehicle.

The road made a right-angle turn, and then another, stair-stepping its way into some obscure alcove off the Tsala Apopka chain of lakes and marshes. Marsh bordered it, and sometimes water covered over by water lilies. The population of this county was increasing about as rapidly as in any region of the nation, but some alcoves remained relatively wild, and this was one of them. It was hard for developers to get a real foothold in marsh, partly because of the new wetlands laws.

Frank finally got there and pulled into the decrepit yard. This was definitely a remote site. Apparently there had been plans for a development, but the developer had gone bankrupt or lost interest, and never followed up. The tenants, stuck with dirt instead of pavement, had simply hung on, unable to afford a move. The house was a mobile home set on concrete blocks, with weeds growing around and under.

He saw the animal as he got out of the car. It did indeed seem to be what was left of a raccoon, for the black fur mask was there. But now it was only a pelt, and not a good one, for there really was no hide under the fur. Just a membrane sagging over the bones.

The woman came out. She was nondescript, beyond youth, and in worn clothing, her hair a sweaty straggle. No air conditioning here! That trailer-house probably got hot as hell when the sun touched it. "That's it, officer," she said, glancing distastefully at the remains. "It was there when I came out this morning, and it wasn't there last night. Someone must have baked it in an oven and then tossed it here."

"I don't think so," Frank said. "I talked with a man a few days ago who had seen a rabbit in the same condition. There have been a number of such reports over the past few weeks. It seems to be something that happens to them on their own." He squatted down to inspect the thing more closely—and felt himself getting an erection. He stood again, quickly, to avoid embarrassing himself. "Why don't I just take this off your hands, ma'am? If it happens again, you just call."

"Take it away!" she agreed, relieved. He saw now that under that homely outfit she had a rather petite and healthy body. He chided himself; was he so hard up for love that he was seeking any pretext to get excited?

He fetched a plastic bag from the car and managed to set it over the bag of bones and close it without touching anything. He picked up the bundle.

"That other report," she said. "Who—?"

"Caretaker of the Middle Kingdom Ranch," he said, seeing no harm in the information. After all, this was nothing official. "It's not far from here, as the crow flies."

"I've heard of it," she said. "Thank you for coming, officer."

"That's what I'm here for," he said, and got into his car. He was concealing his jubilation at finally getting direct evidence of what he had only heard described before. A bag of bones: indeed it was literal! Now maybe he could get a lab analysis—in the line of duty.

❖ 3 ❖

NONE WATCHED THE sheriff's car depart with mixed feelings. She had called about the horrible offering in the yard, but her real need was for some relief from the drudgery of her life. Her husband's job kept him away most of the day, and his supposedly secret affair with Helen kept him away much of the night, and when he was home he might as well have been away. Her son wasn't much better; he treated her like a perpetual maid while he read his comics and talked on the phone with his friends. Neither of them seemed to regard her as a person. She wished she could just step out of her situation and into a new and better one, like a peasant girl adopted by a royal family.

The phone rang. That would be Paris, to tell her he would be late getting home. He was good about that—so she wouldn't get nervous and notify the police he was missing. The last thing he wanted was a police search for him!

She lifted the receiver. "Yes?"

"I'm staying over at Abner's tonight, okay, mom? Thanks." He hung up.

Not Paris, but Jame, her son. Same story, only he wasn't having an affair. Not at age ten. She hoped. Actually she wouldn't have begrudged him an affair, but it could be awkward. The world did not understand about the sexual needs of the young.

Her thought about her husband resumed. The Other Woman's real name wasn't Helen, of course; she didn't know her identity, and didn't care to. Œnone had just named her that, in her mind, for good reason. She had rehearsed the whole scenario in her imagination often, but had no one to tell it to. So for now it was enough just to remember that in mythology, Paris had deserted his wife Œnone for the beauteous Helen. Perhaps the names didn't match in real life, but they fitted perfectly in her pained fancy.

The phone rang again. This time it was Paris, and sure enough, he would be late returning: don't wait up.

"Then sleep on the couch!" she snapped, her anger overflowing, and slammed down the receiver.

She was immediately sorry she had done it. It wasn't that he didn't deserve it, but rather that she had given herself away. She should have remained in control. Now he might seem to have some slight justification for his infidelity, and she hated that. She had never denied him sexually; indeed, she had offered him everything, constantly, and kept herself in shape to make it appealing. He had simply grown bored with her, as everyone did. That was her curse: to be the proverbial petunia in an onion patch, and to have the onions ignore her.

She returned to her laundry, a seemingly perpetual chore. Her husband and son might seldom make it home, but their dirty clothing did! Her whole life was a chore. How had she gotten into this rut, when she had so much to offer? Her great hopes for life had deflated like the body of that raccoon that had appeared on her lawn. The deputy said that there had been other cases, such as one on that big Middle Kingdom Ranch, so maybe it wasn't juvenile malice. That was both reassuring and alarming. If kids weren't doing it, what was?

A shiver ran through her. Was there a monster of some kind roaming the area? That was all she needed, out here on a nowhere cul-de-sac!

But a monster that ate a raccoon might not be a threat to her. Anyway, Donjon would stand guard. In fact, it might be a good idea to bring him in the house tonight, just to be sure. Or maybe right now.

She went out and around to the back where the big mongrel dog was chained. She patted the shaggy head and unsnapped the chain. "Come on in, Donjon; I need a good guard tonight!" Actually, he tended to sleep so soundly at night that only something extraordinary could make

him stir, let alone growl, but he was still a good deal better than
nothing.

In the evening Donjon was restless. She took him out for a nature
walk, and he sniffed avidly at the spot where the raccoon had been, but
did not seek to explore beyond the yard. Yet he remained uneasy,
getting up frequently, sniffing something in the air, and lying down
again unsatisfied. What was bothering him? A bitch in heat somewhere, too distant to leave a clear signal? The dog did seem to be a bit
aroused. Well, if the bitch showed up, Œnone would let him at her;
she would not deny any creature his sexual satisfaction.

Œnone was, by her own observation, unusual among women in
that she did not merely tolerate sex, she craved it. But at age thirty-five,
with an indifferent husband, she was reduced to her own devices. It
was at night that she hated Helen most, not because she had tempted
Paris into infidelity—he needed little temptation, just acquiescence—
but because there was not enough left over for Œnone. Paris typically
came home and conked out, his battery discharged, and nothing
she could do could recharge it. He just wanted to be fed and left
alone.

Fortunately, Œnone had an acute imagination. She could lie down
and give it play and in due course become quite excited. With a little
help she could climax. But there was so much more to sex than mere
climax. She wanted the interaction, the hunger of the male, the passion and the gratitude. She wanted to be held close, to be desired, to
have her sleep interrupted by his recurring hunger for her body and her
love. Paris had always been a loss in that larger sense; once he got it off,
he slept. She wondered what Helen saw in him. Certainly he had no
flair of personality, and he was, at age forty, no handsome hunk of a
man.

How had she gotten herself married to such a creature? Paris never
had had much more to recommend him than a regular job as a
carpenter. She knew why he had married her: he had knocked her up,
being more amorous in courtship than ever since. But why had *she*
married *him*? She had known from the start that he was no phenomenal prize.

Actually, she knew why. She just didn't like to rehearse it. She had
been so desperate for a man of her own that she had taken what offered
without much question. She could not say even at this point that she

had been mistaken. Would any other man have married her? If only her desire had been matched by glamour!

So she watched the TV, then stepped over the snoring dog and made her way to the bedroom. She locked the door, making good on her threat to make Paris sleep on the couch. Some threat, when she craved his passion far more than he craved hers! She couldn't even assert herself without messing it up.

She stripped naked, avoided the mirror, lay down, and put her imagination to work. In her fancy she was twenty years old, ultimately luscious, and the object of the insatiable desire of every man who beheld her. Three naked youths were fighting to see which one would have the first chance to clasp her body to his, their penises so hard they hurt. If they didn't settle it quickly, more than one of them would spurt on the floor.

She settled it for them. "You first," she murmured, indicating the one whose erection seemed about to burst. "Then you—and then you. Be quick about it!"

The first man leaped for her, too far gone to indulge in any pre-liminaries; he simply lodged and thrust, his member geysering the moment it touched; he slid in on the lubrication of his own flowing semen. That had been close!

In a moment he was spent, but she was not. "Give the next a chance," she told him, and he rolled off just in time to avoid getting inadvertently sodomized by the too-eager penis of the next-in-line. This one managed to complete one full thrust before spewing out his fluid. Then he had to move over for the third, who had time for several thrusts in the well-greased channel before shooting off his own load. There was so much of it that it foamed out and around, dripping to the mattress.

But that was only the warm-up. She was feeling unusually sexy tonight, even for her; normally she preferred some pretense of restraint in her dream men before they seduced her.

She took on the first man again. Now, so soon after his first effort, he was much slower, and he gave her a lot of attention before he was able to climax again. He kissed her breasts and ran his hands over her buttocks as his member hardened, and finally, gently, but with infi-nitely mounting passion, he entered and pumped and climaxed.

Still she needed more. She took the second man, and climbed on him, and teased him into erection, and brought him to a pitch that exceeded the first session, until he begged her to finish him off. But she made him wait a bit more, until his desperation for the culmination was agonizing. Then she lowered herself on him, and clamped her legs tightly together, and hung on while he bucked and jetted. "Oh God, oh God, oh God!" he cried, clasping her to his muscular young torso with all his strength, torn by the delicious urgency of it.

By the time she got through the second round with the third man, he was blissfully unconscious and she was asleep. It hadn't been the best of nights, but neither had it been the worst. The three had done their best; it was not their fault if they were unable to match her level of sexuality. They were, after all, mere dummies.

Still, she would have thrown it all away, in favor of one meaningful kiss by a real live man she respected. But where was she ever to find such a man—and if she did, why would he be interested in her? There was the crux of her humiliation. The only man with whom she had ever shared true love was long since dead. Because of her.

She woke at dawn, as she always did, not needing an alarm. She got up, used the toilet, washed up, and dressed quickly. She was an early bird, and she liked to see the sunrise. She brushed out her messy hair, though that seemed pointless; who cared how she looked?

Had Paris come home at all? Sometimes he didn't. She would be disappointed if he hadn't, because her ploy of locking the bedroom door would have been wasted, trumped by his high card. Even though it was a foolish gesture, it would be better to have it properly made. Her daytime satisfactions were few enough as it was. She was still feeling sexy, despite her amours of the night, but knew that her chances of doing anything about it were something on the nether side of nil.

She entered the living room and paused, uncertain about what she was seeing. There was something on the floor, but it wasn't Donjon. Or was it? She peered more closely at the mounded fur. Then she screamed.

It was the dog—reduced in the manner of the raccoon. His eyes were thinly filmed sockets, with the gray-white of bone beyond. His fur lay piled on a skeletal frame. There was no flesh remaining.

The monster had come and consumed her dog—while she lay sleeping in the next room. What would have happened if she had not locked the door?

Paris had not come home; the couch was bare. Now she was relieved. She didn't want him or her son to see this. She wasn't sure why, and didn't investigate her motive. She just knew that this matter had abruptly become far more serious, and she had better keep it quiet until she knew how to handle it. She was oddly calm, her emotions insulated after the first scream. What was she to do?

She 1·.·ded to bury the dog. She didn't want the deputy coming around and seeing this, either. So she fetched a shovel and managed to lift the thing onto it, and carry it grotesquely dangling outside. The worst of it was that she felt phenomenally erotic as she carried the inert hulk. She was fascinated by sex, sure enough, but never with animals or with the dead; this was bizarre! Was she going crazy?

She set it down and used the shovel to dig a hole in her flower garden, deep enough to hide what it had to. Then she put the bag of bones in, and covered it over, spreading the extra dirt around so that there was no mound. She scooped leaves and bits of grass across, so that there was no sign of disturbance. She had concealed the evidence.

Then she went inside and checked the floor. The thing had come up cleanly; there was no trace remaining. Even so, she didn't want to walk there. She hauled a small spiral rug over and laid it over the spot. It was done.

Now she paused to ponder. She had reported the raccoon the moment she spied it; why had she done the opposite for this more serious case? She hadn't paused before, but now she needed to understand her motive before she went further.

Well, she had thought the other was a prank, so she had seized on the pretext to involve the authorities. It was her husband she wanted to report, so that the deputy would burst in on him amidst his intimacy with Helen, and he would have to yank out his laboring member and cover up while she tunneled under the sheet, blushing all the way to her tender derriere, which couldn't quite make it under cover and was smiling invitingly at the deputy. "We had a complaint about something foul here, and I guess I see it," the deputy would remark, staring at the burning crevice.

"Well, you see, officer, it was like this. She needed some carpentry done on her bed, and—"

"Looks more like carpentry on her ass," the deputy would respond with a knowing smirk. Helen would die of embarrassment, or maybe bare-ass-ment, and never speak to Paris again, let alone show him her cute pink bottom.

But that was a daydream, and of course it had come to nothing. But Donjon's horrible demise was reality, and it had happened right inside her house. If she had called the sheriff's office this time, it wouldn't have been Helen's pert buns the deputy saw, but the gruesome remainder of the dog. He would have Questions, and might even suspect Œnone of doing it. By the time that was untangled, Paris would be in on it, and forewarned, and there would be no chance to nab him with his doxie.

But that wasn't the whole of it. She hadn't wanted Paris to know of this, or her son, Jame. Why? Because, she realized with a chill, this was a serious threat. If it could take a dog, it might take a boy, or a man.

She sank into a chair, appalled. Did she want the monster to take her family? Daydreams were one thing, but reality was another, and she was wary of the boundary between them. She dreamed of freedom, true, but knew she would never have it. Without Paris's income she would be broke, and what would she do then? She had no love for him, but she needed him. Even his affair with Helen protected her to a degree, because it kept him honest in other respects. He paid the bills so that there would be no stink about anything; he wanted to make no disturbance that could call attention to his secret life. The plain fact was that Œnone was better off with Paris, affair and all, than she would be without him. She knew that no prince was coming to carry her away to a fairyland kingdom—and if one did, he would probably cheat on her.

She would have to warn Paris about the monster. He could decide whether to call the sheriff's office. He might prefer not to, because it would attract too much attention, but that would be his business. She would have done the right thing. It was important to do the right thing, always, regardless of one's secret thoughts; what was difficult was deciding what the right thing was.

A car pulled in in the afternoon. Œnone didn't recognize it. She noted as it turned that the plates were out-of-state. A lost tourist? No one who was anyone came here by choice!

A woman got out. She looked older than Œnone, and heavier, and she wore better clothing: the female version of a suit, which was surely oppressively hot in this climate. But what did she care? She drove an air-conditioned car.

"Mrs. Brown?" the woman inquired. She had dark brown hair and eyes that almost matched, as if God had employed the same paintbrush when coloring her genes.

Œnone nodded. Outsiders did not know her inner identity. Was this a sales representative for some exotic product? Use our Magic Creme, it will make you so incredibly sexy that you'll have to beat off men with a cattle prod. You'll have to wear a chastity belt just to get your grocery shopping done. WARNING: wash it off at night, or your husband will have a heart attack trying to copulate continuously. One woman overdosed on it, and was gang-raped at the Sunday morning church service. Another applied it by accident, thinking it was sunburn lotion, and when she went to the beach in her string bikini—

"I am May Flowers," the woman said. Apparently she was serious, for she did not smile. "I am a free-lance journalist researching a story. I understand that you found something unusual yesterday."

The raccoon! The last thing Œnone needed was a feature story on the matter! But they didn't know about the dog, and she would not tell them. Only the raccoon, which was little enough. And that other case, at the Middle Kingdom, which might serve as a suitable distraction.

So Œnone told the woman about the raccoon and the sheriff's deputy, and gave no hint of the rest of it. "The deputy said that there was a similar case at the Middle Kingdom Ranch," she concluded.

"Thank you," the woman said, making a note on her pad. "You have been very helpful."

Fat chance, Brown Eyes! "You're welcome."

Then the woman returned to her car, and it drove away, air conditioning and all. Œnone felt sweaty, but wasn't even jealous; what was the point in wishing for what would never be hers?

❖ 4 ❖

MAY FLOWERS NODDED as she drove away from the farmhouse. That woman was hiding something; she had a guilty look about her. She had been too free with details on the dead raccoon, as if covering for something else. Had there been more than one case? But why would she tell about one and not the other?

The woman's eyes had flicked to the garden beside her house, at the outset. May had not remarked on it, but had made sure to inspect that area closely while talking and listening. Sure enough, the earth had been recently disturbed, and covered over with leaves. There was no sign of a new flower put in, so something must have been buried there. What would that be?

What else but another bag of bones. Not too big, because the disturbed region wasn't large, but not that small either. The family was supposed to have a dog, but none had been in evidence; that seemed the most likely prospect.

Why would the woman choose to conceal the death of the dog, after reporting the raccoon? May could see no good reason, which suggested that there could be a bad reason. Well, she would ascertain the facts of the situation in due course.

The woman had mentioned the sheriff's deputy and the Middle Kingdom Ranch. That deputy was certainly someone to interview, but not just yet. May wanted to get as much information as she could on her own, before going to the authorities. That way she would be able to tell how much they were concealing.

Right now she was on her way to the Middle Kingdom. She had been headed there all along, but had been scouting around first. Her presence here was no coincidence; her employer had called and told her to get on it, and she had done so immediately.

As she drove, she thought about her relationship with Mid. He seemed to be oriental, though she had never actually met him. He seemed to be fabulously wealthy, but she had no concrete evidence to support that impression. He had rescued her from an awful pass, and now she worked for him and liked it.

Back in the beginning her name had been April Mays; her parents had evidently had a sense of humor that she could have lived without. They had divorced and remarried elsewhere, and she had shuttled between them, and finally gained adult status herself with relief. She had married hastily, in the belief that this would seal off her past and guarantee control over her life. She had been the classic example of the smart-woman, foolish-choice syndrome. Not just because of the name: the man she had married was named Bull Shauer, pronounced "shower," making her April Shauer. If only that had been the worst of it!

It started gradually, so that for a long time she mistook its nature and made apologies for it, thinking it was somehow her fault. But finally she recognized the pattern: spouse abuse. The man had a mean streak and an insecure streak that came out only when he knew a person well and was sure of his ground. He was a wife-beater who never hit quite hard enough to make it obvious. He built up his self-perception by beating down hers. She was stuck in the worst of marriages.

But it had taken her ten years to recognize this, and almost ten more to do something about it. First doubt, then shame, then fear had suppressed her, though she cursed herself for letting the most promising years of her life fritter away during her protracted indecision. She had cause for divorce, she knew, and for a significant settlement. But she was ashamed to admit that she had been so stupid, and if she had sued for divorce her colossal folly would have come out, and all the "I told you so's" would have their vindication. Her foolish pride had ruined her life. As his nature got worse, so did her fear of him. He would kill her. She couldn't divorce him. She had to escape him. So she had run away.

But by that time she had been thirty-seven years old.

The job market had turned out to be hellish. Theoretically there was no discrimination against prematurely aged women. In practice it meant that some other pretext was always found for denial. She had completed a college education during her childless marriage, and had worked off and on as a journalist, but now she couldn't draw on those credits. She had changed her name from April Shauer to May Flowers—who would believe it?—and gone to a state she had never been to before. That anonymity protected her from the vengeance of her supposedly wronged husband, but also made it impossible to draw on her credits. She could not seek formal employment, because she had no ID she was willing to use.

Then she realized with horror that she couldn't even renew her driver's license, because the old one would betray her identity. She was lucky she hadn't been cited for any traffic violation, or had occasion to show her license in any other connection. She was living on borrowed time in more than the monetary sense.

Had she been twenty years younger, she could have turned to prostitution. It wouldn't have been worse than her marriage. As it was, her choice seemed to be between starvation and crime.

She pondered, and came up with an alternative. She had some money—she had not been so foolish as to take off broke—and it would sustain her for a few more weeks. She got busy and researched and wrote an article, free-lance, for the local newspaper. She was competent, and the paper was small; it could use what it could get. The pay was low, but better than nothing.

She sold her car in another town, trusting that no one would do a records check that went that deep, took the money in cash, and thereafter destroyed her driver's license. She would use public transport thenceforth.

She wrote other articles and mailed them off to other papers. She did generic articles that could be sold to several noncompeting publications. She managed to finesse requests for her social security number by giving a wrong one and pleading an error of memory. She got by, barely.

The local paper offered her a job. She declined, preferring, she said, to maintain her freedom. That was true, but not in the way it was intended to sound. She would have loved the security of the regular salary, whatever the level. But not at the price of identification and discovery by her husband. So she continued to scrape along, until Mid contacted her.

He had telephoned. How he knew of her she had no idea. Perhaps he had a staff devoted to finding such things. He had offered her a job with a nominal salary and complete expenses, her confidence kept. He had repeated enough of her history so that she knew he knew her identity. He guaranteed no illegalities and no awkward favors of any type. "I am not your husband," he had said bluntly. He merely had occasional need of a competent journalist.

So she had accepted, two years ago, and it seemed in retrospect to have been the best decision of her life. When Mid had said that her expenses would be covered, he had meant all of them, and in style. She had to travel, researching obscure things for him, but she always stayed in the best hotels, not by her choice but by his. His staff made the reservations before he even notified her of the assignment. All she had to do was go.

As the assignments became more complicated, Mid sent her a credit card made out to her current name. It was like magic; there seemed to be no restriction on it. She was careful not to abuse it, of course, but she appreciated the trust. She wished her husband had been like that!

As time passed, she realized that she was helping Mid increase his fortune. She was in effect his eyewitness reporter, ferreting out details that only a journalist would think of. Not only did this provide him with a broader and deeper perspective than another might have had, it sometimes gave him the hitherto obscure key to the situation. She did have a talent for getting at the essence; it had served her well in her prior career, and it served her employer well now. None of her articles were published, but she didn't mind; she read in the newspaper of new acquisitions by Middle Kingdom Enterprises, and knew that her input had been heeded. Mid allowed her anonymity and a comfortable life-style, and she was more than satisfied.

After a year, the subject of driving had come up. He had had an assignment for her that was in the Canadian hinterlands, where there was no public transportation; she would have to drive. "But I have no license!" she protested.

"I will provide it, and the car," he said.

Sure enough, in two days both had been delivered, in the name of May Flowers. How he had done it she hesitated to imagine, but she didn't argue. She had wheels again.

The car seemed ordinary on the outside, but it had been upgraded inside. It had quality upholstery and a phenomenal motor; it was a tiger in lamb's clothing, and a wonderful pleasure to drive. She tested it briefly on a lonely highway, but her nerve gave out at ninety miles per hour, not close to its limits. Thereafter she drove sedately.

She drove to Canada and did her research and turned in her report. It was negative; what might have seemed like a promising investment was deceptive, and was no bargain. She hoped he would not be disappointed.

She drove back home and phoned the 800 number which was hers: 0618, the date of the founding of the T'ang dynasty. "Mission completed," she told the answering machine. "Where should I leave the car?"

A day later Mid called back. "Keep the car." That was all. By this time she knew him well enough, for all that she didn't know him at all, to understand that this was her reward for saving him a bundle; he had avoided a bad investment that could have cost him millions, and he rewarded well those who served him well. This beautiful machine was hers.

She had been working for Mid for two years now, and would be satisfied to continue indefinitely. She had all the independence and luxury she wanted, and was doing the kind of work she liked. The current assignment was like a southern vacation, combined with the delight of challenge and mystery.

A man's body had turned up, Mid had advised her, on his estate in central Florida. He had been reduced to skin and bones. There had been evidence of similar treatment of animals before, but this was the first human being. Her assignment had two aspects: first, to find out exactly what this was; and second, to keep his name and property out of it.

May understood. This was one of Mid's private retreats, where he could retire in perfect privacy at will. A local, state, or national story about mysterious bodies would bring a horde of curious folk, ruining it. He had probably sunk a million dollars or so into setting up this retreat, and he didn't care to have some freak scandal nullify it. Her experience in setting up her own false identity gave her empathy; one bit of news in the wrong place could destroy all that she had made.

She intended to get the full story, and to keep Mid's name and property out of it. All else was secondary.

She had researched carefully, of course, but there was little advance information to be had from afar. She would have to get close to it and develop her own leads. Meanwhile, she had three names: George Demerit, caretaker of the Middle Kingdom Ranch, who had found the body; Frank Tishner, local deputy sheriff who was investigating the matter; and Jade Brown, who had made the most recent report. One down, two to go. Already it was growing more intriguing.

She had fathomed something of the pattern of animal deaths. They had started perhaps three months ago, in the vicinity of the juncture of three counties in Florida: Marion, Sumter, and Citrus. The earliest known was in the Seven Springs vicinity, largely covered by one of the big private ranches whose proprietors discouraged intrusions by the public. She had discovered why: hunters liked to boat up Gum Slough and poach what they could along its banks, and litter along the way. Since it was legally an open-access waterway, so that boaters could not be barred, and the poachers did not do their poaching while the authorities watched, it was a problem. May's sympathy was with the property owners; they, for whatever selfish reasons, were at least protecting the environment and the wildlife. Fencing had appeared, and trees had mysteriously fallen across the river, making it barely navigable, while legal action continued. There were unverified stories of guns going off, further discouraging camping. This was a lovely wilderness region, but no place for a casual visit. It was, in fact, a subtle war zone.

Thus it was not surprising that the number or antiquity of the early animal deaths was unknown. It could have been happening for a year before the first was spied. So she knew of only the recent episodes, which were scattered and uncertain. However, there did seem to be a pattern.

Some predator, whether animal or man, had come up the river, and when the river ended in a spring, it had migrated to land. It had taken what prey it could, gradually moving as the region was depleted, and broadening its appetite. It had moved closer to the main river, the Withlacoochee, then crossed it. Now it was marauding in the wilderness regions of the Tsala Apopka chain of lakes and marshes, and had come at last to the Middle Kingdom Ranch. Where, it seemed, it had graduated to larger prey: man. Evidently it still did prey on animals too; to it, man was merely another animal. That was a bit chilling in itself.

She knew already that Mid had suffered a stroke of blind misfortune. The chances of keeping a man-killer out of the headlines were virtually nil. The best that could be hoped for was a swift stop to the

depredations so that no hue and cry developed. That meant identifying
the killer and locating it and nullifying it—soon. Was it possible? She
would do her best to find out. This had the promise of being her most
challenging assignment yet, which was an encouraging indication of
Mid's confidence in her. She would try her best to live up to it.

She arrived at the entry to the ranch, which was not that far from
Jade Brown's house; both were off State Highway 200. She drew up to
the closed gate and touched the call button. In a moment the gate
swung open, which meant that the caretaker, George Demerit, was on
duty. As the one who had reported the dead man, he should be her
most important source, if he was communicative.

The drive was beautiful. It was fenced throughout, with young pine
trees crowding close in against the road. She spied a big box tortoise
scrambling along beside the asphalt. She had always liked that kind,
perhaps because of its habit of minding its own business when challenged, closing up in its shell. There was also a magnolia tree, with a
single lovely bloom; she hadn't realized they bloomed this late. Live
oaks extended their branches over the drive, forming a canopy. Mid
certainly had taste in his private retreats; she would love to live in a
place like this!

She rounded a curve, and the house came into view at the top of a
slight hill. It was large, with two stories, and the fence which had
paralleled the road looped around it to form an immediate yard at the
crest of the hill. There was a small barn beyond, and there appeared
to be a pool enclosure behind. Not palatial, but certainly beyond the
means of a middle-class family.

A man stood at the front door, waiting for her. He looked about
thirty, with sparse brown hair and a thin body, but healthy: the runner's torso. He wore sneakers, blue jeans, and a short-sleeved gray
shirt. Not used to people; even as he waited for her, a stranger, there
was a certain diffidence, almost a fear. A loner. She would be able to
bully him to a degree, but would have to watch it; loners could be
dangerous when pressed too hard.

Her background information confirmed it. He had been pretty much
isolated all his life. The one intelligence score on record indicated an
IQ of 90, but there could have been a foul-up in the testing. Some schizoid tendency. Not aggressive, just odd. Mid must have seen qualities in
the man that others had not, exactly as he had in May herself.

She parked the car and got out. "I am looking for George Demerit,
the caretaker."

"Here," he said guardedly. He seemed ill at ease.

"I am May Flowers. I am a journalist. I work for Mid."

Her last sentence had effect; she saw him tense, then relax. "How?" he asked.

"I investigate things for him and make reports. At the moment I am investigating bags of bones."

He gazed at her, his gray eyes seeming to focus for the first time. She knew he had told nobody but Mid, so now he knew she was legitimate. But he didn't seem to know what to do.

She prompted him. "May I come in? I'm not used to this heat."

He nodded, and opened the door. She walked in and felt the chill of the air conditioning. What a relief!

Inside there was an entry hall, with a carpeted stairway up and access in three directions. The floor was teak parquet of a vintage style; either this house was older than she thought, or Mid had picked up an odd lot. She turned to the left and entered the carpeted living room. There were vertical blinds on the windows, sandalwood moiré, and the carpeting was sculptured berber. The chairs and couches were of knotty pine with rust-colored cotton cushions, except for one chair upholstered in blue; what had happened there? Overall, not as fancy as she might have expected of her employer, but it was possible that he hadn't paid attention, and had allowed the builder to put in whatever was most readily available. Men were like that. It would do, for an unoccupied domicile.

She sat, more or less forcing the man to do the same. It was evident that he was not comfortable in this part of the house; he was more of an outdoors type, leaving the interior alone except to make sure it was in good condition. "Mid told me you found a man."

"Yes."

"There seems to be a pattern of animal deaths of this nature, but this is the first man. What did you do with him?"

"I hid him."

He certainly wasn't unduly communicative! "Where?"

"Put him in the mine."

"An abandoned mine shaft?"

"Open pit."

"Won't that be seen by someone?"

"No."

"How did you deal with his truck?"

"Took it to the river, tossed the key in."

She nodded. "So the police would assume he drowned."

He nodded.

"I think I had better see the body." She hardly relished the notion, but she knew that she would see details that others did not.

He shrugged.

She stood, seizing the initiative again. "How far is this mine?"

"Mile."

"Can we drive there?"

"Halfway."

"Then let's drive halfway." It was a chore getting anything out of this tight-lipped man; he seemed to want only to be left alone. It would be pointless to ask him for a full description of the body; he would just say, laconically, "Dead," or something similarly obvious. "I'll drive."

She walked to the door, and he followed. The heat smote her again as she opened it. How had anyone lived here before air conditioning?

Demerit hung back. Then she realized that he was punching in the security code, arming the alarm system so that no one could enter the house in his absence without setting it off. That was, of course, his job: to see that nothing happened to Mid's property.

There was a whistling. Then the man stepped out and drew the door closed, and the sound stopped. He brought out a key and locked the door. That made a triple defense in his absence: the distant front gate, which had to be keyed open, and the mechanical lock, and the security system. She would feel safe in a place like this, even if it was isolated.

She got into the driver's seat. Demerit walked around and took the other seat. The car was an oven; five minutes could do it in weather like this. She started the motor, and in a moment the car air conditioning came on, delivering a wonderfully cold blast of air.

She pulled the car around the paved loop. "North?"

He nodded. So she drove north, back along the lovely lane. This would be very much like paradise, if only it weren't so hot! Probably it was very nice, indeed, in the winter season.

"Here," he said as they approached the right-angle turn half a mile along, near where she had seen the tortoise.

She drew to the side at that corner, leaving room for another vehicle to pass hers, though she doubted there would be any other. How would it get in? She turned off the motor with regret. She knew she wasn't going to enjoy a half-mile walk in the heat, but duty was duty.

They got out. Demerit led the way north, squeezing through an almost invisible gap in a hedgelike fence and forging onward. She tried to follow, but the prickly foliage caught at her suit. She definitely wasn't dressed for this, but was determined to see the body. "Slower!" she called, lest he travel blithely on out of sight.

He paused while she hauled herself through. It hadn't occurred to him to wait, before she called to him, and it didn't occur to him to try to help her now. She realized that there was no malice here; he just didn't seem to relate to others well. She had not encountered a man quite like him before.

"I am not used to this pace or this heat," she said. "You will have to proceed slowly enough to accommodate me."

He nodded, and set a slower pace.

This was better, but still her feminine shoes slipped in the bare patches of sand, and burrs caught in her stockings. She was going to be a mess before this was done! Well, she had asked for it; she should have come prepared. It was no good deciding that Demerit should have warned her about the roughness of the terrain; he simply didn't tune in to the needs of others.

"You like this work?" she inquired a bit breathlessly.

"Yes."

"You are mostly alone?"

"Yes."

"With the animals?"

Now he smiled. "Yes."

"It must have been horrible, finding that rabbit."

He considered. "I like them, but I like the fox too."

"Oh, I'd love to see a fox!"

"There's one, but I hardly ever see her. The rabbits are out all over the road, in the morning."

"So you accept nature's way. Rabbits are nice, but the fox has to live too."

"Yes." But though the word was brief, his attitude had warmed. She had shown some understanding and appreciation of his interests, and so had made herself more companionable. It was elementary—but she *did* wish she could see those animals. If only they weren't out here in this oppressive heat and these awful burrs. Now there were deerflies buzzing her, actually banging into her face in a most annoying fashion.

Then something huge circled her head, causing her to stop moving, alarmed.

Demerit looked. "Dragonfly," he said. "They're okay. They eat

deerfly." He held up his hand, and the dragonfly perched on it as
if tame

May stared. "Why, yes, it's beautiful!" she breathed. The insect was
several inches long, with a dark blue torso and four spread translucent
wings. Its monstrous eyes shone like polished metal, moving around.
"How did you tame it?"

"I guess they see me around a lot, so they figure I'm one of them,"
he said, pleased. "I like them, and the fireflies at night."

"Oh, it's been years since I've seen a firefly flash!"

"They're here. I can show you one field where they congregate, so
you can see twenty at a time."

"If I'm here long enough, I'll take you up on that." Even sweltering
as she was, she realized how much she missed the occasional delights
of her childhood. This estate was a kind of paradise. She wondered
whether Mid came here often, just to appreciate the quiet sights.

They went on. May was sweating to an unladylike degree, but there
was no help for it. She followed the man under copses of oaks, past
palmettos, and through more stands of growing pine trees. It was only
a few minutes, but she knew that hours of reserve energy were being
expended.

They came to the mine. This turned out to be a monstrous and
awesome pit, frightening in its abrupt depth. She could see the tops of
trees at the outside ground level, as if they had just fallen in alive,
swallowed by an abrupt sink-hole. She had become accustomed to the
generally flat terrain or gentle slopes of Florida, and this was a shocking
contrast.

There was a way down, however, where the old mining wagons had
gone. They walked down it, May finding the descent no easier than the
approach had been.

Finally, in a thicket in the depths, where the shadows made a pre-
mature dusk, there was the body. Demerit pointed it out, then stood
back, letting her wedge in between the saplings to get a good view.

Even in shadow, it was an awful sight. Much of the body was
obscured by the clothing, but this was in sufficient disarray to show
some of the torso, including part of the pelvis. It was as though the
man had opened his trousers to urinate and never closed them again.
Now there was no genital region at all, just a thin film across the bony
structure. Similarly there was no abdomen, just the webbing over the
backbone and ribs. But the head was the worst: filmed eye sockets and
nose holes and jaws, as if the man had been inhaling a large soap

bubble. Overall, she would be hard put to it to imagine anything more grotesque.

What had happened to the flesh? Skin of a sort remained, translucently thin, and bones, and clothing, but no muscles, fat, organs, or brain. It was as if the man had been dipped in a vat of acid that dissolved all living tissue and nothing else. How was that possible?

She sniffed. There was a faint, peculiar odor, not unpleasant, neutral, interesting. Not rot; there seemed to be nothing remaining to rot. But not perfume either. The residue of the acid?

She found herself thinking of sex, incongruously. This was odd, because her interest in this aspect of human endeavor had never been strong, and her experience in marriage had done nothing to enhance it. Certainly she could live without it. Why should the subject occur to her now? Because the boneman's fly was open? She was no curious adolescent! Yet it persisted, making her wish she could get into bed with a handsome man and become completely physical.

She backed away from the body, getting clear of the thicket. As she did, the unwelcome subject faded like the chimaera it was.

But her keen investigative instinct would not let go. Was her stray thought coincidental? Or did it somehow relate to that smell? She disliked the notion, but she had to check; it could be important.

She forced herself to approach the body again. She put her face close and sniffed, harder than before.

A heady feeling coursed through her. She definitely craved sexual expression! The man wasn't important, just the act. No romance, no subtlety, just penis and vulva. She wanted wild abandon.

She withdrew again—and again it faded. There was little doubt now: there were pheromones here, setting off whoever got close enough to inhale them. Did they have an effect only on females, or on males too?

She had to know, because her report would be incomplete without it, so she set herself and asked. "Mr. Demerit, when you got close to the body, did you experience a reaction?"

He looked at her, evidently dismayed. He did not answer.

"I am not trying to embarrass you," she said. "It is my duty to ascertain exactly what is going on here, and to report to Mid. This could be important. For example, something could have been used on the hunter, to attract him sexually, luring him into a trap. Some of that substance may still adhere to his body. It may be a danger for any other person. We have to know. Did you feel it?"

Reluctantly, he nodded. "But it's wrong," he said.

"Wrong to lure a person to his death that way. I agree. But knowledge of the danger could save your life or mine."

"No. Wrong because—" He did not finish.

He was really distressed, and now she realized that it was not simply because he disliked talking about sex with a woman or a stranger. There was more, and she had to go for it, objectionable as the matter was to her.

"Because why, Mr. Demerit? I do have to know, and Mid has to know, but no one else does."

"Because I'm . . ." he said, his following words mumbled and incomprehensible.

"I didn't hear. Because you're what?"

He tried again. "Impotent."

That made her pause. "You can't react—but it made you react?"

He nodded miserably.

This could be significant indeed, as a confirmation of her conjecture. "Mr. Demerit, let me explain what may have happened, and I will not talk of this elsewhere. You may have a psychological condition, as some men do, and there is really no shame in it; it happens to most at some time in their lives, and the equivalent to women. I suspect I suffer from something similar myself. But pheromones can cut through that and have an effect anyway. They are not psychological, they are physical. They make the body react on its own. So this is evidence that this is the case here; that body was doused in pheromones, and we can feel the lingering effect."

He was surprised. "You too?"

"Yes, I felt it; that's why I asked. I assure you I am not keen on sex, so I was suspicious when I felt that particular effect. I think we have learned something important, though this is hardly what I anticipated."

He looked relieved. "I thought I was turned on by a corpse."

She smiled. "No. There is nothing psychological here. It's a chemical influence, and evidently it affected the hunter and brought him to his death. And I think we had better get well away from here before nightfall, because if whatever did this to him stalks at night—"

He nodded emphatically, and turned to retrace their route. She followed, not objecting to the pace. She was getting scared herself.

She made it up the steep slope of the ramp at a rate she had hardly thought possible, and followed him at a brisk pace back the way they had come. She no longer noticed the scenery; she just wanted to get back to her car, her bastion of safety. The thought of being consumed by a monster horrified her, but the thought of being lured or compelled sexually by it was worse. Was it like those exotic plants that imitated the sight and scent of female insects, so that the males of those species tried to mate with the surrogates and were caught? Could this monster emulate the male as well as the female, so that creatures of either sex were vulnerable? She greatly feared this was the case, and she most emphatically wanted not to become a victim.

The ground seemed to tilt, sending her stumbling. She lurched past a small pine, almost colliding. When she had been told to drive to Florida, she had visualized hotels along white beaches, with graceful coconut palms, their fronds waving in the sea breeze. This was far different, here in the interior! Oaks and pines and deep mine pits. But there certainly was sand! And heat.

She tried to go on, but the globe tilted again; it was all she could do to keep her feet. What was happening?

Then Demerit loomed close. ". . . matter?" he asked.

"I'm all right," she said, and took a step, and found the sand coming up at her.

"Heat stroke," he said. "Get you to shade." He put his hands under her arms and hauled her, feet dragging, to the impressive shade of a spreading live oak tree. Spanish moss dangled down in masses like stalactites, forming a partial canopy.

"No!" she protested, pointlessly.

He propped her up against the trunk. ". . . fetch water," he said. "You rest. I'll be back."

She struggled to rise. "I don't—"

"Wait there," he said. "Won't be long."

She realized that this made sense. Heat stroke? It was possible. Her suit was sweat-sodden, but her hands were dry; she wasn't sweating now. Exhaustion, perhaps. Now that she was sitting still, in shade, she felt better. Probably it wasn't serious, just a combination of things, which was passing as she relaxed. But she probably would do best to wait for his return.

Then she remembered the monster. Suppose it stalked her during Demerit's absence?

❖ 5 ❖

$\mathbf{G}$EODE LEFT HER under the tree, flushed and fainting. He didn't like her, but she had done him one favor: she had clarified what had happened when he moved that body. Pheromones—that explained a lot. Smell-traces that set someone off involuntarily. It was what brought all the male dogs when a bitch was in heat. It had nothing to do with appearance or personality; it was just a straight signal to the genitals. So it had made him have an erection, even though he couldn't do the same with a woman. He only wished he hadn't had to tell her.

But she was working for Mid, and he worked for Mid, and he had put in the report about the dead hunter. He had to cooperate. At least now it wasn't just his responsibility; the Flowers woman could decide what to do about the hunter. If Mid had sent her, she was competent; she would know what to do. Just as soon as he got her some water, and got back to her car, so she could be on her way.

He was moving fast, now that he was alone. He had learned to run with a minimum expenditure of energy so that he didn't get as hot as he might have, but on a day like this there was no way to avoid sweating. He should have realized that the woman couldn't keep the pace. He hoped he had stopped her in time; heat stroke was no casual business, but she hadn't quite reached that stage, and should be all right if she stayed in place.

He passed her car at the corner and ran on down beside the road. In another five minutes he reached the house. The alarm went off as he unlocked and opened the door; he stepped in and punched 1206 to make it stop. He fetched a canteen, filled it, punched 12 to arm the system again, and headed for his bike; he could make it back much faster and cooler on that.

The door-chime rang. Geode paused while it completed eight bongs. That meant the far entrance gate. Who could be coming this time?

He could ignore it, and the visitor would go away, assuming that no one was here. But Geode didn't like to do that; he was here to attend to whatever needed attending, and not many cars came here without reason. For all he knew, it could be Mid himself. He had better see what it was. But he couldn't spare much time, because that woman was out there alone, and so was the monster, and he didn't know how avidly it stalked people. Mid might not care what happened to a poaching hunter, but he would care about his investigator!

He compromised. Opened the door again and shut off the alarm. He punched 01 to open the gate, then rearmed, closed the door, and continued to the bike. He would intercept the car on its way in, and with luck be rid of it quickly so he could get to the Flowers woman.

He rode swiftly up the road, winding around the edge of the planted slash pines, and to the north-south straightaway leading up to the corner. He saw the parked car.

Oops! The visitor would have to pass right by that on the way in. Well, what did it matter? This was a private drive, and a private car could be on it if Geode didn't object. He needed to offer no explanation for it.

Then he saw that the incoming car had stopped just west of the Flowers car. What was it doing?

But as he came closer, he understood. It was Deputy Tishner! The worst possible visitor right now!

He rolled up to the two cars. Tishner was standing outside, noting the license tag. He glanced up at Geode. "Friend of yours?"

"No." But he knew that wouldn't put the man off.

"Then it must be a trespasser. I'll buzz the station and have a tow truck out here to take it away."

"No!" Geode protested. "I know the owner. Just—" He couldn't think of anything to say. He knew Mid didn't want Flowers's presence here known, because then someone might catch on why she was here.

Tishner contemplated him. "Demerit, come clean. You lied to me before, and the only reason you're not lying now is you can't think fast enough. What's going on here?"

Geode was at a loss. He had never been apt at dealing with people, and the authoritative ones were the worst. He couldn't tell the truth, and he couldn't evade it, and he couldn't afford any long delay.

"Got something to do with that missing hunter?" Tishner prompted. "Now don't try to lie again; I can see I'm on to something here. Come clean, and we'll get along fine."

That was what Geode couldn't do. But what *was* he to do? He was in trouble either way.

"Let me tell you something, Demerit," Tishner said. "I'm on two cases now. One's the missing hunter, and I've traced him here, or close to it. The other's the bags of bones. Are they connected?" He stared at Geode, and read the truth there. "Yeah, I figured they were. And your boss doesn't want a noise, to mess up his hideaway. I'll make you a deal: you tell me what you know, and I'll keep your boss's name out of it. I know you didn't go out killing any poachers, you're just covering up on orders. I don't know what this car's doing here—but I'll bet it's related. You help me, I'll help you. Deal?" He put out his big hand.

Geode considered. He knew there was no way to get rid of the man now, but he wasn't sure how much he could tell him. "I'll take you to someone who knows," he said.

"Okay." The deputy sheriff pushed his hand forward, and Geode had to take it. They had a deal, of a sort.

"She's in the forest, a quarter mile. Heat stroke, maybe. I was taking water to her."

"I'll help you get her back here. Lead on, MacDuff!"

The man thought he didn't recognize the allusion to Shakespeare. Geode put his bike in low gear and headed north. The deputy followed afoot, making fair time in the sand, but expending a lot more energy. They squeezed through the hedge and moved on. In a few minutes they reached the live oak.

The Flowers woman was there, in good order. Geode stopped the bike and handed her the canteen as she stood. "He intercepted me. You'll have to talk to him."

She unscrewed the cap and drank. By that time the deputy huffed up. Geode hoped she had figured out what to say.

"Come on, woman, it's hot out here," Tishner said. "Let's get you to your car, and we'll talk. I know something's up, and I figure you must work for Middleberry and you know something I need to know. Here, I'll give you a hand." He reached for her elbow.

She rejected it. "I'm all right. I merely became fatigued."

"And you sure don't want to be beholden to a man for anything," Tishner said.

She glared at him, but did not debate it. It was evident that they didn't like each other any better than Geode liked either of them.

As they trekked back toward the cars, Tishner repeated what he had said to Geode. "So I think you're better off working with me than against me," he concluded. "If I have to run down the rest of this myself, I won't owe you anything."

By the time they reached the cars, the Flowers woman had evidently made up her mind. "All right, I'll talk to him," she said to Geode. "You may stay or go, as you choose."

Geode was relieved. "I have to check the rest of the ranch." He mounted his bike and rode off, back into the forest.

❖ 6 ❖

F RANK SAT IN his car with the
woman, running the motor and the air conditioning. She did indeed
seem to have suffered heat exhaustion, and he knew that something
extremely compelling must have brought her out there in her good
clothing, as she obviously hadn't been forced. Demerit was hardly one
to force a woman, anyway; as far as he could tell, the man was either
homosexual or asexual, having little interest in other people of either
sex. It didn't matter, as long as he stayed out of trouble, and apparently
his job as caretaker of the Middle Kingdom suited him just fine. But
the presence of this woman indicated that something significant was
afoot, and it was just Frank's blind luck that he had arrived in time to
catch her.

The woman's color improved as she got cool. She became more
alert and relaxed, sizing him up. He was sizing her up too, as he did
routinely with anyone he encountered; it was part of his business. She
was evidently no dummy. She was about his own age, heavyset but not
really fat, like him. Her hair and eyes were brown, like his, except that
they were rich instead of pale. It was as if she had emerged from the
mold more recently, and had not been so far faded by the sun and
heat. She was about five-six in height, and despite her age and heft,

46

healthy. Probably only the unaccustomed heat had brought her down; she had simply misjudged how hot it was this far south in summer, with the humidity of the lake region making it worse.

"I do work for Middleberry," she said. "And there is something important afoot. I was going to interview you anyway, in due course."

"Oh, you know who I am?" He was accustomed to dealing with folk who saw him as an anonymous figure in a uniform.

"I make it my business to know with what I am dealing."

With what, rather than with whom. He suppressed a flicker of irritation. "Okay, I'll play. Tell me something about me that doesn't show."

"You're a whistle-blower," she said. "You suffered the usual fate of the kind. They couldn't actually fire you, so they relegated you to the hinterlands, and if you give them any pretext at all, they'll can you. Your wife has little sympathy with your attitude."

Frank was amazed. "You *do* know! But how?"

"There are files on everything, if you know how to get at them. I checked the records on the local authorities, and you were the most recent transferee. I checked your prior record, and it was outstanding— until you turned in your department for graft. You learned about what passes for justice the hard way."

"Just the way you learned about men," he said, taking a flyer on her attitude.

"Bad marriage," she agreed. "Not exactly the same as your experience, but perhaps the effect was similar. Mr. Tishner, I do have information I think will interest you, but I do require confidentiality. Can you guarantee it?"

"As you say, Miz—what's your name?"

"May Flowers."

"As you say, May—and you can call me Frank. I'm not being friendly, I'm being off the record, okay? Let's leave the full names out."

"Frank," she agreed with a chill smile.

"As you say," he said once more, "I've been through the grinder, and I guess you have too. If I rock the boat one teeny bit, I'll be out, and this is the only job I know, let alone like, and I've got a family to support. So I'm on a close leash. When I came up with this thing about bags of bones—and I think that's what we're talking about—I got the word: I can investigate it all I want, mostly on my own time or as part of legitimate activity, but I can't go public with it on my own. I have to report it, and someone else will decide what to do with it. Probably it'll just be buried, because they're trying to encourage tourism, and bones don't necessarily do that unless they're ancient. In fact, I think they'd be just as happy if I never reported at all. But if there is a threat to the folk here, I'd better be on it, because we both know who'll get the axe if I hide something that then embarrasses the tourist bureau. So I can guarantee confidentiality right up until something blows, and then I can't guarantee anything. Not for you, me, or my marriage."

"I think we understand each other sufficiently," she said. "Tell me what you know of the bones, and I will tell you what I know—off the record. We may indeed profit by pooling our resources."

Frank told her about Demerit's rabbit and the Brown woman's raccoon and the prior pattern of cases. "Now a fool hunter's disappeared," he concluded. "I traced it back to this region, and I figure it could've happened here, and Middleberry told Demerit to cover it up so's nobody would come poking around the Middle Kingdom. If the same thing that got the animals got that hunter, this is a live case."

"Mid," she said. "We call Middleberry Mid, off the record. You're right; it did get the hunter, and Mid did make the caretaker hide the body and move the truck. Neither Mid nor Demerit has any complicity in the death, merely in the concealment of it and its locale. Mid sent me to investigate, and that is what I am doing. We were just returning from a viewing of the body."

Confirmation! Frank tried to mask his excitement, but knew it showed anyway. "You actually saw the remains?"

"I did. Definitely a hunter's clothing, but only bones remaining, with a thin webbing covering them. No flesh at all. A faint, peculiar odor. And—" She hesitated.

Something clicked. "An erotic reaction?"

"That's it. I conjecture that the monster uses pheromones to lure its prey, and to pacify it. Such chemical substances can be extremely powerful as agents to modify behavior, and if the monster somehow manages to emulate or manufacture pheromones that cause its prey to relax, or sleep, or to become sexually agitated—"

"You're saying it doesn't have to have big teeth!" Frank exclaimed. "I wondered how it could go from rabbit to man! Either the one would be too little for it, or the other too much. But if it could make any size prey just lie down for it—"

"Precisely. There was no sign of violence done to the body, paradoxical as that may seem in the circumstance. The bones were not separated or broken; the skeleton appeared to be intact, as was the clothing. The, uh, trousers were open, as if—"

"As if he was urinating—or trying for sex!" Frank finished. "Maybe he thought it was a super-sexy woman!"

"Apparently the pheromones are generic and non-sex specific. They seem to affect a number of species who should have different, um, tastes, and to have similar impact on male and female. I'm no biologist, but that strikes me as unusual. Either some extremely sophisticated chemical technology is involved, or the monster has an organic capacity of emulation beyond anything we have encountered before."

"Maybe so," he said. "But even so, some of this is hard to swallow. An animal might be tricked or caught, but a man's no dummy. There may be stories of the old sirens, who lured sailors to their destruction, but in real life even the sexiest woman won't tempt a man to his immediate death. Not if he sees it coming. A hunter out poaching's got to know that if he sees a nymph out here in the brush, something's got to be fishy. He's not just going to grab her unless he's pretty sure she's human. So does this monster talk? Does it kiss? If it can do that, what's it doing out here instead of in the big city, where prey is a lot more common?"

"Could it be alien in origin?" she asked. "A literal flying saucer, with equipment to project something tempting, visually, audibly, and olfactory? All that would be required would be the semblance of something desirable, enough to cause the man to investigate. Then he could be caught in a net or whatever, and, um, drained."

Frank shook his head. "Won't wash. If aliens came in a saucer, they wouldn't just hover it in place while they checked out a man, then leave him where they found him. Either they'd take the whole thing, and dissolve the bones too, or they'd talk with him and let him go. They wouldn't stay in sight any longer than they'd have to, and they wouldn't leave such grisly evidence of what they'd done. I don't see any intelligence or technology operating here, but I can see some sort of animal eating its fill and leaving what it couldn't eat."

"I agree," May said. "But what sort of animal could it be? I saw no sign of eating, no blood. How could it get all the flesh out without breaking the skin?"

"Maybe the lab report on that raccoon will tell," he said. "But I think we've got more to worry about than exactly how it's done. Something's out there, and it used to feed on animals, but now it's tasted human flesh, and that could mean real trouble. Middle—Mid may not want a commotion on his ranch, but this thing could blow up beyond anyone's power to control."

"If no more hunters come on the property," she said evenly, "there will be no more deaths here. Mid won't mind if a scandal blows up somewhere else. There is no tangible evidence to tie that hunter in to this property. Would justice be denied if that body turned up somewhere else?"

Frank considered. "Like where?"

"Like where do you want it?"

"In the brush near where his truck was found?"

"Perhaps in two days?"

He nodded. "Could be."

She smiled grimly, but with less chill than before. "However, that is merely one episode. There have been others, and may be more. I believe we should remain in touch."

"Where can I reach you?"

She dug in her purse and produced a business card. She wrote the local number on the back. "I'll be out and around, but a message left there will catch me in due course. Where can I reach you?"

He pondered. "Sheriff's office isn't safe. Better be at home. My wife generally knows where to reach me."

"Your wife may not appreciate calls for you from a woman."

"She doesn't care what I do, as long as I hang on to my job. In my work I get calls from all types."

"Very well." She tucked herself together, getting ready to return to her own car. "One other thing. When I talked to Jade Brown earlier today, I could tell that she was concealing something. She was shaken. I think the monster has struck again, perhaps closer. I have no pretext to go there again; do you?"

"I can make one. I can go there tomorrow. You think another raccoon?"

"Larger, I think. She had buried something in her flower garden. Why would she call the sheriff's office the first time, and conceal the evidence the second time?"

"Good question. I'll see what I can do."

"My interest, of course, is in protecting the privacy of my employer.

But until I know exactly what is threatening it, I am not free to depart. I must also make a full report to Mid. I don't believe that violates the spirit of our understanding."

Frank laughed, a bit hollowly. "Tell him if this gets me fired, I'll need a job."

"I will do that," she replied seriously.

Taken aback, he did not answer. She climbed out and went to her car. He waited while she started it, turned it around, and drove back down toward the house. Then he turned his own around and headed toward the gate.

This had been some session! No, he wasn't going to report any of this, yet. He'd follow up with the Brown woman, whom he remembered as a mousy type, then with the search at the end of Turner Camp Road. It would be better if someone else actually found the body. He should be able to arrange that.

But that would have to wait until tomorrow. He had routine business today. Already his radio had a Signal 46, which meant a sick or injured person, and it was in his territory. "Ten twenty-six," he acknowledged, and headed for the address. He didn't care what kind of minor junk they put him on now; he was on to something that could be truly significant, and that gave his dull life meaning.

Next morning he drove to the home of Jade Brown. She came out to stand by her door as he parked. She was every bit as nondescript as he recalled. Her hair was lank and drab; it might once have been auburn, but now was closer to mop color, and not a new mop either. Her eyes were the washed-out green of the polluted sea on a cloudy day. If she had a figure, she concealed it under a baggy, pocketed work dress. Yet there was an odd intensity to her, as if some live-wire spirit were prisoned within the dull housing.

He eased out of the car and approached her. "Hi there. Remember me? That raccoon two, three days ago."

"Yes, officer," she said nervously. "Do you know what made it die?"

"Lab report not back yet; takes forever when it's not a hot case. But there've been other recent reports, with larger victims." He stared her in the face and put it to her directly: "Do you have anything more to tell me?"

She squirmed like a truant child, and that trapped spirit fought to burst out, but could not. "I—"

"What did you bury there?" He pointed to the disturbed site in her garden. "That wasn't there last time."

She was caught, unable to evade so direct a challenge. "My dog, Donjon. He died."

"I wouldn't figure him to be alive under there," he said cruelly. "Like the raccoon?"

Again it paid off. "Yes," she said, flinching. Now host and spirit were one: afraid.

"And you figured no sense in bothering me again?" He was giving her an out, knowing that he would get the story now.

"Yes."

"He was outside?"

"No, inside. I—found him there in the morning. Just skin and bones. It was awful!"

"Inside?" That startled him. "Where were you?"

"In the bedroom. The door was closed. I—it doesn't go after people, does it?"

How much should he tell her? "You never can tell with something like this. Best not to gamble. How'd it get in?"

Her mouth opened in retrospective horror. "I don't know! The windows and doors were closed. I didn't think of that before!"

"Closed? You sure?" Now Frank himself was getting nervous. He knew, as she did not, that the thing had sucked out a man, but that had been outside, in the forest. Was it now coming inside? "Ma'am, if you don't mind, I think I should take a look at your house, find out just how it got in, and close it up."

"Yes!" she agreed, frightened.

They checked the house, outside and in. The house was in good repair; he remembered now that her husband was a carpenter. But it was a mess inside; she was no housekeeper. Yet it was tight; there was no obvious entry other than the doors or windows.

Frank scratched his head. "Lady, I can't figure it. How big was your dog?"

"About thirty pounds, maybe forty. He was fair-sized."

So it would take a predator of perhaps twice that mass to make a good meal of him, maybe more. A man didn't eat half or or even a quarter of his weight at one sitting, and neither did a tiger. Call it a hundred pounds. How could something that size get into a closed house without doing damage?

"You don't have a chimney?" he asked.

"No."

"Were the doors locked?"

"No, I was expecting my husband to return."

"How alert was your dog?"

"Not very. But he would bark at strangers."

"So if a strange man opened that door, the dog wouldn't just lie there?"

"That's right. Only if my husband—"

"How did he get along with that dog?"

She shook her head as if shaking off something unpleasant. "My husband has his failings, but he liked that dog. He wouldn't do—that. And if he did, how could he have left just the skin and bones? And why would he go away and leave the dog like that?"

"Ms. Brown, I don't like this much better than you do, but I think I'd better ask. Do you get along with your husband okay?"

"He's not here much," she said tightly. That spirit was back, twitching at minor muscles of her face, wanting to say a whole lot more. She had a marriage problem, sure enough.

"I mean, would he do something like this to spite you?"

"Oh. No, never. He'd—take another woman."

So that was it: the man was two-timing her, and she knew it. "So it must have been someone else—or something else." He decided that in fairness he should tell her something. "Look, ma'am, there's a suggestion in the other cases that sex appeal may be involved. I mean, if your dog was male, something with the scent of a female dog in heat—so he wouldn't bark. But it wasn't a dog, but something else."

She stared at him, not a whit reassured. "Something like a dog?"

"Maybe not like a dog at all," he said quickly. "We don't know what it's like. Only that it kills. And it maybe can attract anything by—well, by making a sexy smell. I don't want to alarm you, but if it can get in your house—"

She was already thoroughly alarmed. "You mean it could come after me?"

"Well, I didn't say that, exactly. But look, do you have somewhere else you can go, maybe for a few days? Till we run this thing down?"

She shook her head no, pale and drawn. She had not been exactly pretty to begin with, and was less so now. "Anyway, I couldn't leave my husband and son here."

He was getting to feel guilty. "Do you have a gun?"

"No. They hurt more friends than foes."

"Right. But maybe if you take a knife with you tonight—I don't want to upset you, but if that thing came into your house—at least lock the doors. Maybe the dog knocked the door open, and the thing came in and got the dog, and then it left and pushed the door closed. The point is, your bedroom door stayed closed, and you were okay."

"Yes." Volumes unspoken.

"Do you want me to check on you tomorrow? I can swing by."

She seemed tempted, but demurred. "We'll be all right."

"Sure you will," he said with false assurance. He tipped his hat, feeling guilty, and headed back to his car. Maybe the monster wouldn't strike twice in the same place.

❖ 7 ❖

OENONE WATCHED HIM go. She was terrified, but knew there was really nothing the deputy could do. What good would it be if he checked back by day when the monster came at night? But he had given her good advice: to arm herself, and keep her door locked. She hoped the officer caught up with whatever it was soon so that she could relax. Her life had been dreary and pointless; now it was worse.

Her son came home on the school bus. She was both relieved and worried. She needed company, and he was that, but she didn't want him put in danger. She would have to warn him.

"Jame," she said as he barged in the door.

"Can't stop now, ma," he said over his shoulder. "Got a load of homework."

But what could she warn him about? He already knew the dog had died; he just didn't know how. Did she really want to make him feel as uneasy as she felt, when there was so little she could do about it? She was torn, and the default decision was silence.

Paris was out again, as usual. Jame didn't comment; he just bolted down his supper and headed back to his room. At least he wasn't worrying!

After Jame was asleep, she checked the house thoroughly, making sure all the doors and windows were firmly closed. Then she retreated to her bedroom, surreptitiously clutching the large bread knife. She felt foolish, but also afraid; she did need this bit of reassurance.

She lay on the bed, dressed, the light on, the knife on the table beside her. What kind of a thing could come into a closed house? For she knew that Donjon hadn't pushed open the door; the dog had been so satisfied to be inside that he wouldn't have stirred short of an earthquake. The wind hadn't blown it open; it had not been locked, but it had been latched. Something had come in, somehow, silent, deadly. It could come again. Did it have hands to turn knobs?

She tried to relax, but could not. She tried to summon her eager young men, the ones who found her so compulsively sexy that they simply could not restrain themselves, but on this night they had evidently discovered Helen instead.

Helen—damn that woman! Paris might not be much, but she certainly could use him at home tonight! Helen was making a widow of her, without any of the compensations, such as being free to go somewhere else. Whatever could she see in the man? Paris was short, balding, going to pot, and generally inattentive. He was just about the worst a beautiful young woman could do.

Could it be that Helen wasn't beautiful or young? That would be even worse! It was understandable to lose a man to a sexy temptress, but humiliating to lose him to the opposite. No, she had to picture Helen as lovely. Maybe she wasn't just young, but childlike. A nymphet. Out for the thrill of it, seducing an older man. That type existed—oh, didn't she know it! But what an irony to do it with Paris.

Œnone pictured herself as the nymphet. She wore a gauzy nightie, and her legs were well fleshed but her breasts remained relatively slight, in the manner of the maturing but not yet quite nubile girl. As the man appeared, she turned over on the bed, negligently letting her nightie fall askew, so that one leg showed up to the buttock. Oh, what firm young flesh! What a tight round bottom! The man wasn't supposed to notice; he was just passing (a bedroom? That couldn't be!) by. She must be working in a store window, putting up a bedroom display, checking the draperies beyond the bed, but they were hard to reach, so she sort of stretched out on the bed and rolled over, careless about her dress, which somehow remained the nightie, and achieved the same effect. The man was outside the store, passing by on the street, but he paused, looking in the huge storefront display window, peering at her slender yet nicely formed legs, seeing right up to the crease of her full buttock. That excited him. She somehow couldn't get the drapery right, so kept squirming on the bed, unconscious of the way her nightie rode up farther, baring the other leg past the calf, the knee, the expanding thigh, right up to the shadowed cleft between the rounded mounds of her innocent clean butt. The man didn't want to be obvious, but he just couldn't leave the vision of that delightful posterior. So he pretended to be checking his timepiece or looking for a paper in his pocket, but he kept watching. She made one more stretch for the curtain, the hem of her nightie drawing up completely over her bottom, showing her panties, which were stretched so tight they were translucent. (But how had he seen the halves of bifurcate derriere, then? Well, the panties were almost invisible from this angle.) Then at last she completed her business with the drapery, and was ready to get off the bed, but she had to wriggle backward to get off it, and her nightie dragged on up across her back. Realizing her dishabille, she rolled over and sat up, in the process baring her breasts, which in this position weren't really that small, and were finely formed. Then she saw the man. Oh! Her hand came up to her mouth. What had he seen?

He'd seen too much. His face was now twisted with lust. He simply had to have her! He tried to come right through the sheet-glass window, but could not, so he slid along it, his crotch bulging, finding his way to the store door, his eyes fastened on her body. Those petite breasts, which had seemed unformed only because she had been mostly supine, those round buttocks—he had never seen anything that delicious before, and never would again, and so now was the moment. She, perceiving his excitement, marveled. If she had been able to rouse a man to such a pitch by accident, what might she do when she tried? Well, she would find out! She hauled her nightie up over her head and off, and scooped off her panties, heedless of others passing by the store outside who were now pausing to watch. Let them see how it should be done! She flung back her lustrous tresses and faced the side where the man was lunging through the door, fumbling with his belt, trying to get his pants off or open or something, heedless of the growing audience outside. The very smell of him was sexy. Her legs were lifted on the bed, her knees bent and slightly separated, so that a stray shaft of light struck down between them and—

Then she remembered something. The deputy had said that the monster might attract prey by making a sexy smell. She woke, abruptly chilled.

She was on her bed, in her clothing, her knees lifted and her legs parted, with the lights on and the knife within reach. All was quiet.

She had exited a perfect dream on a false alarm. Furious, she tried to return to it, but it was no good; the mood was gone, the man was gone, the store window was gone. She had to drift back to sleep alone, no teenage temptress, just in her desultory mid-thirties. Any man who saw *her* in a store window would yawn and keep walking.

She woke again in the wee hours. All was as before, but something bothered her. There was a bit of a noise, or a smell, or something, fading but eerie. A *presence*, not malign, just there—when it shouldn't be. Was she imagining it? She had a good imagination, too good at times. How could she be sure?

Well, she could just check. If the monster were in the vicinity, she would catch it. She picked up the knife, oddly unafraid, even experiencing an almost sexual titillation, and went to the door.

She turned on the light in the main room. There was nothing there; it remained exactly as crowded and messy as ever. She wasn't much of a housekeeper, she knew; she ought to do something about that. But somehow something else always seemed to be more urgent at the moment—as was the case now.

She checked the kitchen, just in case she had left something on. All was in order—or at least proper disorder. Paris obviously had not returned, again; he would have been here for a snack before plumping down on the bed.

That left Jame's room. He normally slept soundly until the crack of dawn, and then exploded into activity.

She went there and put her hand on the doorknob. She opened the door a crack and peered into the darkness.

The smell was stronger here, though still faint. She remembered her vision/dream of the night, cut off at the point it had been about to explode gloriously into sex. What a feeling!

Now she remembered: Donjon had had an odor like that when he—the deputy had said something about sex appeal being involved. This smell made her feel sexy—yet it could also mean that—

Abruptly appalled, she threw open the door and turned on the light. She blinked at its sudden brightness, then looked at the bed.

A small skeleton in pajamas lay there.

Œnone screamed, backed out, and slammed the door. She charged back into her room, slammed the door, and leaped onto the bed. The kitchen knife she still held stabbed into the mattress. She grabbed the sheet and hauled it over her, hunching down to hide her head. She willed herself to the safety of sleep. That usually didn't work, but this time it did.

She woke after dawn, tangled in the sheet, in her clothing, the knife still embedded in the mattress beside her. What a nightmare she had had!

But why was the house quiet? Jame should be banging around, and would soon be demanding breakfast.

Suppose—? But no, that could not be! She would dispel that notion right now. She threw the sheet off, put her feet down, and stood. Then, reconsidering, she leaned down to recover the knife. Armed, she went out.

The lights remained on, as they had been all night. If she had dreamed it, who would have turned them on? She went to Jame's room.

She knocked, "Jame! You overslept!"

There was no answer. Fear rose in her, to the level of her heart, which began to beat so hard that her shirt quivered in front. It couldn't be!

She held her breath and opened the door. She looked in.

The skeleton was there.

She had tried to deny it, to make it into a dream, but now she knew it was not. When fantasy came up against reality, reality generally prevailed. The monster had come and taken her son.

Her gaze drifted to the window. It was open.

She had closed that window yesterday, making the house tight. Jame must have opened it, being a fresh-air fiend, and she had not realized. There had been access to his room from outside.

The monster had come in and taken Jame.

At night she had been terrified and tried to flee it, to deny it. Now it was day, and she was rational. The shock of it numbed her. She had to make a decision in a hurry, lest she do something foolish and make it worse.

When the raccoon had been taken, she had called the sheriff's department. When the dog had been taken, she had sought to hide it, but somehow the deputy had known anyway. Now her son had been taken

She should report it, she knew. But would they really believe it was the monster? Or would they think that she had somehow done it herself, practicing on the the dog and then going after her son? It might not be rational to kill her son, but by the time Paris got through talking with them, she would seem like a complete mental case and be committed to an asylum, and Paris would be off with Helen.

No way would she get Jame back, regardless.

She fetched the spade, went to the back, and dug out an azalea bush. She was careful to set the dirt on a plastic tablecloth so it did not mark the surrounding soil, and then to put the bush on it when she had it out. She might have damaged a few roots, but she had balled it so that not much harm was done. It would survive nicely, just as if transplanted. She deepened the hole, taking similar care with the extra dirt.

Then she went inside, hauled in the corners of Jame's sheet, and lifted so that the body was tumbled into the center. He wasn't very heavy without his flesh; she had no real trouble carrying him. She hauled the impromptu bag out and set it into the hole where the bush had been. She pushed it down, folding over the excess sheet so that none was out of the hole. Then she filled in some dirt, covering it. Then she put the bush back in where it had been, and filled in dirt around it until things were level. This time she made sure that there was no sign of disturbance; she sprinkled a few dry leaves around and pressed some into the soil. It should take a better eye than the sheriff's to tell that anything had changed here. After all, the azalea remained right where it had been before.

She took the excess dirt, wrapped in the tablecloth, to an old large laurel oak and bundled it into a ground-level hole in the trunk. She might need some of that dirt again. No one should think to look here, and if they did, what would they find? Just innocent dirt. The job was done.

No, it wasn't. Now she had to devise a way to explain her son's disappearance. The school authorities would think he was playing truant, and Paris would inquire. She would have to tell them that something had come up suddenly, and that he had to visit relatives in another state for a while. No need to transfer records; he would be back in a couple of weeks, and yes, she would see that he made up the lost work.

This was crazy! She was covering for the monster. Why was she doing it? Wasn't she much more likely to be locked up the moment they found the body, as they surely would in time, than if she had reported it at the outset? She was making herself look guilty.

But if she reported it now, everything would happen now, and she'd be in trouble immediately. This way it delayed the reckoning, and gave her a chance to figure a way out. She might have to flee the state, to assume a different identity, so that they would never catch her. Could she do that?

She had to believe she could, if she had to. It would be better than rotting in an institution. At least she would have a chance.

What relatives was her son visiting? It would have to be her brother and his wife. She did not get along well with him, for a reason they never discussed, but by the same token it gave her a certain power over him. She would have to invoke that now.

She looked up his number and dialed it. His wife answered. The wife was innocent, and Œnone was not about to burden her with any part of the truth.

"Jade Brown here," she said briskly. "Tell George that Jame is visiting you for a couple of weeks."

"But we can't—" the woman protested.

"He isn't really," Œnone clarified. "But you must say he is with you, if anyone asks. Tell George; he will understand. With luck, no one will ask."

"But—"

"Just tell him," Œnone said firmly, and hung up.

George would not understand what his crazy little sister was up to this time, but he would know he had to play along. He had learned long ago about playing along. She had not bothered him in years; he was getting off lightly.

So it was done. Now she could relax.

Œnone sat down at the kitchen table and dissolved into tears. Jame was dead! She had held off the full impact of the stunning reality, doing what she had to do, but she had been running on desperation. Now the grief overwhelmed her. Jame had not been the best of boys, but he was far from the other extreme. He had been somewhat of a comfort to her, just by his presence, as her relationship with Paris had fallen apart. She had not tried to hold the family together for the sake of the child; the child had tended to make bearable what otherwise was not. Now that small bastion of support was gone, and she did not know how she was going to survive.

Yes, she did. She was going to seal it over, into a disused person-

ality, one she could remember but would not truly feel, as she had
done before. It would be as if some other woman's son had died,
eliciting sympathy but not true involvement from her. This would
enable her to function appropriately, without being overcome by emotion. Drab little mother would fade away, leaving a new slate. This
would take time to perfect, but she would do it; she did know how.

In the afternoon a car pulled in. Œnone recognized it: that journalist woman who had come asking about the raccoon. Had she somehow gotten wind of what had happened since? That seemed unlikely,
unless the deputy had told her.

Œnone had been crying; a glance at the mirror showed her eyes
discolored and swollen. She had been working on her new aspect, but
loss and grief could not be muscled down in an hour, let alone the
physical evidence of it. How was she to hide that?

She dived for the refrigerator and hauled out an onion. She found
a small knife—her big one was still in Jame's room, where she had set
it down when tending to him—which would really look damning!—
and sliced the onion in half.

She picked up a half and carried it along as she went out on the
porch to meet the woman, hoping to get rid of her quickly. "Is this
important? I'm rather busy at the moment—"

The woman eyed her, and the onion. "Mrs. Brown, I think it is well
that I came here. You have obviously lost more than a dog."

"I'm making salad!" Œnone said, waving the onion.

But the woman would not be blunted. "The monster has been here
again. Whom did it take this time?"

Damn her intuition! "I don't have to talk to you!"

"Mrs. Brown, I think you had better. May I come in?" The woman
pushed on by her, entering the house, ignoring the onion. Œnone
realized belatedly that it was a sweet onion, with very little tearing; in
her hurry she hadn't noticed.

"What right do you have to barge in here?" Œnone demanded,
flustered.

"I am a journalist," Flowers said evenly. "I'm good at it. I do my
homework. Why didn't you testify against your brother?"

Œnone stared at her. *She knew!*

The woman smiled coldly. "That was, shall we say, just a warning

shot. I will tell you this much about me: I was an abused wife. I have
an excellent notion what you went through, and why you don't care to
talk about it. I have no interest in embarrassing you. I just must have
the truth about what's going on here. Tell me everything, and I will
not only keep your secret, I will help you."

At the moment this woman reminded her very much of her husband! She dealt strictly on her own terms, making a bargain that might
seem fair to her but hardly impressed the other party that way. She was
dealing from power, and that tended to be hard on the powerless.

But Œnone seemed to have no choice. "The monster took my son,"
she said brokenly.

"And you did not report it?"

"They might think I did it."

"I know you did not. I was afraid of this. Once the monster attuned
to human flesh, it found human beings easy prey. We have to find it
and destroy it."

"Can't—can't the police do that?"

"The police don't know about it. This thing is not public knowledge, and we intend to see that it does not become so. The one body
that was found by the river was too far gone to indicate much, and the
news was not given to the paper."

"A body?"

"Apparently a hunter. A sheriff's deputy discovered it yesterday,
near where the hunter's truck was found last week. For all they know,
it could have been picked clean by ants. But just in case it was hom-
icide, they are keeping it under wraps. They don't know what we know:
that a monster is stalking people. Now, where was your son, and what
did you do with his body?"

Numbed anew, Œnone showed her. Apparently if she had reported
it, it still wouldn't have become public. Because, it seemed, monsters
were bad for tourism. Unless they were harmless to people, which this
one wasn't.

"You did well," Flowers said. "But I think you had better get away
from here. The monster has now struck three times here. We shall try
to intercept it before it strikes again, but meanwhile you are surely in
danger. This house is too isolated; the monster evidently strikes where
there is little danger of discovery. I realize it is hard to plan effective
action when your son has just been so horribly killed, but it is necessary."

"I have nowhere to go," Œnone said. With that she gave the lie to her wild notion to flee and change her identity. What would she eat, where would she stay?

"And too old to make it as a lady of the night," Flowers said. "I understand rather better than I care to. But perhaps I can come up with something."

"Anyway, I can't just go and leave my husband here," Œnone said. "He would—"

"Make a row," Flowers agreed. "I know that type too. Then I suppose you will have to remain here, but I am not at all at ease about this. Lock yourself in when you sleep, and beware of anything that seems erotic."

"I could have used that advice before I got married," Œnone said with a wan smile.

Flowers returned the smile. "So could I, long ago. We do learn the hard way. I will stop by again tomorrow, hoping you have no further news."

Œnone nodded agreement. She hadn't liked this woman from the start, but that was changing, and she was relieved to have her situation understood. Flowers knew about the monster.

The woman got up and left the house. In a moment her car started. Œnone remained at the table, dry-eyed for the time being, uncertain how she should feel.

8

MAY DROVE AWAY from the house, ill at ease. She had to find out about the monster, and protect Mid's estate from the notoriety its presence would evoke, and she was trying to do that. As long as the monster hunted in this particular region, it was her responsibility, and she tracked its depredations assiduously, doing what Deputy Sheriff Tishner—Frank—was not fully free to do. But the cold logic of her loyalty to Mid did not submerge the increasingly difficult human aspect. That woman, Jade Brown, was in a situation roughly analogous to May's own of five years ago, caught in a bad marriage. True, the husband was not beating her, he was merely neglecting her in favor of a more attractive woman, but the underlying desperation was similar. Now it was complicated by the presence of the monster. Jade Brown was all too likely to be the next taken.

It was not her business to help people in trouble, and May had schooled herself to deal with people toughly, as objects rather than as feeling entities. But the Brown woman was too close to what she understood, both in her marriage and in her proximity to the monster. May's heart was being touched despite herself. There, but for the grace of God . . .

Perhaps it was the background information she had so recently come across. She had done what she routinely did, and researched in some depth the person she knew she would have to deal with again. Mid's resources had facilitated this. Expecting to find dull history, she had been surprised.

Jade Brown had been molested as a child, first by her brother and likely her father, then by a neighbor. She had not complained; apparently she had not realized the significance of the situation. Then her brother had discovered the business with the neighbor, and reported it, and thrown Jade Brown's life into phenomenal notoriety. There had been a dramatic trial. The neighbor had been convicted, thanks to Jade's innocent testimony. That had seemed to be the extent of it, but May knew better. She knew that the neighbor had in effect taken the fall for what the father and brother had done, and that the other two had thus escaped prosecution. Jade had been returned to her family, where quite possibly the abuse had continued.

Was there really a difference between a child locked into an abusive family and a woman locked into an abusive marriage? Perhaps there was, but the parallel struck to the heart of May's buried humanity. She *had* to help Jade Brown!

She knew a house where the woman could go. But it wasn't her place to authorize it. Perhaps not her place even to suggest it. But she suspected she was about to push her luck.

She drove the looping roads to the Middle Kingdom Ranch. She would discuss this with Demerit and then decide what to do. She also had to call the sheriff's deputy and tell him of the death of the Brown boy; that was a shocker that really pinpointed the continued presence of the monster. They had to do something about it quickly, because at this rate it would soon be impossible to conceal it. But how could they dispatch a thing who hunted so silently and unpredictably? Certainly they weren't going to go out into the night with flashlights and wait for it!

She pulled up at the gate and pressed the call button. In a moment the gate opened. Good; that meant Demerit was at the house now. She drove on down the lovely lane. Something about young pine trees made her feel good; she didn't know whether it was the sight, smell, or sound of the wind through their branches, but the associations were nice. Look—there was a huge owl, just sitting on the metal fence, its great dark eyes watching her pass. It wasn't even afraid of the moving car!

She reached the house, nestled in the jungle-like forest; she wouldn't care to hike through that region! She had had enough trouble in the relatively open sandy section of the northern part of the estate; here, with the clustering palmettos and dangling liana vines and thickets of whatever hiding all manner of bugs and reptiles, she would be in trouble immediately. As it was, she had gotten a number of itchy bites on her legs from her prior outing; these had turned out to be chiggers, and it seemed they would take a week or so to settle down. The wilds of central Florida were best admired from the sidelines.

Demerit stepped out. "I have a report and a request," she said. "Let's go in and talk." Then, as he nodded, she added: "I saw a big owl."

"Did it have ears?"

"Ears?"

"Tufts of feathers on its head, like animal ears."

"No, it was smooth-headed, and huge. Its eyes were like pools."

"That's the barred owl," he said. "That's its territory, by the road, when the little creatures come out to forage at night. It knows a moving car is safe, but it spooks if you stop."

"Oh. I'm glad I didn't stop."

"We have a great horned owl that's even larger." He was positively loquacious when he talked about the wild creatures!

Inside, seated in the otherwise unused living room, she put it to him directly. "The monster has taken another human being, a child this time. This will not be made public because the boy's mother concealed the fact; she was perhaps afraid that the authorities would blame her. She has a bad marriage, with the husband in charge; she may have been justified. But I fear for her, and want her elsewhere, both for her sake and to prevent another death from blowing this case open. This brings me to my request: will you provide sanctuary for this woman?"

Demerit looked startled. "I don't—" he said, without finishing.

"You don't relate to women well," she agreed. She had done spot research on him, too, and knew that he had at one time been institutionalized. He was not dangerous, just different. Schizoid, the report said, but that was uncertain; as was too often the case, they hadn't really known the nature of his problem. "She is no threat to you. She is desperate and not pushy, unlike me." She delivered one of her brief cold smiles. "She did not ask for this, and does not know I have it in mind. She's not much of a housekeeper, and no young beauty. I think you could pretty much confine her to one room and bathroom and the kitchen, and ignore her. No need to give her the security access code; she would remain nonexistent to outsiders."

"But—"

"But Mid must give approval. Yes. He will do so if you request it. In any event, since she would become your responsibility, it is essential that you acquiesce. I want you to think about it, and if you agree, you can call Mid, and I can bring her over. This would be temporary, until the monster has been dealt with; then things should return to normal."

He still looked troubled and uncertain.

"Call Mid," she suggested. "Maybe he'll say no. Then you need have no awkward feelings about the matter."

He nodded, relieved. He got up and walked toward the phone.

"Oh, I didn't mean right this instant," May said. "You'll need time to think about it."

"Not if he says no."

She spread her hands. She was pretty sure Mid wasn't going to say no. Mid would quickly ascertain that this was her request, not Demerit's, and know that she had reason.

Demerit punched the number. "The monster got a child," he said, evidently to the answering machine. "Also, may I install a woman in the spare room?" He hung up.

May was privately impressed. The man was competent; nothing schizoid there. So why had he been institutionalized? The record had been frustratingly vague on that detail, as though the authorities had known the diagnosis wasn't valid.

May stood. "I'll check in tomorrow if nothing else happens. So far we've managed to keep the lid on, but it will be chancy if that monster isn't stopped soon. I'm going to ask Mid for an extermination specialist. But I hope to get the woman clear first. Otherwise—"

The phone rang. Demerit leaped to answer it. "Geode." He stood, listening.

Geode? Had he mispronounced his own name? Perhaps she had misheard.

"May Flowers," Demerit said. "Yes." He extended the phone to her. This was faster than she had expected! She took the phone. "May."

The familiar voice of her employer answered. "This is your doing?"

"Yes."

"Why?"

"Two reasons. First, I fear she will be the next victim, because the monster is evidently stalking her premises, and that will be the dickens to conceal. She lives about three miles as the crow flies from the Middle Kingdom, so the notoriety could be awkward. Second, I feel for her." She was nervous as she said that; she had never given such a reason for any prior request.

"Tell her not to make a mess."

"Thank you, Mid." She was vastly relieved.

He clicked off. May set down the phone. "He allows it."

Demerit actually smiled. "He knew right away I wasn't asking for myself. He asked who put me up to it, and I said you. Then he asked if you were here."

"He catches on like lightning," she agreed. "He knows that neither one of us would cross him. Very well, I will shop for some groceries, so that no suspicion will be aroused by your having to buy extra. Anything special she needs, I will obtain. I will caution her about disturbing things here. I hope she likes to read; daytime television can be mind-deadening."

"I won't have to stay around?"

"You won't even have to see her, Demerit, if you don't want to. She will be in hiding, a virtual prisoner. But that's better than being dead, I think. You should proceed about your business exactly as before, arousing no suspicion. Your life-style should change very little." She glanced at him. "But you know, it might not hurt you to get to know her. She's not an aggressive sort, and I suspect she's lonely. Her husband is having an almost open affair with another woman, and her child is dead. You may not need any support from the opposite sex, but she does."

He was nonplussed. "Women—I don't—"

"For God's sake, you don't have to sleep with her!" she snapped. "Just talk to her, show her a bit of sympathy. She's like a person recovering from a serious injury, only it's emotional, not physical. I think she will need to talk to somebody. Someone nonthreatening. You are ideal. Just sit there and listen. You might learn something."

"Listening I can do," he agreed.

"Good. Now I don't know when I'll bring her, but it could be as early as tomorrow. I'll have to see about covering her tracks. If I can, I'll spirit her out of that house, and her husband will return to find a message that she's gone to Timbuktu with her son. He'll hardly miss her; he's usually elsewhere. The monster won't find any more prey at that house, and if we're lucky it will move on to another region, or Mid's exterminator will catch it and kill it."

She moved on out the door. "I'll try to bring groceries today; when will you be in?"

"Dusk."

"Good enough." She braced herself, and opened the door to the heat. She hoped she was doing the right thing. If something went wrong with the Brown woman, May's job would be on the line, and she would pay heavily for her sentimentality.

❖ 9 ❖

GEODE SHOOK HIS head as the
Flowers woman drove away. Suddenly she had foisted on him a house-
guest, and if that guest did any harm to the premises, he would be the
one in trouble. Yet there was also an unholy temptation in the notion.
He did not relate well to women, but neither did he relate well to men.
He didn't understand normal people, and they didn't understand him.
The Flowers woman, pushy as she was, related to him about as well as
anybody ever had, except for Mid, whom he had never met. If this
other woman was just an ordinary person who was willing to talk to
him without getting impatient, and just wanted someone to listen, he
would listen and like it. Listening made few demands. If the woman
was lonely—well, so was he. He stayed clear of other people because
interactions always got awkward, not because he wasn't interested. If
the woman didn't want to talk to him, then he could just ignore her,
as suggested; his daily rounds did take time.

He wondered if the Flowers woman knew that he wanted someone
to talk to. She seemed pretty sharp, in her uncompromising way. She
was intent on her job, certainly, but maybe she did see some around
the edges of it.

Also, he had heard what she told Mid: "I feel for her." The pro-

71

fessional coldness of the woman had been cloven asunder with those words. Sympathy moved her. Then she had said, "I suspect she's lonely." And that she needed someone nonthreatening to talk to, to have listen to her, and that he was ideal for that.

That animated him. The notion that he could actually be good for someone else, for a woman. No one had ever suggested that before. For whom was May Flowers actually doing the favor—the woman, or him? Did it matter?

He closed up the house, armed the alarm, and set off on his rounds on the bike. He had a lot to think about, and this activity was an excellent time in which to think.

At dusk the Flowers woman did come with several bags of groceries, which she stored in the main refrigerator—the one that Geode didn't use. "If anyone asks, these are yours," she told him. But of course no one would ask; no one should be here to see it, other than those who already knew. "Tomorrow I'll ask her."

Geode, normally a good sleeper, had a restless night. He kept thinking about the visiting woman, imagining her already there in the spare room, going about her business, watching TV, eating, sleeping. He had been so long without company, it was hard getting used to it— even though he knew it hadn't happened yet. What was her name? What did she look like? He knew only that she was "no young beauty." But she was married and had a young son, so she couldn't be too old. About his own age, perhaps. Did it matter? Not really. She would be company; that was all that counted. For a week or two he would have company. He would try not to turn her off. In the early days he had not understood what made others avoid him, but after the mental hospital it had been clear. He had a fair idea what not to say or do now. She might accept him as a normal person.

In the morning the deputy sheriff came again. "Any news?"

The Flowers woman had told him about the monster, and the man had agreed to keep it quiet. Geode would not be in trouble for moving the truck and the body. Indeed, he had had to move the body again, to the bushes near where he had left the hunter's truck (it wasn't there anymore), so that another deputy could find it. There had been no news report; as far as the authorities were concerned, the hunter had died in some freak accident, and the ants and vermin had had time to pick his bones clean. Maybe later the story would come out, but for now it was under wraps because they were still investigating.

"Did the Flowers woman tell you about the boy?" Geode asked.

"Yeah, she called."

"She wants to hide the woman here."

"Now, that she didn't tell me! What woman? Why?"

"The boy's mother. Flowers is afraid she'll be next, so she wants her here until it's safe."

The deputy nodded. "Makes sense. That makes three times the monster's struck at her place. Just plain luck her window was closed, maybe, or it would've taken her too. If Middleberry—you call him Mid?—if he sends an exterminator, maybe it'll be over soon, and you, me, the Brown woman, and Flowers'll be out of trouble, and no harm done to any of us." He paused, reconsidering. "Well, except for her son. Too bad about that. But who would've thought it would come right in the house and take a kid?"

"This house is better guarded."

"It sure is! Well, if it's okay with Mid, it's okay with me. You take care of her, Demerit." The officer seemed to find something humorous.

"What—what is she like?"

"The Brown woman? She's a mouse. A bedraggled housewife. Mid-thirties, sort of worn down. I guess a bad marriage will do that to you. Quiet. But I'll say this for her, she had the guts to bury her son and keep her mouth shut. Must be more to her than shows. Maybe you'll find out, eh?"

Geode didn't know what was meant by that. "I probably won't see her much. She'll hide inside, and I'll be out on my rounds most of the time."

"Sure." The sheriff's deputy shrugged. "Well, keep me posted. When that exterminator man gets here, I want to see him. And if the monster takes any more meals here, sing out."

Geode nodded. But his mind was less on the monster than on the mouse. He liked mice, as he did all wild things. A woman like a mouse—he could like her too.

The deputy started his car and moved on around the loop. Geode watched him go, glad to be rid of him.

◆ 10 ◆

FRANK SHOOK HIS head as he left the loop behind. Funny man, that Demerit! There seemed to be a blankness about him, as if he were halfway in some other world even when directly talking to a person. But harmless.

Then, stretched across the pebbled asphalt of the drive, he saw something that wasn't harmless. He screeched to a stop before running over it. It was a rattlesnake, about five feet long and so thick through the body it reminded him of a python. Sure, he'd heard tales of much bigger rattlers, but this one was plenty big enough!

He waited, but the reptile just lay there, not coiled. It was taking in the sun. The pattern was bright enough, but not truly diamond; it was more like a series of brownish patches. The rattles were plain too, but dull. The fact was, this creature was neither resplendent nor aggressive; it was in its drab housecoat, relaxing.

Frank turned his wheels sharply and pulled slowly around the snake. He had to ride on the weeds and dirt at the edge to do it, and he knocked down a few dog fennel and a pokeberry plant in the process, but he made it. Then, after he was safely past, the snake moved. It brought its head about and glided slowly off the other side of the drive.

It was as if the damned thing had dared him to run it over and now

74

was contemptuously departing, having proved its point. Well, so be it; Frank wasn't much for killing anyway, and he knew that all wildlife except maybe stinging flies was protected on the Middle Kingdom Ranch. So it was a poisonous snake; so it wasn't menacing him, and he didn't have to menace it. What would be the point of squishing it under his tire and losing all cooperation from the Middle Kingdom folk? What would be the point even if this wasn't a wildlife sanctuary?

He drove on, and his chain of thought resumed. That was a good notion the Flowers woman had, to hide the Brown woman there. The security system was intended to discourage human intruders, but it was so tight that it should give the monster pause too. If the monster even knew she was there.

What Flowers surely had in mind was to clear the woman out and lay a trap for the monster. Why the monster hung around there no one could guess, but since it did, that was the place to catch it. Maybe they could wrap this whole thing up in the next two days. Then Frank could make his report and get some credit, and everything would settle down.

What *was* causing the trouble? They called it the monster, but that was just a name for something unknown. Could it be a deranged man with some kind of hypodermic that dissolved flesh? What did he do with the flesh? Did he trundle a tank along and save it up for some mad experiment? It would be nice to catch him at it!

But Frank couldn't dwell on the matter. There was a lot of small business crowding his schedule, and this monster investigation was still off the record. The authorities didn't want to know about it. That set of bones by the river was bad enough; they hadn't liked that at all, but had agreed that it wasn't enough to make a commotion over.

For now, Frank wanted the monster kept quiet. It was his baby, as it were; he wanted to see it through on his own, and that wouldn't happen if it suddenly started making headlines. It was intriguing as hell, this business of sucking bodies bone-dry; he'd never heard of anything like that before. He intended to be on the scene when they caught the monster, whoever or whatever it was.

But meanwhile he had to carry on with the routine.

"That woman called again, Frank," his wife announced. "She says there's been another feeding at the first house."

Frank, about to sit down to breakfast, changed his mind. He grabbed his hat. "Damn!"

"What's this all about?" his wife asked.

"Nothing you'd want to know!" he said, hurrying out. He'd been busy for three days, and forgotten to check on the Brown woman. Now it had happened!

He careened his car onto the street and turned north. Why hadn't Flowers gotten that fool woman out of there? Now it had hit the fan, for sure!

But the Brown woman was standing outside her house when he screeched in. "God!" he exclaimed. "I thought you'd—"

"Not me," she said. "My—"

"Don't say anything!" Because what he knew for certain he'd have to report. "Let me check around, see what I can see." Because now he realized that it was her husband who'd been taken. How would they cover that up?

He walked around the house. There was no sign of disturbance, just a faint smell. He found himself getting an erection. Brother! That was the monster, all right.

Another car pulled in. There was the Flowers woman. She'd had farther to drive, so had taken longer even though she'd had a head start. He walked briskly across to her. "I haven't gone in. Listen, I think you'd better get that woman the hell away from here! The smell—"

She nodded. "She wouldn't go before. But I think now she will. And I think we have some work to do here first."

"Put it in a bag, take it with you," he said. "There'll be people poking around here. I'll have to put in a missing-person report. This thing won't hold together long! No, I have a better idea. Clear her out and don't come back, then phone in an anonymous query about this house. That'll make it official, but there'll be no traces."

"I understand. Thank you, Frank. I'll do what is necessary."

"You'd better! We're getting in deep."

"We certainly are." She turned and walked toward the house.

He returned to his own car, got in, and started the motor. He could be canned for this, covering up a killing! But his superiors didn't want any big news about any monsters, and he didn't want to tell them. Maybe it would seem that the Brown family had taken off together. That the woman had found out about her husband's affair, and made him take her on a sudden vacation, well away from temptation. Or something. Anything, just so long as the truth didn't come out!

He drove out. At least he'd have time for his breakfast now. The trouble was, he wasn't very hungry anymore.

◆ 11 ◆

ŒNONE TURNED TO the journalist.
"Why wouldn't he listen?"

"He's an employee of the county. If he sees something significant, such as a dead man, he is obliged to report it. He has agreed not to do that, so he has to avoid seeing it."

"But doesn't he want to catch the monster?"

"Yes, Jade. May I call you that? I think we shall be working closely for a time."

Œnone hesitated. She wanted to conceal what the monster had done here, and protect herself from what the law might do to her, and this woman was helping her do that. But that was because the woman had an agenda of her own; it wasn't friendship. So she did not tell her real name. "Yes."

"And you call me May. Now, I asked you to let me take you to a place of security before, but you demurred. Now you must go."

"Yes." Œnone had hoped to maintain a pretense of normalcy, but now that her husband was gone, she would have no way. She had to take what was offered, and worry about the future later.

"I have a plastic bag in my car," May said. "And gloves. I hoped

77

there would be no more deaths, but I prepared, just in case. Are you up to helping me load him?"

"I loved my son. Not my husband. I know the monster is near. I want to get away from here." Understatements, all. She was running on unreality again, doing what she had to, until it was safe to collapse. The moment she had a chance, she would adjust reality to reflect a temporary absence by her family, so that there would be no pain of death, only of separation. It was the sort of thing she was good at: revising realities. But others did not understand, so she didn't speak of this. If only the monster hadn't struck again so soon; she hadn't really gotten her mind-set straight from the loss of Jame, and now she had to do it over. She was in emotional trouble despite her ability to adapt.

They entered the house. There was the body, laid out on the couch. Œnone had locked her bedroom door because of the monster, and he must have come home in the wee hours and concluded that she was mad at him—a good enough conjecture—and so just slept where he could. And the monster had gotten him. It must have come for her, and took him instead. So Paris had done her one favor, in the end. Such as it was.

He had been a corpulent man, but now was just a skeleton in undershorts and T-shirt. The bones of his toes stood up at one end of the couch, and his skull rested at the other. It looked as if he had been dead for three millennia, with just the suggestion of desiccated skin. She almost liked him that way. Paris had wooed Helen three thousand years ago, and now both were skeletons, as was fitting.

They donned the gloves and slid the plastic bag up over the body, starting with the feet. Œnone lifted, and May slid, and it proceeded well enough because the bones weren't that heavy. There was a faint aroma associated with it, not unpleasant, and it triggered notions of sex. But she knew about that now and ignored it. She wondered whether May Flowers was experiencing a similar reaction, and concluded that she was; pheromones cared nothing for attitude.

Soon the bag lay on the couch. May folded it in the middle and carried it out to her car while Œnone straightened up the couch, making sure no evidence of her husband's presence remained. On May's instructions, she left everything else untouched. She was departing in the clothes she wore and with her purse, nothing more.

She went out to the car. May was already in it. She started the motor and pulled out. "The presumption is that person or persons unknown abducted your family and drove you to some other point, not close by," May said. "Your house is undisturbed, as if you had no intention of leaving. They will check everything in it, of course, but there will be no evidence where you went. This sort of thing happens not infrequently, I'm sad to say."

"Where are you taking me?"

"To the Middle Kingdom Ranch."

"Where the other animal was killed?" Œnone asked, dismayed.

"Where the other man was killed," May said evenly. "Now you will have to know: I came here at the direction of the owner of that property, when that man was found, because there is to be no adverse publicity. The ranch is a secure private estate, intended for the owner to use as a retreat at such time as he chooses. He is a rich and perhaps powerful man, probably with enemies, and he guards his privacy scrupulously. You will refer to him as Middleberry when you talk to others, if you do, and as Mid when you talk to me or the caretaker. I asked him to let you stay there because it is the safest place for you I can think of. The monster may be there, but I doubt it can reach you in that house."

"But how will I eat?"

"I have provided an assortment of groceries. There is also the caretaker, a strange man but not a dangerous one; simply ask him for what you need, and one of us will provide it. If you simply wish to talk with someone, ask him whether he cares to listen; he may, but will not volunteer. He is—diffident about women, you see. You may consider it a vacation at a remote resort. Once we have dealt with the monster, you will be free to leave."

Œnone thought about that. Free to leave—but where would she go, with her husband and son dead? With no income and no marketable skills? She had remained in her bad marriage because she had no alternative; now she was out of it, but her alternatives had not improved.

What could she do? She would have to exist one day at a time, and see what happened tomorrow.

The drive was not long. They came to the gate marking the Middle Kingdom Ranch, and drew up to the keypad mounted on a pole, like a parking meter. May touched a button, and in a moment the metal gate cranked open.

They drove down a lane lined with young pine trees. Then it turned, and they followed it into a region of overhanging live oaks interspersed with magnolias and more pines. Finally the house came into sight, big

and beautiful, white with green shutters. A modern-day palace! It was
hard to imagine that she would be staying at such a residence!

A man stood outside. He was about six feet tall, lean in jeans and
short-sleeved shirt, with brown hair and a diffident look. That would
be the caretaker, precisely as described. May had said he wasn't dangerous, but of course that depended. May was a lot more competent in
such respects than Œnone was.

They stopped. They got out. May introduced them. "George, this
is Jade Brown. Jade, this is George Demerit. He will have to let you in
the house; only he knows the alarm code. Let's show you to your room;
then we'll see to the disposition of the bag."

Œnone stood facing Demerit, realizing that this was as awkward for
him as it was for her. Neither knew what to say.

But May did. "George, lead the way."

The man turned and entered the front door. Œnone followed, and
May after her. It was hot outside, but cool inside. There was a carpeted
staircase. They went up that. At the top were three closed doors. They
trooped around to the left, where there was another door and an
offshooting hall, all carpeted. Down that hall were more doors, and
the man opened one on the left. It was a nice room, with a made bed
and a dresser and mirror and closet. There was a large slow fan in the
ceiling.

"The bathroom is the next door down," May said. "The kitchen is
downstairs. You will want to treat the premises as if no one is here;
don't leave anything that any visitor might see to suggest that you are
here."

Œnone nodded, somewhat overwhelmed. What a change from her
small, hot, crowded, messy house! It was as though she had stepped
into another world, leaving her family at the old one. And that was the
way she would frame it. This was a far hotel, and no one had died. She
was a peasant girl mysteriously brought to a strange, lovely palace.
What awaited her here?

"Now we must hide that bag," May said to the man.

The two of them departed, leaving Œnone to herself. She sat on the
bed, making her adjustment of reality. As she did so, she felt better.
She would be able to function now. She had started the process of
adaptation internally, and had it abruptly facilitated externally; what
she had feared would be difficult had become easy.

After a bit she went out, turned left, and went down the hall. It
ended abruptly at what she recognized as a sliding panel; something

was beyond, but she was not supposed to go there. The bathroom was just before the panel, to the left; it was actually the next room to hers, though the doors were fifteen feet apart, with a small closet between.

The bathroom was as clean and nice as the room. The floor was kaleidoscope-patterned vinyl, with an absorbent carpet near the opaque window. The curtains were feminine. There was a toilet, a marbled counter with an inset basin, and a six-foot mirror paralleling it on the wall. A flowery curtained shower and wood clothes hamper which doubled as a seat completed the set, except for a closet.

She shut the door, then used the toilet. The water in it was blue. When she urinated, the water turned green. When she flushed it, dark blue flooded in, banishing the green. The relatively colorless act of elimination had become colorful!

"I am in love with this apartment," she breathed.

She ran water to wash her hands and face. There was a white hand towel beside the sink with which she patted her face dry. But being clean did not improve the rest of it: she looked forty, with her drab gray dress and lank brown hair. The lines of her drabness were etched into her face. She was growing old without ever having truly experienced youth.

She went out and down the stairs, feeling the spongy softness of the carpet, running her hand along the smooth wood rail. So this was the way the wealthy lived! She would imagine that she was a rich girl, taking all this as a matter of course, not even noticing it except perhaps as something incidental, something commonplace and dull. What luxury, to imagine an attitude like that!

She did not see the others, so took a moment to explore, hoping they would not mind. The short hall at the base of the stairs led to the kitchen, replete with elegant wood cabinets on three sides and a counter that opened to the family room beyond. She checked the refrigerator and saw the groceries: milk, lettuce, bacon, orange juice, bread in the bin below, frozen staples above. In the adjacent cabinet were cans of beans, soup, applesauce, and the like. It would do. Who had paid for this?

She went into the family room and saw beyond it into the pool. The water was clear and blue and looked horribly inviting. It had been so long since she had gone swimming! But of course this would be off-limits for her; she was supposed to stay in her quarters, and sneak down to eat every so often, not disturbing the premises. She would do that, keeping her fancies to herself. She had been a poor housekeeper, but that was because she had had no reason to be good; neither her husband nor her son had cared. Now, in this new, clean, perfect residence, she would be the perfect housekeeper. Perhaps, in her fancy, that was why she had been brought here: to maintain the environs of the King of the Middle Kingdom. No, not King; Emperor. Whatever.

She continued her tour, discovering a small library room lined with books. At least she would be able to read! It really didn't matter what books were available; her tastes were eclectic, though she had a weakness for sexy romance, which she was sure would not be in strong supply here. Still, she noted a matched set of the works of George Bernard Shaw; that would do nicely for a time.

She circled back to the front door and crossed the hall to the living room, where the carpeting resumed. Adjacent to it was the dining room, and beyond that was another short hall whose floor was wooden squares—what were they called?—parquet. That led to both a front and a back exit, and to another closed door. Those closed doors lent mystery to the house, though they were surely innocent. Here was the beauteous, naive, newlywed wife, brought by her sinisterly handsome, rich, taciturn husband to this isolated estate and told that she had the run of it, except for *that* door. Naturally her curiosity burgeoned! But she knew she must not, for if she did, something truly awful would happen. Yet how long could she contain herself? Though it be the end of her, she had to know what lurked behind that one door!

Behind her, beyond the living room, the front door opened. Œnone jumped. But her guilt dissipated as she turned and went to the front.

May and Mr. Demerit were back, both sweaty. They had evidently taken the bag somewhere and hidden it securely. Now their job was done.

May looked at her. "I will have to get you some clothing," she said matter-of-factly. "I'll do that now, and return in two or three hours. Will you be here, George?"

"I have to do my rounds," Demerit protested. "I delayed them this morning because you called."

"Four hours, then?"

Demerit looked out of sorts, but couldn't get out of it. "Yes."

May turned to Œnone. "In the interim, you go to your room and sleep or something. Do not answer the door or the phone; you are nonexistent. George will leave the alarm system on, so that no intrusion from outside is possible."

"Is it all right if I read a book?" Œnone inquired hesitantly. "I saw a set of Shaw—"

"You can't walk around the house," Demerit said. "You'll set off the motion detectors."

Motion detectors! The security was more sophisticated than she had realized! "Could I get a book now, before you turn it on, and read in my room?"

"Yes. Your room and the bathroom are all right. But don't go beyond, or open a window. If you set off the alarm while I'm away—"

"I understand!" she said quickly. That was the very, very last thing she wanted to do. The alarm would end her fancy before it was fairly started!

She went quickly to the library and took the first volume of Shaw. She didn't know what was in it, but was sure it would hold her. She went upstairs and to her room, carrying the book. She closed the door, sat on the bed, and opened the book to the first play. This was *The Doctor's Dilemma*, with the note "No Performance Recorded." Now that was interesting. Why write a play and never perform it? She turned the page and encountered a preliminary essay, "How These Doctors Love One Another!" It turned out that what was described was quite the opposite; these doctors hated one another. Maybe that was why it couldn't be performed: the AMA had squelched it.

Fascinated, Œnone was soon oblivious to the rest of the world. Shaw could do that to her. What a writer that man was! How she would have liked to get him alone at night in a house like this! She was barely aware of the sound of May Flowers's car starting up outside the window.

❖ 12 ❖

"Make sure you are back," May told Demerit firmly. "I'll need to be let in, and she can't do it. I realize you don't want to be left alone with her, but some contact is inescapable. She can't even eat until you turn off the internal sensors."

"I'll be back," he agreed.

"Remember, she's been through a lot. You don't have to hold her hand, but try not to be insensitive."

"I'll try," he agreed, not smiling.

She went to her car. The faint lingering aroma of the body remained, inciting a passing thought of sex. What an imposition that was: to be handling a grotesque body and have to think of sex at the same time. They had stashed it in the barn, up in the loft, behind some cardboard boxes, and stacked some boxes on top of it. No one should think to look for it there, considering that no one else knew it existed, or that it had been transported here. It should keep until Frank Tishner decided what to do with it. The barn had been sweltering, hotter in the loft than below despite the aeration provided by the soffit, and she had practically burst out with sweat. Demerit hadn't; he seemed to run cooler, somehow. Perhaps it was a function of his mental detachment.

She started the motor and felt the blessed air conditioning. She pulled around the loop. As she headed away from the house, she saw Demerit emerge and close the door carefully, and get on his red bicycle, which was parked near the side entrance. He certainly didn't want to be near the Brown woman! But this was a necessary thing, hiding the woman; it would protect both her life and the privacy of this estate.

She reached the gate and touched the OPEN button. A person could not get in without either knowing the access code or having a special beeper or being let in, but it was easy for anyone to get out. Of course, a truly determined person could simply crash his car through the gate, flattening it. But that would set off the alarm, and shortly the police and the fire department would arrive. There was no percentage in that, for an intruder!

She passed through, and watched the gate close after her in the rearview mirror. This certainly was a secure estate, and she liked that. Mid did things right.

She was about to drive south into Inverness, but changed her mind; why would a portly woman like her buy dresses for a much smaller frame? She had sized Jade Brown up by eye and had a fair notion what would fit her. The woman was actually better structured than the casual observer would think; she might be a mouse, but she could be a sleek one in the right fur. So May turned north on 200, heading for the river and the next county. She would do her shopping this time in Ocala, which was larger, and where no one had seen her around. She would put it on her charge card, which Mid would replenish; he had known when he agreed to let the Brown woman stay that there would be expenses.

Let's see: several simple, light print dresses should do, and some jeans and blouses for outside; she knew the woman would not stay cooped up inside all the time. Just so long as she remained concealed from anyone who came in.

She returned with an excellent wardrobe. There was a certain joy in such shopping, even though it was not for herself, and she had rather overdone it. Perhaps it was the thought of that woman, abused emotionally if not physically, with so little to look forward to. Then the monster coming and wiping even that out. It was so easy to identify with her hopelessness; May had been through it herself. Someone needed to do something nice for her, and this was May's pretext. The rest of the time she would be her usual tough, businesslike self, getting her job done, and actually Jade Brown was now part of that job. But in this one thing she was indulging herself, doing her bit to rehabilitate a forlorn woman, if only for a week or two.

Demerit was back, because the gate opened as she buzzed. She drove on in and to the house. Then she started unloading.

The man came out. "Carry this up to her room," May said, handing him an armful of dresses. He did not protest; he simply took them and went back in.

May hauled out her bags of shoes, underclothing, and accessories. She had even splurged to the extent of jewelry. It was cheap—there were, after all, limits—but attractive. The subject might not be much, but modern cosmetics and foundations could do more than many men and some women believed. It was said that clothes made the man, but it was even truer for women. They were going to make this woman.

Was she being foolish? Yes, certainly. But an inner need had been evoked, and she would play it out.

Jade Brown appeared. "This—what—?"

"You can't occupy a house like this in clothing like that," May said emphatically. "Suppose the owner came here unexpectedly, and you looked like that?" There was, of course, little if any logic in this, but it sounded authoritative, and Jade did not challenge it.

May bustled up with the bags and set them on the floor in the room. "Now, you survey this stuff tonight, and put some on tomorrow. I will be by to help you if you need it. Don't ask George; he won't know a thing about it. Now, have you eaten?"

Wordlessly, the woman shook her head.

"Well, you're surely competent there; go and fix yourself supper while I hang this stuff up in your closet." She smiled fleetingly. "Don't worry, I won't pry into any of your things, or steal anything."

The woman turned and walked down the hall, as submissive as the man. May was bullying her, she knew, but it really was better to get this set up, and if the woman ate while May was here, at least she could be sure that she was fed. Demerit was unlikely to think of anything like that. What he did at night she didn't know and was hardly curious about; for all she knew, he could live on wild berries and sleep in the swamp. She intended better for Jade Brown; she meant to see that things were properly organized.

She felt, actually, somewhat like a fairy godmother.

In twenty minutes she had everything put away. She went downstairs and found the woman completing a perfectly competent can of lentil soup. Well, that might not be ambitious, but it would be filling.

"I have other errands," she announced. "But you should be all right for the night. Don't be concerned about George." She glanced back to be sure the man was not near. "He's impotent. He won't bother you. But if you care to talk to him, I think he'll listen."

Actually, it was not her way to blab people's secrets, but in this case she felt it was appropriate. The woman had just lost a philandering husband, and would be dependent to a considerable extent on a strange man who controlled access to the house. She would naturally be concerned about his possible sexual approach, especially considering her own history of abuse as a child, and this would reassure her. Demerit was not an ordinary man, but he was no molester of women.

"Remember," May admonished in conclusion, "you must be invisible. Do not answer the doorbell or the phone. When anyone other than Demerit or me comes, you hide. Don't leave any of your things outside your room."

"I understand," the woman said meekly.

"And tomorrow I want to see you in one of those new outfits. They should fit you, and they're adjustable."

Jade looked uncomfortable. "You know I can't pay—"

"I know. I did this on my own. Wear them."

She nodded, in much the way Demerit did. May exited, bracing herself against the heat, and went to her car. She would have to do something about that faint lingering odor of the monster in the car; it was disconcerting, to say the least.

⬦ 13 ⬦

GEODE WATCHED MAY Flowers depart. He felt a thrill of nervousness. He was alone for the night with Jade Brown. Of course it didn't mean anything; she probably wouldn't even talk to him, and certainly he wouldn't bother her. But the idea of it was electrifying: association with a woman who was not on her way somewhere else. May Flowers had said Jade might want to talk. Probably that was just to keep him from forgetting her, from locking her in or out, but he would like it if she talked to him. He might have said so before, but had been too nervous to approach her, and his daily rounds did offer an excellent pretext to avoid the matter.

Now his round was done, and he had no pretext. But he still couldn't approach her.

He reentered the house and closed the door. He wouldn't arm the security system yet; he didn't want the woman setting it off by accident. Once he knew she was settled in her room for the night, he would arm it.

He turned—and there she was. She was, as the deputy had said, mousy, but that hardly mattered; she was a human being. "Mr. Demerit," she said hesitantly.

He tried to speak, and could not. He could relate to pushy people,

88

like May Flowers, because they carried the ball right to him, but it was harder here. So he nodded.

"I—I borrowed a book from the library. Was that all right? I mean, I think you didn't say no, but May was there, and maybe I shouldn't have taken it."

Now he could talk; she had asked him a direct question. "Mid doesn't mind, if you don't hurt the books. I read them all the time." Which was about ten times as much as he thought he would say; it had just flowed out, like water under pressure.

"Oh, I was careful not to smudge it! I—I had to stay in my room, and I didn't have anything to do, so I took the first volume of Shaw and just started at the beginning."

"*The Doctor's Dilemma,*" he said. He had read them all, and found them all fascinating.

"Oh, you *do* read them!" she exclaimed. "You weren't just saying that!"

"I have a lot of time to myself," he explained. *She was interested.*

"So do I. Even before—before my family went away. I read anything, but I love the great writers, and Shaw is one of the greatest."

"Yes. The essays too." No one had expressed interest in anything he was interested in, before.

"The essays too. The man had uncanny insight into everything he touched."

"Yes." She had said it better than he could have.

"But I must not keep you from your work," she said apologetically. "I just wanted to be sure—"

"My work's done." He wished he could just stay here, having her interested, and never do anything else.

"Well, your supper, then. You have been very kind, very nice about my intrusion, and I won't bother you further."

"I don't mind." So much was whirling in his mind, but almost all of it choked off at his mouth.

"But I know you have to eat, and—" She paused. "I am competent at cooking. May I fix you something? I would so appreciate being useful!"

"No need." He wanted to say yes, but didn't really know how to. He had not had a meal with a woman in a decade.

"Please, I'd like to, if you don't mind. I'm—the truth is, I don't like being alone, especially now."

To have a woman want to be with him! It was hard to believe this was happening—which meant that it might not be. He didn't want more trouble. How did he know what was polite and what was sincere? "I—I don't know," he stumbled.

"You have something special that you eat? I don't mean to interfere. I'm sorry if I—"

He could see no better way to do this than just to say it. That might be a mistake, but what else was there? "I don't know whether I'm supposed to accept or not."

"Supposed to?" she asked blankly.

"If you're being polite, and I'm supposed to say no."

"Oh, Mr. Demerit!" she exclaimed. "I'm not being polite! Please say yes!"

"It's all right?"

"Oh, yes! Why should you think otherwise?"

"People don't want my company. I don't know how to be with people."

"Well, I want your company, Mr. Demerit! I don't mind how you are with people."

It did seem all right. He took the plunge. "Yes."

"Oh, wonderful!" she exclaimed, and he felt another thrill, as if something truly momentous had occurred. "Come, I'll see what I have. What do you like?" She led the way toward the kitchen.

"Anything." Anything she wanted to fix for him would be a novel experience.

"You are easy to please, Mr. Demerit! Should I call you that? Can we be less formal?"

He shrugged. "May Flowers calls me George."

"I couldn't call you George," she said. "Even if it is your name. Don't you have some other name?" She was bustling in and out of the refrigerator, doing things, female fashion.

"Why?"

"George is my brother's name. I don't like him."

The implication staggered him. She didn't want to call him by the name of someone she didn't like. Did that mean she liked him? "I call myself Geode."

"Geode! That's beautiful! A stone, so drab on the outside, all crystalline inside! Some people are like that, and surely you are too!"

What joy to have her understand! "It's from my name."

"Yes, of course. 'George Demerit' run together. But the image is the stone, isn't it?"

"Yes. The stone. Do—uh—"

She paused in her bustle. "Yes, Geode?"

"Do you want to see it? The stone?"

She actually clapped her hands. "You have a stone? A real geode?"

"Yes, in my room."

"Oh, yes! Let me see it."

He lurched off. In a moment he brought the stone back. It was about six inches long, weighed about five pounds, and was pitted like a meteorite outside. But it was only half a stone, cut across the center and polished so that the crystalline center was exposed. "It's just quartz," he said. "But I've had it all my life."

"It's beautiful!" she exclaimed. "It's you, Geode! All gruff and sober outside, perfect inside!"

"Oh, no, I'm not—I mean, it's perfect, but I'm—" He couldn't formulate his demurral.

"I understand! What I mean is that no one can tell from the outside what a person is like inside, and maybe a person looks stupid or mousy outside, but there's so much inside that may be beautiful if you just understand."

"Yes!" What a perfect way of putting it!

"Then I will tell you my secret name too, Geode. I am Œnone. That's ee-NO-nee, not 'onion', though I may have layers to peel." She was cutting an onion under water as she spoke.

This was too much for Geode to grasp all at once. She had seemed so shy, and now seemed so open. "Not Jade?"

"No more than you are George. Shall we be friends, Geode?"

Was she teasing him in some way? His doubt returned. Who wanted to be friends with him?

She paused in her activity. "Did I offend you? I didn't mean to. I apologize if—"

"No!"

"But I said something wrong?"

He struggled with it. "I don't have friends."

She resumed her activity, evidently relieved. "Maybe you have one now. Why do you say that?"

Was this folly? He wanted to tell her, but feared the consequence. It was so nice being with her like this, watching her bustle, he didn't want to alienate her. He shook his head, neither yes nor no, but confusion.

"But I am prying," she said. "I didn't mean to do that, Geode. You don't have to tell me anything you don't want to. Would you like me to tell you about me? I mean, my name?"

"People don't like me, when they learn," he said with difficulty.

"You see, my husband's name is Paris. That's where it started. That's really his name. In Greek mythology, Paris was married to the nymph Œnone. So I became that. Am I talking too much?"

"No."

"Œnone is a rather sad figure. Because Paris—do you know about him, mythologically?"

Geode thought. "He—Helen?"

"Exactly. Helen of Troy. Paris left the nymph for the face that launched a thousand ships. Œnone was not completely pleased. But how could she compete with Helen?"

She evidently wanted something of him, but he wasn't sure what. "I guess she couldn't."

"Yes. So she just kept to herself. What else was there to do? So she didn't have many friends. Paris had a good time while Œnone suffered."

"I keep to myself," Geode said.

"Yes. Like your namesake. All the good things are inside."

"I don't know if they're good."

"Would you like to tell me?" She looked at him and smiled, and it was like a splatter of sunlight from the surface of a dark pool.

He still wasn't sure, but decided to tell her. "I see things. Hear things. But I guess others don't."

"Good things?"

"Just things." He swallowed, then said it: "Animals who talk to me."

"And they called you crazy," she said.

"They put me in a hospital."

She nodded. "When I was little, my Raggedy Ann doll talked to me. Nobody believed. So I learned not to tell them."

"Yes," he agreed with a rush of feeling.

"Another time I told them something, and they did believe. That was worse."

"Yes. First they thought I was just trying to get attention, and laughed at me. But when they believed—" He paused, getting it straight. "When they believed I believed, they put me away. Until I told them I didn't believe."

She thought for a moment as she worked. "I must tell you something, Geode. I don't want to, but I have to."

He was silent, knowing what was coming. He had told her, and it had been a mistake. He should have known better.

"I have nowhere to go," she said. "I have no money, no marketable skills, no hope. Suddenly I am in this dream house, like a poor peasant girl who has been mistaken for a lost princess. What is she to do?"

"I don't know."

"She is going to try to act like a princess, so as to fool them just as long as she possibly can, because once they catch on, she will be out on the street and her life will be over."

He stood there, watching her, not understanding what she was getting at.

"If the King's butler tells that girl something strange, will she laugh in his face?"

That he could answer. "No."

"That's right. Because she doesn't want to offend anybody in the palace. So she will believe anything he tells her, so long as it is not inconsistent with her being a princess. Do you understand?"

Now he did. "You won't laugh at me."

"Yes. But I am not to be trusted. Oh, I will behave perfectly, and be the very model of the princess, but what is in my heart you cannot trust, because I don't want to be thrown out. I need your favor, and I will do anything to get it and keep it. I am like a hungry cat, purring at your legs so you will feed me and let me into your house. Can you live with that?"

Geode was troubled. "I work for Mid. If he says you stay, you stay. If he says you go—"

"But he will let me stay if you want me to."

"I guess so."

"So I will try to make you want me to."

"You don't have to—"

"Beginning with this," she said, setting a sculptured salad down on the dining-room table. She had somehow fashioned it from lettuce and tomato aspic and carrots and beans. It was beautiful.

He sat at the table, then realized that it was a one-person salad, and the only one. "But you—"

"I ate before. Now it's your turn. What would you like to drink? We have milk and orange juice."

"Juice. But—"

"Coming up. Dig in while I prepare the next course."

"But you don't have to—"

"Yes, I do. Now settle down and let me play my part."

She really did want to do this, he realized. So he started eating, and let her do it her way.

It seemed that only a moment had passed when he finished what turned out to be a very nice meal concocted of simple ingredients. Œnone was sitting opposite, watching him. She had washed his dishes and put them away as he finished them.

"Do I talk too much?" she asked abruptly.

"I like to listen."

"May I be candid again?"

Geode had not known what to expect, and his fancies had been fragmentary. The reality was infinitely more detailed and fulfilling. Whatever she wanted to say he would hear. "Yes."

"I do not want to sleep alone. May I sleep with you?"

He stared at her. Again, he couldn't answer.

"I realize I'm not much," she said. "But whatever I am I will offer you, only for your company this night. Do I affront you?"

"I—I don't know what you mean."

"I want so much not to be alone that I have no scruples about it, no inhibitions. If you want me as a companion, I will be that. If you want me as a sex object, I will be that. Only let me be with you, and I will do for you whatever you ask, to the extent of my power to do it."

"But I can't—"

"If I could make myself beautiful for you, I would. I will certainly try. I realize I am not eighteen, but neither am I sixty. Perhaps in the dark—"

"I'm impotent!" he said, hating the word.

She was not fazed. "Would you let me try to make you potent?"

He was amazed. "You would do that?"

"I would."

He knew this was crazy, but the dream of becoming normal took hold of him. "Yes."

"Let me change, and I will join you in a moment."

She had spoken most plainly, but this was hard to believe. He nodded.

She left the dining room and went quickly upstairs. In a surprisingly brief time she was back, clad in a negligee.

Geode stared. She had been, as Tishner had said, mousy. She had been transformed. She had let her hair loose and fluffed it out, and put on some makeup, and the negligee made of her body a hazy, floating form showing a bit of cleavage. The lines of her face had faded, and her eyes were no longer pocketed but shadowed.

"You're beautiful!" he exclaimed. It was an exaggeration, but not much of one. "Pretty" would have been a better word. Yet the change was so great that a stronger word was required to satisfy it.

"You are kind," she said.

He just looked at her, taking in the change. Perhaps she remained a mouse, but now she was sleek and soft and interesting.

"How would you like me?" she asked.

He just shook his head. His belief simply could not make the jump.

"Would you like to dance with me?"

"I can't dance."

"I don't do it well, but I could show you the steps."

"I—I don't know what to do."

"Then stand," she said.

He stood. This was surely a dream!

"Put your arms around me."

He did so, clumsily. In a moment she might burst out laughing, but until then the dream remained.

She embraced him. "Kiss me," she said, lifting her face.

"I don't know how."

"Purse your lips, close your eyes, and bend your head forward."

He followed instructions. Then he felt her lips against his. She was kissing him on the mouth! He was so amazed he lost his balance. He pulled her with him, involuntarily, and the two of them fell against the wall.

Appalled, ashamed, he opened his eyes and tried to pull away. But she clung to him. "The first time is never perfect," she said. "All things must be learned. But perhaps we should practice lying down."

"I—" He was afraid he was losing touch with reality entirely.

"Your room or mine?" she inquired.

"I have to go out."

Her brow furrowed. "Now?"

"To—" He knew it was wrong to say it to a woman.

But she caught on. "The bathroom?"

He nodded, embarrassed.

"You don't use what's inside?"

Somehow it always got like this when he was with another person, all awkward and stumbling. "It's just water, and the plants, they need it."

"Oh, Geode, now I understand! You fertilize the plants! How thoughtful."

Had he somehow managed not to offend her, again? "You aren't mad?"

"You like plants," she said. "Why waste a lot of water flushing a toilet, when the plants can really use the nitrogen? It shows how sensible you are. By all means, go out. I don't think you want my company at the moment."

She really did seem to understand, the first one ever to do so. He went out the side door into the closing darkness, found a familiar azalea bush, and urinated at its base. Then he returned, and washed his hands in the half-bathroom just inside that entry.

Œnone was there, just beyond. "Your room or mine?" she repeated.

She didn't let go—nor did he want her to. She was pushing him the way everyone did, thinking him dull-witted, but she was pushing him in a wonderful new way. "Here." He opened the door to the wing where he stayed. He normally left the main house alone, only checking it to be sure everything was in order. Whenever Mid came here, the house and trees would be ready.

"Oh, the forbidden door," she murmured.

"No, that one's upstairs."

She put her fist to her mouth as if startled. "It is?"

"The security closet. It's always on unless I turn it off with a key, so nothing can be stolen. There isn't anything in there, but Mid has it set up so if there ever *is* anything he can use it."

"Oh. Of course."

He reached for the light switch near the door, but she demurred. "Let's be in the darkness, for now," she said. "I was afraid of the dark, alone, but I'm not afraid with you."

Geode had no concern about the dark; in fact he rather liked it. He liked it even better now. "Can you see?"

"You can guide me." She took hold of his elbow.

He guided her in a few steps, where the wing divided into two rooms, and then to the left, where his bed and belongings were. "Here."

"Lie down, and I will join you."

He stretched out on the bed, on the left side, facing right. She lay on the right side, facing left. She moved into him, her body touching his at thigh and chest. Her left hand came up and found his head; then her face was there, and she was kissing him. He felt as if he were floating through warm fog, yet also lying on the bed with her.

"You see, we can't fall over," she murmured.

He had to laugh, and she laughed with him. It was the first time he could remember laughing with a woman.

"Let me see if I can make you potent," she said. "Take off your clothes."

He did not protest. He was beyond that, in this unreal darkness. He rolled off the bed, unbuckled his belt, dropped his jeans, stripped off his shirt, and removed his underpants and socks. He lay down, naked.

Her hand touched his chest, locating him. Then she lay against him again, her body warm against his. She was naked too; she had removed her negligee and slippers. "All that a woman can be to a man, I will be to you," she murmured, and kissed him.

Then, after a moment: "Am I boring you?"

"No." Far from it; he had never before had such an experience.

She moved against him, pressing him back, her breasts sliding across his chest. Her hair fell down, tickling his neck. She kissed him once more, lying on top of him, her legs falling outside his.

"You really are impotent," she said.

"Yes."

"But when you handled the—what the monster left—what then?"

"It—I—it got hard," he said, remembering, surprised.

"And when you sleep, alone?"

"Sometimes it does," he said.

"So it is psychological, not physical."

"Yes."

"But I am not finished." She drew up her legs and lifted her body, straddling him on the bed. She moved down, exposing his crotch. Then her hands found his member. It was soft.

"There are ways," she said. She moved down farther, then began kneading his penis and stroking his testicles. Then she put her mouth down. She licked him, and stroked him, and finally sucked on him, but there was no hardness.

She paused. "I must ask; forgive me if I offend you. Are you homosexual?"

"No. I like women. But they don't like me."

"Ah, so you don't really believe I want you. That nulls your circuits. Let's try it the other way around." She lay down beside him. "Get up on me, sitting as I was, and run your hands over my body."

Geode obeyed. "My breasts," she said. "Don't avoid them. They may not be world class, but neither are they nonexistent; they merely flatten out as I lie on my back. Take handfuls, knead them, gently."

He did so, and thrilled to the experience. "Now my thighs," she said. "Run your hands down, outside, now inside. No, don't shy away! Go up where they join. I am spreading my legs wide. Here, you must let me do it; put your knees together inside mine. Yes. Now move your hand up. Do you feel where it is wet?"

"Yes. Am I hurting you?"

"No, Geode. You are making me want you. My body is ready for yours. Is yours ready yet?"

"No."

"Would you like to use your mouth, as I used mine?"

"I don't know how."

"Put your face down. Here, let me guide you." Her hands came up and caught his head on either side. They brought it down until his face was in her crotch. "Now lick."

He licked. He found it fascinating and enjoyable, but his member did not get hard. It was as though the nerves between his head and his penis had been cut.

"Ah, Geode, I love it," she said. "But it is your potency I am striving for, not mine. I must have you in me, or I have failed. Lie down again, put your arms around me, and we shall consider."

He obeyed. Soon they were embraced, their legs intertwined, her head nestled against his neck and shoulder. "I thought I could make you react by sheer force of body," she said. "I was mistaken. Would you rather sleep alone?"

"No!"

"I really don't know how to deal with impotence. I'm no psychiatrist. I suppose I should make you tell me your childhood secrets, to find out what inhibits you. But I fear that would be a mistake, as it seems this physical approach was. I came at you too hard and strong and invoked your defenses, and you cannot perform, though I think you want to."

"Yes!"

"But I have only begun to fight, Geode. Only let me stay with you, and I will find a way to make you potent. I promise."

"I like this, even if—" He did not finish, hoping she would understand.

"It is as if you are hungry, and you are at a bakery, and you can smell the sweet rolls, but your mouth is wired shut."

"Yes." She was so good at the right imagery!

"We'll get your mouth open, Geode. I will stay close to you, and I will break this barrier. If you just let me."

He lay there, embraced, feeling as if he were floating again, all the way to the moon. She had already given him more than he had ever had before.

✦ 14 ✦

He DREAMED THAT he had dreamed of a woman lying naked with him, and awakened to know it as a dream, for what woman would ever do that? He felt enormous regret, actually sorrow. In his dream she had offered everything, and he had been unable to take it. Why couldn't he have done it in the dream? When would he ever have a better chance? He had been a fool, even in his own imagination!

He woke, chastened, and felt beside him—and found her body there. It was real! He wanted to kiss her, but didn't dare; she might be angry, and disavow everything.

In the morning she remained, lying beside him. The dawn was expanding, and his eyes were adjusted; he could see her well enough. She was beautiful, in her fashion. Her breasts heaved with the gentle rhythm of her breathing, and one of her legs overlapped his. She was all woman, so desirable—and he so inadequate.

He got up and went to the bathroom to wash. When he returned, she was awake. "You didn't change your mind?" she asked worriedly.

"I would like it like this forever," he said.

"Forever, for now. I will fix you breakfast."

"No need."

"Unless you tell me no in quite explicit terms, I will do it. I must get to know you, Geode, so I can discover how to make you potent." She donned the negligee as they talked, concealing nothing from him. Her breasts, as she had said, were not big, but neither were they small, and they bounced intriguingly as she put the light garment on over her head. He saw that her stomach had a pattern of scar tissue.

"You—don't eat first," he blurted.

She smiled. "I will eat with you this time, if you wish." She poked her feet into her pink slippers and hurried toward the kitchen.

By the time he got there, she had milk and canned fruit and dry cereal out. Her hair had been brushed; she must have found time to go up to her room and do that too.

"You—did your—did he hurt you?" he asked stumblingly.

"My husband? He hurt me only by ignoring me, after our child. I don't like to be ignored, as you might have noticed."

"But you—your stomach—"

She pulled up her negligee, exposing her legs, stomach, and breasts. She glanced down. "Oh, that! Those are stretch marks!"

"What?"

"When I had my baby, my abdomen contracted, but my skin didn't quite make it back. The marks of that stretching remain. I agree they aren't pretty; that's why I prefer darkness for lovemaking. I was so busy trying to seduce you I forgot about them."

"Trying to—?"

"Do you suppose when I do this it's an accident?" she asked, lifting the material to breast height again. "Touch didn't do it last night, but sight might. Does it make you react?"

He looked at her breasts. They were as perfectly formed as any he had seen in pictures. "I wish I could. I want to."

"I wish you could too! It's been so long since any man was interested in me, and there is so little time. You're sure there's no reaction?"

"Everywhere but there," he said sadly.

"I meant to wake and watch you in the night, to catch you when you got an erection, but I was so tired I slept right through. But tonight—"

"It wouldn't work. Even in my dreams, I can't do it."

"Well, I will keep working on it, if you let me."

"I—I just like to be with you."

"Well, I am trying very hard to be pleasant. Just warn me when I talk too much."

"I like to listen."

"I mean, I can talk a blue streak, all about everything I've read and feel and dream, and I can bore people to sleep. I'm trying to hold it down, but it keeps bubbling up. So when I do that to you—"

"No one ever wanted to talk to me before."

She paused. "You mean you really don't mind?"

He tried to frame it, lacking competence. "When you—last night you talked to me—paid attention—you didn't have to take off your clothes or anything, I liked listening."

She gazed at him, and her eyes shone. "Oh, Geode, I think you have just paid me the nicest compliment! Do you mind if I kiss you?"

"I like that too."

She got up, came around the table, squirmed onto his lap, put her arms around his shoulders and neck, and drew his head in to hers. She put her lips to his, then paused. "Open your mouth," she said.

Surprised, he did so. She put her open mouth to his and pressed hard. Her tongue came through and touched his.

Astonished, Geode froze, not in horror but for fear that anything he might do would disrupt the experience. For the first time, with a woman, he felt the tug of a reaction.

She withdrew. "Did I go too far?"

"I think I started to get hard," he said, awed.

"You did? Oh, Geode, I'm so pleased!" She let go, grabbed his head, and pressed it to her bosom.

He felt the warm resilience of her two breasts, his chin at the décolletage of her low negligee, his mouth and nose across the cleavage formed by the pressure of his face. Her left nipple pressed against his right cheek. He felt another tug. He was reacting to a woman!

In a moment she realized this. "Yes! Definitely!" she exclaimed. "Let's go to the bedroom—no, that's too far away. Here." She lifted her negligee, spread her legs, and sat on him, face to face. She reached down, opened his fly, and squirmed closer to make the connection.

But it didn't work. His nascent erection fled, and no penetration was possible. Œnone collapsed against him, her head beside his. "It got to be too much like sex," she said. "The spontaneity was gone."

"But I wanted it!" he protested.

"Yes, but your unconscious censor doesn't. When I kissed you, when I hugged you, that was emotion, not sex. That was all right. Then I got too physical, and turned you off."

"But I really liked what you did! You were so—so expressive. You liked me."

She lifted her head. "I forgot the act, I was myself," she said. "I showed real emotion, and you picked up on that."

"You—it wasn't real?"

She stared into his eyes. "Oh, Geode, I told you last night. I don't want to be thrown out on the street. I'm trying to please you, I'm trying very hard. I'm not usually like this. I never threw myself at my husband like this! But you're not used to this, you want what's real, and I'm not giving you that." Her eyes overflowed. "Geode, I'm sorry. I'm toying with your emotions and hurting you."

"But—but when I complimented you, weren't you pleased?"

"Yes! I was thrilled! You liked what wasn't part of the show—" Her eyes widened. "I kissed you with real passion, the way I wanted to. And then I hugged you, so happy. Geode, those things were *real!*"

"And if you loved me, for real—"

Her streaked face froze. "I never said love! I stayed well clear of that word. I can't—there was never love in my marriage, it was for convenience—and now I need a place to stay—I never deceived you in that!"

He continued to look at her, feeling a lump in his throat. She *had* told him. She had been fair.

"And there's the key," she said, her tears still forming. "You are physically impotent. I am emotionally impotent. If I could give you what you truly want, you could be potent with me. Your unconscious understood better than I did."

"But you must like me a little," he said.

"And you reacted a little. Geode, that's a very long way to go, and it is no proper course."

"I want to go there!"

"But, Geode, consider the future! Once they catch the monster, I won't have to hide, and I won't be able to stay here with you. I am poison, Geode! You don't want to love me. You want to use me, to have experience, and forget me after. That's the male way."

"I read somewhere—it's better to love and lose than never to love at all."

"You would love and lose, Geode. I don't want to do that to you."

"But otherwise I don't have anything!"

"I think you still don't understand. When I leave here, I expect to be dead. There is no life for me out there, and perhaps there never was. I shut out the past and have no future. There is only now. Touch my body as you will, but keep your emotion clear, or you will be left with nothing, with less than nothing."

He knew she was trying to spare him, but he couldn't let it go. "You said—you said I shouldn't love you. But you could love me."

Her mouth dropped open. "That's right! I have it backwards. As long as you don't love me, it doesn't matter how I feel. That is, I could love without hurting you. I can't be hurt, because I'll be dead."

"Just talk to me," he said, not liking her conclusion.

"Geode, I fear you mean to cheat. You want to be loved—and to love."

She had him dead to rights.

She leaned against him, thinking about it. He put his arms around her, so glad for the feeling of holding her close.

After a time she lifted her head again. "I would like to love before I die."

"I think I—I was lost when you first talked to me."

"About twelve hours ago," she said with a rueful smile. "You loved anyone who was willing to be close to you."

"Yes."

"But you still couldn't *make* love. For that you need mine, mismatched though we must be."

"Yes."

"Shall we seek love, then?"

"Yes!"

She laid her head on his shoulder again. He felt the shudder of her sobbing, and felt the heat of her tears. Once more he felt the tug of a reaction. The pretense had been abandoned; now they were going to try it for real.

He felt moisture on his own cheeks. That was odd, because he could not remember when he had cried before.

At last she lifted her head again. "We must start over," she announced. "We've been going at it all wrong. The seduction must wait."

He nodded.

She climbed off him and drew the hem of her negligee down. He put himself back together and zipped his fly. "I will change," she said. "What will you do?"

"I have to wait for May Flowers to come. Then I will go out to check the property."

"May I come with you?"

"I don't think you could keep up."

"Please, Geode, is there some way? I don't want to be apart from you."

This time she hadn't pleaded fear of being alone. He could not deny the present phrasing. "Maybe I could run and you ride the bike."

"Oh, yes, I rode a bicycle when I was a girl! It's much easier than running."

"Yes."

"I'll wear jeans. But for May Flowers, a dress, I think. Do we care if she knows?"

He hadn't thought of that. "I'd rather no one knew."

"Exactly. When we exchanged our real names, we entered a private world. The princess and the prince."

"Prince?"

"In our world. When we make it. It is no business of any other person."

"Yes." How well she understood!

"Geode, in anticipation of this disaster, may I kiss you again?" But she didn't wait for his answer. She stepped up to him, leaned down, and kissed him chastely but infinitely sweetly on the lips. Then she broke and headed for the stairs.

He sat there, bemused. Every kiss was more effective than the last, no matter how she did it!

Then he got up and went to brush his teeth. He normally did this after every meal, but had never thought of it last night.

When May Flowers arrived, Geode was checking the lawn around the house. It would need mowing soon; he had to pick out the sticks that inevitably fell from the surrounding trees, so that they didn't get hurled around when the mower passed. Œnone was secluded in her room.

"How did you two get along?" May inquired briskly. She had another bag of groceries.

Geode shrugged. "Okay."

"You are about as communicative as a gopher tortoise. Is the house open?"

"Yes."

She went in, carrying her bag. After a moment he followed. It was, after all, his business to keep an eye on any strangers in the house.

Œnone came down the stairs. She wore a green dress, with a matching bow in her hair, and green slippers. She was so lovely that Geode blinked.

May paused. "My dear, you are transformed!"

"Thank you." Œnone proceeded to the bottom. "I can take that. Thank you so much."

"I can put these away for you."

"No, please." Œnone took the bag from her, almost by force. Geode knew why: May Flowers would surely notice that twice as much food had been used as seemed appropriate, if she opened the refrigerator or looked in the cupboards.

"Well, then," May said. "It certainly is an improvement! You must have had a good night."

"A wonderful night," Œnone agreed. "This is a beautiful house. I'm used to sweating in my sleep."

May smiled. "Air conditioning is addictive."

"Yes, I was very comfortable." Œnone carried the groceries to the kitchen and began putting them efficiently away.

"Well, then," May repeated. "Since everything is in good order here, I'll just depart, and check again tomorrow morning." She turned to Geode. "You have to go out on your rounds?"

"Yes. I waited for you."

"And you will lock the house?"

"Yes. Mid requires it."

"But won't the internal motion sensors be set off by her presence in the house?"

"I will cut them out."

She nodded. "Then no one can intrude from outside, and she will not want to go out herself."

He shrugged.

May stepped back out and walked to her car. But as she did so, there was an eight-beat chime. She paused as Geode hurried to press the signal to open the distant gate.

They waited. Evidently Flowers was not about to depart until she knew who was coming. It was probably Frank Tishner.

Œnone quickly completed her chore of putting groceries away and hurried upstairs, with a fleeting glimpse at Geode that make his heartbeat flicker; they had a secret. She would hide in her room until the visitor was gone, knowing that Geode would not leave without her

What a joy it was to have that secret! It made his rather dull life bright. Œnone had been ten times what he might ever have hoped for.

Geode closed the door and waited on the front portico. "She's hidden?" May asked from the car.

"Yes."

Then the vehicle arrived. It was a battered black van with shaded windows. May looked at Geode questioningly, and he shook his head; he had never seen this one before.

It pulled to a stop behind May's car. A small, middle-aged man got out. His outfit most resembled old army fatigues, but they were quite clean and neat. "I am the exterminator," he said. "You are?"

"May Flowers, the journalist," May said. "I sent for you. This is George Demerit, the caretaker."

"For whom do you work?"

"For whom do *you* work?" she returned evenly.

"Mid. And you?"

"Mid," she said. "You came to rid the house of termites?"

"That, too, if necessary. But I am more interested in bones."

"You are also an archaeologist?"

"May we cease fencing?" he asked with irritation. "My name is Cyrano, and I am a forensic entomologist. Geode found the first set, you saw them, Mid sent me to analyze them. You were supposed to have the last set for me. Did you?"

"Geode?" she asked sharply.

"Mid calls me that," Geode said. "Others don't know."

"So this man is legitimate," she concluded. "Very well, show him the body, Geode." She seemed unpleased.

"It's in the barn," Geode said.

May returned to her car. "I will call in later. I shall want a full report."

"We all require the fullest information," Cyrano said. "I shall interview you before making my report to Mid."

She got in her car and drove around the loop and away. Cyrano's lips quirked. "She's miffed because Mid told me your code name and not her. He just forgot, I'm sure; he's a busy man. Let's see that body."

Geode hadn't liked May Flowers much, but he liked this man. He was assertive without being pushy, and he had set May back. Geode led the way to the barn.

"Let me pull my lab in," Cyrano said. "I'll park it behind, where it won't show from the house. This may take some time."

Geode opened the gate to the barn. Cyrano got in his van, started it, and pulled it carefully through. Geode closed the gate behind, while the van moved on to the barn and beyond. There wasn't much space there, but enough for the van. It was entirely hidden from the loop, which was all the average visitor should be on.

He walked up and opened the side door of the barn, which was beside the van. He climbed the wooden ladder to the loft, which had not yet achieved its daytime heat. "Here," he said.

Cyrano ascended behind him. He went to the body, helping Geode uncover it. He hauled the bag out to the uncluttered part of the loft and peered in. He sniffed. "Interesting," he remarked.

Geode nodded, knowing what the smell did. He was getting an erection himself. If only he could have a whiff of that when he was with Œnone!

"Very well," Cyrano said. "I will haul this to my lab in the van and work there. Why don't you check on me in an hour, when I'll have a better idea where we stand?"

Geode nodded. This would delay his tour of the property, but couldn't be helped. The man was doing Mid's business.

He climbed down the ladder and went out.

◆ 15 ◆

CYRANO WATCHED THE man go, then made a silent whistle. He had anticipated something odd, but this was beyond his expectation. That first sniff had told him: potent pheromones! This man had been treated to biological compulsion such as was normally unknown in the human species. The enclosure of the plastic bag had concentrated it, of course, but the body had been dead for over a day, and stored in this heat. There was almost nothing left of the flesh, so there should have been very little of the chemical remaining. Even that little bit had been enough to give him an instant and almost painful erection. He understood from Mid that it had a similar effect on women. That was remarkable indeed. He had not truly believed it until he sniffed it himself.

What other surprises did this desiccated body have to offer? He would soon find out. He folded the bag, clutched it under one arm, and made his way down the ladder. He carried it out of the little barn and put it in his van. Here in the shade of barn and forest the van would not overheat, and he could perform his initial tests efficiently. He left the sliding door open, and opened the other doors, so as to allow any breeze to refresh the air inside and keep the heat down. He had air conditioning, but didn't use it unless he ran the motor, and that wasted gasoline, so he avoided it when he could. He brought out a stool and sat on it, using the floor of the van as his operating table. He donned new gloves, set out his kit, and went to work.

He slid the bag off the body and gazed at it. The thing was no more than a skeleton, with a membrane covering it under the man's pajamas. An incongruous sight, a pajama-clad skeleton! He carefully unbuttoned the top and got it off, then did the same for the bottoms. The whole of the skeleton was now open to view.

The membrane covered all of it. Even where the bone was solid, as on the skull and pelvic girdle, that membrane extended. It completely surrounded the body, bones and hollows and all.

Was it tight? If so, there could be gas trapped inside that would be invaluable for analyzing. He could try to capture a vial of that. He would also clip as much of that membrane as he could and save it. The main thing was the bone, which appeared to be intact. He could perform only the crudest of tests out here, and he was already pretty sure they would not be relevant to this case. This was the most unusual body he had heard of!

His hands went about the routine mechanisms, collecting his samples, but his mind ranged back to the circumstances of his life which had brought him to this unusual case. He had been a veterinarian, and satisfied with it, but his curiosity about obscurities had gotten him into mischief. For example, when sent to inoculate a herd of cattle against a routine infection, he had wanted to know the pattern of that infection; how had it spread here, what were its dynamics? Could it be controlled better by isolation than by inoculation? Or could the disease itself be modified to become benign? What about the worming? Worms were endemic, but rather than poisoning them in the animals every six months, why not prevent them from ever getting in? Many maladies were spread by insects; surely it made sense to deal with the insects, instead of allowing them free access to the animals. He had constantly to dose horses against the larva of the deer botfly. The female botfly would hover around the horses' legs and glue her yellow eggs on them; those eggs were harmless in that stage, but a few days later, when they hatched and the larvae began to crawl, the horses would rub their legs with their noses, and the larvae would transfer to the mouths and thence to the digestive system for the next stage. That was where the damage started. The cycle could be broken simply by brushing the eggs off with a stiff brush or pumice stone, but it was hard to do because they were firmly glued on and the horses didn't like to stand still for it—and in any event, another botfly would soon be by to deposit more eggs. So it was easier simply to medicate the horses regularly—but still it seemed to him that it would be better if the botflies never got at the horses in the first place. Prevention was so much better than treatment.

Unfortunately, effective prevention would reduce the need for treatment, and fewer veterinarians would find employment. Cyrano's notions incited covert hostility. He persisted, but could not make headway against the entrenched attitude. He discovered that the attitude and practice of the average person were firmly anchored in that person's perception of his self-interest. He lost his position and found it hard to get another; word had spread. He was not charged with anything tangible, and probably others did not even properly fathom their underlying motives, but pretexts occurred and he was unemployable in this profession. He lacked the financial backing to go into practice for himself. But the truth was that his interest in veterinary medicine had diminished, and his interest in insects had increased. He changed specialties, though he was now beyond the flush of youth, and became an entomologist. He could not be blacklisted as a student. But his savings gave out, and he was faced with the prospect of giving up without completing his course of instruction.

That was when Mid entered the picture. Mid offered him money to complete his program, and a position thereafter at an excellent stipend. But there were two stipulations: he must specialize in what Mid chose, and he must become anonymous. He would publish no papers, he would make no headlines; he would work only for Mid.

It seemed not the best of bargains, but also not the worst. He seemed to have no enticing alternative. So he agreed, without complete enthusiasm. He assumed a new identity for his work with Mid: that was when he became Cyrano, the literate dueler. He dueled not with swords but with concepts and microscopes.

Thus he took many more courses than he had anticipated, in more subjects. But he emerged with a considerable background in organic matters. His actual degree was in entomology: the study of insects. But had learned a lot about anatomy, human and animal, and forensic procedures.

It seemed that some of Mid's operations were being sabotaged, but the proof was difficult. Cyrano investigated the death of a prize horse and discovered fly larvae that indicated the animal had not died when or where it was found; it had been poisoned, then transported to another state, where it had supposedly and mysteriously expired. That made the difference; Mid was able to ascertain when and where the deed had been done, and who was in charge of the horse at that point. That person had disappeared, and Cyrano had not inquired further. He was getting to like his employer better, though he had never met him.

Another case involved the death of a person. This appeared to be innocent, an unexpected heart attack, and there had been no investigation, but Mid wanted to know the cause. Cyrano was given four hours with the body, privately, before the cremation. He discovered a pattern of larval development that was unusually rapid. This was inconclusive, he had reported to Mid, but it answered the description of cocaine residues in the tissues.

Mid had made an abrupt and intense quest for cocaine, having several employees involuntarily tested. Cocaine was found. The person involved left Mid's employ in a hurry and was not heard from again. Cyrano had been given a vacation in Hawaii and a significant bonus: Mid had his ways of expressing favor.

It had been ten years now, and Cyrano's doubts about working for Mid had long since faded. He had been involved in more interesting challenges than any ordinary employment would have provided. The work appealed to him, grisly as it sometimes was. Where else would he get to run tests on a mysterious human skeleton? Cyrano was now moderately rich himself, thanks to Mid's generosity, and could afford to retire. He had no intention of doing so. He wanted to continue working for Mid, and he was fully committed. He was loyal to the death.

He heard someone coming. It was Geode. He glanced up. "Yes?"

"You said to check back in an hour."

Cyrano glanced at his watch, which was a fine expensive timepiece, one of Mid's little gifts. An hour had indeed passed; it had seemed like five minutes! But his hands had been busy, and he had his preliminary samples, as well as a perpetual erection that was now no joy at all. He needed a break.

"Yes. I will take this specimen away for further study. But I had better interview the one closest to the living person. I believe she is here?"

The man looked uncomfortable. "It's supposed to be secret."

"Geode, I've worked a long time for Mid. He tells me everything I need to know. He told me you had the body of a man, and were hiding his wife at the Middle Kingdom. I understand the need for secrecy perfectly, and will tell no one of her presence, and you will tell no one that this body ever was here. Not because we care about each other, but because Mid wants it private. You work for him; you understand how he is."

"Yes." Geode was visibly reassured.

"Bring her out here. I'll need to talk to her only a few minutes. Then I'll be on my way, and with luck we'll never meet again."

"But aren't you here to exterminate the monster?"

"Indeed I am. But first I have to understand it. Then I will hunt it, and kill it, and take its body away, and your life will return to normal. I prefer to work alone, as I think you do."

"Yes." The man turned and walked toward the house.

Cyrano shut down his operations and moved away from the van. Now at last his erection subsided. What effective pheromones those were! If a perfume company ever bottled them, it would make a fortune, making its lady clients truly irresistible. Fortunately, the effect lasted only while the pheromones were actually being inhaled. But how much worse would it be with the living monster? For it was a monster; Mid had called it that, and what it had done to that body was virtually incredible. There was no residue of flesh at all; all of it was gone, and the surface of the bones had been etched by some powerful reducing agent. Probably the monster could dissolve bone too, but lacked the patience to bother because of the diminishing returns. So it withdrew and moved off, leaving the discards.

What was it? Nothing Cyrano had encountered before, certainly! He knew of no earthly creature that could do anything like this! Dissolving a body and consuming it, all except for the hard parts. No animal operated that way. Except—

He stopped still. Except an insect. He remembered his first sight of fireflies, flashing in the dusk, so beautiful. Perhaps it had been that sight that had turned him on to insects, even as a child. He had grown to other pursuits, but that image of the flashing fireflies had always lured him back. Yet part of what had turned him off the subject, for a time, was the way the firefly fed. It used digestive acids to dissolve the body of its prey, then sucked in the fluid. Later he had come to accept the differing ways of other creatures, and to respect them; he was no longer repulsed by such digestion. Was it any worse than putting undigested food into one's body and breaking it down internally and defecating the residue, as mammals did? So the firefly had become beautiful again to him; he had learned tolerance.

So it *was* done by earthly creatures. But what kind of a firefly could make a man its prey?

A big one, obviously. A big, biiig one!

"Oh, damn!" Cyrano breathed in awe and delight. This case had suddenly assumed a new dimension!

Geode returned with a woman. Cyrano watched them approach. She was of middle height and slight build, in her thirties, and might have been winsome in her prime but was so no longer. Her figure wasn't bad, actually; she didn't run to fat. But the description Mid had relayed certainly fit: she was a mouse, timid, unassuming, nondescript. The kind of person no one noticed unless he had to.

But she had information he wanted, so he noticed her, for the moment. She had been close by when the man was taken, and might have some additional hint of the nature of the firefly.

The woman paused, and he saw she was gazing at the colorful dragonflies that hovered in the vicinity. She smiled with passing delight, and her face became pretty. Even a mouse might have her moments, he realized.

They came to stand before him. "You are?" he asked her, ignoring Geode, who was similarly easy to ignore.

"Jade Brown. The body is my husband."

"He was a fat man?" For there had been a certain deformation in the skeleton suggesting that.

"Yes, at the end."

"Maybe two-hundred-thirty pounds?"

"Yes."

"Where was he when he died?"

"On the couch in the living room."

"Was a door or window open?"

"No."

"Could one have been opened, then closed?"

"Yes. But I don't think it was."

Cyrano nodded. He had expected something like this. No huge firefly could have flown in, fed on the man, and flown out. More than a closed door prevented that! "Did you smell anything?"

"The smell—it makes it sexy."

He affected surprise. "For you too?"

"Yes. May Flowers felt it too."

Mid had mentioned that detail, perhaps not realizing its significance. Pheromones that acted similarly on male and female! Who would have believed it! "Even a firefly doesn't do that!"

"What?" she asked.

He realized that in his excitement he had spoken aloud. "The monster. I think of it as a firefly because of the way it dissolves flesh and consumes it. A big one."

"But fireflies are lovely, like the dragonflies," she protested.

"Not to their prey. If dragonflies started biting us the way the deerflies do, we'd hate them just as much. Actually, all insects are interesting, once you appreciate their qualities."

"A big firefly," she repeated. "Yes, that makes it easier."

It was time to get back to the subject. "Did you hear anything when your husband was taken?"

"No, I was asleep. I didn't know he'd come home. He—" She grimaced, and didn't finish.

"Was there anything on the couch under the body?"

"No. He was just there, in his pajamas. And that smell."

"It seems to me that the pheromones—the smell, as you put it—should have been much stronger when the thing was feeding. It should have suffused the house. You weren't aware of it?"

She looked embarrassed. "I did have sexy dreams."

"But not enough to wake you?"

"No. And when I woke it wasn't so strong. Not till I got close to the body."

So the creature didn't broadcast the pheromones, but used them only at immediate range. Unless her bedroom had been airtight. Interesting. Why should it go to the trouble of developing such a potent all-purpose lure, and then not use it to bring in prey? Something was missing here. "Thank you. I'll be on my way." He turned and went to the van. It would be a pain, driving with that odor pumping him up in the closed van, but the day was getting hot and he wanted to get the body to a safer and cooler place.

❖ 16 ❖

ŒNONE WATCHED THE van back out and drive through the gate as Geode held it open. She hadn't wanted to talk to the man, but she was a guest in Mid's house, and what Mid wanted, he got. But it had been interesting. A huge firefly? Surely not a flying creature, but something that ate as a firefly did. Did it flash also? A flash that only its victim could see, or maybe smell? For certainly she had not smelled it, not consciously anyway, any of the three times it had raided her house. Four times—there was the raccoon too. But she had smelled the bodies. If the firefly made them react that way, and what she smelled was only the trace aftermath— well, no wonder they didn't flee it! Maybe the smell was just a bit of solvent or something, used to dissolve the flesh, and the actual pheromones were there too, associated but not the same.

So she had sexy dreams, not even realizing their source. Not that she needed any encouragement; sex was always on her mind. It was hard to believe that other women weren't the same way, but she had learned long since that it was so. With men it was another matter, of course—except for Geode. Was that an irony, or an opportunity? Had he been turned on the way other men were, he probably wouldn't have taken this job, and she would not have encountered him. So it was, after all, her fortune. She had access to the man other women didn't want—and he wanted her as other men didn't want her, though he could not implement it. Yet.

Geode returned to her as the van disappeared down the drive. "We can go now, if you still want to."

"I just want to be with you," she said sincerely. And that was true. Four times the monster had struck at her house, and she was the only one remaining associated with that residence; the firefly was coming for her too. She didn't dare spend a night alone; all the others had been taken in their sleep, except perhaps the raccoon, and she wasn't sure that wasn't the case there too. She had to be with someone to guard her, and Geode was the one. She had spoken truly when she told him of the peasant girl in the castle. But also when she agreed to try to love him. The notion was thrilling: to love, once more, before she died. Then at least she would die fulfilled.

He walked to the house and fetched his red bicycle. "This is made for off-road cycling," he said. "Wide tires, eleven gears. It will get you there."

She looked at it. "Eleven? But it has five gear wheels on the back, and three on the front. Doesn't that mean fifteen?"

"They overlap," he explained. "You aren't supposed to mesh the extremes; it angles the chain too sharply, and makes it wear." He pointed to the largest front gear wheel and the largest rear one, and she saw how they did not align; indeed, the chain would be hard put to it to bridge between them. So he didn't use the four most stretched combinations. It made sense after all.

She got on the bike, pushed off, and pedaled. it worked! She remembered how to ride. She saw that the brakes and gearshifts were on the handlebars, the front ones on the left, the rear ones on the right. She tried the rear derailleur as she pedaled around the paved loop, and in a moment the chain clunked onto a different sprocket and the pedaling got faster. Then she had to use the brake, because she was going down a slope too fast.

By the time she had completed the loop twice, she had the hang of it. The bike was light and responsive, and the wide tires really held the pavement. She could go anywhere on this little machine! But she was glad she had changed to jeans after May Flowers left, because dresses just weren't made for bicycles.

She returned to Geode and stopped. "I've got it," she reported. "Lead, and I'll follow."

He led her back toward the barn. Now she was on yellow-brown dirt, the kind that normally torpedoed the thin tires of bicycles. She worried, but the tires held. This thing really was made for off-road travel!

Beyond the barn a path led into the jungle. Geode jogged along it as it wound between the trees. Now she had to go carefully, because the clearance of her handlebars was slight. But the tires handled the leaves and roots of the path as well as they had the dirt, and she kept going. She was keeping his pace, using a fraction of the energy.

He ran on past hanging liana vines and oaks large and small, with clusters of palmettos throughout. Here and there, struggling for light, were little magnolia trees; she recognized their broad leaves. Here there was a green mossy trunk on the ground, there the sandy remnant of some old tortoise burrow. She had lived several years in Florida, but had never really seen the deep forest like this.

The small path debouched into a larger trail, one that might handle a car in a pinch. Geode ran up this one, picking up speed. She followed, pedaling faster now that she had room to maneuver. In fact, she had to change gears so that she wasn't pedaling uncomfortably rapidly.

They came to a clearing—no, it was a region of small pines—and Geode abruptly turned off and stopped. There was an old bathtub with a red pitcher pump mounted at the end, and beyond it an open pole barn.

She stopped and watched as he brought out a green plastic pitcher from near the pump, dipped it in the tub, and poured water into the top of the pump. As he poured he worked the handle, and after a bit the priming worked and water gushed out of the spout. He pumped water into the bathtub, filling it to the level of its overflow hole.

"What's that for?" she asked.

"The horses and burros," he explained. "They don't like to have to go down to the lake to drink."

"You have horses here?"

"Yes. I put feed out for them in the evening."

"Could I see them?"

"Maybe. They're shy around strangers. Maybe after a few days they'll let you see them. They make friends more readily if you have carrots."

"I must come with carrots!" she exclaimed.

"You like animals?"

"I always liked horses. Now, with you, I like all animals."

"Maybe they'll like you," he said. "The three burros can be any-where. I call them Burrito, Frito, and Dorito—that's the female. Burrito is very friendly, once he knows you. Mostly they graze among the slash pines here." Then he set off again, loping up along an alley between the planted pine trees.

She pumped the bike along after him, brushing through the tall dog fennel and clumps of bahia grass. Then she spied another kind of plant. "Oh! Blueberries!"

He paused. "Huckleberries—they're black. Blueberries are blue. Here." He indicated another bush, where the berries were indeed blue. "We have blackberries too. I come out here and eat them, sometimes."

"I want to be with you next time!"

"The season's passing; not many berries left."

"I'd like to come here and just walk through the pines."

"The chiggers will get you."

"Chiggers?"

"Little red bugs. They dig into the skin, and a day later you feel the itch, and the spot takes a week to fade."

"I must be getting them now!" she exclaimed, horrified.

He looked abashed. "I didn't think of that."

"But do you get them? You're out here every day!"

"I run. I get sweaty. They don't seem to like the way I taste."

"There must be more to it than that!" she protested. "A bug isn't going to turn up its nose at you if you're its only chance for a meal. You must wash off after you run."

"Yes."

"So I'll wash off too. If that works, I'll never have to use repellent."

He nodded, then turned and resumed his run. He seemed indefat-igable; he had obviously been doing this for a long time. He had the distance runner's body: lean and lanky. She had heard of "runner's high," with runners deriving a sense of well-being from the hormones the strenuous exercise produced. It was supposed to be akin to the highs produced by chocolate, and by sexual activity. She liked the latter two; he liked the first. They were not that far apart.

The pines trees were in endless rows, and ranged in size from knee height to about twenty-five feet tall, depending, it seemed, on the nature of the soil. They must have been planted together, and those that fell on good ground prospered. There were patches of white sand where none grew, and at the edges of such patches were small ones, and larger ones beyond, until they got into one of the excellent patches. Passion flower vines grew among and on them, their big, lovely, purple flowers like opening umbrellas. The dark green tops of the trees were framed against a beautiful blue sky, fading to gray near the horizon. A flight of half a dozen birds was passing, in a somewhat ragged V formation. It was at once completely ordinary, and extraordinary. She had seldom been out beyond the range of houses, she realized; it was a different world.

Geode slowed and pointed. She looked, and saw a big gopher tortoise. It hissed and pulled in its head as she passed. But she looked back a moment later and saw it moving along rapidly enough, snapping at blades of grass. She felt good for having seen it.

But now she was developing a pain in her stomach. "Geode!" she gasped. "I have to slow—I can't keep up with you!"

He stopped running. "Side stitch?" he asked.

"I'm afraid so. You've given me every advantage, but I'm just not in the condition you are. If I can rest a moment, I'll try to do better." She stood where she was, aware how her heart was beating; she had been working harder than she realized, pedaling along the path.

"I used to get them when I started," he said. "Takes years to toughen up, and when I push it, it still happens, sometimes."

"That tortoise—are there many of them here?"

"Yes. They have their burrows on the high ground. Other animals use them too; they call the gopher tortoise the 'Landlord.' "

"Other animals?"

"Mice, rattlesnakes, maybe rabbits and burrowing owls—I'm not sure about them."

"Rattlesnakes!"

"They don't mean any harm. If you see one, let it be. Just don't step on it. Coral snake too; that's the pretty one."

"Coral snake!" she exclaimed. "Doesn't that have the deadliest poison of them all?"

"Close to it. But it's mostly harmless."

She shook her head, bemused. "How can it be harmless when one drop will kill you?"

"It's a small snake, with a small head; its teeth are pretty weak. If it bit you on the leg, it couldn't get through the denim. You'd have to pick it up in your hands—and then it wouldn't bite you, if you didn't squeeze it. It's no threat to man; it uses its poison for prey its own size. I wouldn't hurt a coral snake for anything."

"I didn't know," she said, chagrined. "I've got all these civilized ways, which really aren't so civilized. I assumed that poisonous snakes had to be killed."

He shook his head in emphatic negation. "No, never! Never! They have to make their living in their own way, same as we do. I don't care about it that way, but they are beneficial to man; they eat rodents."

"I will not forget," she promised, with a rush of emotion. "You are teaching me."

"And the big indigo snake is really beautiful," he continued. "Maybe six feet long, thick like a python, all black except for a bit of red in the chin. When I see one of those I just stop and watch."

"I hope I see one." She wanted to share everything of his in this alternate world of the Middle Kingdom.

"They're around, but rare." He glanced at her. "Can you move now?"

"I'll try. I'm really sorry about slowing you down like this; I didn't mean to be a drag."

"It's the first time anybody cared to come with me. I don't care how slow it gets."

"Thank you, Geode. It's wonderful being with you in your world."

He started running again, and she resumed pedaling. This time he went slower, and she kept up more readily.

They came to a metal fence and gate. Beyond was a paved road. It looked familiar. "I—I think I've seen that before," she said, perplexed.

Geode turned his head and smiled. "It's the corner of the drive. The house is south." He pointed.

She reoriented. "Oh—this lane through the pines must be on the diagonal! So it forms a triangle with the drive."

"Yes. The rest of the ranch is north." He turned north, away from the corner, and resumed his jog.

The trend seemed upward here. She shifted to a lower gear, making the pedaling easier, and was able to keep up; she was getting the hang of it, though she feared her legs would be sore tomorrow. It didn't matter; she had asked to come along, and she was going to keep the pace somehow.

She brushed by a patch of grass. Something stung her on the calf. She reached down to brush it away, and it stabbed her hand. "Oh!"

Geode stopped. He nodded. "Sandspur."

Oh, of course; she had encountered them many times before. She just hadn't been thinking of them now.

Geode used his fairly husky fingernails to pull the spurs from her jeans, then took her hand and worked out the one she had slapped. His touch was gentle and competent. "Thank you," she said.

"I should have warned you."

They resumed, and now she was careful to avoid the reaching spikes of sandspur.

The vegetation changed. Here, instead of small pines, there were mixed oaks, some of considerable size. The path wound up, skirting palmetto thickets and patches of sand. But then they came to another planting of pines. These were smaller, and seemed to be of a different kind.

"Longleaf pine," he explained, seeing her perplexity. "They grow in a 'grass' stage until they have enough mass to move, then they shoot up their trunks and become regular trees. Protects them from grass fires, so you'll see stands of natural longleaf where other trees have been burned off."

"But then why isn't the other part planted with this kind?" she asked.

"The slash pine? It's a good tree too. They thought it was the best, and the longleaf won't start well from seed. Have to use tublings, mostly. So they planted mostly slash, only the soil was wrong in a lot of places, and it couldn't make it. That's what happened here; they had to cut it off and start over with longleaf." He grimaced. "Fool authorities for a long time wouldn't classify it as a tree farm unless the pines were planted in rows, so natural-seeded longleaf didn't count, and good trees were taken out in favor of ones that couldn't make it in the dry soil. Now they're catching on, and the trees don't have to be in rows, but it'll be a long time before you see a lot of tree farms with mature longleaf."

"That's the longest speech I've heard you make!" she said, smiling.

"No one wanted to listen before," he said, taken aback.

"Fool authorities," she said. "They don't listen."

Surprised, he almost laughed. "You really care about trees?"

"I do now."

"I mean, when you're not playing your game."

"It stopped being a game this morning."

He looked at her. She was now riding beside him as he slowly ran.

She nodded her head affirmatively. It was obvious that he was not accustomed to having anyone take him seriously. To him, this relationship was as much a fantasy as this ranch was to her.

"If you want to stop for a moment, I will kiss you," she said.

He considered that for a moment, then slowed, then stopped. She stopped the bicycle beside him, put her feet on the ground beside the pedals so that her legs held it up, turned, caught his shoulders, and drew him in to her for the kiss. The position was awkward, but the novelty was a thrill. He was glowing with sweat, and so was she; it didn't matter.

"You said you liked to listen to me," she said. "Well, I like to listen to you too. Out here you are in your element."

He shook his head, in wonder rather than denial, and did not speak. In a moment they resumed their travel.

He glanced at a large pine tree. She looked too, but saw nothing. "What is it, Geode?"

"That's where I found the hunter."

She felt a chill despite her sweat. "The monster was here?"

"Yes. In the night, maybe. I found his truck further over."

"The monster's truck?" She made a stifled giggle. The grotesque mergence of concepts had to be alleviated somehow.

"The hunter's truck. Mid had me drive it to another place so there wouldn't be notoriety here."

Œnone had been genuinely enjoying this strenuous excursion. Now there was a pall. "Please, let's not stay here!"

Wordlessly he went on. She followed, managing to keep the pace as they passed islands of full-grown laurel oak and extensive regions of tiny pines. Then, abruptly, there was a section of tall pines of the prior variety—and a horrendous pit. The thing seemed to be several hundred feet across and anything up to a hundred feet deep. Trees grew down its steep slopes and in the bottom.

"The mine," he explained. "Limerock. They took it out and left the hole."

"But aren't they supposed to reclaim the land after they've done mining?" she asked.

"Yes." He ran on.

She looked down into the awesome hole in this otherwise almost level land. Probably this excavation predated the laws; even so, she understood that enforcement was a mockery. But this great hole was probably far more impressive than the original land had been. Florida didn't have ragged mountains, it had the opposite: ragged depressions.

She kept pedaling, and gradually her interest in the aspects of the ranch diminished; she just wanted to get through without collapsing. She focused on Geode's back, and followed. It was as though she were in a tunnel, the vegetation forming its walls.

Her mind turned inward, as it so often did. She had seen a great pit; what might be down in there? A whole community of folk who never saw the outside world? People with different customs and cares, perhaps not evident at first. Elven folk, even; elves could be the same size and appearance as ordinary folk when they chose, and sometimes as a matter of indifference or mischief they did so choose. Perhaps one day a man from the outer world went down there and walked into the village, not realizing how different it was. There was an auction proceeding, and as he arrived he saw a pretty girl holding up an object that appealed to him, an elegant vase that would do for flowers. It was blue, or purple, reminiscent of lapis lazuli; perhaps the seller did not realize its worth.

He bid on it. All he had on him was a ten-dollar bill, so he bid that. To his surprise, he took it; no other person bid. So he went up to the table and laid down his bill, and the girl came with the vase. She gave it to another pretty girl, then turned to the man and smiled.

"But that's my vase!" he protested. "I just bought it!" For it seemed that they were about to auction it off again.

"Not so," the old man at the table said. "You bought the girl, not the prop."

The girl stepped forward and took the man's arm. "But—" he started, bewildered.

"Sorry, all sales are final," the old man said. "You bought her, you take her home. If you don't like her, sell her or kill her."

"But I couldn't do that!" the man protested.

"Didn't think you could," the old man said. "Now clear out; you're holding up the next sale."

And so the man departed the pit, with the girl. She was a truly lovely creature whose every breath was suggestive. In fact, she looked much the way Œnone did, in her prime. She had spoken no word, but it was obvious that she knew what was what, and soon—

The bike bumped over a root and Œnone almost skewed out of control. She recovered, but the thread of the story was lost. Damn!

Then there was an opening to the left, distracting her for the moment. It was water! They were passing the lake, or a river. And there was a house—but not the one they had started from.

"You look bushed," Geode said, slowing to a walk. "I don't want you to get heat stroke."

"Where—where are we?"

"Cabin at the far corner. I have to check, make sure there're no squatters." He went to the door, brought out a key, and unlocked it.

She leaned the bike against the wall of the house, as there was no kickstand. She followed him in.

It was a somewhat ramshackle cabin, with kitchen, bedroom, and an enclosed porch. There were bare mattresses on the floor. "I'm afraid to lie down," she remarked. "I might never get up."

"I guess I went too fast," he said. "Lie down; I'll wait."

"No, I don't want to hold you up." This wasn't politeness, it was grim determination.

He smiled. "I'm not much good in your world. You were nice to me. Now you're in mine. I'll be nice to you." He plopped down on a mattress.

"You make such sense!" she said, and collapsed beside him. She put her head on his chest, her arm on his shoulder, and let her strength ebb. What a delight to relax!

After a moment, he put his free arm up and across her back. She listened to his heart beating.

The affair had turned sour, and her guilt waxed inversely as the romance waned. How could she, a married woman, have done this thing? What had seemed so exciting at the outset now seemed sordid. She was sorry she had ever gotten into it. Her husband was ten times the man her lover was, and she knew that now. She had betrayed the man she loved, and was ill with self-loathing for it.

There was no help for it: she would have to tell him. She would make a clean breast of it and beg his forgiveness, and if he threw her out, well, it was his right and she had brought it on herself by her foolishness. But what a loss to her it would be! Yet she couldn't keep silent, for that would make a mockery of their relationship; there had to be honesty between them, however painful it might be.

She nerved herself and broached the matter that evening. "Dear, I have something to say that I fear will not please you, and—"

"Oh, you found out!" he exclaimed.

"What?" She was nonplussed.

"About my indiscretion, over now. I really wanted to tell you, but I was so afraid of losing you, the only woman I ever truly loved. Now you have found out, and it's too late for courage. I wish it were otherwise!"

He had had an affair? At first she felt a surge of anger. But following hard on its heels was relief: he couldn't condemn her, if he had done the same!

Nevertheless, honesty compelled her. "I didn't know," she said. "What I have to confess is my own indiscretion. I—"

"You?" he asked incredulously.

"Me," she agreed. "I—"

He looked almost relieved. "Maybe—would it be amiss if we simply let things cancel out, without going into details?"

"Why, yes, if you feel—"

And so it was that they devoted the night to love instead of confession and recrimination. He stroked her hair and she kissed him, and their marriage prospered thereafter.

It was only much later that she learned by chance from another source that her husband had never had an extramarital affair. Then she realized that she had been mistaken: he was not ten times the man her lover had been. He was a hundred times.

Œnone woke abruptly. "Oops, I slept!" she exclaimed.

"Nobody ever wanted to sleep with me before," Geode said, smiling.

"But you were supposed to continue your rounds! I delayed you!"

"It was the greatest hour I ever had, except for last night."

She lifted her head, gazing at his face. "Mine too, I think. I've wanted so much to be with a man, held by a man, not just sexually but for myself. It's been a long time, and I'm very hungry for it."

"I stroked your hair," he said.

"Oh, I didn't know! You should have woken me up for that!"

"No, I wanted you to sleep."

"I was joking—I think," she said, remembering her dream. Tenderness, for the sake of nothing else. "Come on, I have delayed you too much. We must complete your rounds."

He sat up, nodding. "Maybe we can come here again sometime. When—" He shrugged.

"When we can make it," she said, understanding.

"Or just to sleep. I like being with you so much, it doesn't matter what we do."

"You are my dream man," she said.

He shook his head, not believing it.

"No, I'm serious. I've always wanted to be with a man who just wanted my company, all the time. I didn't think any existed. Now here you are. Well, you shall have my company as long as you want it, and when you get tired of it, it's still been nice, very nice."

He stood looking at her, as if trying to say something, but not being able to get it organized. "Anything you want, take," she said. She went to him, embraced him, and kissed him.

"I think that was it," he said.

"That's only the beginning of it." She let go and went out of the cabin, determined not to make her mistake of the night before, trying to push sex on him when he wasn't ready. It wasn't that he objected, but that the foundation had to be set before the structure could be built.

She had not really looked around before, being too tired. Now she saw that there were cedar trees near the cabin, and an earthen ramp extending into the river. The swollen trunks of cypress grew at the water's edge, and indeed, some way into the water.

"We could take a canoe," Geode said.

"So I could rest my legs? But then you'd have to leave the bike here, and wouldn't have it when you needed it next time," she said. "No, I'd better finish my ride, though I'd love to canoe with you tomorrow."

He nodded, his usual response when it would do.

They resumed the circuit. Geode went slower yet, and she followed on the bike, picking up more of the scenery now. They were on a car-drivable road, and the bike had no trouble with the tire-wide tracks; she could virtually coast along many stretches. That helped, because her legs were indeed tired.

The road looped south and west, leaving the river and bordering parts of the lake. She caught glimpses of water lilies and reeds and occasional sections of open water. There were some purple flowers there, but those weren't passion flowers; they were vertical. She would learn their identity in due course.

At last they came to a metal gate, and beyond it was the paved drive. They had made a complete circuit, and apparently looped around the house, and were coming at it from the north. Geode unscrewed the little link that locked the gate, and let her through, then screwed the link tight again.

She walked the bike up to the house, where he took it and put it away in the alcove. Then he unlocked the side door—and the thin wail of the alarm started. He hurried through the house to the alarm pad, and in a moment the alarm stopped. She knew that if he hadn't done it within thirty seconds, the system would have dialed the police and fire departments, notifying them of a break-in.

He returned. "It's noon," he said. "You can rest. I'm not going out again for a while."

"No, I have to fix you lunch!"

"No, you don't. I'm used to doing for myself."

"What do you fix yourself?"

"Can of beans."

"I can do that!"

He shook his head. "I've got to shower. So do you. The beans can wait."

He was right. She was dripping sweat. "Would you like to shower together?"

"Do you want to?"

"Yes."

"Okay." Then he smiled. "The bathroom down here doesn't have a shower; I usually use the one upstairs. Yours."

"Then it was fated," she said.

He led the way through the door to his room, but this time turned to the right. There was another staircase she hadn't known about. They went up. At the top was a panel, which he slid into the wall. Beyond was the hall, with her bathroom at the beginning. She had found out what was beyond the forbidden portals!

They entered the bathroom, closed the door, turned on the air exhaust, and stripped. Soon their clothing lay on the floor in two sodden piles. "I will run those through the laundry," she said. "I hope you have a dryer, because I can't hang my clothing out to dry in the sun; that would give away my presence the moment anyone saw it."

"There is one," he said.

She turned on the shower, waited for the water get warm, then stepped in. Geode hung back. "You too," she said. "And bring the soap."

The soap bar was beside the sink. He picked it up and stepped diffidently in with her. The water blasted down on them both, refreshingly. She felt the fatigue and tightness in her legs easing. She took the soap from his hand and rubbed it over his body, then hers. Then she put her arms around him, rubbing her slippery body against his.

"You feel so good," he said. But he didn't get an erection. Well, it had been worth the try.

Then they heard the sound of the chime. Someone was at the gate!

Geode jumped out, dripping, and ran naked from the bathroom. He was going to buzz the visitor in. Œnone quickly rinsed herself off, including her matted hair.

Geode returned. "I have to get dressed!" he said.

"No, you don't," she said. "You've been out on your rounds; you were taking a shower. Just wrap a towel around yourself; they'll understand. I'm the one who has to get dressed, so if I should have to meet anyone—"

He nodded. He stepped back into the shower as she stepped out, and quickly rinsed off the remaining soap. He turned off the shower. Then he wrapped a towel around his middle and went downstairs, while she patted herself dry. Of all the times for someone to arrive!

Œnone picked up both sets of clothes and dumped them in the hamper, shoes and all. Then she stepped around to her room and quickly dug out new underclothing and a brown dress. She could change in a hurry when she had to. In moment she was petitely garbed and was brushing out her hair. It was wet, and there would be no concealing that, but of course she could have been washing it. Nothing directly connected her with Geode.

She heard a car pull up outside. There was the faint murmur of dialogue below. Then Geode's raised voice: "But I can't bother her, sheriff! I just got out of the shower!"

Deputy Tishner! He knew about her being here, but not about her relationship with Geode.

The house intercom came on. "Ms. Brown, you up there?" came Tishner's voice. "I need some information."

She found the talk button. "I will come down."

Then she walked down the hall to the main staircase, and down to the front door.

Tishner was there. "You're looking good, ma'am," he remarked.

"May Flowers bought me new clothing."

"So I see. Look, they're putting the heat on about your disappearance, especially your boy's. I mean, you and your husband could've gone somewhere, but the boy's supposed to be in school."

"A family emergency came up," she said. "We sent my son to stay with his uncle George for a few days, and then my husband and I left without warning; there wasn't time to notify anybody."

"But your car's still there."

She had forgotten that. "It wasn't running well. We took a bus—" She hesitated, for he was shaking his head in negation. Bus service wasn't great here, and it could be checked. "We—a member of the family came in his car, and we just got in with him and drove away. I know we should have notified someone, but it was so sudden—"

He nodded affirmatively. "Your brother—will he confirm?"

"Yes."

"What's his number?"

She checked in her purse and found the number. She gave it to him.

Geode appeared, now dressed. Tishner glanced at him. "Sorry to pull you out of your shower like that, Demerit. This just came up. I don't know how long we can keep the lid on. That exterminator—did he get here?"

Geode nodded.

"He took the body?"

Another nod.

"Did he say anything about it? I mean, what did it?"

"He said he had to get it to his lab. But he thought it was a firefly."

"A what?"

"The way a firefly eats. Dissolving."

"Oh. Yeah. Well, I'd better talk with him, because it's my ass on the line—excuse me, ma'am—if that thing dissolves any more men. We've got to get rid of it, then maybe we can patch over what's happened."

"I don't know where he is," Geode said. "May Flowers asked for him, and Mid sent him."

"Then maybe I better talk to Flowers."

"Yes."

"Will do." Tishner nodded to each and departed.

Œnone turned and walked up the stairs. She would not approach Geode until she knew the sheriff's deputy was well clear.

❖ 17 ❖

FRANK SHOOK HIS head slowly as he drove away from the house. Neither the man nor the woman seemed to appreciate just how awkward his position was! That monster—a firefly?—was killing folk right and left, and he had to keep a lid on it, and when the shit finally hit the fan, as seemed inevitable, he was the one standing square behind it.

He was, incidentally, surprised at the change in the woman. She had been such a homely mouse; now she was petite and not unattractive. It had to be the clothing; the Flowers woman had bought it for her, and evidently had known what she was doing. And that man Demerit didn't even notice! He had been off taking a shower while Jade Brown was turning pretty. Well, it was really none of Frank's business. He had his own job to do, and as long as the Brown woman stayed hidden so she couldn't be interrogated, his job was that much easier. What a mess this thing was becoming!

First, he'd have to get the Brown alibi straight. That disappearance could blow the thing wide open.

He returned to the office. Some quick research on the phone got him the identity of Jade Brown's brother, George Faulk. He lived in Georgia, which was just far enough away to make any direct contact

131

unfeasible. Good. Frank didn't know what Jade Brown had on him to make him cover for her; maybe he was just a loyal family man.

He called the number. He got a woman. "This is Deputy Sheriff Frank Tishner calling from Citrus County, Florida," he said. "I have a question relating to Jade Brown, who I understand is George Faulk's sister. Is Mr. Faulk in?"

It turned out he was. A gruff masculine voice came on the line. "What do you want?"

"Mrs. Brown and her husband are missing," Frank said. "We are trying to determine whether there has been foul play. We understand their son is staying with you."

There was a pause. "That's right."

"Are the Browns joining you too?"

"Not exactly. Something came up."

"Something like what, Mr. Faulk?"

"A family situation. Frankly, sheriff, I don't think it's any of your business."

Frank was momentarily set back by the use of a word so similar to his name. "Only if there has been foul play, Mr. Faulk. Are you telling me that the Browns have gone elsewhere? That there has been no foul play?"

"Yeah. Satisfied?"

"I'll have to be. Thank you, Mr. Faulk." He broke the connection— and looked up to see the sheriff.

"That Brown disappearance?" the sheriff inquired.

Frank grimaced. "Yes. I located the woman's brother in Georgia. Man has a bad attitude. He says their boy is staying with him, but won't say where the Browns have gone. It seems to be some family thing."

"Not our concern, then. Probably some skeleton fell out of a closet, and they had to hotfoot it over to hide it."

Skeleton . . . "Maybe so," Frank agreed. "Want me to investigate further?"

"No, as long as there's no evidence. Just keep an eye on their house until they get back. We've got enough to do without looking for trouble."

Which was exactly the answer Frank wanted. He had made a token investigation, been balked, and for the time being had no further responsibility.

"Anything more on those shrunken animals?" the sheriff asked.

Frank shook his head. "There seems to have been a number of

them. Just skin and bones, nothing else except maybe a bit of fur. I'd really like to make a more organized search for—"

"No way! We don't want to stir up a big commotion about what's probably some kind of anthill eating out wild animals."

"No commotion," Frank agreed, having received the second answer he wanted. He was following the spirit of that directive far more faithfully than the sheriff realized. The lab report on the raccoon had been inconclusive; they admitted that they couldn't determine the cause of death, and asked for a fresher specimen next time. Ha-ha!

He watched the sheriff amble off. The man was quite a character. He was a rancher and a hunter, but he enforced the laws relating to both. There had been the case of repeated vandalism on an isolated property; kids were breaking down the gate to a lot and partying there, stealing the lock and leaving the gate hanging open. Almost impossible to catch them in the act. But it happened that some of the sheriff's steer were grazing in an adjacent property. Periodically they would find a way through or around the restraining fence and graze on the vandalized lot. So the sheriff had simply let it be known whose cattle would be let out on the street if that gate wasn't tight . . . and the vandalism had abruptly stopped. No unpleasantness, no threats—but the kids in question knew exactly who would be on their tails if a steer got killed because of a certain open gate. The sheriff got his fence patched, of course, but he didn't bruit that about. Law enforcement of the indirect persuasion—and it worked.

Then there had been the matter of the deer. That one had happened near the Middle Kingdom Ranch, actually, where the sheriff had a few horses. A wild deer had befriended the horses, and took to grazing with them out in the open, visible from a nearby highway. The sheriff saw that and acted immediately. He went to the neighborhood tavern where the hunters hung out, and made an announcement: "Now, I'm a hunter myself, and I've bagged my share of deer, in season. There's a deer grazing in plain sight beside the highway, with several horses. Those horses just happen to belong to me. I want folks to know that any friend of my horse is a friend of mine, and if anything should happen to that deer I'd be a mite perturbed." Then he departed. Thereafter the deer led a charmed life. People came with cameras to take pictures of it, and hunters rode by with rifles in their cars, but nothing happened to that deer. Hunters understood indirect persuasion just about as well as teenagers did. Not one of them wanted a perturbed sheriff on his tail.

Frank smiled, remembering. The sheriff had told him to let the Brown case slide until something else developed, and to do the same for the animal bones. The sheriff didn't like a commotion. There would be no commotion if Frank could possibly help it. He had more than his job on the line now.

In due course he was back in his car, on other business. In the course of that business he stopped to make a call at a pay phone. He was in luck; he caught the Flowers woman in her hotel room. "Got your man's report?"

"Preliminary," she said. "Can you talk now?"

"Yes."

"He has confirmed my suspicion of pheromones, but he believes they serve as a pacifier, not as an attractant. In open air they dissipate and break down rapidly."

"Pacifier? You mean those victims think they're having one big fuck?" He was trying to jostle her, because despite their deal he didn't much like her, but it didn't work.

"That is his conjecture. The bones have been partially dissolved by some type of acid he hasn't been able to place, probably the same that dissolved the soft tissues. He is sending samples off to our employer's laboratory, but it will be a few days before those reports return."

"Our lab threw up its hands on the raccoon."

"Mid's lab will be more competent," she said coldly. "The exterminator doesn't want to move until he knows what he's up against; he never botches a job. But he says that as far as he can tell, this monster is something alien to his experience."

"You mean a monster from outer space?"

"More likely from under the sea. A true alien would find our flesh poisonous, I think, and this one obviously likes it very well and knows how to get it. So it is bound to be a creature of our planet, but one we have not before encountered."

"I'd like to see that monster!" Frank exclaimed.

"I suspect that if you did, you would shortly be dead. There is no evidence that any of its victims had any power against it."

"I'd like to see it dead," Frank amended. "And if it looks like a gigantic firefly—"

She made one of her cold laughs. "To be sure. At any rate, he thinks there should not be any more people taken for two days. He believes that the monster requires three days to properly digest a meal the size of a man, based on the frequency of past episodes, unless it is feeding on large animals like cattle in the interim. You had better check on that, just in case."

"Right. Missing cows."

"What is the status of Jade Brown?"

"Covered. Her brother in Georgia says her son is with him, and that a sudden family matter called her and her husband out of town. Take that for what it's worth."

"It is worth an alibi for you; you cannot be expected to know when a person on the phone is lying."

"Right. I have been instructed to let it and the animal bones ride until further developments. The woman herself seems to be doing just fine; she looks human in that dress you bought."

"I thought she might. Any evidence of association with Demerit?"

"No, not that it matters. He's a cold fish. He was in the shower while she was in the dress; he met me wet, in a towel—" He paused. "But I just remembered. Her hair was wet."

"Wet?"

"Combed out, but wet. She must have just washed it."

"At the same time as his shower?"

"Why not? So she wanted her hair clean."

"If I understand the layout of that house correctly, and I believe I do, the bathroom with a shower at that end of the house is the one she uses. I doubt very much that he would trek to a shower at the far side of the house. He seems most diffident about not using the main house; he saves it for his employer."

"Well, there's a bathroom with a sink downstairs at that end. She could've used that."

"So when you came to the door—it was the side door?—he dashed down from the upstairs shower while she dashed up from the downstairs bathroom?"

"What are you getting at, woman?"

"I suspect they are getting along better than they care to advertise."

He pursed his lips. "Could be, now you mention it. What do we care? It's their business, isn't it?"

"It is better that they get along together," she said. "If the woman cares for Demerit's opinion, she will not expose him to embarrassment. That facilitates our effort to keep her disappearance, and the reason for it, quiet."

"Yeah, I guess so," he agreed. "Well, keep me posted, and I'll keep you posted. I want to know everything about that firefly."

"Don't we all," she said, and hung up.

✦ 18 ✦

MAY SET DOWN the phone. She regretted having to give full information to the deputy, but she had made the deal, and the man was essential to the preservation of secrecy. He was useful too, in his fashion; he had established the alibi provided by Jade Brown's brother. He had also indicated that Jade and Demerit were, after all, getting together. She had given Tishner a practical reason for that, but she had an impractical one too. She had suffered a foolish sentiment, a feeling of camaraderie with Jade Brown, because of the evident abuse. Jade had suffered it in childhood, and suffered a different sort now. From bad childhood to bad marriage— how could May let that pass unchallenged, knowing how unpleasant a marriage could be? The woman deserved a bit of happiness in her life, and since she had to hide anyway, it made sense to combine the two. This might be the only unprovoked good deed May did this year, but she wanted it to be effective. Perhaps she was succeeding.

She checked her notebook of listings. She had pretty much caught up on the monster investigation, in part because she knew a great deal more about the monster's last attack than she could allow to be known beyond Mid. She could relax until Cyrano got a handle on the nature of the monster.

She smiled without humor. He had called it a firefly. What a contrasting image! Imagine saddling the pretty and harmless firefly with such a concept. Still, it did fit, in its fashion. A creature who hunted by night, flashing sexual signals.

It was good to take it easy, for a change. She seemed to have been on the go since this assignment began. Maybe now she could take a midday nap.

She kicked off her shoes and lay on the hotel bed. At times like this she regretted not being married. Well, technically she remained married, but that hardly counted. She wasn't turned off marriage, just marriage to the wrong man. With the right man, there would be pleasures to be had, ranging from conversation to the comfort of a warm body adjacent during the night. She was alone by necessity, not by choice.

But she was forty, and beyond the stage that appealed to men. Her figure was now solid, and so was her attitude. She was no man's doormat, now, and planned never to be so again. So even if she were available, she wouldn't find anyone suitable. Independence was certainly better than being locked to the wrong man.

Before long she was asleep, enjoying her interlude.

A harsh knocking woke her sometime later. May got up, feeling a bit dizzy, and went in her stocking feet to open the door. What on earth could this be—a fire alarm?

It was worse. She stared, appalled.

"Surprised to see me, April?" the man asked, smiling. "Well, everything's fine now that we're together again." He pushed into the room. She gave way before him, for the moment tongue-tied.

It was her husband, Bull Shauer. After three years, he had found her.

What was she to do? She knew this was disaster. It was as though her passing thought of him had summoned him, in the fashion of the devil.

He closed the door and set the lock. "We have a lot of catching up to do, April," He remarked conversationally. At age forty-two he remained a handsome man, literate and fair spoken. He had fooled her long ago, and she had never had much of a taste for handsome men since.

He pulled an easy chair before the door and sat in it, stretching out his long legs. She would not be able to get past him, and it was the only exit other than the window. He had her trapped, and it would be hell to escape, if she could manage it at all.

"You're looking good, April," he said, smiling in the manner that once had charmed her. His wavy light brown hair bobbed gently as he moved his head. "Or should I call you May now? That was clever: April Shauer to May Flowers. I wish I had imagination like that."

May coughed, trying to get her throat clear, but panic constricted it. "How—how did you find me?" she wheezed.

He flicked a hand negligently. "Does it matter, my dear? Surely you should be relieved that your long sojourn in isolation is over. I am here to take care of you."

"I don't need—" she started.

"I am sure it has all been a misunderstanding. But I am a forgiving person. I harbor no grudge against you. Come home with me, April, and all will be forgotten."

"No!" she choked.

"Ah, but there's yes-yes in your eyes, my dear. Come, sit on my lap, as you did of yore. I'm sure you'll remember how much our marriage has to offer, if you will just relax a bit." He gestured her toward him with four fingers, his eyes as mild and gray as summer clouds. But such clouds could turn into violent storms without notice. How well she knew!

Her glance fell on the phone. If she could call out, summon the police, anything—

"But if the mountain won't come to Mohammed, Mohammed will go to the mountain," he said, rising easily and coming toward her.

She could try to get out the door, but he would catch her before she got it unlocked. It was better to maintain her poise. "You know it wasn't working between us, Bull," she said, managing to achieve a normal voice.

"There may have been misunderstandings, but I'm sure those are over," he said. "Here—I have brought wherewithal for a libation." He reached behind him and brought out a hip flask.

He had always been worst when he drank. How well she knew the pattern! Three years had vanished as if a mere blink, and everything was horribly fresh. The python had made eye contact with its prey.

"Fetch glasses, my dear," he said. "We shall celebrate our reunion."

She moved to the bathroom, where there were water glasses, feeling partly like a zombie and partly like a trapped animal. She *had* to win free! But how? Nothing seemed to offer. She looked at the window, but found it barred against possible opening by children. The hotel wanted no family accidents! No escape there.

She brought the glasses to him. Maybe someone would come! Or call. Anything to interrupt this dread pattern. She would flee to the end of the earth the very moment she had the chance.

As if in answer to her prayer, the phone did ring. She jumped toward it, transferring the second glass to her left hand.

Bull moved smoothly but swiftly. His hand came down on hers, on the phone. "April, we don't need that interruption. Let it ring; they will assume you are out."

Indeed they would! Helplessly, May let go of the phone. It rang four more times and died along with her hope.

"That's better," Bull said. He guided her other hand to the bedside table and made her set down the glasses. Then he poured the whiskey into each, an inch deep.

He lifted one. "A toast!" he said, smiling again.

Reluctantly, May lifted the other. Suppose she threw it in his eyes, and escaped while he was blinded? No, his reflexes were better than hers; she probably wouldn't score, and if she did, she would only provoke immediately what would otherwise take time. She was better off stalling.

"To us!" he exclaimed, and sipped his drink.

"Us," she agreed faintly, sipping her own. She had hated whiskey ever since her first encounter with his use of it. The very smell of it made her want to retch.

"But you look so, if you will forgive me, frumpy and formal in that outfit," he said. "Why don't you change to something more feminine?"

"I don't have anything feminine." But she knew that would not stop him.

"Your nightie, then. We'll call it an evening gown. I always loved the feel of it, and of you in it."

He was going for sex! She hated that, too, for his way was not fun. But it might stretch things out, and postpone the violence long enough. She would have to do it.

She set down her drink, returned to the bathroom, stripped as slowly as she dared, and donned her nightie. She turned—and found Bull standing in the doorway, watching her.

"You've lost some weight," he remarked. "Too bad; I prefer full-bodied women."

"Maybe you should go find one, then," she retorted.

He moved so quickly she couldn't react. His open hand caught her across the left ear. She cried out, reeling, and fell against the bathroom cabinet, feeling the corner gouge at her right eye. She sank to the floor, to her knees, and then to all fours, her head ringing. She stayed there, her hair hanging down across her face, unable to think of what to do next. Now the pain began, welling up, but she did not make a sound. He had made her cry in the past, but her three years of developing pride stiffened her reaction.

A spot of red appeared before her. She stared somewhat stupidly at it. It occurred to her that it was blood. She put her hand up to her eye, and her fingers came away wet. Yes, she was bleeding.

"Sorry I had to do that," Bull said. "Now mop yourself up and come to bed." He turned and walked away, satisfied that he had made his point.

Oh, yes, he had done that! He expected no resistance and no back talk from her. The penalty for infractions was pain. How could she have forgotten, even for an instant? He wanted nothing less than her complete submission and humiliation, and perhaps somewhat more.

She had to get away from him! But how? The desperate question still had no answer. Bull was not a stupid man, however gross his other faults might be. He had found her, after three years, and he intended to make her pay for her temerity in leaving him. He would have all the bases covered.

She hauled herself up and faced the bathroom mirror. Her left ear hurt, but no damage showed. Her right eye was somewhat numb, not yet discolored, but the gouge just below it was leaking blood. She wadded and wet a paper towel and dabbed at it, flinching. She would have a black eye, but her sight didn't seem to be impaired. She smoothed it over with a bit of cream, hoping this patchwork would do. She was starting to get a headache, probably as much from tension as from the physical blow, but that was the least of her concerns.

The bleeding abated; it was more bruise than cut. She brushed her hair, smoothing it into dark brown curls around her ears. Then she went over her brows and eyelashes, framing the brown of her eyes. Bull was less likely to hit a pretty face than a plain one. She also adjusted the nightie to show the upper rondure of her breasts. Her breasts were full and they sagged; she would make an abysmal score on the pencil test. But partial exposure could be quite kind.

She had to escape, but it would be no easy thing. Her best chance was to obey Bull implicitly until an avenue opened. After drinking, violence, and sex (in that order), he usually slept. Then she might be able to sneak away.

She entered the main room, taking a breath to enhance her figure. He was right: she had lost weight since fleeing him, but she remained what was most delicately described as full-figured. She was no fresh young thing. So why *didn't* he go for something young and shapely? With his appearance and manners he could hook a girl of any age, and it would be some time before she learned the downside. Just as it had been with May.

But she knew the answer. Not all women accepted Bull's kind of treatment. He would be taking a definite risk that one of them would file charges and make them stick, and he would be marked even if he got off. After that, any repetition could land him in deep trouble. He would be unable to indulge his particular appetites safely. May, on the other hand, had the spine of a jellyfish in this regard. She had made a mistake with him, and had never been able to admit it to any other person. Her whole effort was not to expose him, but to escape him. Thus, protecting her secret shame, she protected his too. She would cover up for the blows and the degradation. He knew that. She was his safe harbor.

Also, there was an element of pride. He felt affronted that she should have asserted her independence by escaping him, and he wanted to erase that insult. He had married her, and by his reckoning, that made her his property. Unfortunately, to a considerable extent society and the law supported that view. So a man beat his wife; she had probably asked for it. If she didn't like it, she could divorce him.

How much easier said than done! May no longer honored the forms, but she had been born Catholic, and the notion of divorce appalled her. Bull knew that too.

"Finish your drink, April," he said from the bed. He had stripped naked, which made it evident that he had no erection. The mere sight or proximity of a woman didn't do it for him; his tastes were more channelized than that. He lay on his back, relaxed.

She approached the bed and picked up her hated drink. She tried to imagine it was brandy, but her imagination failed her. She associated whiskey with all things foul—in other words, with Bull Shauer.

She gulped it and blinked, feeling the sting of it. Meanwhile Bull reached around her derriere, and she schooled herself not to flinch; handling was better than violence. She had to please him, for the next hour, so that she could emerge from the far end of this tunnel and recover her freedom. She had, in fact, to put aside all thought of the future, for he could read her feelings, and make her pay for them. He was her personal devil, who truly knew how to make her suffer.

"You're my woman, April," he said, sitting up, drawing her in, and putting his face to her bosom. "You always were and you always will be. Now are you ready to apologize for annoying me?"

It was his way. How well she remembered! If only it would stop there! "Yes, Bull."

"Very good, April. Do it."

"I apologize most abjectly for making a smart remark and causing you distress, and I promise not to do it again."

"Thank you, April." His mouth nuzzled her left breast through the thin material of the nightie. Then he drew the décolletage down and bared her nipple. "And the other?"

"I apologize also for deserting you for three years."

His lips closed on her nipple. "And?" he said around it.

"And I promise not to do it again," she said, tensing.

His teeth closed savagely on her nipple. She stifled her scream of pain, so that only a thin squeak and rush of air passed though her nose. If others heard her scream now, they would know, and she couldn't stand that. This was part of the torment he inflicted: forcing her to cover for him, though she hated him.

"You were lying," he said, licking the blood welling around the nipple.

"I was lying," she agreed, blinking out the tears of pain and humiliation. It was no good to deny it, for that would only bring more punishment, and indeed, it had been a lie. He had forced her to lie, knowingly, because she hated falsity almost as much as she feared him.

"You deserve anything I give you," he said, kissing the nipple.

"Yes I do, Bull," she agreed.

"You're a fucking bitch, April."

She felt his teeth poised again. "I am a fucking bitch," she echoed. He knew how she hated either to hear or to use that language.

His hand slid down her leg to the hem of the nightie, then up inside until it cupped a buttock. "And you want me to fuck you, don't you, bitch?"

She gritted her teeth. "I want you to fuck me, Bull."

His fingers pried in between the cheeks of her posterior, touching her genital region. "And I am going to oblige you, April. Take off your outfit."

At least he wasn't hitting her, this time. Maybe he would just do it and go to sleep. She lifted off her nightie and stood within his grasp, naked.

He stood, disengaging. "Stand where you are. Lean over. Put your hands on the bed."

She didn't like strange positions. He knew that too. But she turned and bent over, putting her hands down. He played his hands over and around her bottom, massaging her buttocks, then running a finger into her vagina. She was wet, not from desire but from a perverse reaction to his punishment. She hated the notion that she could be a masochist, but somehow she did get a sexual reaction to his abuse.

He had an erection now. There was no question about him: he was a sadist, and he was sexually turned on by her physical and emotional pain. He poked his finger into her again, and brought it out, and put it in again, evidently transferring fluid to his member. To facilitate entry? Hardly; he had never been that kind. It must be just to make her know she was his, even to this disgusting familiarity.

He touched her with the wet tip of his member.

A cold shiver passed through her. Suddenly she realized his intent. "Oh, no, please, Bull!" she said.

"Are you begging, April?"

"Yes, I am begging," she said, knowing it was useless but unable to stop herself. "Please, not that way!"

"But you see, it's been three years," he said in a reasonable tone. "Something special is called for."

"Please, please, no," she whispered.

He pressed in. It hurt more than physically.

"Please, please," she continued, gritting her teeth against the awfulness of his penetration, knowing that he delighted in this pleading, but meaning it all the same.

He thrust harder. The pain increased. Her arms gave way, and she collapsed onto the bed, but he was right with her. She gasped as his weight pressed her flat, but his terrible thrusting continued.

Finally she felt the spurt of his climax, and knew that this aspect of her punishment was mostly done. But when would the memory of it ever pass?

After a time he slept—but not before he had confiscated her purse, her clothing, and her luggage. He had everything jammed under the bed, and his arms overlapped the edges. He had had military experience; he slept lightly when on guard. She would not be able to get anything without waking him, and it would be exceedingly foolish of her to make the attempt. She had the freedom of the room, but she couldn't dress, couldn't drive her car (the keys were in the purse), and had no money. And if she did go out despite all this, what would she tell anyone else? She would die before she let the truth be known: that she had suffered herself to be sodomized.

And Bull Shauer knew it. He had really fixed her, this time. He had bound her morally as well as physically. He well understood her scruples. He knew she would have to behave herself, by his definitions, to prevent him from doing it again. He would allow her to maintain the semblance of decency as long as she gave him no trouble at all.

Yet he had misjudged her, slightly. He thought she would remain with him, once he had humiliated her and broken her will. But she had had three years of independence, and in that time she had thought about her past life, and she had concluded that death would be better than a return to it. But she was not the suicidal type.

That left two alternatives. She could flee despite the feeble chance she had to make it good—or she could kill him.

She considered the two seriously. Killing him seemed to be the better choice, for then she would be free of him, no matter what. But she had no weapon—and if she somehow succeeded, she would be a murderess, and doomed to trial and imprisonment. At the very least, her guilty secret would be exposed, for they would examine her medically. She couldn't stand that. This, too, Bull surely knew; it was why he trusted her. He figured that life with him was better than the alternative, and that she had the sense to know it.

So she would flee, hopeless as it seemed. She went to the bathroom and took a towel. It wasn't the full bath size; it wouldn't cover her completely. She wrapped it about her waist and tiptoed to the door. She worked the lock with excruciating care, avoiding any noise, her eyes fixed on Bull.

It clicked open. She froze, but Bull did not wake. She cracked the door open and peered out. It was late afternoon, and no one was in the hall. There was a phone at the end; it was there she would make or break her chance to escape.

She eased out and closed the door. Barefooted and bare-breasted, she walked down the hall; if anyone came she would pretend she had been trapped outside her room by accident after a shower. Such things happened.

She reached the phone. She would call Mid—no, she would get his answering machine, and have to wait for a callback, and that could be in thirty seconds or in twelve hours, binding her to this phone throughout. That was no good. She needed someone local who could help her quickly, and who would keep his mouth shut.

That abruptly narrowed it down to one. Fortunately, she made it a policy to memorize numbers she depended on. She dialed Deputy Sheriff Tishner's home number.

It rang; then Tishner's wife picked it up. May squared her shoulders and her voice. "This is May Flowers. May I speak to Frank Tishner, please?"

The woman didn't answer. Instead, May heard her call to another person. "Frank, it's that reporter woman."

In a moment he picked up the phone. "Something new?"

"No. Frank, I'm in trouble. Can you pick me up immediately at the hotel?"

"Trouble?" he asked, startled.

"Personal trouble. Bad. I'm naked and must hide. Can you help me?"

"This isn't a joke?"

"Believe me, it isn't. My husband found me. He—he's a brutal man."

There was a pause. "I'll be there in fifteen minutes. Exactly where will you be?"

"In the hall if he doesn't wake. If he does—can you arrest me or something?"

"I'll get you out of there," he promised. "On my way."

Weak-kneed with relief, she hung up the phone. Fifteen minutes— that was her window of freedom. Once Frank got her away, she could contact Mid, and things would get put back together, somehow.

Now she felt her injuries. She might have a concussion from the blows to her head; her right eye was throbbing, her left breast was burning, and so was her rectum. She feared something had been torn.

She would need to get to a doctor—yet if she did, he would find out, and that could not be tolerated. So no doctor; she would have to hide out and recover on her own, hoping that no permanent damage had been done.

She was also standing in a semipublic hall, with a bath towel around her waist and bruises which were surely beginning to show. If anyone came by in the next fifteen minutes—

She cast about desperately for some hiding place. All she saw was a broom closet. That would have to do. She hurried down to it and opened the door. It was tiny, filled with mops and vacuum attachments, but there might be just enough space for her. She moved things to the sides, squeezed in, and pulled the door closed.

But in fifteen minutes she would have to come out—and Bull had taken her watch too. How would she know when?

She counted seconds. With each sixty, she closed a finger into her left palm. When she finished the fingers, she started with her right hand. Then with the left again, this time stretching the fingers out. When she finished that, she knew it was time. She would have to go out and—

And what? Go half naked down the stairs and out to the street to flag down the deputy? Some private pickup that would be! No, she would have to wait in the hall, hoping he had the sense to come in.

She put her hand on the handle—and discovered the door was locked. It was one of those one-way doors, openable from the inside only—only the hall was the inside. Nobody was supposed to close the door from the closet side! She could not get out.

She stifled a surge of panic. She could scream—but the first person to hear might be Bull. Anyone else would be almost as bad. Open the closet to discover a forty-year-old, battered, bare-breasted woman? She did not want discovery!

She heard the heavy tread of someone coming. Was it a stranger, or Frank Tishner, or Bull? It was time, but Tishner might be late. She had one chance in three: should she cry out or keep silent?

The steps halted. Was it Frank, wondering where she was, or Bull, doing the same? Should she speak, and risk being recaptured and punished more horribly than before, or be silent and risk losing her chance to get away? She could do neither; she was in an agony of indecision.

"May?" The voice was muffled.

It was Frank! "Here!" she exclaimed—and realized too late that it could be Bull, toying with her, using her adopted name to fool her.

A hand came down on the knob. It turned. The door opened, and light flooded in. Blinded, she could make out only a solid male figure.

"God, he really beat you up!" It was Frank's voice! Now she could see him more clearly.

She hugged him. "Oh, Frank, I'm so glad it's you!"

"Uh, sure," he said, embarrassed.

Then she recoiled. "What am I doing?"

He held out an overcoat. "Put this on. Best I could do on short notice. Just walk with me; no one will notice."

Numbly, she did so. They went down the stairs and outside—where her bare feet touched the hot pavement. "Oh!"

"Gotcha." He turned, put his arms at her back and knees, and picked her up. She knew she was no lightweight, but he was strong; he heaved her into the air. He carried her the few paces to his car.

She caught at the handle and yanked the door open. He set her down at the edge of the seat, and she slid in. The operation was clumsy, and her towel was dislodged, but that was not of much moment at this stage. Frank closed the door and walked around to the driver's side while she yanked as much of the towel up and across her front as she could.

"I'd better take you first to a doctor," he said.

"No! No doctor!"

He looked at her, pausing as he was about to turn the key in the ignition. "May, your left ear's bruised, you right eye's bleeding, your left breast is swelling, and you walk as if you've been raped. Let the doctor confirm the fact that you've been physically and sexually assaulted, and we'll put your husband away. It's got to be done now."

He was one observant cuss! "Frank, I can't, I just can't. He's my husband and I can't testify against him. I've just got to get away from him!"

He started the motor and pulled carefully onto the street. "And change your name again, and start over somewhere else?"

"Mid will help me! I just have to stay away from Bull!"

"You never struck me as a frail, fainting creature. Not like that Brown woman. The man is a wife-beater! Why won't you let us help you?"

"I can't, Frank. Believe me, I can't. Please, take me somewhere I can hide until Mid decides what to do."

He shook his head. "Damn it, we can't prosecute if you won't testify! But it stinks to high hell!"

"Thank you for helping me, Frank," she said quietly.

Scowling, he drove on out of town. In due course he pulled in at a house somewhere beyond. "My wife will help you while I see about getting you into hiding."

She nodded. They got out, and she walked on the cool grass beside the drive until reaching the shadow of the house.

Frank took her to the front door. He opened it a crack. "Hey, Trudy, I brought her here. We need your help."

Trudy appeared. She was a woman of about May's own age and heft, with short, straight black hair. "Here?"

Frank gestured May in. "May Flowers," he said. "My wife. Trudy, she doesn't have anything to wear. I don't know what to do for her."

Trudy frowned. "Well, come to the bedroom, then," she said to May.

May followed her to the bedroom, which was homey and neat, with twin beds. So they didn't sleep together.

Now Trudy got a better look at her. "Your face!" she exclaimed. "What happened?"

"My husband found me."

"Husband?"

"We've been married eighteen years. I've been apart from him the last three. He wasn't pleased."

"Let me get a cloth and some—you need to see a doctor!"

"No, I just need to get away from him."

Trudy got the cloth and dabbed at the eye. "He hit you?"

"Yes."

"How could you stay with a man who did that?"

"I couldn't get away. I supposed I hoped it would get better, but it didn't."

"If any man hit me, I'd be gone instantly!"

"Frank doesn't get violent?"

"Him? Never! He hates domestic violence. I just wish he hated job insecurity as much."

"Job insecurity? He seems secure enough to me." But May knew what the woman was talking about; it was just that she did not find it expedient to reveal her research.

"He insists on standing up for what he sees as right. It's cost him two jobs, and if he throws this one away, I'm leaving him. I can't stand the disruption of moving, starting all over again, losing all my contacts."

"I'd trade for mine," May said sadly.

"Let me see the rest of you. I think my clothes should fit you. We're about the same size."

May removed the coat. Trudy stared at her breast. "He did that?" May nodded.

"And he raped you?"

"Technically, no. I didn't resist."

Trudy shook her head. "Frank gets all upset about abuse. I knew it happened, but it didn't mean anything to me. Now I begin to understand. You've got to take him to court!"

May simply shook her head no. She preferred to let others believe it was fear that restrained her, rather than the whole truth.

Trudy dug out bra, panties, skirt, and blouse. They fitted reasonably well, but her lacerated left breast hurt when constrained.

"Wait, I have an old maternity bra buried somewhere," Trudy said. "We never had children, but at one time we thought we might, and I got it." She rummaged in a closet, found a package of old clothing, and pulled out the bra. It was huge, with flaps allowing exposure of the nipples for nursing.

May put it on, opening the left flap. That helped; her swollen nipple looked awful but suffered no extra pressure. The blouse was loose enough to accommodate it without touching. The skirt had good elastic, so adjusted well enough.

Trudy tried one of her shoes on her, but the fit was uncomfortably wrong. She rummaged and found an old pair of sneakers; these were large, but tight lacing made them suffice. May was back in business, after a fashion. "Thank you," she said. "I will return these to you when I can."

"No, don't bother," Trudy protested. "I had no idea what you'd been through! I wish you'd at least see a doctor."

"A doctor would have to make a report. I can't have that."

"You're protecting that monster! How can you do that?"

"Shame," May said simply.

"I can't understand that!"

"I'm glad."

They went to the living room. Frank was waiting. "I have a place for you," he said. "It's not much, but it should be safe."

"Thank you. Can we go there now? I'm very tired."

"You've got to see a doctor! There could be internal bleeding, and that eye—"

"Please, can we just go?"

He threw up his hands, literally. "Come on."

She followed him out. She eased herself into the seat and leaned back. She had not been fooling about being tired; she was about ready to pass out. But one comment of his stuck in her mind: internal bleeding. She hadn't thought of that. The penetration had been so hard, there could be a tear. That would not only complicate evacuation, it could—

She stifled the thought.

After a period of stupor she came to, to discover them at the gate of the Middle Kingdom Ranch. "But I don't want to intrude on—" she protested.

"You aren't." he glanced at her. "You did a nice thing for that Brown woman."

"She was an abused wife. Not physically, but that's not the only component of the syndrome. I happen to be in a position to know."

He nodded. "I understand. It's nice to know you have a human side."

"All too human," she agreed listlessly.

They arrived at the house. George—no, his name was Geode, she remembered—came out. "I can lead you in," he said.

"No, I don't want her bumped worse than she has to be. Take her in yours, and I'll follow. Then I'll know the route."

Geode nodded. He went into the house. In a moment one of the garage doors rolled up, and a car backed out. It was a small foreign-make station wagon marked 4WD. It headed a short distance down the lane, then turned left at right angles onto a dirt trail. It stopped.

Frank pulled up behind it. Geode was out opening another gate by hand. This trail was within the fenced portion of the ranch; May had not known it existed before.

Frank got out and came around to help her out. She tried not to wince as she moved her legs, lest it betray the nature of her discomfort. Her innards were pulsing with dull pain, making her feel a bit like retching. Abdominal injury did that, she knew.

She walked to the station wagon and got in as Geode did. It was odd to see him driving; she had seen him only afoot or on the bike before. She got the seat belt buckled and tried to relax. If the man noticed her distress, he gave no sign.

He moved the car forward, down a trail overhung by trees. It seemed to go right into the water of the lake, but then it turned left and paralleled the bank. Tishner's car followed.

The trail curved tortuously around the edge of the marshy lake. Geode drove slowly, easing over the bumps, but May felt them anyway. She learned to put down her hands and lift her body just before they navigated one, easing the shock to her posterior. It helped, but not enough.

After what seemed like an eternity of convolutions, the trail forged inland and became straighter. They picked up speed. Finally it entered a region of large oaks, and then a clearing where—was it a dream?—two brown ponies stood.

Geode pulled up at a ramshackle cabin. He got out and went to unlock its door.

Frank stopped behind the station wagon and got out. He opened May's door and helped her out. This time she could not avoid staggering; only his firm hand on her elbow kept her on course. He guided her to the door and in.

It was desolate inside. There was a kitchen of sorts, and a main chamber with mattresses on the floor. It was hot, but she didn't care; she eased herself down on the first mattress and lay there, hardly caring about appearances. This place was isolated and safe, because it was on Mid's estate; that was all that counted.

She stared at the ceiling, and consciousness faded.

19

GEODE GAZED AT the woman lying there. "She's hurt," he said.

"Beaten up and raped," Tishner agreed. "Concussion, maybe damage to that eye, a chewed-up breast, and I think when he raped her he hurt her inside. She could have internal bleeding. But she won't see a doctor; she's ashamed to let it be known how that man treats her. I've seen it before, too often. She needs medical attention, but I gave my word no doctor. We'll just have to chance it."

"Would she see Cyrano?"

Tishner's jaw dropped. "The exterminator?"

"He's a vet too."

"By damn, man, maybe that's a notion! He's in on the secret, he works for Mid, and she knows him. Maybe he could help her some."

"I'll call Mid and ask him to send Cyrano."

"Good enough, Demerit! You do that." He looked again at the woman. "But you know, I don't like leaving her alone like this, with no food or anything."

"I'll bring some from the house tonight."

Tishner went to the window air conditioner. "This thing work?"

"Yes."

He turned on the unit. It cranked up and began blowing air. "That'll help some. Okay, you bring her some food, and maybe bring Jade Brown too; May needs a woman's help, and she helped Brown. I'll bring in food in the morning; you let me in and I'll go right around without bothering you at the house. You can check on her when you do your rounds too. I just hope she's okay."

"Yes."

"She's a good woman, Demerit. I didn't like her, but now I know something about her. I don't want her hurting."

Geode nodded. "We'll come to her tonight."

They went out. "The key—leave her the key," Tishner said.

Geode went back in and set the key on the kitchen table.

Tishner got in his car and looped it by the ponies, who gave way cautiously. Geode paused to fetch a carrot from the store at the house, broke it in half, and gave a piece to each horse. The small one was the bolder of the two; the larger one remained wary as long as strangers were near. "Keep guard," he told them, then returned to the station wagon, not waiting for their answer. He drove it down the trail, back toward the house, about two miles distant.

He wondered exactly what the man had done to May Flowers. As he understood it, sex didn't normally lead to injury, but she looked injured. He wished he knew more about it. But even if he had been potent, what woman would have been interested in him? He would have to ask Œnone, for she surely knew everything he didn't.

He arrived back at the house and went in. Œnone appeared as soon as the door closed. "What happened, Geode?" she asked anxiously. How wonderful it was to have her at the house; his life had assumed an unfamiliar state of delight since she had come.

"She was beaten up and raped," he said. "She won't see a doctor or let Tishner report it. We must bring things to her."

"Oh, yes, now I will do for her what she did for me!" she agreed. "But why didn't you bring her here?"

"She didn't want to interfere with us."

She gazed at him without speaking for a moment. "Then she knows," she murmured.

"I guess so. I have to tell Mid, and get Cyrano to see her."

"But Cyrano is here to kill the monster."

He nodded, and went to the special phone that was only for Mid. Œnone hesitated, then went to the kitchen.

He got the answering machine, as expected. "May Flowers has been raped and savaged by her husband," he reported. "She is in the cabin. She won't see a doctor, but we fear for her. We think Cyrano might help her." Then, after a pause, he added, "She is a good woman. Œnone and I are going out to see her tonight, and Frank Tishner tomorrow. We want to help her. She put us together. We hope you will send Cyrano."

He set down the phone. That was as close as he could come to asking a favor of Mid on his own.

Then he went to check on Œnone. She was busy packing a bag with groceries that May had brought her. "And does she have water there?" she asked.

"Yes."

"And anything to read?"

"No."

"Find something Mid won't mind."

He checked Mid's shelves. It was all right for him to read the books, because he was careful, but he wasn't sure about removing a volume from the house. Still, May worked for Mid too. He found a novel, *The Shattered World* by Michael Reaves; that was old enough to be expendable, he hoped, if she liked fantasy. If not, he would try another.

He returned with the volume to the kitchen. Œnone was ready. "Now we go," she said.

They went. Before long they were at the cabin. "It's so much quicker by car!" Œnone exclaimed. She had not complained, but he knew she was stiff from her arduous ride around the ranch. He watched covertly as she walked, to see whether any of that stiffness showed, but all he saw was how well formed her legs were in the jeans.

Inside they found May lying where he and Tishner had left her. Œnone went immediately and knelt beside the mattress. "May, it's me, Œnone!" she said.

May stirred. "Who?"

Œnone evidently realized that she had slipped. "Jade Brown."

May blinked. "Œnone—the way he's Geode?"

"Yes. Please, you are hurt and we want to help you. How do you feel?"

"Awful. I need to—" She broke off, looking at Geode.

"Take a walk, Geode," Œnone said without looking at him.

Oh. The bathroom. He fetched a carrot and went out, but the ponies were gone. He walked out along the earthen pier, gazing at the slow gray curve of the Withlacoochee River, and at the stand of cypress trees growing at the verge. There were giant stumps of bygone cypress further in, five and six feet in diameter, but the current ones were hardly more than a foot at the point their trunks narrowed.

The river was divided here, with a series of marshy islands on which more cypress trees grew. Actually, the islands might be because of the cypress and the communities of creatures their massive root systems supported. Cypress knees projected from the water, long a mystery to man. It seemed that the knees started as ordinary roots; if they were in aerated soil they grew downward, but if they were in water they grew upward until they found air, then grew down again. People had conjectured that they served as sources of air for the roots, or that sunlight on their surfaces signaled the seasons for the tree, but there was no conclusive evidence.

Geode had no problem with it. It was obvious to him that the primary purpose of the knees was to brace the tree in insubstantial soil. Ordinary trees could grasp the firm soil with their roots and be strongly anchored against their primary challenge, the wind. Wind put a lot of force against the extensive surface of a tree, and it was usually wind which finally brought down a tree, after it was dead and could no longer defend itself. They eased it by making their leaves flexible or needle-shaped, so that they offered little resistance to the passing air, and their branches and even their trunks had enough give to allow them to bend with the wind and spring back undamaged after it passed. But the heart of it was their root system, which held their vulnerable upper sections in place. Except when the soil was not solid, but muddy, or even covered by open water. That represented a challenge which defeated most trees. They could get oxygen down into the roots, just as they could get water up to the leaves; that wasn't the problem. But the anchorage had to be below, and mud was no good. Cypress reduced the surface it presented to the wind by being thin, almost like furred sticks growing up. But that wasn't enough. So the cypress used the outrigger system, sending its roots first out and then down, spreading them wider to gain leverage. Then the anchorage of the mud sufficed; the membrane of the rootlets themselves firmed it, and the leverage of their spread braced the tree despite the softness of the soil. How did they know when to do this, and how far to reach out? That was where the genius of the system showed: the farther underwater a root started, the farther it had to grow to reach the surface. Since it grew at an angle, that meant it went farther out. Once it was high enough so that the seasonal fluctuations of the water level never covered it entirely, it made its turn and grew down until it found the soil. Then it made the best anchorage it could, in the manner of any tree, reaching deeply and spreading out its feeder rootlets. It had become a flying buttress whose placement provided the leverage the larger tree required.

Geode liked all trees, but he had special respect for the cypress. Trees were not smart in the manner of men, but they were geniuses in the manner of trees. They could grow in terrain that excluded other trees, so they had little competition. They could grow in dry soil too, and did, without their knees, but there they were competing with the myriad other species adapted more perfectly to that dry land, and were at a disadvantage, and tended to be squeezed out. So, in the larger sense, they owed their prosperity and perhaps their survival to their knees. If the water rose, owing perhaps to a shift in the river or the pattern of rainfall, other trees would die, but the cypress would survive. That deserved respect.

If the cypress were lost, the ecology of the waterfront and swamp regions would change. All the species of fish and insects that existed in the protection of those knees would perish. There might be types never discovered by man, hiding there, that would be rendered extinct if their habitat were eliminated. Geode didn't need to know exactly what they were, he just needed to know they had their fair chance to live their lives and do their things. His mission in life had come upon him slowly, but now it was clear: to protect the wildlife that remained on the planet, any way he could. Mid gave him that chance, here at the Middle Kingdom, and he would carry through.

That led him to thought of the monster, the firefly. Was it a wild creature? If so, he should protect it too. But his news of it had summoned Cyrano, who was here to kill it. Was this right? Yet if the monster lived, and continued preying on people, there would come a massive monster hunt, and they could burn down the entire forest and dredge the river and fill the swamp, just to get rid of the monster. Then the firefly would truly have brought the fire! The Middle Kingdom would become a wasteland. So it seemed that if the monster wouldn't go away, it had to be killed, to protect the ranch and all the natural creatures it harbored. Geode didn't like it, but he appreciated the logic of it.

He saw a ripple at the verge of the water. There was an alligator, moving smoothly in quest of prey. One thing about the alligators: they made intruders cautious. Except for the poachers, who wanted their hides for expensive shoes. Geode would prefer to see the hides of the poachers made into shoes, or stretched out on boards in the fashion of rattlesnake skins. He visualized an alligator talking to a rattlesnake in front of a board and boots: "You should have seen the fight he put up!"

In a sense, the firefly was doing that, turning the tables on the poachers. A hunter had sneaked onto the property and become the prey. It was simple justice. Geode couldn't help liking the firefly, some.

He walked back to the cabin. A pair of wrens poked in the grass beside it, indefatigably looking for bugs. He liked wrens too; they were bold little birds, almost tame, and if a door was left open they would come in and explore. Once one had been caught inside; he had had to explain to it that this was an accident, and it had forgiven him. When he split wood, preparing it for the fireplace at such time as Mid might arrive, the wrens would poke about the billets, seeking the bugs dislodged from the bark. That was just as well, because bugs were no good inside the house. They had no way to forage or hide, so they died. It was better that they live or die cleanly, nature's way.

He knocked on the door, in case the women weren't finished. Œnone came to let him in. "I don't know how much is physical and how much psychological, but she's not well. We must do something for her."

Geode was willing, but had no idea what to offer. He followed her into the main chamber, where May now sat up on the mattress, propped against the wall. It was true: she did not look good.

"We brought you a book," he said, knowing this was inadequate. "It's a good fantasy novel." He had been carrying it all this time, unconscious of it. *"The Shattered World."*

Her dull eyes swiveled to cover him. "Thank you, Geode. It sounds appropriate."

There was a silence.

"Maybe I could tell you a story," Œnone said. "If you aren't up to reading."

Surprise lighted May's features momentarily. "You tell stories?"

Œnone was embarrassed. "No one ever cared to listen."

"I am a captive audience," May said. But she smiled.

"I will tell you of Œnone." Œnone reached up and loosened her hair, shaking it out into an auburn mass.

Geode was interested. He sat on the other mattress and watched her. And was duly impressed.

◆ 20 ◆

ŒNONE WAS A nymph of Mount Ida. Like a hamadryad, who was a spirit of a particular tree, she was a spirit of the mountain, immortal as long a she remained with it but unable to live apart from it. Mount Ida was, in an overwhelming sense, her mother.

Mount Ida, as Œnone knew it, was a many-splendored region. Associated with it were misty glens and ridges covered by pines and flower-covered slopes. A stream coursed down it, falling through cataracts toward the Ægean Sea. For centuries Œnone roamed the protective recesses of the mountain, knowing neither joy nor sorrow, for she had no experience of the mortal realm.

Then a small party came to Mount Ida. A nurse brought a wrapped parcel and laid it on a ledge, exposed to the sun. The party departed. Œnone, curious, went to see what they had left—and was astonished.

It was a mortal baby boy! Apparently he had been left here to die, unwanted. But he was a marvelously pretty baby, and she had ruth on him, and picked him up and carried him to the home of a shepherd who lived at the foot of the mountain. She could not let herself be seen by an adult, for adults did not believe in mountain spirits, so she left the baby at the door and faded away. But she watched from cover, and saw the shepherd's wife come out and find the baby.

"Oh!" she exclaimed. "It is the answer to my prayers! Zeus has granted me a baby!" Then Œnone knew that she had done the right thing, for the woman would take good care of the foundling.

Thereafter Œnone watched, for she had touched a mortal person and thereby assumed a bit of mortality herself, while yielding part of her immortality to the baby. She had not realized that this would be the case, for she had been innocent of the ways of mortality, but gradually she came to understand. The baby had been fated to die, and she had saved him not merely by carrying him physically to the shepherd's home, but by yielding part of her immortality to him, counteracting his fate. That part of her nature which enabled him to live also attached her to him, for he was now part of her as much as she was part of him.

The shepherd called him Alexander, and he grew in due course to handsome manhood. This happened quickly, by Œnone's terms, for to her twenty years was but an instant. He became a shepherd, and spent much time on the mountain slopes, and she watched him constantly, drawn by the part of her that was him. She saw that though he was breathtakingly handsome, he was shallow of character, having little interest in anything other than his immediate pleasure. She assumed that this was normal for his kind, and this did not surprise her. It was, after all, the way of mountain spirits, for they had no souls.

One day he was injured in an accident occasioned by his own carelessness, and his leg was bleeding. Œnone came then and put her hand on the injury, and it healed.

"Who are you?" he inquired.

"I am Œnone, nymph of the mountain."

"What magic is this?"

"No magic, only the natural healing I do for injured animals. I did not want you to hurt." For though she had little understanding of the human condition, Œnone hurt when any creature of the mountain did. Thus her act of healing was as much to relieve her own distress as to relieve his.

"Oh. Thank you." He got up and went about his business.

Then he noticed something. He looked back at her, verifying it, and called to her. She could not resist him, and came to him. He was clothed, in the manner of mortals, but she was not, in the manner of nymphs. Her charms were those of youth and health, for a nymph never ages after her maturity. Her waist was small, her breasts were full and upstanding, her legs were marvels of rondure and symmetry, and her auburn hair flowed down about her like a living cloak that nevertheless concealed nothing. He gazed upon her, and into her eyes, which were as green as the verdure of the slopes of Mount Ida, and he took her in his arms, and she could not resist the lure of his visage and his mortality. And so it was that he brought her down from the high slopes, to the low slopes, and married her, and lay with her, or perhaps it was the other way around, for his adoptive parents were strict about the amenities, and she committed the folly of loving him.

For every human emotion costs a nymph more of her immortality. Œnone lost some when she had ruth on him as a baby, and more when she loved him, but she could not help herself. He swore his love for her, and seemed happy, yet there was a mystery about him, and the unraveling of that mystery was to ruin their life together.

For Alexander wanted to know his origin. He knew he was adopted, and he was dissatisfied with the bucolic life, for there was too much honest work entailed, so he hoped for some way out. He asked Œnone if she knew, and she discovered that she did. She had not realized before that she knew, but she was of the mountain, and the mountain knew many things, and it spoke through her. "Yes, you are Paris, son of Priam, king of Ilios, and Hecuba, his queen."

He was amazed. "Then I am a prince! But how came I here?"

Again she learned the answer as she spoke. "Hecuba dreamed she was to bring forth a firebrand. This meant that the child she carried would bring destruction to Priam's house. Priam sired fifty children, so could spare one, and they sent a nurse to expose the newborn one on the mountain, that he might die without actually being killed." Then she added from her own memory, "But I saw you there, and took you to the shepherd, who raised you as his own. Now you are grown, and you are indeed a prince."

"Well, then, I must go to Ilios and claim my heritage!" he exclaimed.

"But what of me?" she asked. "I cannot leave Mother Ida!"

"Nobody asked you to," he said. "Prepare me a pack with staples, for I will set off on the morrow."

Œnone was saddened, but she loved him and wanted him to be happy, so she prepared the pack. That night he made love to her three times, because it occurred to him it might be several days before he encountered another woman, and in the morning he set off for Ilios, a city to the northwest. Œnone mourned to see him go, but hid her feeling so as not to disturb him. She was learning the human condition.

A week later he returned. "They welcomed me!" he said. "They had long since gotten rid of that false prophet and regretted throwing me away. I have reclaimed my position."

"Then why did you return?" she asked naively.

"No woman there looked as good as you do."

She blushed, in the mortal fashion, taking it as a compliment. He promptly threw her down and had his pleasure of her, and three more times during the night, catching up on the rest of the week. She was happy again. She was regretful only that she was unable to bear him a child. But that was the province of mortal women. She was not yet sufficiently mortal.

Then trouble came, deceptively, from afar. The goddesses had a contest to ascertain who was the most beautiful among them, and decided that it should be judged by the handsomest mortal man: Paris of Ilion, the city otherwise known as Troy.

So it was that three formidable goddesses came to Paris at Mount Ida and required that he choose which one among them should be awarded the Golden Apple of victory. Œnone knew immediately that this was likely disaster, and tried to warn Paris, but he was too flattered by the attention to heed her.

It started after a passing storm, when the rain was fading and the clouds were dispersing. A rainbow appeared, spanning the peak of the mountain, brighter and richer than any seen before. Paris and Œnone gazed at it, entranced, fascinated by its surrealistic intensity.

Then a part of it detached, and formed a smaller rainbow within the arch of the first, closer to where they sat, and then a yet smaller one that seemed almost close enough to touch. The colors swirled and coalesced and became the rainbow-hued skirt of a young woman garbed in the manner of distant Crete. Her feet and breasts were bare, and her skirt was horizontally tiered, and her black hair was bound about with golden chains. She walked toward them, her toes not quite touching the ground, and in her hand she carried the shining gold Apple.

"Iris, messenger of the gods during discord!" Œnone exclaimed, recognizing her. For Hermes was the messenger when the gods intended harmony.

But Paris's eyes were on the visitor's décolletage, and on the Apple, and he had no concern for the implications of her presence. "What may I do for you, lovely creature?" he inquired eagerly.

Iris stopped before him. "Take this Apple, Paris. You must award it to the most fair among goddesses."

He took the precious fruit. The Golden Apple was far heavier than a normal one, and more lustrous, and he wished he could keep it for himself, but realized that the gods would not permit this. "Must I then return it to you so soon?" he asked gallantly.

But Iris was immune to such blandishment. "Three contend for the honor," she said. "Behold, here is the first." She broke into bands of color, which swirled briefly and faded out.

A brilliant peacock flew toward him, landing and spreading its tail so that light splayed out as if from a prism. A golden cloud formed above it, and lowered majestically to the ground, obscuring the bird. Then it dissipated, and its mists formed into towering columns supporting a magnificent pavilion girt with colorful murals of animals. In its center was a golden throne, and on that throne sat a beautiful woman, resplendent in queenly robes whose every embroidery was the lifework of the most skilled artisans.

Œnone recognized her, because the mountain did. She was Hera, queen of the gods, daughter of the Titan Kronos and granddaughter of Ouranos, who was the sky itself, and sister and wife to Zeus, the king of the gods. After her had been named the ancient Heræan Games for women, after which the more recent and inferior Olympic Games for men were patterned.

"Give me the Apple, Paris," Hera said, "and I will give you riches beyond measure, power such as your father never knew, and greatness before all mortals."

Paris held the Golden Apple, sorely tempted. But he remembered that there were three contestants, and it behooved him at least to see the other two before accepting the gift the queen offered.

Aware of this, Hera retreated some distance, and the next appeared. This was a warrior-maiden wearing silver armor and carrying a spear. Yet so cunningly were silver slippers, skirt, cuirass, and helmet fashioned that she was strikingly beautiful too. This was Athene, goddess of war, handicraft, and wisdom, after whom the great Parthenon was named. "Yield me the Apple," she said, "and I will give you prowess in battle, and knowledge, and wisdom to use your powers well. I will enable you to know yourself and to follow the right course always, becoming a champion of the way of law and freedom, standing always upright. Your reputation shall be as fair as your face, your heart courageous and pure."

"Give it to her!" Œnone cried, recognizing that this would replace Paris's greatest weaknesses with strengths. But Paris's attention was more on her firmness of limb and torso than on her words; he had never been overly keen on rightness as opposed to self-interest. He did not answer.

Then Athene made a strategic retreat and gave the vanguard position to the third goddess, who now approached in the form of a truly beautiful woman. This was Aphrodite, born of the foam that gathered about the severed parts of the emasculated god Ouranos when his son Kronos castrated him with a sickle. She was therefore the goddess of erotic love. The Babylonians had known her as Ishtar and worshiped her with ritual prostitution. She was the one Œnone feared the most.

Aphrodite walked slowly toward Paris, and pythons would have envied the way her hips undulated as she strode, and her bosom heaved with rippling swells like those of the hungry sea. Her hair floated like the foam of her origin down about her pearly shoulders and the upper contours of her phenomenal breasts, showing now one curve and then another, each more seductive than its neighbor. She walked on violets where there had been none before, and her dress was of such perfect silk that it glistened like a second skin. From her rose the scent of ambrosia, the elixir of life itself, the food of the gods that conferred immortality.

"Judge me, Paris, as I am," she said, and with a gesture of exquisite aplomb she threw off her garb and stood before him as the most perfect of women. "And for your trouble I shall give you the fairest and most loving mortal woman."

Paris, blinded by the beauty of her body and her promise, extended his hand in the manner of a somnambulist, presenting her the Golden Apple. Queenly Hera's visage clouded with affront, and wise Athene shook her head at his folly and retreated. Aphrodite accepted the Apple, leaned forward to kiss him once on the lips, and said, "She is Helen of Sparta. I will guide you to her acquisition. Speak my name when you are ready for that challenge." Then she turned and walked away, her rear view as generous and appealing as her front view, for those who liked that type. Œnone didn't care for it, but Paris remained mesmerized until she disappeared from the bower.

"O Paris, my love, go not to Sparta!" Œnone pleaded, for she borrowed from the mountain a certain knowledge of how things were, and knew that nothing good would come of this. "You can only involve yourself and your country in ruin!"

"Tell me of Helen," he replied, indifferent to her concern.

Dutifully, Œnone drew on Mother Ida's knowledge and spoke of Helen. "One day Leda, the lovely young wife of Tyndareus, king of Sparta, arguably the leading city of Greece, walked beside the water and was spied there by Zeus, king of the gods. Smitten by her beauty, he approached her for a liaison. But Leda was a virtuous woman, and rejected his advance. Enraged by such astonishing treatment, Zeus assumed the form of a great swan and attacked her. He beat at her with his wings as she fled, and caused her to fall; then he landed on her and drove his bill at her face. When she spread her legs in an effort to scramble up, he forged between them and ravished her. His lust abated, he flew away and forgot the matter. Leda was too ashamed to confess to her husband that she had been raped by a swan, so she concealed her horror and pretended that nothing had happened. But she had conceived by Zeus, who was the most potent of males in any form, and in due course laid two eggs (at that point her husband may have been suspicious), from one of which hatched Helen. Rather than allow a scandal, Tyndareus claimed the children as his own, and Helen grew into the very perfection of womanhood and married Menelaus, who became king of Sparta. There she remains today, and soon enough he will see about begetting a child or two upon her, trusting that they are not birthed as eggs."

"Then I must go quickly to rescue her!" Paris exclaimed chivalrously. "Aphrodite! I am ready!"

The goddess appeared, smiling knowingly, and extended her hand to him. "No!" Œnone wailed, but she was helpless. Paris took the hand, and there was a flare of light, and when it faded, Œnone was alone in the bower.

"O Mother Ida!" she cried to the mountain, as reported by Alfred, Lord Tennyson. "Hearken ere I die!" For she was dangerously close to mortality now, having loved too well and foolishly. "Paris swore his love to me a thousand times!" But now he was gone.

And so it was that Paris went to Greece, and beguiled the beauteous Helen, and abducted her and carried her away to Troy. The Greeks were so affronted that they gathered together a great army and besieged Troy for ten years, finally overcoming it by trickery. They were in fact part of the effort known to historians as the Peoples of the Sea, whose depredations weakened the civilized Hittite and Egyptian empires and were a nuisance to Crete. Dark ages were to fall in these cultured regions—all because Œnone had saved a baby who should have been allowed to die. All this she learned from the mountain, too late; she could have known it in time to prevent it, but she had never thought to inquire.

Paris earned the contempt of all who knew him by his shallowness and cowardice, and Helen turned out to be similarly shallow and vain. The entire effort was for nothing. Paris tried to hide as the Greeks took the city at last, but he was wounded by a poisoned arrow shot by Philoctetes, who had been laid up for ten years by a serpent bite but who possessed the magic arrows of Heracles that were required for the finale. Even so, Paris managed to escape to the countryside—some hint he might have garbed himself as an old woman to hide—and came again to Œnone, beseeching her to use her nymphly healing magic to preserve his life.

But by this time Œnone was pretty upset with him. It had, after all, been ten years. She hardened her heart and refused. His servants took him away. Then, just like a mortal woman, she reconsidered, and repented her attitude, and agreed to heal him. But it was too late, and he died. They laid his body at her feet, and she was consumed by remorse. She knew then that her own death was soon upon her, for too much of her had been lost with her false lover. What now for foolish Œnone?

❖ 21 ❖

M AY WAS OVERCOME by emotion. "Oh, Œnone, was it like that for you? I never realized!"

"It is only a story," Œnone demurred.

"You called your husband Paris," Geode said, similarly moved. "And he had an affair with Helen. Now Paris is dead."

"But that doesn't mean you have to die!" May said.

But Œnone just glanced at her, and down. "We must return to the house," she murmured. "Geode is supposed to be there, to keep watch. But we will return first thing in the morning, to be sure you're all right."

"Thank you," May said, still awed by the facet of the woman's character that had been revealed. She had thought of Jade Brown as a mouse, and had hoped to bring some little pleasure into her life, but now realized that Œnone was some other type of creature. For as she had told of the various characters in the mythology, she had emulated them, becoming Œnone, Paris, Hera, Athene, and Aphrodite. For a moment she had even been the bare-breasted messenger-goddess. The woman lived her story. Now, with her Paris dead, was she determined to die herself? May was very much afraid that the woman's ready adaptation to this new situation was because she believed she had no future. Why grieve for others when your own life is ending?

The two of them went out, and in a moment May heard the station wagon start up and move off. She was alone.

She roused herself and went to the door. It was deep dusk now; and darker in the house. She hadn't noticed, as Œnone told her story, but now she felt vulnerable. Her innards seemed to have settled down, but she had no confidence of health. Œnone had helped her use the toilet, but it wasn't merely bruising, outside or in, that concerned her.

She closed the door and turned back into the house. She found a light switch and flicked it. Then light came on. Thank God Mid kept the power on out here!

She returned to the mattress. There lay the book they had brought her. Well, she needed something to distract her. She eased herself down, picked it up, and began to read. It turned out to be true to its title: a fantasy of a world which had been shattered into many fragments, all moving along more or less together, with people living on the various pieces.

Shattered, she thought. Like her life. Like Œnone's life. A firefly had come to destroy Œnone's family, and a different monster had come to destroy May's current life.

She couldn't concentrate long on the reading. Her attention kept hovering like a vulture, waiting to light on a forbidden topic. The thing that loomed worst now. Finally she gave up and confronted it.

The word was AIDS. Bull had raped her anally. Had it been just to degrade her—or had he been out to kill her? If he had AIDS . . .

How could she know? It would take months or years to manifest, and then it would be too late. In fact, it was too late now, if she had it.

Which meant she could do nothing about it, and should put it out of her mind. But how much more readily decided than done!

She got up and went to the kitchen, where she fixed herself milk and bread and jam; that was the extent of her gustatory ambition at present. Then she returned to the mattress, lay down, and slept.

In the morning she used the facilities again, and ate another anemic meal. She wasn't feeling better, but at least she wasn't feeling worse.

She stepped outside the cabin and took a slow walk around the immediate premises. There was a huge twisted-trunked red cedar tree right beside the cabin, overshadowing it, and a kind of earthen pier projecting into the river. It was actually a rather nice region, excellent for both hiding and convalescing. There were giant spiderwebs in an old shed nearby, complete with the biggest spiders she could remember seeing, and a phenomenally colored grasshopper. This was the heart of nature.

Then there was a motion. She was startled, then saw that it was two brown ponies, one large, one small. They approached her cautiously, as if hoping for a treat but aware that strangers were not to be perfectly trusted.

She smiled and returned to the cabin. She grabbed two slices of bread and took them out. She proffered them to the ponies, who abruptly decided that she was a friend. This was the way to start a morning!

Abruptly the ponies turned away, retreating nervously. "What's the matter?" she asked.

Then she heard the rumble of an approaching vehicle. Oh— someone was coming. They had heard it before she did.

She retreated to the house and watched from the window, just in case. It turned out to be two vehicles: Geode's wagon and Cyrano's van. What was Cyrano doing here?

Œnone jumped out of the station wagon and ran to her. She was in one of the dresses May had brought for her, and looked fluffy and fetching. In fact, she was surprisingly pretty, almost nymphlike. May was almost certain now that things were working out between her and Geode. Maybe the woman wasn't thinking of death, but of a new life. A transformation to a better situation.

"Mid says Cyrano should look at you," Œnone said.

"But he's a vet!" May protested.

"But he can keep his mouth shut."

May considered. She needed to remain hidden, and she had a serious question. Cyrano just might have an answer. She also did not feel very good, purely physically; the night's rest had done her some good but not enough. She nodded.

"We'll unload more supplies and leave him here," Œnone said.

They did that. Soon May was alone with Cyrano. "What is it you propose?" she asked warily.

"This is a bit out of my department," he said. "But when Mid learned what had happened to you, he seems to have been annoyed." He made the briefest of smiles, and May knew why. None of them had met Mid, but their dealings with him by phone indicated an imperturbable man. Mid's unvoiced pleasure led to significant rewards, and his unvoiced displeasure was dangerous. If he had let annoyance show, there was apt to be hell to pay.

"With whom?" she asked.

"With Bull Shauer." He set down his medical case, opened it, and brought out a small package. "I think Bull would be best advised to travel immediately and secretly to Tasmania; that might purchase him another week of life. But just in case you should encounter him again, use this."

May took the package. "What is it?"

"Hypo with animal sedative. Stab him with it, and within a minute he will lie down and sleep. Then get out of there and report to Mid. You will never see Bull again."

"But I couldn't kill him!" she protested.

"I said it's a sedative. It won't kill him, it will just put him down for an hour or so. It wears off rapidly enough, without ill effect. Giving you time to get cleanly away."

"But then he'll be after me again!"

"Not once Mid knows his location."

She pondered that. She decided not to inquire further. She knew that Mid could order a death, and probably would in this case. No one brutalized one of his employees with impunity. It wasn't as if Bull was worth saving. All she could do was stay clear, and never speak of it again.

"One thing I would like to know," she said with difficulty. "Does Bull have AIDS?"

"The autopsy will show," he said, and the implicit assumption was chilling. In Cyrano's mind, Bull was already dead. "Now I must check you. I find the prospect no more appealing than you do, but Mid wants to know."

May thought of protesting. Then she thought of trying to oppose one of Mid's directives. "Inside," she said.

She stripped for Cyrano much as she had for Bull, and with not a lot more equanimity. But she prided herself on being able to do what needed to be done, and this did need to be done. She had refused to see a doctor, and this was the alternative.

He checked her eye and breast. "Use this," he said, giving her a tube of ointment. She didn't ask what it was; it was surely intended for animals, but would work as readily and safely on a human animal. Then he checked her genital region.

"He didn't do it that way," she said through her teeth.

"So I see." He paused as he opened another kit and donned gloves. "This much needs to be said: sodomy is an accepted practice in many parts of the world. It may be one of the more widely used contraceptive measures. Some women even come to prefer it, perhaps because of that safety factor. That, of course, is changing, as AIDS becomes endemic in Africa; it is no drug-related, or gay-related, matter there. So many would not consider there to be any shame attached to it. It is evident that you feel otherwise—but it seems to me that the shame should attach to the perpetrator, not to the victim." His rubber-gloved fingers probed, then entered. Then he used an instrument. "Bruising, no actual tearing," he said. "It will heal. Use this." He brought out more ointment. "If he has no venereal disease, you're home free. Even if he has, the odds are against your contracting it. AIDS is especially vulnerable; it can't survive long at all if there is no blood-to-blood contact. I would rate your chances of not having it as about twenty to one—even if he has it. I think it would be best for you to think of Bull as never having existed."

"Certainly I won't be advertising my encounter with him," she said grimly. "But you seem quite confident about his incipient demise."

"I am," Cyrano said, glancing up at her.

She felt a cold wash of emotion. Suddenly she knew who had been assigned to dispatch another monster. "He never existed," she agreed.

Cyrano put away his things. "And we never talked," he said. "Remain here until you receive news, then dispose of the hypo where it won't be found."

She nodded again, and started dressing. For all its outrageousness—being given an internal by a veterinarian!—it had been what was necessary. Her secret was preserved, and she was reassured that she had no serious injury. The matter of venereal disease would be checked soon enough. And if Bull should find her, she now had a defense. That was reassuring.

Cyrano left the house and got into his van. May, feeling better, went to see about something more to eat. Half a load had been lifted from her mind.

❖ 22 ❖

CYRANO DROVE HIS van back along the bumpy forest trail, pondering. The woman had been savaged, sure enough; her brutal husband deserved what he was going to get. Cyrano would have no compunction about putting the man away; he was in the business of exterminating vermin of any type that bothered Mid. He had the impression that Mid liked May Flowers. Oh, there was nothing personal in it; Mid liked anyone who did good work for him. Mid liked Cyrano best of all, because Cyrano did what he was told without limit. Had Mid told him to dispatch May Flowers, he would have done it, but with regret. He would handle Bull Shauer's case with no regret.

Nevertheless, there was an aspect to this case that bothered him. It had come about by chance, but it was nevertheless chilling. May had gone to the isolated cabin to escape her husband—but that put her alone in the very heart of the territory hunted by the monster. How many nights could she remain there without being taken?

Cyrano had considered mentioning this to Mid, but had decided to wait until he saw the actual site, lest he give a false alarm. Now he had seen it, and he was sure: that cabin was not tight, and it was close to the water, and its mattresses were on the floor. The monster had already taken prey from more difficult terrain than that. Now he would have to ask Mid to move her, and this he disliked doing.

Suppose Mid told him to let her remain there? And to say nothing about the matter?

Cyrano was afraid that this was exactly what Mid was going to say. Because May Flowers represented a perfect lure for the monster. When it came from her, Cyrano could catch it, and the job would be done. May was the perfect Judas goat—or sacrificial lamb.

But the monster was like nothing Cyrano had encountered before. He was afraid that he would catch it too late: after it fed, instead of before. He would not dare stay too close to the cabin, because that would alert the monster, but if he stayed too far away, it might get her. He didn't know its parameters; if he misjudged it, he would lose it or let it feed.

He would have been happy to take the gamble with someone else. But May was a fellow employee, and she had been badly treated by her brute of a husband. She didn't deserve this risk. It was bad enough that she had possibly been exposed to AIDS; the firefly was a more immediate threat.

Well, he would try to argue. But if Mid wanted it that way, Mid would have it that way. Cyrano was very much concerned that that was the way it would be.

He saw bird flying up out of the way. It was large, with a gray and white pattern on its back and tail reminiscent of an old-style mattress. It was a red-shouldered hawk, flying silently and skillfully through the tangled lattice of twisted live oak branches. Cyrano admired predators like that; they were efficient and beautiful, unlike man.

In due course he came around to the gate and the house. He parked and knocked. Geode opened the door.

"I have to call Mid."

Geode nodded. He gestured in the direction of the phone, then went outside. He would not deliberately eavesdrop on another person's talk with Mid; it wasn't done. Cyrano entered, went to the phone in the living room, and dialed his number. Mid could tell who was calling by the phone that rang; he would answer this one.

Sure enough, it was no answering machine. The receiver was lifted, and there was silence on the line.

"Cyrano. May will recover; her injuries are physically superficial, emotionally more difficult. She is concerned about possible infection by venereal disease, but this seems unlikely. I gave her medication and defense."

"Is she safe?" Mid asked.

"No. She is alone in monster country." He braced himself; he knew how Mid's mind worked.

"Decoy."

"It is risky. We don't know the capabilities of that creature. The firefly could readily take her. I would prefer to move her out."

There was a pause. Then the dread directive came. "Leave her. Ambush the monster."

Damn! "Done."

Mid hung up. Cyrano put the phone down. He turned—and there was the Brown woman. Damn again—she must have overheard. He had forgotten that Demerit wasn't alone in the house, and this woman didn't know the conventions.

"That was Mid?" she asked. She was looking rather pretty in an off-the-shoulder dress; he was surprised by the change in her since his prior time here. It was as if she had lost twenty pounds and ten years.

"I report to him," he agreed gruffly.

"Will he help May?"

With uneasy relief he realized that she had not heard enough to know the situation. Mid had given his order, and Cyrano had responded, "Done." He could conceal the truth from her. He didn't like doing it, but she really had no need-to-know, and this grim matter was best kept quiet.

"I checked her, and she is injured but will recover. I gave her some medication, and a few days' rest will do the trick."

"Maybe she should come here, instead of being out there alone. I could help her better here."

"Mid said to leave her there."

"With the firefly," she said.

So much for concealment! "I will try to intercept it."

"I don't think I'd like working for Mid."

"He looks after his own. He was angry about what happened to her."

She just looked at him, and he felt small and grimy. He turned away from her and went out the door, where Geode waited. "I have to go back and watch," he said gruffly.

Geode didn't comment. He went back into the house quickly, as if hearing something.

Cyrano went to his van, climbed in, and sat for a moment before starting it. What could he tell them? Mid had said to leave May there.

He had to do what he was told; they knew that. Meanwhile, he would do his best to intercept the monster before it reached her. He didn't want it taking any more people! He wanted to catch it, perhaps not kill it; he might take it away with him and study it at length, for he was certain it was a most fascinating creature. The idea of simply killing what might be a representative of a unique species was appalling—which was why he was glad that he, and not some ignorant sheriff, was working on the case. But to have one of Mid's own serving as the bait—there had to be a better way.

He made a short sigh and dug out his ignition key. It was time to go and set his ambush for the firefly. He wished he had a better notion of what it looked like.

He started the van and pulled around the loop. But as he did so, another vehicle came in. It was a sheriff's car. Think of the devil!

He waited for the car to clear the joining of the loop so he could pass by and turn down the dirt trail, but the car stopped right at the wrong place, blocking him. The door opened and the deputy climbed out. He was a solid man of about forty, with thinning brown hair and a tired expression. He came around to Cyrano's door.

"Frank Tishner here," he said. "You're the exterminator?"

"Yes."

"You figured out what's doing it?"

"Not yet."

"You looked at May Flowers?"

"Yes."

"You're not much for communication."

Cyrano nodded.

"Listen, I set it up to put her in that cabin. But overnight I remembered the firefly. I don't want her there anymore."

"You'd rather have her back in town while her husband remains at large?"

"No. I'd rather have her here at this house."

"So would I. But it's not my decision to make."

"Well, maybe it's mine."

Cyrano shrugged.

Tishner returned to his car, and got in, and pulled it out of the way. Cyrano moved on beyond the loop, then turned into the dirt road. Mid had said to leave May there, but if the deputy took her out, that was not Cyrano's doing. Maybe it was for the best.

~ 23 ~

FRANK DREW UP to the door. It opened and Demerit emerged. "I don't like that cabin," Frank said. "Could she come here instead?"

Demerit spread his hands. "Mid said no."

Jade Brown appeared. Tishner almost did a double take. She looked much better than before. Now she was in a low-cut pink dress that showed more breast than he had believed she possessed. May Flowers had thought that Demerit and Brown might have something going, and that had seemed possible. Now it seemed that Demerit would be a total fool if he didn't have it going, because Jade Brown had become one petite piece of flesh. The lines of her face had smoothed, and she seemed animated in the manner of a person who had discovered religion.

"But you don't work for Mid," she said.

"I don't have anywhere to put her. We're agreed that she can't go back to town. If she can't come to this house—"

"She's bait for the monster," Brown said.

"This is how Mid treats his employees?"

"He treats us well," Demerit said. "But we have to do what he says. We're going to watch that cabin until the monster is caught."

"I wish I could! But I've got other business." Frank shook his head.

175

"Look, she needs stuff, right? I got a few cans of things, I'll just drop them off."

They nodded together. Frank wished he knew what their private relations were!

He returned to his car and drove it down the dirt road, following the exterminator's tracks. As he maneuvered through the winding reaches, he thought about May Flowers.

He had seen her just about naked when he took her out of the hotel. Because the view was unintentional, it had had a special quality. She was a solid woman, but well enough formed for all that; in fact, impressive for her age. Then she had impulsively hugged him, taking him for a friend, though their relationship had been slightly on the hostile side of business. What her brute of a husband had done to her—that had made Frank angry. He knew she didn't want any notoriety, so he had gone along with her preference. But he wouldn't have minded arresting that man for spouse abuse and rape, and if he resisted, Frank wouldn't have minded shooting him. No animal like that should be allowed loose!

But mainly it was that single glad hug, as if he were her best friend. It had caught him completely by surprise, and he hadn't known how to react, so he had ignored it. Yet after things settled down, he still felt that hug. His wife didn't hug him like that. The passion had long since gone out of his marriage, and it survived mainly on sufferance: as long as he held his job. Trudy would decamp the moment he lost it. She had given him notice, and he believed her. She had no sympathy with his stands of principle. It wasn't that she was unprincipled, just that she was removed from the situations that he was close to, and her values differed. What he called principle she called looking for trouble.

In short, that hug had made him think of May as a woman rather than as a business contact. That change of perception was having an insidious effect on his outlook. Perhaps it would come to nothing, a passing fancy. He knew May didn't have any interest in him. But he had to see to her welfare in what little ways he could.

So he had gone shopping, unasked, for her. Now he would deliver the goods to her, and perhaps she would be pleased. If not, at least he would see her again, for what that was worth.

He noticed after a time that he had lost the exterminator's vehicle; he should have caught up with it by now. That meant that the man was hiding, setting up to try to trap the monster. Frank was right with him on that; he just didn't like the bait being used.

He came to the cabin and stopped. He got out, then reached in back for one of his bags. He carried it to the door and knocked.

She answered immediately. "I heard you coming," she said. Her eye was now thoroughly discolored, but the rest of her was in a too-tight dress. She had had to use one of the ones she had bought for Jade Brown, and even with spot altering it just wasn't close to her size. There was a pad over her left breast, tucked into the dress. He understood the reason for these, but it remained a striking contrast. "Is something wrong?"

He was jolted out of his inspection. "I thought you might need some stuff," he said, abashed. Before, he hadn't cared what she thought of him; now he did.

"Oh, did Œnone make Geode do more shopping for me?"

"Who?"

She grimaced. "I used wrong names. I meant—"

"The Brown woman, and Demerit?"

"Yes. They have special names. She told a story about Œnone, and after that—please forget that I gave them away."

"No, I can see it. We've been calling each other by our first names, and they should also. May I bring this in? I shopped myself; I don't know what you need."

"Oh, of course. That's very nice of you."

She moved back, and he carried the bag in. "It's just some lettuce and apples and stuff; I really was guessing. But—" He shrugged.

"Do you have a moment? I don't want to take you from your work, but—"

"I shouldn't be away from it, but—"

"Sit down; I won't hold you long. It's just so nice to have company, however briefly. I'm not used to being helpless like this, and—"

They were seating themselves on the mattress; it was what offered. "I'd better tell you straight," he said. "I don't like you being here."

"But you set it up!"

"Yes. Then I realized that it could make you bait for the firefly. I don't want that to happen to you."

She took a deep and somewhat shuddery breath. "I was trying not to think about that."

"I'd like to get you out of here, but I don't know where to take you."

She smiled somewhat wanly. "It would be ironic if I fled one monster only to fall prey to another."

"The exterminator is mounting guard, but I don't trust this. That firefly—"

"Cyrano," he said. "We call the exterminator Cyrano. As far as I know, he's competent. So Mid decided to leave me as a tied lamb, to bring in the predator?"

"That seems to be the size of it. Look, maybe my wife would understand if I took you home."

She paused, glancing at him. "Would she?"

"No. But I can't leave you here!"

"Forgive me if I misinterpret, but it almost seems as if you have some personal feeling here."

"I'm sorry. I apologize. But I guess I do."

"I had understood that we were hostile associates, united only by our interest in the firefly."

"We were."

"What changed?"

"You got in trouble. You were glad to see me. You hugged me. I know it meant nothing, but—" He shrugged.

"So you came to see whether I might be amenable to something?"

He scrambled to his feet. "No. This is going wrong. I'll get out of here."

"No, wait. I didn't say I objected."

He froze. "I just had to see that you were all right. That's all." But it wasn't all.

"Frank, you helped me when I needed it. You were the only one I felt free to turn to, and I didn't like imposing, but—"

"I was glad to do it. Look, is there anywhere else you can go?"

"I think not. My job here isn't finished. Frank, I acted impulsively, but I realize now that there was some substance to that impulse. I had no business calling on you, but I must have known that you could be prevailed upon. I am flattered if I made an impression on you. I realize what a sight I was—and what a sight I remain."

"You're a good sight. You won't go?"

"I'm afraid I won't. But I do appreciate your concern. I am coming to appreciate qualities in you that I did not perceive before. But you are a married man, and I'm an independent woman, normally. I think we are in a situation where appearances may be deceptive."

"Yes. I guess I'll have to leave you here. But I don't like it."

"Will you come again tomorrow?"

"Do you want me to?"

She nodded. "Yes, Frank. I want you to. You don't need to bring anything."

"Maybe I should bring you a gun," he said.

"I'd shoot myself in the foot. As far as I know, the monster never took anyone who was alert."

"But you have to sleep!"

"I know. I wish I had company—no, no, don't volunteer! I'd love to have you, perhaps for more reasons than one, but that isn't right. But I think I have to brave this night myself, as I did last night."

"Yeah. Maybe so. Damn, I hope you're okay!"

"That's sweet of you, Frank."

"That's straight fear!" He went out, before he could say anything else that might be even more stupid.

He drove back along the trail. "Exterminator—Cyrano—you keep good watch tonight!" he muttered. He felt stupid and guilty and mixed up. What business did he have getting emotional about that woman? So he had seen her bare-breasted; that shouldn't have been more than a passing thrill. So he had carried her mostly naked to the car, and felt her bare flesh. So that was in the line of duty. She had been beaten up and raped—but he had seen that before too. She had been glad to see him; what else could she have been, in that situation?

Yet she had not objected when she misconstrued his purpose in visiting her at the cabin. That suggested that she returned his illicit emotion. That the spark of her joy had signaled a deeper change of feeling. Of course such speculation was treacherous, considering the situation. They were both, after all, adults, and not young ones. Still—

He reached the house. Demerit was there. "She won't leave. I don't like this at all. How sharp is this guy Cyrano?"

Demerit—Geode—spread his hands.

"That's what I thought. Listen, I helped put her there. I have some responsibility. If she gets taken—"

Jade Brown emerged. Œnone—yes, that did seem to fit her now. "If she gets taken, we'll all be responsible," she said.

"She told me your names," he said, apropos of nothing.

"We're in this together," she agreed.

He nodded. "I'll check tomorrow. Can you folk—?"

"Yes," she said. "Geode will go there. Maybe I'll go there for the night. I've had experience with the firefly."

Frank began to move. "That'll help, maybe." He returned to his car and drove off. His feelings were mixed, about all of them, especially himself.

❖ 24 ❖

G EODE SIGHED. HE could see that Frank Tishner didn't like it, but like the rest of them, he was stuck.

"He likes her," Œnone said as they went back inside.

Geode was astonished. "Him? Her?"

"It happens. We know, don't we? We can check on her when we go on the rounds."

"Better wait till afternoon. Sometimes Mid calls in the middle of the day, and I'm supposed to be here."

"Then we shall wait," she said brightly. "It's the night we have to fear."

"Yes."

"What's next, then?"

"Every month or so I have to clean the pool."

"Then we shall clean the pool!" She led the way toward it.

Geode followed. It was amazing how much nicer things were with her along.

The pool was about thirty-two feet long, sixteen wide, and ranged from three to eight deep. There was a Jacuzzi extension at the shallow end. It was enclosed by a screen, the yard and trees visible beyond. Its deck was pebbled in brown.

"Oh—there's a dragonfly caught in here," Œnone said.

"They get in," he agreed.

"Maybe I can get it out. There's nothing for it to eat in here." She picked up the net and went after the insect, but it avoided her teasingly.

"They don't like to be caught," he said. "But they're pretty tame."

She set down the net and put out her hand instead. The green dragonfly lit on it. "Oh! you're right!" she exclaimed, pleased. She walked carefully to the screen door, opened it, and put her hand outside. The dragonfly flew away.

"We have a frog too," he said. "A black one. It got in somehow, and I don't think Mid would mind, so I let it be. It takes a swim maybe once a day, and hides behind the flowerpots the rest of the time."

"That means the water's good," she said.

"Once I checked the pool at night, and there were two tiny tree frogs sitting on the floating thermometer," he said. He liked telling her things because she liked hearing them. "I took them out; they don't forage in water."

"I've seen them on windowpanes. They're the cutest things."

Geode got out the brushes and the pole with the broomlike brush at the end. He started brushing the growing algae off the sides. This was the tedious part of it, because it was necessary to hold the brush in against the side while shoving it down to the bottom—without overbalancing and falling in himself. The job couldn't be rushed; the brush tended to skip out from the wall, leaving a patch of algae. He had let the pool go too long, and not watched the balance of chemicals closely enough; there shouldn't be so much growth.

"Where should I start?" Œnone asked, picking up a brush.

"It's hardest to get it right at the waterline," he said.

She squatted at the edge and leaned down, brushing vigorously. The greenish color faded, leaving the white wall clean. She moved over, scrubbing the next section.

Geode was sweating before he was half around the pool, for this was vigorous work and the temperature was about ninety degrees Fahrenheit. Œnone was warming up too.

"Is it all right to swim?" she inquired, pausing.

"Yes. Just so long as the pool gets cleaned."

She stood and doffed her clothing. "You'll be more comfortable too," she said.

"I don't swim," he said.

"You don't?" She was surprised. "Would you like me to teach you?"
That had not occurred to him. "Yes."

"Then undress and come in. I won't let you drown."

Geode had never gone naked outside or by day. But she had set the scene. He set down the brush and removed his own clothing.

Œnone stepped down into the pool. "Oh, that feels good now!" she exclaimed.

Geode joined her. They waded into the shallow end and down to the halfway line. She turned to him. "How much do you know about it, Geode?"

"I've seen people swim, but it doesn't seem to work for me."

"Maybe they tried to teach you by the sink-or-swim method. That's guaranteed to teach children the fear of water. They may learn to swim, but they never do it voluntarily after that."

"Well, yes, but that wasn't all."

"Let's sit down," she said. She waded to the Jacuzzi region and sat on the submerged concrete bench by the bubbling jets of water. Geode followed.

"What was it?" she asked.

"A fish talked to me."

"How wonderful!" she exclaimed. "A mermaid?"

"No, just a regular fish. It said it didn't like the chemicals in the water."

"So you got out, and when they asked you why, you explained about the fish and what it said?"

He nodded, embarrassed.

"And they laughed at you."

He nodded again.

"So you never learned to swim," she concluded. "But now you will, Geode. And if you see that fish, show me. I won't laugh."

"Maybe the fish wasn't there. I know real fish don't talk. I—they say I have trouble telling what's real from what's imaginary."

"I wish I did!" she said.

He looked at her, surprised. "You do?"

"I would swap my imaginary life for my mundane life in a moment." Then she glanced at him. "Until I came here."

"You don't think I'm crazy?" She had reassured him before, but he had to ask again.

"What is the evidence of your craziness?"

"They put me in a mental hospital."

"They did that? Why?"

"When I told a doctor about talking with animals. He askeᴅ questions, he seemed to understand. Then he asked me to talk with someone else in the hospital, and I went there, and I couldn't get out. When I tried, they put me in restraints. After three months when they asked me if I still talked with animals, I told them no. It wasn't true, but I didn't like it in there. Since then I haven't told anyone but Mid."

"Why did you tell him?"

"He knew about the hospital. He understood. He gave me this job. I had to tell him the truth."

"And now you have told me the truth."

"Yes."

"The difference between us is that I learned earlier than you did to keep my mouth shut. Mostly. I learned to see that line between reality and fantasy. You learned only to say you saw it. You know that animals don't admit to talking to people, and people don't admit to talking to animals, so it doesn't matter what the truth is, you have to deny it."

"Yes."

"But you can tell it to me. I may not see or hear what you do, but I understand."

"Yes."

"Just as you understand about me."

"Yes."

She got up, turned, sat on his lap in the water, and kissed him. "I love it here with you, Geode."

"I—may I kiss you back?"

"Yes, you may, Geode, if you want to. Anytime you want to. I will let you do it by yourself."

Hesitantly he embraced her in the water. Her body was slick and wonderful. He moved his face toward hers, afraid she would turn away, but she waited for him. His lips touched hers. She neither helped nor hindered his effort. He withdrew.

"You never did that before," she said. "With anyone."

He nodded. The touch of their lips had been almost unreal, but now his pulse was accelerating. He had actually done it, as she said, by himself!

"You think that I may be like an animal, not really doing this, according to others."

"Yes."

"So we won't tell anyone else."

"Yes." He was relieved.

"Do you know about the little mermaid?"

"Who?"

"Then I will tell you. A simplified version, because it isn't my own story. A little young mermaid was following a ship, when a handsome prince fell off. No one saw him; he had been walking the deck alone at night. He couldn't swim, and was drowning, so the little mermaid went to rescue him. He was unconscious, so she held his head up so he could breathe. He looked so wonderful that she fell in love with him. She couldn't climb up on the ship, so she bore him away across the sea and toward the nearest beach. But she lacked the strength to bring him all the way there. She begged the lord of the sea for strength to do it, and he granted it, but he set a condition: she would die the day the prince married anyone else but her.

"She brought him to the beach, near a great palace, and pushed him up on it, but she could not follow. So she left him there, and watched, and saw a lovely princess come down and find him there and wake him. Naturally he thought she was the one who had saved him, so in due course he married her, and the little mermaid perished, her deed unknown."

"She died?" he asked, upset.

"It is the fate of those who love foolishly."

"But if the prince had known—"

"It is ironic," she agreed. "But sometimes they do know, and still they do not treat their nymphs well."

"I would never do that!" he protested.

"Today ordinary folk deny that mermaids ever existed. They say that they are confusions of sightings of manatees. So any little mermaids who love mortal men do so at their own risk."

He gazed at her, almost seeing her as a mermaid, with the sturdy tail of a fish. He embraced her again, and kissed her, and this time she responded.

"You are learning how," she said.

"I want to."

"I want you to." Then she bounced off his lap. "But I must show you how to swim!"

He joined her in deeper water. "Now first let's try the dead man's float," she said. "Toward the shallows, so you can always put your feet down and stand. Watch me." She took a breath, held it, shut her eyes, stretched her arms up over her head, fell forward, and kicked her feet vigorously. Her body did not sink; it floated slowly toward the edge of the pool. When her outstretched hands touched the wall, she put down her feet, lifted her head, and took a breath.

"Now you try it," she said. "If you sink to the bottom, we'll try something else."

Geode copied her exactly. In a moment he was facedown in the water, kicking his feet, going nowhere. But then he felt the pool wall. Surprised, he put down his feet and lifted his head. He had traveled the same distance she had!

"You did it!" she said excitedly. "For that the mermaid gives you a kiss!" She splashed into him and delivered it.

"But all I did was float," he protested, pleased.

"That's halfway there." She waded out again, standing breast-deep. Her breasts floated. "Next lesson: same as before, only this time move your arms." She demonstrated, assuming the same pose. She fell forward, kicked her feet in the dead man's float—but then stroked with her arms, first one and then the other lifting out of the water and cutting down through it. This time she moved forward much faster, and had to stop after just a few strokes.

He waded out and tried it. His effort was clumsy, but he did do it.

"And so you swam," she said. "Of course, it takes longer to learn to breathe while you do it, but you have the essence. Here, let me hold you while you try."

They set up chest-deep, and she put her arms around his torso, holding him up and in place while he tried kicking and moving. His left arm kept banging into hers, but his right worked effectively.

"Maybe backstroke is better," she said. "Try this." She demonstrated an easy float on her back, only kicking her feet. He tried it, and again it worked. He was amazed.

"So now you can swim," she said. "We'll practice more, of course, but you can see how easy it will be."

"Yes." He had never imagined that it could be so easy!

Now, thoroughly cooled off, they resumed their scrubbing of the pool. Geode climbed out and worked with the long-handled brush, while Œnone continued around the upper section with the hand brush.

When they had it done, they practiced swimming again. Geode was glad to do it, but also glad for the chance to be naked in her arms without the need to try for sexual expression. It was much easier to enjoy her company and her embraces when no further performance was expected of him.

At last they emerged, and dried, and dressed. It had been a wonderful midday!

Geode looked at the clock and blinked. An hour and a half had passed, when he thought it was half an hour! He was late for his rounds.

Œnone came up beside him. "Did I hold you too long? I'm sorry."

"No, it was great! But—"

"I understand. You can make your rounds twice as fast without me, and now you need to."

"Yes."

"Then you had better go alone this time. Next time I'll be more careful. It was just so nice being with you, I didn't think of the time."

"Yes," he said gratefully. "Uh—"

"You don't have to ask, Geode," she said, stepping into his arms and lifting her face.

He kissed her. This, too, was a continuing amazement. Today he could swim, and kiss her, and he wasn't sure which was the more significant accomplishment.

"I'll make it back as soon as I can," he said. "And, when, tonight, uh—"

"Anything you want, Geode; you know that."

"I mean, would you tell another story?"

That caught her by surprise. "You like my stories?"

"Yes."

"I'll be glad to, Geode!"

"Thanks." Then he went out the side door, got on the bike, and set off. He would get a real workout this time! He had to be back by four, in case Mid called. The phone had an answering machine, but it was much better to be there, because Mid didn't like to wait.

❖ 25 ❖

ŒNONE WATCHED HIM ride away. She had told him the truth: she had enjoyed their session in the pool as much as anything she could remember in the past year, except for her night with him. She had felt guilty about being in this nice house, and about taking up his time, though she knew he liked it; now she was doing something useful, teaching him one or two skills that would serve him well in life. In short, she was beginning to pay her way.

She hadn't really meant to tell him the story of the mermaid; it had just come out, familiar as it was. She hadn't given the more elaborate version, in which the Little Mermaid was granted the ability to have legs and walk on land in exchange for what turned out to be her death sentence. But either version was certainly true to her life, as she saw it. She was here on the sufferance of Geode and his employer, and when they decided they had had enough of her, she would depart—and perish. Like the little mermaid, she had in effect to marry someone, for she had no survival on her own, once committed.

But after allowing for everything, she had had a wonderful time in the pool, and she hoped they could do it again, many times. His impotence didn't matter there; they had had a job to do, and a lesson to learn, and there was no stress. Yet the suggestion of romance had

187

not been proscribed. She had gotten him to kiss her, and that was nice
progress, for him. She knew he liked her to kiss him, but his problem
was not with feeling, but with initiation. When he became confident
enough to kiss her without asking or apologizing, he would be a giant
step toward the achievement of the other thing, which she could not
do for him.

There were dishes from lunch. She washed them, gladly. Anything
she could do to make his life easier, and to justify her presence, was
good. Her life at home had consisted of such chores, and they had
been dull; now they were bright. She had been a poor housekeeper not
from ignorance but from futility. It was different here.

But there was this matter of May Flowers. May had arranged to
bring Œnone here, and thereby lifted her from the skids of hell to a
sojourn in paradise. Now May was set out as bait for the monster. That
wasn't right!

The phone rang, in Geode's room. Œnone hurried to answer it—
then realized that she wasn't supposed to, because she wasn't here, officially. But this was Mid's phone, the one that only he called on, and
he knew she was here. Geode was the only one supposed to answer it.

Yet, somehow, she never paused. She plunged into the room and
scooped up the receiver. "Please, let her come here!" she exclaimed.
"Don't let her be food for the firefly!"

A vaguely oriental voice replied. "Who are you?"

"Œnone. You let me be here."

"Where is Geode?"

"He's on his rounds. He is hurrying to be back in time for your
call."

"What do you do?"

"Me?" The question surprised her. Actually, this whole conversation surprised her; she should never have picked up the phone! "I—I
tell stories."

"What have you done here?"

"Here? Today? I helped clean the pool. I took a dragonfly out. It
wasn't right to let it be trapped where it couldn't survive."

"Are you a dragonfly?"

She laughed uneasily. "Me? No! May is! I'm just a firefly. No, not
even that; the firefly's not innocent anymore, it's a monster. I'm a
glowworm, the female of the species. I glow only in the dark; by day
I am nothing at all."

"What is Geode?"

"He's a rock, of course, with all his wonderful qualities locked inside. I am trying to fall in love with him." This was absolutely crazy! But she couldn't stop. "I mean he's someone stable, and I'm trying to perch on him so I can be stable too."

"Did he tell you his history."

"He hears animals speak. I wish I could. Oh, Mr. Mid, please let May come here! She's worked for you so loyally—"

"Tell me a story."

She didn't dare question this odd request. What would interest a fabulously rich tycoon? She pictured herself as such a person, tuning in, and let her fancy fly.

"Once there was a businessman who paid his tax and had a big refund coming, but the Internal Revenue Service misread it as an unpaid tax. It acted without verifying, sending him a demand for immediate payment plus penalties for tax evasion. He wrote back that it was the other way around, that he didn't owe them money, they owed him money. But this was rebuffed by a badly programmed computer. The IRS refused to see their error, let alone admit it to a taxpayer. He wrote again, presenting the figures—and they seized his bank account in lieu of the payment they said he owed. Now, he was a peaceful man, but this annoyed him. For one thing, his routine business checks were bouncing because the bank wasn't allowed to honor them, and his clients were getting upset and his business was suffering. So he mortgaged his estate and got the money to fight them, and he took them to court and got a restraining order against the IRS, not to harass this man anymore, and to pay court costs and a punitive penalty, because the judge saw that the businessman's figures were right and had been right all along. But the agency responded by auditing the judge's tax return! Now it was the judge who became annoyed, because he was an honest judge with twenty years on the bench and he knew what he was doing, and he had never even thought about cheating on his tax. So he hit the Revenue Service with a citation for contempt. But the Service claimed it was immune from that, and demanded possession of all his records for three years back.

"About this time a fearless journalist with dark brown hair and eyes got interested. She researched the matter, and then published a story which made local and then state and then national headlines. There was a terrific public outcry, and a spreading tax rebellion. Then the IRS decided that there had been a slight clerical error, and it dropped the case and forgot the matter. But by this time Congress was responding to voluminous mail from all over the country, because it seemed that a lot of people had suffered similarly, and they wanted corrective legislation or a class-action suit. Congress passed a bill which severely curtailed the Service's right to threaten or impound, and imposed a schedule of automatic penalties for any future errors the IRS made. 'It's time the tax man stopped harassing honest citizens and started doing its job right,' Senator Smogfound declaimed to national applause. The President saw the lay of the land and signed the law. And so the businessman was vindicated, and he received fifteen proposals of marriage from starlets and lived happily ever after. They never audited him again."

There was a pause. "Granted," Mid said, and hung up.

"What?" But she was too late.

Then his meaning registered. She had begged him to let May, whom she had put into the story as the journalist, come here to the main house. He had agreed!

She returned to the dishes, elated. Mid must have liked her story, foolish as it was. That might save May's life.

She thought about Geode. So he had been institutionalized. But he was not crazy, only misunderstood. She had spoken truly when she reassured him; she was a creature of imagination who had learned to stifle it, externally. Geode had not—until getting in bad trouble for it. He was very much her type of man, so serendipitously discovered. She could be happy with him, even if it weren't for this lovely wealthy estate with which he was associated.

But the curse of her nature was on her. She was Œnone, the doomed nymph. She might have a momentary flare of hope and joy, but inevitably she would perish. Paris was already dead. She might flirt with another man, but any permanence was illusory. The best she could do was thrill to it while she could, and try not to hurt the ones with whom she associated. In this case, Geode, and May, and maybe Frank Tishner.

She found herself crying. She knew why. May and Frank she might avoid hurting, but Geode had to love her in order to be healed. He had to know she loved him so he could love her. When she died, Geode would be hurt. There was no way around that.

If only she could have made him happy without love! To have teased him into sexual performance, made him a man, without tying into his deepest heart. Then she could have faded away without real harm. But he was more complicated than that, and could not respond sexually without first responding emotionally. He was like a woman in that respect, while she was like a man. So it had to be love. She only hoped that the curse of it was not greater than the blessing of it. For herself it hardly mattered, because she expected no suffering beyond death, but for him it did.

The tears continued. She wept for him, but perhaps also for herself. She had in effect died when Paris did, and so was mostly beyond emotion, but she wished that her fate had not been sealed. This was such a wonderful moment, it was difficult not to dream of it continuing forever.

She knew what she had to do. She had to break if off before getting in any deeper. She would have to explain to Geode that she was doomed, and he would be too if this went further. She had to do it right away, as soon as she saw him, because otherwise she wouldn't be able to. It would hurt him, but not nearly as much as her death would later, if this went on.

Her tears abated. She had decided, and that was that. She was a creature of desperation rather than courage, but there was a certain consolation in the decision.

She went to her room, took up the volume of Shaw, and sat on the bed to read it. The book fell open at a page she had already read beyond, but she glanced at it anyway. "The Achilles heel of vivisection, however, is not to be found in the pain it causes, but in the line of argument by which it is justified." Shaw went on to make the point that the good that might come of the deed did not justify it, for a similar argument could justify any crime. A thief could justify his theft by pointing out that it enabled him to spend money and stimulate the economy.

"Oh, I am guilty!" she exclaimed. "I thought the good of teaching Geode love, and my own pleasure, justified the heartbreak I would bring him! I am a vivisectionist!"

At least she had made the decision before the book reminded her! For that she was thankful. She was not entirely derelict.

She found her place and read a bit further, but could not concentrate. She gave it up and went downstairs to wait for Geode's return. He had not set the alarm this time, knowing she might trigger it by accident.

Still restless, she opened the door cautiously and peeked out. The heat struck her; how easy it was to forget it, in the temperate house! She slipped out onto the portico, nervous about being seen. But how could anybody see her? The gate was closed; no cars could come unless they were buzzed in.

She heard something, and jumped. It was a kind of tingling and banging, not loud. She cocked her head, listening, and concluded it came from the chain link fence that paralleled the drive and looped around the house behind. What was happening to it?

She walked cautiously around the house, peering nervously ahead. A sudden crack of thunder jolted her. She looked up and saw the clouds mounding up, their fluffy white shading into gray, and their gray to dark gray. A storm was building, sure enough. Was it gusts of wind from it that made the fence ring?

But the air was calm at the moment, yet the sound continued, irregularly. She followed the fence—and spied a gopher tortoise banging at it. The tortoise was trying to get through it, and every time it tried, its shell banged the wire, making the sound. The whole fence reverberated with each shove, in the fashion of a plucked guitar string, but with less melody. "A storm is coming, and you want to get home!" she exclaimed. "If Geode had been here, you would have told him, and he would have helped you."

But of course Geode wasn't back yet. "Is it all right if I help you instead?" she asked. "Otherwise you'll get caught out in the storm." Not that rain or wind could hurt a creature with a portable house-shell.

The tortoise ignored her. But she went to it, set her hands at the sides of its carapace, and lifted it up. It was solid; it weighed about fifteen pounds. It hissed and pulled in its head as it came up.

She carried it around to the gate, lifted the latch with her knee, and went through. Then she set the tortoise down on the other side. It remained secluded.

"But this is the other side of the fence," she reminded it. The tortoise considered, then extended its neck and resumed marching. She followed it, curious about its destination. It actually made pretty good progress, considering the shortness of its legs. It took sideswipes at the grass growing around the house. Then it came to its burrow and plunged in. It had indeed been coming home.

Well, at least she had managed to do a good deed. She returned to the house. Dragonflies danced in the air around her, as if applauding. Some were brown, some green, some blue. They hovered before her as if curious what she was up to. "And he talks to you too," he said. "I would if I could, but I learned too early and too well."

The storm was wasting no time. Now gusts of wind swept down, making the trees flail wildly. There was a sharp crack as a branch broke somewhere. Œnone knew she should get back inside, but there was something about a storm that fascinated her. Its elemental power seemed to take her spirit, lifting it into the struggling trees. Her dress pressed against her in front and stood out behind, flapping.

She loosened her hair so that the wind could take it too. Ah, yes! This was nature, making her part of it.

There was another sound. She turned—and there was Geode, riding the red bicycle, his own hair stiffening in the wind.

She ran to him. "Mid says May can come here!" she exclaimed. "I talked to him on the phone, and told him a story, and he says it's all right!"

He smiled. "I'll go pick her up!"

"Yes! I'll go with you! But first—"

He waited for her to finish, but she found herself choking instead. How could she tell him now?

But it was now or never. "Geode—I'm doomed—you must—"

"Is something wrong?"

"No. Yes. I mean, you mustn't love me."

He gazed at her. "You don't want to be with me?"

"I want to, but—"

He was silent, but she read his expression: *Without you, I have no life.*

"But it's only been two days!" she said, arguing with what she knew he was thinking. "I am poison for you!"

Still he was silent, but she knew his question: *Did I do something?*

"No! I just—"

A third time he waited: *I know I don't know how to act.*

"Geode, it isn't that! I'm going to die, and I don't want to hurt you!"

Now he managed to get it out. "Mid can get a doctor."

"It isn't medicine, it's the curse. Œnone can't survive. You would only love a dead woman."

Once more he didn't speak, but she heard him: *Then let me die with you.*

She stared at him, knowing he was serious. It was already too late. She had taken him off the cliff, and they were in midair, and she couldn't put him back safely on land.

"Oh, I'm so sorry, Geode!" she cried, her tears coming again. She stepped into him as he stood astride the bicycle, and embraced him, and kissed him desperately. "I should never have started, but I can't stop it now!"

Then the storm broke. A few fat drops of rain spattered down on the leaves and dirt. The two did not break their kiss. Annoyed, the storm washed down in earnest. In a moment they were soaked. It didn't matter.

Their lips finally slid off each other. Water was coursing down their faces. Still they stood, the bike tangled between them, his left cheek to her right cheek. "You better get inside," he murmured at her ear.

"I'll get dry clothing for us both. You get the car."

He nodded, his cheek sliding against hers. She let go, and backed away, then ran for the house, the dress clinging to her legs, making her ungainly. Geode rode the bike around to the garage.

She saw him park the bike in the garage, out of the rain. He would have to go over it in the morning, to prevent it from rusting. She realized that he would strip off his shirt and pants. He didn't want to get Mid's station wagon wet inside.

He wouldn't be sure what had happened with Œnone, only that it had scared him, and now it was all right. She felt guilty for not being able to do what she had to do, but at least she had tried.

Meanwhile she was racing through the house, pulling out dry clothing. In a moment she had changed and gotten a change for him too.

Œnone went to the interior garage door. She had an armful of clothing for him, and a towel. He took the towel and dried, then got into the underpants, trousers, and shirt she provided. He didn't mind getting wet, but it was good to be dry again.

She approached him and combed his hair for him. At this stage it seemed natural.

Then they piled into the car. He started the motor and backed out. The rain beat down on the windshield and hood.

He took down the automatic opener tucked in the sunshade and touched the CLOSE button. The garage door trundled down; he had been careless about leaving it open before.

In fact, he had been careless about a lot of things in the past two days. She knew it was her fault: her attention had overwhelmed him. As long as Mid didn't mind—

"You wanted me to tell you a story?" she asked.

"Yes." He might have forgotten that, but she hadn't. Her story of Œnone seemed to have fascinated him. He had not realized that she could tell stories, and she hoped it added another dimension to his appreciation of her.

"Then I will tell you of the Bad Noble and the Good Girl," she said.

✦ 26 ✦

ONCE IN MEDIEVAL times in a me-
dieval kingdom there was a good nobleman who had many fine sons
and one timid daughter named Teensa. The sons grew up and went
into training for knighthood. The daughter might have been useful as
a match for some scion of another noble, but though she was winsome
enough, she was so shy that she hid her face when any of that type was
present. Her father despaired of finding a husband for her, but she was
his only daughter and she was infinitely precious in his eyes, so he bore
with it.

One day a hunting party from a neighboring region passed by. It
asked asylum for the night, as it had wandered astray in the pursuit of
game and had too many leagues to travel to avoid nightfall. The
nobleman granted it, and the party rode into his castle.

The hunting party consisted of a young foreign nobleman, four
young knights, and a dozen squires, pages, and servants, together with
their horses, dogs, and falcons. The castle staff rose to the occasion. An
excellent dinner was served, much stout ale was guzzled, and stories of
valor were exchanged. Then the visitors went to their quarters for the
night.

Teensa absented herself from the proceedings, terrified of so many strangers. She hid in the stables, garbed as a slops wench, so that no one could find her. Her father made excuses for her absence, saying that she was indisposed.

The visiting nobleman was typical of his age and station in that he cared more about his horse and falcon than the rights of lowborn women. He went out after the banquet to check on his gallant steed, as he normally did, and woe would betide the page responsible if the horse were in any way discomfited. But the horse was in excellent spirit and the servants already retired for the night; the nobleman was satisfied.

Then the nobleman spied a wench. It was evident that she had been admiring his fine horse, as wenches tended to. "Dost thou wish to sit on my steed?" he inquired gruffly of her.

Abashed, she nodded, for it was arguably the noblest stallion in the region, a gift from an alien prince.

"Come here, wench, and I will lift thee up," he said.

She approached, afraid of the man but lured by the magnificent horse. He put his hands at her elbows and with huge and easy strength lifted her up, for he was a powerful man. She bestrode the stallion, and was thrilled; she had never been on an animal like this before.

Then the nobleman reached up to lift her down again. But instead of setting her on her feet, he held her suspended in air. "Now I have done thee a favor," he said. "Does that not require a return favor?"

Uncertain of his meaning, but hoping he meant her to bring some treat for the great horse, she nodded.

He then set her down, but retained his hold on one of her slender arms. With his other hand he ripped away her servant's garb, exposing her body, which was almost as fine in its way as the horse was in its way. He opened his breeches and brought out a tool of horrifying implication. He bore her back against the wall and ravished her without ceremony. Then he dropped her and returned to his chamber for a good night's repose.

Teensa lay for some time where the nobleman had dropped her. At first she was aware only of the pain, then the horror, for she had been raped, when she had never before even seen a man's tool, or known what it was for. She had been too terrified even to scream, not understanding any part of what the man had intended. Now it was too late to scream—and indeed, as she realized what had happened, she knew that she dared not say anything about it to anyone, for a woman, even a nobleman's daughter, who was not a virgin was useless for any good match. So she dragged herself up, staunched the blood with a shred from her dress, and staggered secretly to her own chamber.

Her maid was horrified. "Mistress, what happened to thee?" she exclaimed. "Did a boar gore thee?"

"Yes," Teensa said. "But it was my fault. Swear to tell no one!"

The maid swore, for it was her job to support her mistress in all things. But she was not fooled; she had been ravished enough in her youth to recognize the signs. She provided Teensa with what she needed, and bathed her and clothed her for the night, and said nothing to the other servants.

Teensa wept herself to sleep. But she was, for all her shyness, of noble lineage, and in the morning she rose and pretended that nothing had happened. The visiting party departed, and the normal routine of the castle settled in. It seemed that the ravishing had never happened.

But when the visitors were gone, the maid approached the nobleman, Teensa's father, when he was alone. "I have aught to tell thee, sire, though it distress thee," she said.

"Speak, loyal maid," he said, for he was a tolerant master.

"One of the visiting party ravished a maid in the stables," she said. "Even as thou ravished me when I was young and buxom."

"Thou'rt still buxom," he replied gallantly. "It happens. Why report this to me?"

"The maid was thy daughter."

The nobleman had been in the process of picking his teeth. The toothpick snapped asunder. His fist clenched so hard it became white. "Which one?" he asked through his teeth.

"Sire, I know not. She would not speak of it, and swore me to secrecy. But I have no secrets from thee."

"None at all," he agreed, remembering his erstwhile pleasure in discovering those secrets. "Return to thy duties, maid, and keep this for thyself." He gave her a fine gold piece. "Say naught elsewhere."

"Aye, sire," she agreed. He had rewarded her as she had hoped he would.

The thing was, maids and wenches of low birth were fair game to nobles, but a noble maid was fair game to none. In particular, Teensa was untouchable. The maid had had the fortune not only to serve her master loyally, as she had done in another way in the past, but to earn a reward for providing him with news that cut him to the very marrow. Thus she had a private triple victory, and was well pleased with herself.

The nobleman investigated quietly, and in due course ascertained which visitor had gone to see his horse at what hour. He discovered the faint stains of blood under the hay where that horse had been stabled. He now knew the identity of the ravisher.

But this was no easy matter. A lesser individual he could have had beaten to death; the visiting noble would have done it on request as a matter of simple courtesy. But the nobleman himself—that were not expedient. In fact, no charge could be made, because of the circumstances. First, such a charge against a nobleman would be tantamount to a declaration of war, which would gain no one anything worthwhile. Second, it was obvious that the visitor had not known the identity of the maid. He had taken her for what she appeared to be: a slops wench. As such, she had no rights, and his action was in no way untoward. Had Teensa identified herself, it would have been another matter.

The nobleman pondered a considerable length of time. Then he summoned his most trusted employee, the captain of the guard. "There will be another nobleman in charge of this castle for a time," he told the man. "Thou must serve him during my absence as thou wouldst me, in all things but one. If he abuses my daughter, thou must kill him and flee for thy life. Because I cannot, of course, sanction the killing of a visiting nobleman in my castle, thou must arrange to do it beyond these demesnes, perhaps as a hunting accident. Here is gold to enable thee to survive in a far country when thou dost flee." The nobleman gave the captain enough gold to make him independently wealthy. "Agreed?" For such a directive could not be imposed; it had to be done for loyalty.

"Agreed, sire," the captain said grimly.

Then the nobleman dictated a missive to his scribe. It stated that he had a pressing business excursion of some duration, and requested a noble to govern his castle and demesnes in his absence. He asked whether a particular young nobleman of his acquaintance was available.

It was the nobleman who had spent the night and ravished his daughter. A request of such nature could hardly be declined; there was a geis involved, an obligation of honor. More than the young nobleman knew, perhaps. The man agreed, and in due course arrived with a limited entourage of one squire and one servant; he would, of course, avail himself of the local staff while here.

The host, having announced his incipient departure, delayed only long enough to greet the visitor and introduce him formally to his daughter. Teensa could not avoid it this time; she would be having meals with the visitor and would be under his protection for the duration. So, reluctantly, she got garbed and ready. She had not been informed of the identity of the noble who was to be in charge; she knew only that she was required to defer to him as to her father. Such was the place of even highborn women in those days.

The host arranged it so that the two, visitor and daughter, first saw each other simultaneously, so positioned that the host could watch them both at this moment. "And this is my daughter, Teensa," he said, as she stepped around a screen and came face to face with the visitor.

Each recognized the other instantly. The girl froze in fear, while the man froze with horror. There was now no doubt: he was the one who had ravished her—and he had not known her identity. It had indeed been an accident.

Then each recovered, true to training and breeding. She forced a polite smile and murmured something inconsequential. He nodded graciously and turned away, evincing no further interest. This was as it should be. Both were of noble birth; each knew when and how to keep a secret, and from whom. They were ironically united in this matter. Their lapses had been only momentary, but the host had caught them.

Now for the remainder of his plan. He turned over the keys to the castle, introduced the captain of the guard, and with his retinue departed the castle for the month. It was in other hands than his now.

Teensa was absolutely stricken. She thought her father had unwittingly brought in the very worst person for this job! Now the beast would be able to complete his ravishment and make an end of her, so that she could never tell—and she was powerless to prevent it. She retreated to her chambers and gave herself up for lost.

But when the time came for the evening repast, the nobleman summoned her to the table. This was standard procedure, and she could not deny it. Her maid, knowledgeable in such things, assured her that it was best to follow the forms. She garbed herself appropriately and came down.

She was in terror of molestation, but the noble acted with perfect courtesy. The castle staff was impressed with his demeanor and his dialogue. He complimented her on her appearance, which was indeed outstanding; all that exquisite raiment could do for a woman, it did for her, evoking charms which had been barely apparent during her masquerade as a slops wench. The truth was that Teensa, stripped by circumstance of her self-abasement, was a lovely young woman.

Noticing that she had little appetite, he said to her: "It may be that thou art ill at ease in the absence of thy father. I assure thee that I am here to protect thy interests as his, and no harm will come to thee while I am here, while I live. This is a matter of honor."

"My thanks to thee," she said, not one whit reassured. She knew full well that he did not consider rape to be harmful to a wench. Few men did, whether noble or ignoble.

But to her amazement, it was so. The days passed, and the man made no move to molest her. He treated her always with perfect courtesy. There was no peremptory knock at her chamber door at night. She became fascinated, in the manner of a captive bird, and even allowed herself to be alone with him at one point, though with an exit handy so she could flee. Noting their isolation, he said: "If I have given thee offense in any manner, I sorely repent it, and would make amends were it possible. But I fear it is not." Then he turned away, evidently troubled.

Astonished, Teensa retreated to her chamber and pondered. She realized that the noble could not speak openly of what had passed between them, for that would be a confession of a crime that would require blood to amend. Yet he had in his fashion apologized. She realized further that he had not known her identity when he ravished her, and was now in an extremely awkward position because of it. It seemed that if she did not speak of it, neither would he, for it could not with honor be spoken of. It hadn't happened, as far as the castle was concerned.

Yet it *had* happened, and there would be an ugly reckoning at such time as her father married her to another noble. Her secret could be carried only through the ceremony; the moment she proffered herself for her wifely duty, her husband would discover that she was not chaste, and would be outraged. He would have the marriage annulled, and she would be condemned, and unbearable shame would be visited on her father. Rather than bring that horror upon him, she would take poison before the ceremony. This was the true measure of what the visiting nobleman had taken from her: her married life.

The life of the castle continued. Now less fearful, Teensa observed the noble more closely. He was a great bear of a man, enormously powerful physically, yet he was noble, and possessed the manners of his office. He was also a competent administrator, seeking advice when he needed it, so that the management of the demesnes was satisfactory. She was seeing another side of him.

Then an army advanced into the region. It was a Gothic marauding party, out to ravish the land and take spoils. This could not be tolerated.

The noble summoned Teensa and the captain of the guard. "Have we resources to turn back this ill tide?" he inquired of the captain.

"No, sire. At best we can defend the castle, for they lack siege equipment. They will depart in time, but the lands will be laid waste and the peasants savaged."

The noble turned to Teensa. "What would thy father do in such case?"

"He would offer tribute," she said, flattered despite herself that she should be asked. "He would say it was cheaper than the alternative, though it made him wroth."

"I will do as they father would, this being his estate," he said. "Though it makes me wroth too."

Then he sent out a party with the offer. In due course it returned with the Goth chief's answer. "All thy gold and grain, and thy fair daughter for my plaything." They were not aware that a visiting noble was in charge.

The noble pondered. "The gold and grain they would take anyway, in war, or the equivalent," he said. "But a noble woman is no plaything. I will not accede to this."

"But if they ravish the lands—" Teensa protested, knowing well that he knew she, already ravished, was of little worth anyway.

"Make them this counteroffer," he said to the leader of the negotiation party. "I will meet their champion in single combat. If he wins, the castle gates will be opened to them. If I win, they will depart without warring on us."

The party departed. The noble turned to Teensa. "Disguise thyself and hide during the combat. They must not know thy identity. Thou canst then escape with the peasants, if the gates are opened."

"But—" she protested, aghast.

"I owe it thee."

She realized that he actually intended to do it. He was going to risk his life to spare her humiliation, though he knew that she had no virtue remaining to defend. Such was the requirement of his code of honor, which she had not properly appreciated before.

The party returned. The Goth chief had agreed. There was nothing the Goths appreciated so much as a good fight, and it was certainly an easier way to settle matters than a siege.

The noble girt himself and rode out on his fine horse with only his squire in attendance. He trusted the honor of the Goths. They would not be able to hold their heads up among their own kind if they massacred a single knight after agreeing to individual combat. Indeed, their wagers were being laid out; they were genuinely enthusiastic about this spectacle.

Teensa watched from the ramparts, terrified. She realized that if the noble lost, the castle would not even be defended, and there would be horrible ransacking and rapine. But if he won, all would be salvaged, and the disaster that had seemed unavoidable would be avoided. It was a brave and bold thing the noble was doing.

The opposing horseman approached. The Goths were proud of their horsemanship; they had defeated the Romans because of it, and were the terror of the open ranges because of it. It was hard to see details, but the motions of the horses as they spun about each other were clear enough.

Light flashed. It was the reflection of the sunlight from moving steel. Now they were at swords, striking from their steeds. Then one steed went down. It was the Goth's horse!

But immediately the other rider dismounted and pursued the fray afoot. Strike and counterstrike. Teensa hardly dared look, but could not avert her gaze—and saw little anyway. There was too much dust.

At last one warrior fell, and the other stood. Who had won?

Then the standing one was helped to his steed, and rode toward the castle. It was the noble! They had been saved! Something snapped in Teensa then, and she was so relieved she wept.

The noble had indeed won. The Goths respected a valiant winner, and though they could not applaud an enemy, they let him depart unmolested. They packed up and moved away, hardly marauding at all. They really didn't have to; there were other estates close by, so they could keep their word and honor at little inconvenience. The castle and lands had indeed been spared.

But then news came that the noble was injured. The Goth champion, outhorsed, had been a veritable tiger afoot, and had slashed away the noble's armor and part of his left shoulder before being killed by the terrible counterstroke. The noble had kept his feet and made it to his horse, holding his head high, and the Goths had respected his courage even more. But he was grievously wounded.

Teensa came to him. "I am versed in healing," she said, and indeed she was, for she had tended her father's injured servants many times. She washed and bandaged the shoulder, and sat beside the noble in the dark hours while the fever took him, and held his hand when he cried out with the hallucinations of that fever. It was a long vigil, but in time, thanks to her ministrations, he recovered.

He slept long, and at last awakened. He found her there beside him. "Thou hadst no need to do this," he said.

"Thou didst save my father's possessions, and his honor," she said. For had she been made the plaything of the Goth chief, her father would never have survived the shame. "I owed thee."

"Nay, I owed thee! That was why I did it."

"Then mayhap we are even," she said, turning her eyes demurely down.

"We can never be even," he said. "But I would do anything for thy forgiveness for that of which I cannot speak."

"Why?" She was genuinely curious; but more than that, certain things he had uttered during his fever-madness had surprised her and provided her an astonishing hope. Should he repeat the like in this hour of his sanity—

"Thou art fair. I knew thee not, but now I do."

That was the verge of it. Her heart fluttered. "I forgive thee."

He extended his hand, and she took it. "I would marry thee, if thou couldst trust me that far."

And that was the whole of it.

"Aye." Then she leaned over the bed and kissed him.

When her father returned, the castle was in good order, and the visiting noble was recovering from his wound. After the initial ceremonies, the visiting noble and Teensa approached her father. "I have been indiscreet with thy daughter, and would marry her, that her honor be never in question," the visitor said.

The nobleman turned his gaze on his daughter, frowning. "Did this rogue force himself on thee?" he demanded.

"Nay, father. I love him, and would marry him." And with that half-lie she committed herself. She had protected his honor, and hers, in the manner expected of a wife.

"Then I am constrained to consent," her father said. Then he smiled. "In fact, I deem it an excellent match."

She hugged him, and he nodded. His ploy had succeeded in repairing damaged honor, just as the visiting noble's ploy had succeeded in saving the estate. This was the one man who would never challenge Teensa's chastity at the marriage bed. Indeed, he would draw his sword on any person who even hinted that she was anything but perfect. No one but the host nobleman ever knew the whole of it—except perhaps Teensa's maid, who was wise in the ways of these things, and knew when to keep her mouth shut.

❖ 27 ❖

T HE STATION WAGON had pulled
up and stopped, but the occupants did not get out. May waited a
moment, then went there. Geode and Œnone were within, and she
was talking.

May approached, wondering what this was about. Then she caught
on: Œnone was telling another story!

"And so they were wed, and Teensa went to the noble's castle, and
lived reasonably happily as such things went, and bore fine children,
and learned to be less shy," Œnone concluded. "All because she had
kept her mouth shut and not been unduly influenced by her first
impression."

"But why did the visiting noble treat her so well?" Geode asked,
perplexed. "After what he had done—"

"He had done what a man did with a slops wench," she said. "But
when he learned her true identity, and her father put him in charge,
he was honor-bound to serve the father's interest. It was part of the
code of chivalry. So he did the best he could in an awkward situation.
The father knew he would; it was the daughter who needed influenc-
ing."

Geode nodded. "We serve Mid like that."

Then they became aware of May, standing beside the car. "Oh—we're here!" Œnone exclaimed, surprised.

"I wish I had been able to hear it all," May said. "I did enjoy your story yesterday."

"Oh, May, we came to tell you—you don't have to stay here anymore!" Œnone exclaimed. "Mid said you could come to the house!"

But May shook her head. "Thank you, Œnone. But I think this is something I have to do."

"But the monster—it runs three days between feedings, and this is the third day! Tonight it will come!"

"Yes, I suspect it will. But Cyrano is alert for it, and we need to catch it. If I can help by luring it in, that is what I must do."

"Then I will stay with you, so that one person will always be awake!"

"No, Œnone. You have lost too much already. It is my turn. I will be alert."

"But I am doomed anyway! *I* should be the bait!"

"Doomed? We shall not let you suffer further, Œnone. Go with Geode, tell him another story; I will be all right."

The woman looked troubled, but let it be. "You are a dragonfly, bold where I am afraid."

"A dragonfly! How nice! But I am simply doing what I must; I am not bold." Indeed, she reflected with horror on her inability to oppose her brute husband, even after three years on her own. How spineless could a person get?

So they left, reluctantly, and May was alone again. It was the way she preferred it, for now, until she recovered from her injuries and could show her face in public again. She did not relish another night alone here, but this was indeed their best chance to catch the firefly, and that was what they were here for.

Yet there was now another aspect, which had caught her completely unprepared. Frank Tishner had expressed interest in her. She knew that his marriage was in trouble; his wife had said that. It seemed likely that by the time the monster was dealt with, Frank would lose his job, because Mid's agenda would conflict with the needs of the local county. When Frank lost his job, he lost his wife; that much had been established.

She had not considered Frank as a prospect. Indeed, she had had no serious interest in any future liaison with a man; her experience with Bull had cured her of that sort of thing. Yet now that the subject had been, however inadvertently, broached, she found herself interested.

She did not actually like being alone; she liked independence. She had assumed that the two were inextricably linked. Now she wondered. A man who wasn't brutal, who would let her be herself, strong enough to be himself—there was an appeal to that.

Well, it was probably academic, and she had more immediate concerns. Her body was healing, but she had far to go before achieving either physical or emotional comfort. She didn't like being dependent on others for food and clothing, but had no choice at the moment. It was nice of Œnone to get Mid to offer the use of the main house, but that would have put her with Œnone and Geode, and she wanted them to be alone together. Also, there was indeed the matter of the monster. Who else could she ask to serve as a lure for it? She was on the job here, using her recovery time to its most effective potential. That, perhaps, was her root reason for declining the chance to stay at the main house. She preferred to be in harness, pulling her own weight, and she was doing that here.

The prospect of this night frightened her, without a doubt. Œnone had called her a brave dragonfly—but dragonflies did not fly by night. Fireflies did. The monster was a firefly, and she was its prey. For somehow she knew it would come here to feed, and not elsewhere.

As far as she knew, it had never taken an alert person. But did it depend on natural sleep, or did it somehow lull its prey to sleep? She would find out. The prospect made her distinctly nervous, but she reminded herself that Cyrano was out there watching; she should be safe.

It was midafternoon. She would sleep till dusk, then be alert through the night. It fed at night; she was depending on that. In fact, she was betting her life on it.

She lay down and slept. It was an ability she had developed as a business asset, for her investigations could require odd hours. She knew she would be able to stay awake for the night with this preparation.

She woke at dusk, as planned; the other part of sleeping on command was waking on command. She felt better; she had slept so as to prepare for the night, but it had helped her heal too, perhaps, or at least put a bit more distance between her and her recent horror.

She went outside, gazing at the evening. The ponies were not in evidence; apparently there had been too much recent activity here, so they had moved elsewhere. With a square mile of field and forest, they had many options.

She saw a firefly flash in the shadow. That reminded her of the monster. How close was it now? How close was Cyrano? Suppose it came, and he did not? Could she handle it when alert? She knew it was small enough to get in a window, which didn't seem so fearsome, but large enough to consume a man, which it did. A python could crawl in a window and consume a man! How could she defend herself? Now she regretted declining Frank's offer of a gun. She wished Frank were here!

She heard something. It was faint, so faint she might be imagining it—a high keening, like a tuning fork or a ringing in the ear. Where was it coming from? She couldn't tell. Did the monster make a sound?

She thought of Frank again. What would it be like to have sex with him? A man's fires diminished somewhat as he aged, but plenty remained when evoked. Her husband had demonstrated that! Had it actually been so bad, being sodomized? In some circles it was an acceptable alternate mode of sex. Cyrano had reminded her of that. She had to agree that the perpetrator was more to be blamed than the victim. But she would rather have Frank here, stripping down, doing it normally, eagerly—

A horrible realization came. The firefly! It used sex to pacify its victims! Pheromones. That was why she was becoming so uncharacteristically sexually excited. IT WAS NEAR!

She hurried back into the cabin. Now her decision to remain here another night seemed foolish. She knew of no one who had escaped the monster. She had assumed they were all asleep or unconscious—but maybe they had all tried to have sex with it. What aspect did it assume, to compel a person to come close and to remain while it consumed that person?

Would it seem to her that Frank was arriving, and would she go gladly into his arms for sex—and would they find her bones in the morning? What folly to expose herself here to what she did not understand!

She looked for some weapon, but realized as she did so that it was futile. The best that offered was a broomstick or a small paring knife. Somehow she knew that neither would be effective against the firefly. Would she hit or stab Frank when she was lusting for him? Even if she knew he was only an illusion covering the monster?

But suppose she simply refused to have sex? Would the firefly then be helpless against her?

She remembered the pheromones. She had reacted erotically when she smelled the remains in the old mining pit. How much worse would it be with the living firefly? She was very much afraid that not only would she be unable to fight it, she would welcome its embrace, even knowing it for what it was. Already she was thinking sex again, wanting to embrace a man, to open her legs for his member, to feel him penetrating her. That really wasn't natural for her, but now it seemed completely desirable. It was no use reminding herself that sex was all too often inconvenient, uncomfortable, and messy; she craved that messiness.

Then she heard a motor. Relieved, she ran to the door and flung it open.

The ambience of sex struck her almost tangibly. The keening was louder. The closed cabin had sheltered her from it to some extent. Now she had no doubt at all: it was the firefly, coming for her. All too soon she would desire its approach; she felt the urge mounting, felt her crotch becoming hot and moist. If she saw anything like a penis she might grab it and climb on it. What power in those pheromones!

She saw the lights of a car coming down the path through the forest, blinking on and off as they were interrupted by intervening trees. Surely the firefly couldn't be driving it! Yet if it was in fact a man with a unique method—no, impossible! The car had to be coincidental.

Then the vehicle came into sight in the closing dusk.

It was her own car! The one Mid had given her!

Did that mean Frank had gotten the keys and brought it here to her? Wild hope surged. She could have him and escape the firefly at the same time!

Then she saw the figure inside. *It was Bull Shauer!*

She reeled, emotionally and physically. Everything was happening at once! What could she do now?

But the shock brought some sense to her. One thing about which she was absolutely certain; she did not want more of Bull's type of treatment! Not even pheromones could override her fear and aversion! She had to get away from him.

She knew she could not. Maddened by the pheromones, he would be ruthless. And she—how long could she hold out against the pheromones herself? How long before she welcomed Bull's sadistic lust? That would be horror on horror!

Then she remembered the anesthetic dart. She had it hidden under the mattress. She went and fetched it. Where could she hide it on her person? She tucked it quickly in her hair. She hoped it was effective, because it was her only hope. If it wasn't—

The car pulled up almost to the door. Belatedly May remembered the lock. She rushed up and turned it.

There was a thud as Bull pounded once and tested the knob. Then a pause. In a moment there was a scraping. He was using his knife to jimmy open the latch. The door had no dead bolt.

May ran into the outer chamber as the door opened. There was no help here; the mattresses would only hasten his appetite. She went beyond, to the enclosed porch, but its door had been long since sealed over; no egress there. She was trapped.

She turned back to the main chamber. He was there, smiling cruelly. "You were foolish, April, to think I would let you go so readily," he said.

She knew he wanted to brag. She played the game; it was better than the violence that would erupt if she didn't. "How did you find me?"

"I never lost you, April. I was not asleep when you wrapped that towel around your ass and tiptoed out bare-boobed to hide in the broom closet. I wanted to know what your contacts were. Who would have thought they were a sheriff's deputy and a rich Chinaman! I must compliment you on your savvy in managing men." He frowned. "But I think you know now that if you get close to that deputy again, his livelihood is gone. One call, and he'll pay for your bare titties with his job."

He *had* seen! "You fooled me completely, Bull," she confessed, honestly enough.

"And if you think that asshole in the van is coming to your rescue, forget it. I took him out on the way in."

"What?" she asked, dismayed anew. She *had* hoped Cyrano would spy the commotion and investigate.

"I tied him to a tree. He won't move till I let him move. Maybe in the morning, when we're headed out of here and back home."

"But—" But what could she say? Bull wouldn't give a fig about the danger from the firefly, and indeed, if he didn't know about it, she shouldn't tell him.

"As for the Chinaman, all he wants is privacy. He'll boot you the moment you become an embarrassment to him. So—you will become that embarrassment. But first we'll have a little fun."

"You've already tried to give me AIDS," she flared.

"AIDS? What are you talking about?"

"Weren't you—when you—?"

"When I fucked you in the ass? Hell, no! I don't need any stupid drugs and I wouldn't touch one of those damned fairies! I was just letting you know your ass is mine. And you know that now, don't you, April?"

She nodded, not trusting herself to speak. He had just lifted an enormous burden from her mind. Bull never lied to her; her opinion was beneath his contempt.

"Say it, April."

"My ass is yours, Bull," she said with appropriate reluctance. Actually, her heart was singing, despite her present peril. Bull would beat her, but wouldn't actually kill her. The AIDS would have killed her.

"So bare it for me, bitch." He used the bad words deliberately, aware of her relative fastidiousness about terminology. He was savaging her already, verbally. It would hardly stop there. With part of her mind she noted that the pheromones didn't seem to change his behavior; apparently they couldn't enhance a sado/sexual drive that was already firmly in control.

She removed her clothing, slowly but not too slowly, in the way he liked. Then, naked, she took the pins out of her hair, letting it down. The last was the hypo Cyrano had given her. How could she use it, with him watching?

"Bitch!" he snapped.

Startled, she dropped the handful. The hypo rolled across the mattress. He knew about that too!

"Stop stalling with that shit. Come open my pants."

He wanted oral sex, she realized. He knew she didn't like that either. He hadn't seen the hypo! She approached him and dropped to her knees. Probably the forced humiliation of the position was as important to him as the act he demanded.

Her mixed relief was short-lived. "What's that?" he exclaimed, gazing down.

She froze, not knowing what to say that would not damn her.

"You into drugs now, bitch?" he demanded.

"No," she protested, hope flaring with this miscue.

"Think you can lie to me, you fucking whore? Give it to me."

She got up, then stooped to pick up the hypo. Bull extended his hand to take it from her as she straightened.

Now! she thought. She did what she had never done before, and attacked him. She lunged, stabbing at his arm with the hypo, depressing the plunger as the needle entered the flesh of his forearm.

"You turd!" he cried, snatching the hypo away. "What's in that thing—coke?"

She retreated. Had she scored on a good place? How long did it need to take effect, from a peripheral site?

"You trying to turn me into a druggie?" he demanded, advancing on her. "Instead of shooting up yourself, you shot *me* up? Well, it won't work! One shot doesn't make an addict. Meanwhile, I'm going to ream your ass so hard—!"

He grabbed for her, catching her arm. She spun around and away, stumbling by him, her nakedness making her harder to catch on to, and ran for the other room. But he turned and dived after her, grasping her by the hair. He yanked cruelly back on it, bringing her up short. "You are going to pay," he said.

She turned back, swinging her arm. Her right elbow caught him on the cheek. He grunted and his grip on her hair loosened. She wrenched away and charged the door again.

He was after her again immediately. But she was committed now. She had discovered that she could fight him. In all their years of marriage she had never struck back. Now she was doing it. Maybe the pheromones were giving her some sort of sublimatory courage, translating her detestation of his kind of sex into violence. He would pulverize her, of course—but he would have done that anyway.

She dived out the door, but he was faster. He caught her again, his right hand clutching her shoulder. She turned, trying to spin away again, but his other hand caught her wrist. He yanked, and she came flopping into him. There was no way she could match his strength.

She jerked her hand up, but he still gripped her wrist. She put her face to it and bit his knuckles, hard. There was almost a glory in this, fighting back physically! The end might be certain, but this time he would be scarred as well as she.

"You damned cunt!" he raged, letting go and making a fist.

She stumbled back, turned again, and sprinted barefoot for the car. Had he left the keys in it?

No. They weren't there. She couldn't use it to escape.

She ran again—but her brief pause was fatal. He caught her again. This time he tackled her. She crashed to the ground, turning her face barely in time to avoid the grass and dirt. There was a flare of pain from her injured left breast. He changed his grip, virtually climbing up her, holding her down while he opened his fly. He turned her over, jammed his knee between her knees to force them apart, and came down on her.

But his follow-up was oddly slow. He was trying to have sex with her, and his member was ready, but it was as though he were falling asleep.

The sedative! It was working at last! Bull had run out of steam!

She renewed her struggles, and this time was able to break free of his loosening grip. She drew herself out from under him. Bull remained where he was, sprawled facedown in the grass, fly open, penis out, and stupefied. He had an erection, but nowhere to put it.

She couldn't pause to gloat. She didn't know how long the sedative would last, considering that she probably hadn't given him a full dose. The moment Bull recovered, he'd be after her again. She couldn't trust herself, either; the moment her terror of incipient capture faded, her obsession with sex returned. That big, stiff penis—

She ran to the cabin, entered, jammed on her clothing and shoes, and came out again. The car—she needed to use that! But he had the keys.

She looked at him, lying there. Could she go and pick his pocket for them?

She didn't dare. It would be just like him to play possum, and grab her when she approached. Cat and mouse was his game. And if she got close to that penis again, she would be drawn to it, heedless of the consequence. It was as if she were drunk with sex: she didn't dare drive. Or whatever.

She set out on foot, following the trail into the dark forest. With luck she would make it to the house before Bull recovered. They could set the alarm system, so that he could not break in without bringing the police, fire department, and whatever else. If only he didn't wake too soon!

But even as she ran, she felt the horrible, continuing urge for sex. The smell of the firefly was here—and where was it lurking? Down this trail? Would she stumble into it in the dark? Would her fear of it be greater than her hunger for sex?

How could she know? It was Bull or the firefly. She plowed on, hoping she wouldn't get lost. Maybe she could find Cyrano and untie him, if the firefly hadn't—

She stifled that thought. That couldn't happen, it just couldn't!

28

BULL SAW HER go, but was unable to pursue her. The bitch had stabbed him with her drug hypo, and it had brought him down into a stupor. He had assumed it was whatever she used, coke or heroin, though she'd never been into that stuff before. Instead it seemed to be something to make her sleep—and now it was making *him* sleep. At least, it made his body sleep; his mind was awake, his eyes open. He just couldn't move. What had she dosed him with, curare? That was the stuff the pygmies used, that knocked out the body and not the mind. Surgeons had given it as an anesthetic, and patients had complained that they felt the surgery, and naturally the doctors had dismissed that as imagination—until a surgeon had had surgery under curare. Then he believed. Too bad they didn't do the same thing with dentists, make them feel what the patients felt, so they could stop calling it imagination.

Well, if it was something like that, at least he wouldn't be conscious while being cut up! It would wear off after a while, and then he'd get after the bitch again, and catch her, and make her pay. What kind of sex would appall her most? He'd had her in the ass, so that wouldn't have the same effect next time. He had to make her really hurt, in the mind as well as the body. He had three years of hurting to catch up on.

Maybe bondage: tie her up, burn her tits with a cigarette, make her beg for sex, scream for it, and really mean it to get out of the pain. Then burn her while he was going into her, so her writhing brought him off. He'd heard of a guy who did it with a chicken, holding the bird down, putting his pecker in the avian cunt, then cutting off the chicken's head, so when the bird flapped around and clenched in its death throes, it brought him off. Something like that for April—yes, the notion of her screaming and twisting in pain while he rammed it into her, that was great! She'd pay, oh, she'd pay!

It was getting pretty dark, but he saw something. Heard something too. A sort of high keening. Crickets? It didn't seem the same. He wanted to turn his head and look, but couldn't; peripheral vision was all he had. So it was just a rustling in the grass, maybe a snake, down somewhere beyond his feet, but coming closer.

A snake? There were rattlers in these parts! If one came up and bit him—

He put that aside and thought of sex again. The hell with where and how he fucked her, so long as he did it fast and strong. The bondage could wait until he got the edge off, and she'd think it was over; then he'd tie her and start in again, making her hurt while he got it up for the reprise. His pecker was hard as a rock, poking out from his pants. He'd never been this horny before! He'd fuck her continuously, the way they did in those dirty movies, in the mouth, in the cunt, in the ass and back to the mouth, on and on, coming and coming, let her scream and beg him to stop, let her choke on it, he'd just keep ramming it in. He imagined her lying there, her fleshy legs parted, while he pumped it in continuously, like a fire hydrant, spuming out around her crack, no end to it. She was a solid woman, Rubenesque, ample of breast and hip and thigh, and he liked her that way, a piece of ass that a man could really get into. Sometimes he had the feeling that it would be dangerous to fuck a slender woman; she might split right in half when he wedged his cock into her crack. But not April; she could take it all, and still be there for more. She was big and soft, like a pillow-doil, and pneumatic.

A damned ant appeared by his nose, a little reddish one. He knew about the ants of this region, fire ants, with many-holed mounds, whose sting made a burn that hurt for hours. If that fucking insect stung his nose—

Something touched his shoe. He felt the nudge, but still couldn't see what it was. He really didn't care; if it came within range, he'd fuck it too! The smell of sex was in the air; that was all he cared about.

Another ant appeared. He pursed his lips and blew it away; at least he could do that!

Something touched his prick. There was a fine caress, and a soft surrounding, an enclosure. The pleasure magnified. God—a woman should be like this! This was the finest cunt that ever existed. His pecker got so hard it was bursting, and still the pleasure mounted. The old Roman gods, they must have fucked like this, immortally great, who cared what woman was on the other end of it, they were all just sheaths for the rod, just coming and coming, never-ending sex.

It was like an orgasm, but it didn't just come and go, it continued. It started at the tip of his prick, and swelled into the head of it, and down inside the channel, like semen going backward, making the pleasure follow. Now his entire member throbbed with the sheer joy of penetration—the exquisite bliss of that fluid coursing slowly inside. His pecker felt as if it were a foot long and six inches thick, deep in a hot, slick cunt to match.

Then the ecstasy proceeded further in, following the channel down and around and deep, making the whole root of it resonate. There had never been gratification like this, not in all the aeons of man's existence! He could stay here a thousand years, just letting it happen, transported by the ultimate sensation.

It traveled on into his bladder, spreading its rapture. His whole belly radiated pleasure. He never wanted this to stop. If this was a damn wet dream, he hoped he never woke. He just wanted to ride on its current forever. He was on his way to Fucking Heaven.

Gradually his consciousness faded, as the delight extended up through his body toward his head.

29

FRANK TISHNER STARED down at the body. That was Bull Shauer, all right, the description fit. May Flowers's car was not far from it, as she had said.

The phone had roused him in the wee hours: May, sounding desperate. Her husband had found her; she had stabbed him with the hypo and fled. He had caught her, but succumbed before he could rape her. She had made her way through two miles of forest, following the trail, until it led her to the house. Bruised, scratched, mosquito-bitten, she had pounded on the door, and Geode had let her in. But Bull was still in the forest, and so was Cyrano—and the firefly.

Frank had gotten over there in a hurry. Now he was at the cabin as the dawn threatened—and here was Bull, exactly where May said she had left him, on the ground, facedown. His clothing, and his bones.

The firefly had taken him.

Frank left the body there for the moment and went in search of Cyrano. It seemed that Bull had claimed to have tied him to a tree. Since there was no evidence of Cyrano, that was probably true.

He found the place where the tread marks of Cyrano's van left the main trail. He followed them. It wasn't hard, now that he knew what he was looking for. Soon enough he found the van, parked under a reaching live oak. Not far from it was the man, sitting on the ground, his arms behind him around a small tree, tied. He was gagged.

Frank moved the gag, then the rope binding the wrists. It was a simple tie, but just about impossible to escape.

"May Flowers," Cyrano said, unkinking his arms and chafing his wrists.

"Safe," Frank said. "She got away and called me, and I came out. She would have helped you herself, but didn't know where you were, and couldn't find you in the dark. I think she got lost on the way; took her hours to find the house."

"The firefly," Cyrano said.

"The monster? It got Bull Shauer. I don't know where it is now."

"Thank God I gave her that hypo!"

"Thank God you did!" They both knew it would have been May, otherwise. "Look, we can't advertise that body. I don't think anyone knows where Bull went. As far as the law is concerned, he left town. But the bones—"

"I'll take care of them. My pleasure. Maybe there'll be more to show how it happened, this time."

"His clothing's on, but his fly's open. But he had it open to rape May, she says, so that doesn't mean anything."

"Maybe. But the thing uses pheromones. He could have thought it was a woman."

"Do you have any idea what it looks like?"

Cyrano shrugged. "Maybe like a woman."

"But doesn't it take females too?"

"Female animals. When I catch it, I'll let you know what it looks like."

"It affects human females too. May said it was so strong, she almost wanted Bull Shauer."

Cyrano grimaced. "Which must be about as strong as anything gets. I wasn't nearly as close, but I got a whiff of it, and that was enough."

"But hardly any remained by the time I saw the body. The firefly must turn off the pheromones once it catches its prey."

"For sure. Why waste them?"

"You've had a bad night out here. Will you be okay?"

"I'm alive. That's good enough."

Frank had to agree. If the firefly hadn't fed on Bull Shauer, it would have come for Cyrano.

"Then I'll leave the bones to you. Just so there's no trace. This never happened."

"Don't tell me my business," Cyrano said gruffly. He headed for his van.

Frank went to his car. He paused only long enough to make sure the van was operative, then turned his car around and went back down the trail toward the main house.

"Cyrano's taking care of it," he announced. "None of us ever saw Bull Shauer out here. Agreed?"

They nodded together: Geode, looking the same as usual; Œnone, looking surprisingly radiant; and May, with a shiner, welts, and ill-fitting dress.

"For all we know, or care, he got disgusted because May escaped him, and left town. So there's no mysterious disappearance and no body."

They nodded again.

"And you can stay here, May, until you recover."

"No," she said. "Now that Bull's gone, I can return to my room in town, and resume my activity."

"But you look a sight—no offense."

"None taken," she said, smiling. "But there's no mystery about that. Bull *was* in town and did beat me up. I hid, but returned when he left town. There'll be some talk, but nothing dangerous. I'd like to get my car."

"I don't think you'd better go out there again."

"We can do it," Œnone said. "Geode and I."

Frank nodded. "And take her stuff out of the cabin; better if there's no evidence she ever was there." He held out the keys to May's car, which he had taken from the bones.

Œnone smiled in agreement. The two of them went out.

Alone with May, Frank found things suddenly awkward. "I guess you'll be okay, then. You'll want to rest before you drive in."

"It has been a difficult night," she agreed. "But are you in a hurry?"

"At this hour? No."

"Bull freed me of a double burden," she said. "First, of himself; that is a phenomenal weight off my mind, quite overriding the shock of the manner of his death. Never again will I have to hide. I'll remain nominally married to him, of course, since I can't prove he is dead, but that is no concern to me. Second, he reassured me that he didn't have AIDS. When he raped me, I was afraid—but he said he didn't have it, and in that I believe him. I will survive."

He hadn't realized that she suffered from that particular fear. "I'm glad."

She hesitated. "This—may not be appropriate. But I would like to be in your arms."

"What?"

"You are not like Bull."

His surprise became understanding. He went to her and took her in his arms. She clung to him, and put her head on his shoulder, and he felt her crying. She was in desperate need of comfort, despite her businesslike attitude.

"Oh, the hell with this!" he said.

Now she was surprised. She lifted her face. "I'm sorry. I'm not normally like this. I—"

He kissed her.

At first she responded diffidently, flustered. Then she coalesced and came back with full strength. The lingering barriers came down, and only understanding, need, and passion remained.

They broke, partway, in due course. "Yes, exactly," she said. "I know I'm not much at the moment, but last night when the firefly approached, and its pheromones—I thought of you. I wanted you in a way I have not wanted any man before. I realize that this puts an ugly face on the situation, but for the first time I truly understood sexual passion, and I have not forgotten. So if you—"

"I'm married. No disrespect to you."

"I respect that." She seemed, if anything, relieved. "Then perhaps we should simply talk."

They sat in the living room and talked, about nothing in particular. They did not touch again. But it looked very much like dawning love.

In half an hour Geode and Œnone were back, each driving one car. Geode drove the station wagon into the garage, while Œnone parked before the house.

"Thank you, dear," May said. "You have been so kind."

"You have been kind to me,"Œnone replied.

The two women hugged. Then May got into her car. Œnone took the things out of it, for they would only call attention to May's presence at the ranch. May's things were at the hotel room in town. She would have to get by in the too-tight outfit for a few minutes when she got there, but then she would be able to change.

"I'll follow you in," Frank said. "If you feel faint or anything, just pull over."

"Thank you." May started the car and pulled slowly forward.

Frank returned to his car and followed her. Everything was formal, the way it should be. But everything had changed, and not just with the firefly. He didn't know what was going to happen next, but his outlook had abruptly become more positive.

As they turned left at the right-angle corner, he noticed how the fence there was overgrown by passion flowers, each big and purple. There was passion fruit too, looking like green lemons. He had heard they were edible, but he didn't trust it. Still, it did lend a notion: here in the vicinity of passion fruit, he was discovering a new and unexpected passion. May had confirmed her interest in him, and despite his demurral, he was interested. Oh, she was no nymphlike beauty, but that wasn't the point. He was a lot more interested in character and constancy, and those she had in spades. Yet as far as physical appearance went, she was good enough. In fact, she was a pretty robust specimen. That had been quite clear when she was halfway naked. After all, he was no college athlete himself. Had he not been married . . .

❖ 30 ❖

"I PROMISED TO tell you another story," Œnone said as she fixed him lunch. "I have told you about Œnone; now I will tell you about Eve." She paused, glancing at him. "It isn't really a story; it is history. It is the truth about women, and how they govern men."

He sat watching her, listening. As she talked, he saw what she described, becoming immersed in her framework. He learned about Eve.

It was about a hundred and fifty thousand years ago, between the beginning of the Riss glaciation and the beginning of the Würm glaciation. Eve was born into an isolated tribe in Africa, whose members were confined there by the greater worldwide success of the more robust species of man who were later to be termed Neanderthals. Her people were on the primitive fringe, lacking access to the richer hunting grounds. They had to make do with scavenging from the edge of the great sea, finding shellfish and spearing fish. They were as intelligent as the others, and their language skills were equivalent, but their numbers were too few for real competition.

The problem was that their breeding rate was low. The women of other tribes came into heat every month until bred, so were constantly getting pregnant and producing offspring. But Eve's tribe, driven to the verge of the sea, had survived only by retreating *into* the sea to avoid enemies, including other men. They had adapted by becoming more fleshy, especially their women, so that they could better withstand the chill of the water. The men remained lean when young, going ashore to hunt, but the women's safest haven was shallow water in seaside caves, curling up with their fat babies in the darkness so that others did not know their whereabouts. Those who were able to remain still in cool water longest survived best.

But in the course of this water retreat they had somehow lost something vital. Too often their periods of heat occurred when they were hiding in the water, so that the effect of the pheromones was lost, and their men did not flock to breed them. This lessened the breeding rate significantly, and the tribe barely maintained its numbers. Yet if a woman left the water during her heat, she could attract a neighboring tribesman, who would gladly impregnate her, but would not care for her thereafter. A man of her own tribe would not care for her when it was known that her baby was not of the tribe. Thus foreign impregnation was too apt to be her death warrant. She needed to breed with her own kind—more than she did.

Eve was a mutant, though she did not know it. A genetic defect lurked in her being, and it did not show until she matured. Then it became entirely too evident. Her breasts were prematurely swollen. Normal women's breasts developed only when they were gravid, in time to suckle their babies, as was the case throughout the anthropoid species. They developed partially when the women came into heat, but subsided when fertilization did not occur. Eve's breasts would have been normal for late pregnancy, but were grotesque as permanent structures. What use were they, with no baby to suckle? They did not lactate, they were merely there, incongruous.

But there turned out to be a side benefit to this abnormality. Eve was able to endure the chill of the water better because her prematurely developed breasts insulated her to a degree. Also, the men of her tribe were attracted to women who looked as though they were ready to breed. Thus those with wide pelvic girdles and fatty thighs were more appealing than those with narrow ones, and the nascent breasts of the time of heat contributed to it. In the absence of the proper dissemination of the mating odor, because of the water, Eve's half-hidden breasts seemed to resemble the lesser signal of readiness. There was

normal variation among men, with some being more visually stimu-
lated than others, and Eve was able to attract one of these. He bred her
right there in the water, not waiting for her heat. Actually, he thought
her heat was on her, because he saw the breasts and knew the smell
couldn't travel through the water, and she was so eager for it that she
certainly *acted* as if in heat. The penetration was uncomfortable, and
of course it didn't take, but the lure of her oversized breasts remained,
and the next day he bred her again—and again on the following day.
She learned to make herself ready for him, so that the penetration
didn't hurt despite the tendency of the water to wash away the slick
juices that normally facilitated it during heat. She gave the illusion of
being perpetually in heat, as long as the water drowned out the air-
borne pheromones, and he responded to it with less appetite than those
who were compelled by the smell, but nevertheless persistently
enough. It was a fact that any man could copulate at any time, only
awaiting the readiness of the woman.

Inevitably two things happened. He came to form an attachment to
her, and so became her regular man: what today would be termed the
married state. And in due course she came into genuine heat, so that
the breeding took, and she conceived by him. So her defect turned out
to be an asset, and she bred when those around her did not.

The effect on her tribe was small but significant. Eve received male
attention the whole of her mature life, even when she was well past the
age of breeding, because her aspect in the water gave the illusion of
breedability. Thus she bore babies constantly, many more than usual,
and male protection extended even after she stopped producing babies,
because she always seemed ready to have another. Thus her offspring
were more copious than those of other women, and had better protection, and became more prominent in the tribe.

The majority of her offspring happened to be female—and all of
them grew up with the same genetic defect, because it turned out to be
dominant. Their breasts swelled at maturity and would not subside.
But in the water they did well, both against the chill and with visually
oriented men. They quickly learned to conceal their real state, and to
accept the approach of men even when they did not feel inclined for
copulation, because they knew that repeat servicing was far better than
none. They bred effectively, and had many offspring of their own. The
men were not completely fooled, of course; they knew that breedability
was mostly illusion when the women were not in heat. But they were
satisfied to go through the motions regardless, for there was pleasure in

it apart from the actual fertilization. In fact, the men never had been as interested in the fertilization as in the pleasure of the moment, and these women were very good at providing the latter. For the first time, the women were able to do what the men could: to breed at any time. It was a wonderful equalization of the sexes, which in time would lead to the very verge of full equality, farfetched as that seemed at this time.

Generations passed, and the population of Eve's tribe reversed its trend. Now the tribe was growing in size, and achieving a better competitive position. The women no longer had to hide in the water so much. But by this time the alternate pattern of breeding had become established, and men did not necessarily bother to wait for the pheromones before going to it. In fact, some women had lost their pheromone production qualities, so that their periods of heat were virtually unmarked. It turned out to be a continuing advantage for them to hide their reproductive capacity, because some men did not desire to sire offspring, which entailed some years of obligation. But because the women never looked unready, the men could never be sure when it was "safe" to copulate, and frequently got caught. Conceptions continued.

Gradually Eve's tribe increased, for there were many factors that governed man's success, not just his rate of reproduction. Fifty thousand years later her descendants had spread across Africa, but remained only one of a number of human species. Then the final glaciation came, Würm, slowly shaking up the world. As the glacial surges of ice moved down from the arctic region, the northern tribes retreated south, impinging on the territory of those who had settled there. There was warfare, and admixture, and famine as regions were overhunted. There was a progression of migrations as one species put pressure on another, and the other put pressure on a third, dominoes toppling south. The fair-haired Neanderthal Northmen were on the move, and the disruption of their coming was chronic.

Meanwhile Eve's people were expanding, for now they had a secure population in Africa and were still breeding well. It was not that their population doubled every generation; the effect was far more subtle. But it doubled in the course of twenty thousand years, while other populations didn't, and that meant rapid expansion on the geological scale. Eve's people had continually to find new pastures. So it was that they were always coming into conflict with those who already occupied those pastures. Eve's people had either to remain bottled up or to fight. They became excellent warriors. They were a cohesive group, with constant intercommunication, and were especially protective of their women. This was because their women remained constantly sexually appealing. Other species of man converged on any woman in heat, and bred her madly, and then forgot her for a month in favor of the next woman in heat. But Eve's women no longer came into heat; their reproductive cycles were muted, often entirely hidden from males, and their breasts were forever swollen, so that the lure of their sexuality never abated. A woman kept her man occupied continually, never giving him the chance to wander. So while the women of other species might be slain between breeding cycles, unprotected, Eve's women were never unprotected. Thus they continued to breed at a superior rate. Eve's men excelled at two things; warfare and copulation. In fact, they became the most warlike of the human species, and they developed the biggest proportionate penises.

There was an interglaciation, the ice retreated. The species and tribes of man migrated back north, and the pressure of population was relieved. But then the glaciers advanced again, forcing the tribes back—while Eve's people continued to advance from the south. This happened several times. In some regions, two species lived in the same general terrain, but they never interbred, because Eve's men were no longer compelled by the heat cycle, and found the flat-chested women of other species unappealing. Caught between the ice and Eve's people, even the proud and powerful species of Neanderthal man at last succumbed to the dark-skinned Eve's species. By about thirty thousand years before the present, the greatly varied species of man had been replaced by one uniform species: Eve's children. Then that species branched, becoming fair-skinned like the erstwhile Neanderthals in the north, and black-skinned in the south, and large and small as the local terrain encouraged. But all of them had perpetually swollen breasts on the women and big penises on the men, even after there was really no need to compete by superior reproductive capacity.

So it was that Eve was the mother of modern man. Her genetic pattern is in every living human being. We know this because we have traced the special gene pattern of the mitochondria, which are the power generators of the cell, which are transmitted only from mother to child. The father does not pass these particular genes along. In this sense, only the women matter; the men are genetically forgotten. So we know about Eve, but not about Adam. Her legacy became the guiding principle of mankind: continuous sexuality.

And indeed it has been perfected! A man is a comparatively simple creature, sexually; he is aroused by the signals of the most proximate woman, and will breed with her if there are not contrary constraints, such as another man present. The art and science of sex lie with the woman. Her entire body and manner have become a sexual geography, from her large, innocent eyes and hair that frames her face, neck, and bosom to advantage, to her trim ankles and dainty feet. Her large breasts attract a man's eyes like magnets, but if she is facing away, her buttocks take up the task and hold him just as securely. Her narrow waist and broad hips signal her femininity and ability to breed. The very contours of her limbs and extremities are appealing to the man, and compelling as they approach her center, which is the site for copulation. Like a spiral, her body brings in his gaze and his desire, so that he is compelled to approach and finally enter that central orifice. When she walks she signals, and when she dances she incites. The man is helpless before this array; virtually any healthy young woman who strips and signals any man will compel him to breed with her. She can breed almost anytime she wants to, with any man she wants to. She is the daughter of Eve, who conquered the world by first conquering the male of her species—without letting him know it.

If she does not wish to breed—and indeed, she can be quite choosy about this—she has a variety of ways to turn off the signals. Her clothing, instead of being crafted to show those portions of her body which most incite men to lust, can cover them. Her actions can become negative. For a woman's ultimate beauty is only partly physical; her actions complete it. A woman who meets a man's gaze briefly, then glances demurely down, and her earlobes flush and her bosom heaves and she tilts her head a bit to the side and meets his gaze again, sidelong, as she smiles—that woman is beautiful. In such manner she lures and captures the man of her choice, he being too dull to understand that it wasn't his idea. This dullness has nothing to do with intelligence; the man may be a genius—which is why she wants him—but the signals she sends operate below the level of intellect, and score despite his belief that he is in control and knows better. She talks with him, she listens to him, she flatters him, and finally she offers sex to him, and he is hers.

Eve started it, and her daughters perfected it. Every woman practices it, and so governs even the most reticent man.

"As I am doing with you," Œnone concluded. She stood before him, in a dress that exposed her neck and shoulders and the upper surfaces of her breasts. Her auburn hair came down across her forehead and framed her eyes, which were luminously green. She put her hands on his shoulders, and drew him a bit in to her as she tilted her head and gazed momentarily into his eyes, and away, and back, her pupils dilated, her mouth parted, almost slack, a bit of color on her cheeks. She was lovely.

"But I can't—" he protested, wishing, oh, wishing that he could.

"Because now you know I love you, and it is safe for you to love me."

He stared at her face, and it seemed to blur, and then he was holding her, and kissing her. It was true.

"I have told you of Œnone, and of Teensa, and of Eve," she murmured. "I must still tell you of Nymph. Then we shall make love, if you wish."

"I love your stories, but I don't need—"

"Indulge me, Geode. Nymph is important. But she can wait. We must eat, and go on your rounds; I think there is time today for me to go with you."

"Yes. I want you with me. Forever!"

"I will be with you, while I live."

"Till death do us part," he said, recognizing the allusion. "You are everything to me, Œnone."

"This is the way of love. But it must be guided. And fed. Eat, Geode."

For of course the meal was ready. Obediently, gladly, he ate.

The chime sounded. Geode got up quickly and went to the front door, where he punched in the gate-opening code. Was it Frank Tishner?

Œnone quickly hid the dishes, in case it was someone else and she had to hide.

It was an express delivery van. "There an Onion here?" the driver asked. "This is the address, but—"

"The owner has a sense of humor," Geode said quickly. "Sometimes he puts odd names on things. I'll take it."

The man handed over a small package. Sure enough, it was addressed to Œnone.

The van moved off. Geode brought the package inside. "It's for you," he said, giving it to her.

"Me? But, Geode, no one knows I'm here, except—"

"It's from Mid." He showed her where the return address listed MIDDLE KINGDOM ENTERPRISES.

Amazed, she opened the package.

It was a beautiful gold brooch made in the likeness of a dragonfly, with gossamer wings and turquoise eyes.

"Oh, my Lord!" she breathed, enchanted. "But this can't be mine! I'm not the dragonfly! May is! I must tell her."

"Mid doesn't make mistakes like that," he said. "He must want you to have it."

"Can I call out safely?" she asked.

"Yes, but—"

She went to the phone in the kitchen. "May's number—do we know it?"

"Yes." May had given him a slip with the number, just in case. He gave it to Œnone.

She dialed it. In a moment she was talking to a surprised May Flowers. "This gold dragonfly arrived, and you're the bold day flyer, so I know it is for you," she said.

May laughed. "Œnone, Mid may have gotten us confused symbolically, but he would have addressed it to me if he wanted me to have it. He likes you; this is his way of saying it. That brooch is yours. Ask Geode."

"Thank you. I did." Œnone looked across at Geode. "She says you were right." Then she returned to May. "Oh, May, you must see it! I've never had anything so lovely!"

"Wear it," May said. "I will surely see you soon enough."

Œnone hung up, and saw about pinning the brooch to her dress, awed. To Geode, she looked yet more beautiful in her delight.

❖ 31 ❖

M AY HUNG UP the phone. So Mid had adopted Œnone! That was good, very good. It simplified things. For Mid did not do that casually. Once he adopted a person, he stood by that person as long as that person stood by him. Œnone would not be thrown back into the cruel world she had left.

Things were definitely looking up, after the horror of yesterday. May was now free of Bull, for whom she mourned not a bit, and free of her apprehension about AIDS, and now Mid had endorsed her action with Œnone. All that remained was the firefly. And Frank, of course. If only he weren't married!

But first she would rest. She had had a hard night, and her elation about its outcome could not sustain her indefinitely. She would sleep today, and return to work tomorrow.

The phone woke her late in the afternoon. It was Frank. "There's a lead on what could be the firefly," he said. "I don't know if it's solid, and I'm tied up with paperwork today and tomorrow. Are you interested?"

"I am," she said, trying to shake the fog of remaining sleep from her head.

"I'll stop by and give you the details in half an hour, when I get off duty."

"Thank you." He could have done it on the phone, but she didn't choose to point that out. She wanted to see him.

When he arrived, she was in a bathrobe, fresh from the shower and feeling better. "Come in, Frank."

"Actually, I need to take a statement from you," he said. "We got a call—someone saw your black eye."

"My estranged husband returned and gave it to me," she said evenly. "I managed to get rid of him, and haven't seen him since."

"Do you wish to prefer charges?"

"No. I merely want never to see him again."

He made a note on his pad. "Thank you, Ms. Flowers."

"So we are covered," she said.

"Yes. I'll file a routine report."

"What is the firefly lead?"

"Someone saw a monster serpent down in the Heatherwood section. We have had odd reports from that region before, and none have amounted to anything. But when we get a call, we have to investigate, or make sure it's covered. It's probably just imagination, but if our firefly is a serpent—"

"Give me the address, and I will go there tomorrow morning."

He gave her the address. Then: "I've been thinking about something you said this morning."

"Anything I said, I meant, Frank."

"Well, you didn't actually say it. You implied—and I told you I was married. But after that—"

"You wanted me."

"You got it," he said, managing to flush. "I cursed myself for a fool. I mean, my marriage is on notice, and the moment something happens to ruin this job—I guess I don't want to be single, and that's why I hung on so long. I know you had a bad experience in your marriage—"

"If you're attracted to me now, in this condition, you might continue to be when I recover."

"I don't care how you look!" he said. "You're an independent cuss, and I like that, and you know where you're headed, and I like that. But

you know, if I lose my job, it'll be hell to get another, so it isn't as if
I'm any bargain. So about all I can do is be honest and say yes, you
turn me on, and if you ever repeat your offer—"

He broke off, for she had opened her bathrobe. She wore nothing
beneath, other than a small elastic bandage on her left nipple. "I think
I anticipated you, Frank," she said. "I'm forty, and I'm no slender
starlet, but if you like what you see, it's available."

"I like it. But you're still bruised—that breast must hurt—"

"Yes, I would rather not be touched there yet. But elsewhere, yes."

"Now?" He hardly seemed to believe it.

"Do you want me now?"

"Oh, God, I do!"

"I have discovered that I do not truly enjoy the single life either,"
she said. "I also remember my thoughts when under the influence of
those pheromones. It occurs to me that men are not all the same."

"That's for sure!"

"Take me, Frank. I want it to be you."

"You got it!" He stripped. He embraced her and kissed her, standing, trying not to press against her sore breast. He had an erection
which seemed to be both his pride and his embarrassment; evidently
his wife had not been much for doing things by daylight.

May did not ordinarily go into matters like this, and her interest in
sex was not great. But there was something she needed to know about
Frank, and this seemed the best way to learn it. "How would you like
me?"

"Oh, damn, I don't want to put my weight on you. You want to be
on top?"

"I'm really not the aggressive type, in this regard."

"Are you sure you want to—?"

"Frank, let me explain. Sex per se has never interested me much,
and Bull made it a point to make it unpleasant. But I would do
anything for one I love, and it pleases me to be honestly desired by one
I respect, at this age. You will have to do it, but I will cooperate to the
best of my ability. I want you to enjoy it."

"But if you don't—"

"I enjoy having you enjoy it. That's sufficient."

He tried to laugh. "You are so honest it gets painful. But that's
another thing I like about you. You don't pussyfoot around; I know
where I stand with you."

"There are men who prefer deception." *Or violence,* she thought.

"Maybe if we sit."

"As you wish, Frank."

He sat on the edge of the bed. She tried to spread her legs and put her knees down outside his hips, facing him, but the bed was so bouncy and unsteady that it threatened to dump them. "Maybe if you turn around," he said.

Bull had had her do that. But she kept her face set and turned, and sat carefully on him. His member came up between her legs, and she used her hand to guide it in. Again she was ready, wet inside, even though neither the position nor the act was truly to her liking.

He reached around her to take her breasts in his hands, hefting them as if they were two great nuggets of gold, squeezing the right but not the left. "Oh, May, you are some woman!" he whispered.

Then he was climaxing, his arms locking around her body just under her breasts, his member bucking inside her. "Damn, I came too soon!" he exclaimed.

"It's all right, Frank." *There had been no violence.*

"But I wanted you to have it too! Damn, I'm sorry, May! I didn't realize how excited I was!"

She smiled. "It is a woman's dream to be so sexy that a man climaxes without control. That seems to have been the case."

"You're awful good about it. I let you down."

"No, you didn't, Frank." She stood a bit, to disengage, and reached to the side of the bed to take a tissue to tuck into her crotch. She handed another back to him. Then she turned and pushed him gently down on the bed. She joined him there, lying on her side. "Just kiss me."

They kissed, and this was the essence. Bull had twisted meanness with sex and alcohol, and she was well wary of that. Frank had just enjoyed the sex, even losing control. No alcohol, no violence. He had wanted her to like it, and had been chagrined rather than aggressive when it went wrong. That showed his underlying nature in the way that counted most for her. Perhaps in time, with him, she would enjoy the act. Certainly she enjoyed the relationship.

"I messed up," he said. "But even so, it's the best sex I've had in years. You're special, May."

And that sent a thrill through her that the sex had not. She kissed him again. "Me too. You too."

He laughed, then sobered. "I thought you were joking about it being your best when it was nothing, but then I remembered what your husband did to you. May, it gets a lot better than that!"

"It already is."

They lay there, not talking further, kissing, and kissing again. It had looked very much like love before; now there was no reasonable doubt.

But soon he had to dress and go, for there were appearances to maintain. She remained pleasant. There really was no sexual meanness in Frank; now she was sure. He was safe to be with.

In the morning she donned dark glasses and went to the address in Heatherwood and talked with the man who had seen the giant snake. There was no doubt he was shaken, but considerable doubt as to what he had seen. The man had gone to shoot a raccoon he thought had been raiding his property, and gone near a giant live oak tree, and the coon had become the monster serpent. He had fled, and reported it. He had a fear of snakes, and always killed them when he saw them, but this one had been a monster of such terror he didn't dare get close.

May went next to talk with the owner of the property on which the big tree stood. There was a nice two-story house virtually embraced by the branches of the oak. She paused to admire the tree; it was a phenomenal sight, its massive limbs twisting out in all directions. She remembered how she had climbed on branches like that as a child; this seemed to be an eminently friendly and climbable tree.

Then she went to the door and knocked. A startlingly pretty young woman answered, with lustrous black tresses and a figure such as a starlet would envy.

"Excuse me, I am a journalist investigating odd appearances," May said. "There was a report of a large serpent in this vicinity, and I wondered whether you had any information."

The young woman laughed. "Josh, another one!" she called back into the house. Then, to May: "Come in; we'll explain."

May entered and was introduced to the woman and her husband and her husband's children, a boy and a girl. He was Josh Pinson, and she was Brenna, his second wife after he was widowed.

"There is what I call an ambience here," the man explained. "The property was reputed to be haunted, before I moved here. The neighbors know that, and at times their imagination gets the better of them. I assure you, there is no giant snake, only a giant tree."

He wasn't lying, May sensed, but neither was he telling the truth. It was as though he had a cover story for something that was nobody else's business. Certainly there was no hostility here.

She probed further. "There have been reports of some kind of monster in this county. One that leaves the skin and bones of animals. Do you know anything about that?"

Both Josh and Brenna were mystified. "Nothing like that here," Josh said. "I really doubt that it could happen here."

Again a partial truth, but no ill intent. How curious! Yet she had a deep feeling that it was all right, that the firefly she sought was not in this vicinity, and had never been. She thanked them and departed, mystified. Perhaps someday, when this was over, she might call on them again, and try to fathom what they were so amicably concealing.

So this had been a false lead, but useful in getting her painlessly back into the swing of her investigation. It also reminded her that none of them had any notion of the appearance of the firefly. A giant serpent? That was possible. Certainly it seemed to be almost silent, yet powerful enough to kill and consume a man in a few hours. Did it swallow its prey, then disgorge the bones? No, not when the clothing was undisturbed. And what of the pheromones? She had never heard of a serpent using them to capture prey. So it seemed unlikely.

Pheromones. That reminded her of sex. She had had sex twice in the past week, after having none for three years. Bull had forced it on her, horribly. Frank—she had really led him into it. She had embraced him when virtually nude, thereby giving him a notion which it seemed was easy to give a man, and then had been receptive to his rather fumbling advance. In fact she had offered, and then anticipated, being virtually eager to do it. That was entirely unlike her. She had thought it was just the memory of the sexual ambience of the monster, and her desire to learn whether Frank was safe to love. But could she have been affected by lingering pheromones from her close encounter with the firefly? That seemed possible; sex had suffused the very air in the firefly's vicinity. She had been there, and then Frank had been there, breathing in that atmosphere. How long did it take to wear off?

But she thought it was more than that. Sex normally had an object. When the pheromones had aroused her, she had thought of Frank— and he had evidently thought of her. They had fixed on each other, and that fixation had remained after the urgency faded. Frank, with his tottering marriage to a wife who was more interested in security and appearances than in him. May herself, still recovering from the shock of bestial sex. It was as though she had a need to eclipse that awful event with something proper, or at least pleasurable.

And it had been a pleasure, she realized. Not the detail of it; she had always found sex to be a messy business at best. But the closeness, the camaraderie of the joint effort. A man, it seemed, could not think straight when he had an erection, but once that was out of the way, he became tolerable company. She had appreciated, for the moment, being a sex object. Making a man so eager that he literally could not contain himself. That was a kind of power. But then, with the edge off his physical passion, she had been able to be with him in an unstressed condition. It was that which she most appreciated. In fact, what he had taken to be his error, climaxing too swiftly, had made him apologetic and receptive. It would have been worse had he taken half an hour, prolonging the agony, forcing her to a pretense of pleasure, making it unreal. As it was, no pretense had been necessary.

Frank was at heart a gentle man. She valued that. Perhaps there would be occasion in the future for a longer engagement, with greater privacy, so that the sex would take up a smaller proportion of it.

She thought of Jade Brown—Œnone. It was obvious that she had done something similar with Geode. But he was impotent. Had she been able to get around that, or did she like it that way? May would be able to live with an impotent man, but she had the impression that Œnone was of another nature. Sometimes the least prepossessing women had the greatest appetites. That story of Œnone—May had had no idea the woman could express herself like that! Œnone had improved dramatically in appearance, and it wasn't just the clothing May had provided for her; there was now almost a glow to her, an intensity, an inner joy. She was, perhaps, a woman in love.

Well, it did happen. May was no one to deny it. She had thought she could live alone the rest of her life and like it; certainly she had not seen in Frank any prospect for romance! Then Bull had come, and the firefly, and suddenly things had changed. Whether it was her realization that she was not secure from brutality, so needed the protection of a man, or whether it was the ambience of the firefly and its incitement to lust—whatever it was, she wanted Frank, and would do what she had to to please him.

Meanwhile, Œnone remained at the Middle Kingdom Ranch, and would need more food. Also, May was curious to see that dragonfly brooch. It was perhaps as important to her as to Œnone, because it vindicated her judgment in putting Œnone there at the house. So she would do some more shopping now, and drive out there, nominally on routine business, actually on emotional business.

This time when she drove onto the ranch she spied an armadillo walking along the edge. She slowed, then stopped, watching the armored brown animal. She understood that they rolled up into tight balls when frightened. This one merely paused, then moved on toward the fence when it saw that she was not pursuing it. It found a low spot, pawed away some dirt, and squeezed under. Then it was gone through the trees, vanishing in the jungle.

If a solid and relatively clumsy armadillo could so readily disappear here, what of the firefly? They seemed to be no closer to catching it than they had been before. Should she volunteer to stay another night in the cabin, to lure it in?

She shuddered, but pursued the thought relentlessly. Maybe if this time she could do it with Frank. Then, when the firefly approached, they could do the inevitable sex, then wait alertly for the thing and finally make an end of it. The notion had its perverse appeal. Maybe she would suggest it to Frank. He was almost certain to like it.

She drove on, and came to the lovely house. Geode came out to meet her, and then Œnone, when they saw that it was her. She delivered her groceries, then looked at the woman.

The brooch was there, pinned to her décolletage on the left, calling attention to the swell of the breast. Jade Brown had been a mouse; Œnone was a lovely creature. "It is beautiful," May said. "And so are you."

"You made it possible," Œnone said.

May glanced around. Geode was somewhere else at the moment, not having much interest in groceries, male fashion. "I know it is none of my business, but have you—?"

"Soon."

"I'm glad."

She went outside. Geode was there, just standing. "We seem to be back to square one on the firefly," May said.

"Cyrano's working on it. It will feed again in two days. He will wait for it at the cabin."

"Not alone, surely!"

"He says it won't come if he isn't alone. He knows what he's doing."

"Surely so! But so, it seems, does the firefly."

Geode shrugged. Œnone emerged. "Thank you so much," she said, like a hostess to a departing guest.

"You're welcome," May said, smiling as she returned to her car. Indeed Œnone was welcome! Perhaps it had been her story which had pointed up the distinction between a worthless man and a good one, so that May's mind had sought and found that distinction between Bull and Frank.

She waved as she drove around the loop and out. Œnone, now standing beside Geode with one arm around him, waved back.

❖ 32 ❖

ŒNONE WATCHED MAY go, feeling warm. The woman had done her the courtesy to inquire, and she had answered. Now it was in the open, in its covert way, and she felt free to be close to Geode in company. May had set it up; she deserved to see it.

They had had an excellent tour of the ranch, this time using a canoe to pass around some of the edge of it in the reed- and water-lily-overgrown Tsala Apopka Lake, and along the side of the Withlacoochee River. They had seen an alligator, and a big swimming turtle, but no firefly. Geode liked all living things, even alligators, so now Œnone did too. He had shown her more of his world, and now it was time for her to show him more of hers.

They had supper, then went to his room for the night. "Leave the light off," she said. "This one requires imagination."

He shrugged in that way he had. "Lie on the bed, without your clothes," she said. "I will sit here without mine."

He obeyed. Naked, they shared the bed, in their separate positions, as the darkness became complete.

She took his left hand in her left. "You may not like this story," she said.

He merely squeezed her hand. He liked anything she told him, as long as she stayed with him. That was, of course, a great part of what attracted her to him.

The Trial was well advanced. The Prosecution had presented its case and fairly damned the man; there seemed to be no doubt he was guilty, especially since he had confessed. But the Defense insisted on entering a plea of Not Guilty for him. It seemed that the Defense had a secret weapon, and the Jury was becoming quite curious as to what it might be.

"Your Honor," the lawyer said, "the Defense wishes to present only one piece of evidence, but it is not in our possession. We ask that it be subpoenaed."

"What is it?" the Judge inquired, curious himself.

"Your Honor, it is the 8-mm recording of the Victim's testimony."

There were dropped jaws in the Jury box, and a murmur of astonishment in the Audience. The Judge blinked and reflexively rubbed his ear. "*Whose* testimony?"

"The Victim's. The film is in the possession of the Prosecution."

The Judge suppressed further reaction and turned to the Prosecution. "You have such a film?"

The lawyer for the Prosecution looked abashed. "We interviewed her, of course, Your Honor, but elected not to show the film. She is, after all, a child."

"I know that!" the Judge snapped testily. "If she wasn't, there would be no Trial! Why didn't you show it?"

"We felt it would be inappropriate, Your Honor, and we did not need it to establish our case."

"What is the general nature of it?"

"The Victim, in her own words, establishes the guilt of the Defendant beyond any doubt whatsoever."

"Then what the hell was inappropriate about it?" the Judge demanded. He was quickly irritated by irregularities occurring in his orderly courtroom.

"We just feel it is unnecessary, and could be awkward," the lawyer said inadequately.

The Judge turned to the lawyer for the Defense. "You wish to show a film which will only confirm the guilt of your client?"

"Yes, Your Honor."

"Are you mad? What kind of defense is this?"

"Your Honor, if you will allow the film to be played in its entirety, I believe its relevance to the Defense will be apparent. The Defense asks that this film be shown."

"I find this just about impossible to understand! I remind you that you are obliged to do the best job you can for your client, to establish his innocence of the charge against him. If you instead try to undermine his case and cause him to be convicted, you are betraying your trust and could be held in contempt and disbarred. Do I make myself clear?"

"Yes, Your Honor. I am doing my best for my client. I understand the child has a virtually eidetic memory for detail, and that her statement is most comprehensive."

The Judge threw up his hands. "Turn over the film," he said to the Prosecution.

"But, Your Honor!" the Prosecution protested. "This is a travesty!"

"I will determine that without your assistance," the Judge said grimly. "As far as I'm concerned, you're both crazy! Turn over the film."

"Exception!" the Prosecution said.

"Noted," the Judge said, giving him a curious look.

So the controversial motion picture film was shown in court. The Judge and Jury were mesmerized by it, and appalled.

Nymph was five years old. She had big green eyes and a mop of orangy-brown hair, and was a cute and active girl. But she was pensive as the lady interviewer introduced herself and explained that they were making a picture of this, so that the little girl would not have to go to the big, scary courtroom. "But where is Mad?" she asked plaintively.

"Do you mean Maddock Stoller?" the interviewer inquired.

"Yes, Mad. My friend. Why can't I talk to him instead?"

"Because we must talk about him," the interviewer explained. "It is not nice to talk about a person when he's listening."

"Oh." Nymph considered. "Is he in trouble? Someone said he was in big trouble."

"He may be," the lady said cautiously. "But perhaps what you say will help him."

"Oh, yes, I want to help him!" the little girl exclaimed, brightening. "He's my friend!"

"What you must do is tell me, in your own way, exactly how Mad was your friend," the lady said.

"Okay," the girl agreed brightly. She began to speak, and so eager was she to help her friend that she needed only occasional prompting by the interviewer. With the naiveté of her youth, she held nothing back.

"I was hiding from George. He's my big brother. He was mean to me. So I went into this house across the tracks where we weren't supposed to go so he couldn't find me, and there was this nice man on a bed watching TV."

"This was Maddock?" the interviewer inquired.

"Yes, only I didn't know him yet. I just met him."

"Of course, Nymph. I was just getting it straight."

"He looked at me. He was a grown-up man with sort of frowzy hair and some—some—"

"Beard?"

"Yes. The way Daddy gets when he doesn't shave over the week-end."

"And what did the man do?"

The child assumed the aspect of a grown man, and mimicked his words with uncanny precision, and then her own. She seemed for the moment to become the man, and herself of the episode, her posture changing with her voice.

'Aren't you in the wrong house, miss?'

'I'm hiding from my mean brother. Don't tell him I'm here.'

'But won't your folks miss you?'

'Not till six, when they come home from work. I gotta hide from George till then.'

"You are describing your conversation with Mad," the interviewer interjected.

"Yes. Just like it happened, close as I can remember."

"Very good, Nymph. What did he do then?"

"He sat up and put his feet down on the floor. 'But a cute little girl like you shouldn't be in a place like this. Something might happen to you.'

'Something'll happen to me if George catches me! Promise you'll hide me if he comes.'

'I promise. No one will hurt you here. What's your name?'

'Nymph. What's yours?'

'Mad.'

Nymph laughed, showing how she had laughed then, with that same marvelous accuracy. 'You're mad?'

Nymph smiled a tolerant adult smile, emulating the man she described. She was a consummate little actress. 'I'm Maddock. But that's such an awful name, they just call me Mad.'

'Mad,' she said, evidently liking it. 'That's a funny name.'

'What does your brother do to you?'

'He makes me get on all fours and take down my panties and he pokes a candle or something in my bottom. It hurts.'

'In your bottom? You mean where you use the toilet?' The emulated man seemed to have trouble finding appropriate vocabulary.

'Yes. He says he'll make me shit backward. He's mean.'

'He's mean,' Mad agreed, and she seemed to like him more for siding with her. 'You should tell your mother, to make him stop.'

'Nuh-uh! She'll punish me for lying again!'

Nymph emulated Mad, making a sort of face. 'Your father, then.'

'He's mostly too busy. But he's nice when he has time. He plays with me.'

'That's good. Maybe next time he's playing with you, you can tell him.'

'I don't know. Maybe he'd get mad like my mother.'

'Why should he do that?'

'Well, what he does, it's sorta like what George does, only it's fun with Daddy.'

'The way he plays with you? He wouldn't put a candle up your bottom!'

'No, he's got something else. He keeps it in his pants. It's hot and not as hard as a candle. But he never quite does it. Just when we're having real fun, and I'm going to sit on his thing, he changes his mind and sends me away, and I don't know what I did wrong. I wish I knew what it is, so it would be okay.' The girl stood, and turned to the interviewer as if she were the man. The interviewer had a funny expression, as if she were trying to swallow a bad-tasting worm without making a face. 'Maybe you can tell me, Mad. What's the matter with me?'

'Kid, you better get out of here before it gets out of hand!' she said for the man.

She began to cry. 'Now I've made you mad too, and I don't even know why!'

'Damn it, kid, you're not supposed to know why! I'm sorry I made you cry.'

'All I want is to know what it is,' the remembered girl said. 'How come George hurts me with a candle, and Daddy won't play?'

The girl put on an uncomfortable face. 'Look, kid, there's things little girls aren't supposed to know. A fellow can get in bad trouble just for telling them.'

'You know!' she exclaimed. 'You know what it is!'

'I know,' he agreed. 'I think you need to get out of that house, Nymph.'

'But why?'

'It's hard to explain.'

'I can keep a secret!' she told him.

'Listen, Nymph, I got in trouble once because I did something with a girl. She was a lot older than you, but still too young. I don't want to get in trouble again.'

'I won't tell! I won't tell! Tell me, and I won't tell!'

He shook his head. 'You really want to know, don't you?'

'Yes, I really want to know! Then I could tell George to bug off, and Dad would like me better.'

'A secret,' he said.

'A big fat secret!' she agreed.

'Okay, I'll tell you, but that's all. Your father wants to have sex with you, but doesn't dare, and your brother wants to, but doesn't know how.'

'What's sex?'

'That's when a man and a woman—a grown man and grown woman—get together and do it. Children aren't supposed to.'

She didn't know what he meant. A look of great perplexity showed on her face. 'What do they do?'

'They take off their clothes and lie on a bed and, well, they do it.'

'What do they do? I don't understand!'

'Well, he puts his—I guess you don't know the words—his thing in her thing.'

'Why?'

'Because it's a hell of a lot of fun, kid!'

'You mean like when Daddy plays with me?'

'Yes, only more so. A lot more so.'

'I want to do it!' she told him.

"You said that?" the interviewer interjected, startled. She still hadn't quite managed to swallow her worm.

"Yes. I knew he knew how, so I wanted him to do it with me so I'd know how. Wasn't that right?"

The interviewer seemed to be having a bit of trouble with her objectivity, but she got hold of herself and finally got the worm all the way down. "It was natural curiosity, perhaps right for you. Please continue. I did not mean to interrupt."

Immediately the child resumed her posing, playing the parts of both Nymph and Mad.

'You can't do it,' he protested. 'You're a child.'

She began to cry again. 'You promised to tell me!'

'I did tell you, Nymph. But to get any farther, I'd have to show you, and that's real trouble.'

'I won't tell!' she said. 'Show me!'

He shook his head. 'Damn, I can't believe this. Okay, kid, I'll show you. Remember, you promised. If you tell, I'll be in big trouble.'

'I won't tell! Show me, show me!'

'Okay, I'll show you.' Nymph paused as if uncertain how to proceed.

"He showed you?" the interviewer prompted grimly.

"Yes, only I don't know how to show it. I don't have pants."

"Just tell what happened."

"Okay. He stood up, and took off his pants and shirt. Then he took off his underpants. He had a thing like Daddy's. 'This is my cock. That's what goes in the woman.'

She stared at it. 'It goes where she poops?'

'No. She has another place, in front of that.'

'Where she pees?'

'No, behind that. Right between the two.'

'I don't think I have a place.'

'Yes, you do. You just haven't found it yet. But when you grow up, you will.'

Nymph put her hands to her dress, evidently about to remove it. "You don't have to do that!" the interviewer said quickly. "Just tell it."

"Okay. I took off my dress and panties so I could feel. 'I don't think there's a place.'

'Take my word, Nymph, it's there.'

'Show me.'

'Nymph, this is getting hairy. I like you, really I do, but it's not right to touch you.'

Nymph looked at the interviewer. "But I saw that maybe he really wanted to, the way Daddy did even when he said no. 'Maybe we can play the game Daddy plays with me, only you can show me what's supposed to happen when he stops.'

'It's not right for a man to touch a child,' he said. 'I showed you, but I can't touch you.'

"But then I knew this was a sort of game, because Daddy played like that," Nymph explained to the interviewer. 'Let me climb up on you, and you don't have to touch me, just tell me hot or cold.'

'Hot or cold?'

'Hot if I'm right, cold if I'm not.'

'Oh.' He thought about it. 'Okay, Nymph. I won't touch you at all, so you can stop whenever you want to. But even so, it has to be a secret.'

'Sure.' Nymph glanced at the interviewer. "I was real pleased, because I knew I'd maybe find out something."

"And did you find out something?" the interviewer inquired softly.

"Gee, yes! But it's hard to—maybe if you lay like him, I could show you."

The interviewer hesitated, then evidently decided that duty lay with acquiescence. She was obliged to elicit the fullest possible testimony, without alarming the child. She lay on the floor, supine.

"Yes, like that," Nymph agreed. "Only put your arms up behind your head."

The interviewer did so. The child climbed up on her and sat on her legs. 'Am I warm?'

'Getting warm,' he agreed.

She poked at the interviewer's groin. "What are you doing?" the interviewer inquired in a controlled voice.

"His thing was there," Nymph explained. "I need it."

"Pretend it is there." The interviewer closed her eyes and clenched her jaws.

"Okay. I saw his thing was up on his belly, and bigger than it was. I scooted up and touched it. It got real hard and hot when I squoze it." she made motions as if handling the pretend member. 'Warm?'

'Warm,' he said. 'That goes into the woman, and when things are right, it helps her make a baby inside her.'

'Gee.' This seemed to be real news to her. 'Like magic!'

'Like magic,' he agreed.

She felt it some more, and made an interested face. "What is happening?" the interviewer asked.

"There was a drop of water at the end, real slippery," Nymph explained. 'What's that?'

'It makes it slick so it can go in better,' he said. 'She gets wet too, so it doesn't hurt.'

The child started fidgeting. The interviewer, evidently uncomfortable in more than one sense, inquired again: "What was happening?"

"I was getting really excited, like when Daddy played with me. I felt my place, and it was sort of slippery. 'I want to do it,' she told him.

He sort of laughed. 'Welcome to try, kid. It won't fit.'

"So I nudged up some more, and sort of sat on his thing, and it felt sort of good there, all hot and round. But it didn't go in, because it was sidewise. 'I can't do it,' she said.

'I told you, it's too big for you. Grown women have larger places, so they can handle it, but it would hurt a little girl.'

'I want to do it,' she said again, excited. She glanced up at the interviewer. "This was where Daddy always quit, when I played with him in his lap and his thing was there, and I didn't want Mad to quit, and I was afraid he would."

'It's no go,' he said. 'But anyway, you're at the wrong angle. It goes in endwise.'

'Oh.' The girl pantomimed again, incomprehensibly, provoking another query by the interviewer, who evidently wished this would finish in a hurry.

"I lifted up his thing, but then it was up in front of me. I tried to lie down on top of him, so my place was in line, but I couldn't do anything that way. So I sort of got up, and squatted, like having a poop, and held his thing up straight, and sort of sat down on it, just like Daddy wouldn't let me do." The pantomime made an almost visible penis, erect and huge, in her hands. 'Where's the place?'

'It's right there in the middle,' he said.

"I held it there and sat down more, but then my body went back and they weren't in line again. So I moved up again, and tried it again, and again, and then I found the place, sort of leaning forward and holding it right there." Again she suited her action to her words, her body showing exactly how it was, angled at about forty-five degrees while she clutched the big hot thing with both hands and held it between her legs. 'Am I warm?'

'You're hot!' he said. 'It's there!'

"So I pushed against it, and sort of felt where it should go, and it was super big and hot, and it wouldn't go in. I got my finger there, and sort of spread the slippery stuff around, and it went in a little." She poked under her dress with her finger.

'It's too big for you, Nymph,' he said. 'It's right there, but it would hurt you to get it in.'

'I want to get it in,' she insisted. 'I want to be a real woman so Daddy will like me.'

'I think you've got it in all you're going to. At least now you know how, for when you're big enough.'

'I want it in,' she said. "I poked the slippery around some more, and pushed harder, and got it in some more. It hurt some, but I was real excited because I knew I was getting real warm." She demonstrated, while the interviewer, involuntarily playing the part of the man, visibly gritted her teeth behind her fixed smile.

'Look, kid, you better stop,' he said.

'You promised!' she said. 'You promised to show me!'

'What I mean is, I'm coming,' he said. 'I mean, there's going to be fluid coming out of it, and if you don't want it on you, get away.'

'Does it hurt?'

'No, it just spurts. If you hold it tight there, it may go right into you. So if you don't want it, get away quick.'

'No, I want it, I want it! I want it in me! I want to be a real woman!'

He gave up the argument, which he had evidently not been too keen on winning anyway. 'Then hang on, kid!'

"I hanged on, and kept his thing right at my place with my hand around it, and it swelled up even more, and then it sort of shook, and I felt the stuff coming out of it and into me. I felt it going through where my hand was, like in a garden hose, the water on. I held it real tight, but a little white stuff sort of leaked out. I squoze my bottom real hard, to keep it tight, and I felt real great when I felt that stuff going into me. I was a real woman!" She smiled beatifically. The interviewer's expression was unreadable.

Then his thing got less hard. 'It's over, Nymph,' he said. 'I came, and you got it.'

But when his thing got softer, she grabbed it with both hands and shoved it into her. "Because it was all wet now and smaller and it didn't hurt so much. I kept cramming it in, and I got it all in me." She sat down hard on the interviewer's pelvis, making the lady wince. 'I got it! I got it!' she cried. 'It's all in me, the whole thing! See! See!'

'But it's over,' he said. 'That's all there is.'

'But it wasn't in me,' she argued. 'Just the juice went in. I got the real thing in me now.'

The girl paused. The interviewer, still trying to mask a certain discomfort with the proceedings, prompted her. "And that was all?"

"No, I wouldn't let it be all," Nymph said. "It wasn't in me when it went. I wasn't a real woman."

"But can you be a real woman, at your age?"

"Yes! Yes! I had to, so Daddy would like me better, and George couldn't get me."

"And what happened next?" the interviewer inquired with simulated mild curiosity.

"I held it in me, and it was real soft and slippery and it didn't hurt at all, it felt real good. 'This can't be all,' I said. 'I want more!'

'You can try it, I guess,' he said. 'Put your finger down where it's slippery and rub, right in front of it.'

Nymph still sitting astride the interviewer, put her hand down at her crotch, demonstrating. She touched herself, through her panties, and rubbed slowly. 'Here?'

'Yes. You'll know the place when you find it. It will feel good.'

Nymph experimented, reenacting the experience. Then she smiled angelically. 'There! There! It feels good!'

'Keep doing that, and maybe you'll feel what a real woman feels.'

The interviewer attempted to move the narration along. "So then you didn't have to stay with him anymore?"

"No, no! I kept him in me! He—it—his thing was getting big again, and hard, and I knew if it got out it couldn't get in again, so I stayed real close and didn't let it out, and I kept rubbing, and it felt real good." The child was accelerating the pace, rubbing her panties faster and harder. "I kept stroking it the right way, and his thing kept getting bigger, but it was so slippery because of the stuff that came out of it before, it didn't hurt, and the bigger it got, the better it felt, and I knew if I could keep it in me I'd be a real woman this time!"

The interviewer gave up. "And what did Mad say?"

'You really are getting there, Nymph! I think you're going to come.'

'Yes, yes! I'm coming, I'm coming! I want to come! I want to make warm stuff come out of me!'

'No, a woman doesn't do that. She just has a very good feeling when the man does. He gives it, she takes it.'

'I'll take it! I'll take it!'

Now the child's action was feverish. She bounced around as she rubbed her front, and it was evident that she was getting a real reaction in the course of the reenactment. Then, impatient with the panties, she put her hand down inside and into her cleft, and stroked directly.

"But wasn't Mad's thing too big to stay when it got all the way hard?" the interviewer asked desperately.

"Yes, I couldn't keep it all in me, only the end of it," Nymph confessed, still rubbing vigorously. "It felt awful big and awful tight and awful good. I tried to hold it in, but it just got longer and I couldn't. So I just sat on it as much as I could, as tight as I could." She rose a little on her knees, so that her weight was no longer directly on the interviewer. "Oh, I wish you had a Cock!" she exclaimed.

The interviewer seemed to give herself up for lost. "Pretend that I do," she suggested. "What happened next?"

"I got real hot, and it was so good, it just—aahh!" the child went into an evident climax, her little thighs flexing, her torso shaking.

'You did it!' he said. 'And you've got me into it too. I feel you coming, I'm coming again too! Hang on!' And his thing swelled up like before, and he pushed some, in and out and she hung on, but it was sliding so, she thought it'd come out. 'Lie down on me!' he said. 'Don't let me hurt you! I'll try to keep it slow!'

The child lay down on the woman, her legs spread wide, trailing down across the woman's hips and outside her thighs. Her body moved in an unmistakable rhythm. "And he shoved, and maybe it hurt some, but it was so good too, and I kept it in, and the stuff came out of it again, and into me."

'Now I'm a real woman!' she exclaimed, flush with her victory.

'Now you are a real woman,' he agreed.

The girl put her little arms around the interviewer and hugged her. "It was so good! I just lay there while his thing got small again, and this time it was all right, because I was a real woman, I had done it, I had all his warm water in me, I knew what it was. It wasn't pee, it was sorta white and slippery, and it could make a baby inside my tummy, and I was a real woman for real now!"

Then she lifted her head to look at the interviewer's face. "Wasn't I?"

"Yes, dear, you were," the interviewer said with a straight face, though her lips were thin.

"And I went up on him and kissed him," Nymph continued suiting action to word, kissing the interviewer ardently on the mouth. "Because that's part of it, because I saw grown-ups doing it. I had his water in me, and I loved him just like a real woman."

"And that was all," the interviewer said, as if uncertain whether to believe it.

"Yes. That time." Nymph scrambled off her.

The interviewer got up, somewhat disheveled. She looked less confident than the child did. "There was another time?"

"Oh, sure!" Nymph said eagerly. "Lots of times! Every time I could, I sneaked back to his house, and if nobody else was there, we did it. It was a secret, see; he didn't tell anybody, and I didn't tell anybody. It was just us. It was real fun! We were Lovers!"

"What did you do with him, those other times?"

"Oh, everything!" Nymph said, delighted. "I licked his thing, and he licked my thing, and he made me come with his tongue, and I sucked on his thing and made him come, and we kissed and hugged and everything, and he said I was the best little woman he ever had!"

"He made you do these things?"

"No! I made him! I wanted to do everything a real woman did, and he said he wasn't really supposed to do it with anyone young like me, but I kept kissing him and grabbing his thing, and then he did it. I made him do everything!"

"How many times did you visit him?"

The child pondered. "Gee, I didn't count. Should I have counted?"

"No, dear, I was just curious. So you did it several times."

"Every day I could! Some days I couldn't get away from George. See, I didn't want him to see where I went, because then I couldn't hide from him, so I'd just run around and not go there, so he couldn't see. But I went lots of times—more than I can count." She ticked off her fingers, to ten, and again, not knowing the numbers. "Mad and I are in love."

"What?" For a moment the interviewer lost her composure, as if there had been one straw too many.

"In love," Nymph repeated. "Real women love. Make love, I mean. I didn't care about Daddy anymore, I didn't want him to do it with me, just Mad. Isn't that love?"

"It may be, dear." The woman took a deep breath. "How did it end?"

Now Nymph scowled. "George! George did it! He followed me when I wasn't looking, and he saw Mad, and he told Mommy, and now Mad's in jail, and it's all George's fault and I hate him, and can I go to him now?"

"You want to see Mad?"

"Yes! Can I see him now? I told you everything, so you know it's okay."

"What do you want to do with him, if you see him?"

"I want to get his thing in me again, and hug him and kiss him and everything and make it spout in me, and be his best woman! Just like before. Can I, huh, please? I really, really want to."

"I don't think that's possible."

Nymph stared at her. "I can't see him? But I told you everything! It's all right now!"

"I'm afraid it isn't. You see, Mad wasn't supposed to do those things with you. He will be put on trial."

"But you said if I told you, it would be all right! He would be out of trouble!"

"Nymph, you misunderstood. I said we had to talk about him, and that what you said might help him."

"Yes! Yes! I helped him! I told everything!"

The interviewer's face was grim. "I had thought you might say something else. Something that would help him. Unfortunately—"

Nymph's eyes widened in shock. "You mean our secret—it won't help him?"

"I'm afraid it won't, dear."

"You mean if I'd lied, it would have helped him?"

"I didn't say that, Nymph." The interviewer's eyes were moist, and her lower lip was trembling.

"I didn't help him, I hurt him!" Nymph exclaimed, catching on. "Oh, Mad! I'm sorry!" Her great innocent eyes overflowed as she started to cry. "Oh, Mad, I love you! I'm sorry!"

"So am I, dear," the interviewer murmured, wiping her eyes. "I wish I had never done this."

The courtroom was quiet as the videotape ended. The Jury sat stunned. Several jaws hung slack. One jurywoman was openly weeping. No one had anticipated a story like this.

The Judge refocused his eyes and mopped his brow with a handkerchief. "Is—is the Defense ready to proceed?"

"We are, Your Honor. We believe that this poignant tape establishes that though the Defendant may be technically guilty of the charge against him, he is not morally guilty. He did not seek the girl, he did not force his attention on her. He demurred at every stage, by her own testimony. It was entirely voluntary on her part. In fact, they were lovers, in the truest sense, age no barrier. The law may say he is guilty, but the law is sometimes an ass."

Several members of the Jury nodded their agreement.

Then he turned to the Jury. "If there is guilt here, then surely it is that of the father, who set her up by incestuously toying with her. And of her brother, who practiced sodomy on her with a candle. Remember, it was to escape that abuse that she first fled and found the Defendant. The Defendant never hurt her. He did only what she asked. He gave her what no other man did. He loved her. We may take issue with the manner of the expression of that love, but we cannot deny its reality. She came to him of her own accord, again and again, because what he offered her was so much better than what she received at home. *Her family should be on trial!*"

In the dark, Geode was quiet. "Are you asleep?" she asked softly. "No."

"Did you like the story?"

"No."

"Do you want me to go?"

"No." His hand squeezed hers.

"Then do as you will with me."

"What did the jury decide?"

She nodded in the darkness, then resumed her storytelling tone. "But in the end the Jury, reluctantly, had to go with the Law. They found Mad guilty. They urged leniency. But the Judge was constrained by a mandatory schedule of penalties. Mad was sentenced to a long term in prison."

"What happened to Nymph?"

"Nymph was returned to her family. She showed little emotion, and seldom spoke unnecessarily. The years passed. The first chance she had to get away from the family, she did so, by seducing and marrying the first eligible man she encountered. She maintained contact only with her brother, to whom she sent hostile cards every Christmas. He was afraid of her, and never responded. She became a nondescript housewife and was never heard from again."

"What happened to Mad?"

"Conventional criminals don't like child molesters. He was killed in prison. Nymph blamed herself for that; she had betrayed their Secret, and so had killed him."

· Geode lay silent. After a time she asked again: "Do you want me to go?"

For answer, he pulled her down beside him. He found her face and kissed her. "I think I can do it now," he said.

"Oh, Geode!" she exclaimed. Then she succumbed to a sudden storm of weeping.

Tightly embraced, they slept.

❖ 33 ❖

G EODE WOKE, FINDING Œnone in
his arms. She was sleeping. The bed under his shoulder remained wet
with her tears.

She had told him a remarkable story. There had never been any
doubt in his mind that it was her own. Œnone was a creature of stories
and of alternate identities, and he loved them all. Œnone, whose
husband had lost interest in her and taken another lover. Teensa, who
had been raped but came to love her attacker. Eve, the girl with
breasts. Nymph, with a love affair at age five. She was all of them, to
some degree, but mostly she was Œnone and Nymph.

But who was she now, with him? None of her stories had involved
impotence. He had told her he thought he could do it now, to have sex
with her, and he had thought so, but they hadn't tried it right away.
She had thought he wouldn't like her once he knew her story, but she
could tell him a thousand such stories and it wouldn't matter. Rather,
it *did* matter: it helped him to know her and to trust her. He wanted
to know all about her, because only then could he truly love her.

He thought about his impotence. He had always had it. He had
gotten erections when by himself, but in the presence of another
person, male or female, never. It had been known in his family from

255

the outset that sex was evil. Later there had been classes in school that said it wasn't, necessarily, but they had no force; he *knew*.

He had never had any social life. It wasn't that he was especially shy of girls, just that there wasn't much point, since he knew he couldn't do what it came to in the end. Mostly girls had evinced no interest in him, and he had ignored them. But in his reading and viewing he had come to understand that there was a world he was missing. Now he knew what it was and how it was supposed to be done, but he couldn't do it.

Once a girl had befriended him, perhaps because he was nonthreatening. In due course she had suggested sex, and he had explained that he couldn't get it hard. "I don't believe it!" she said. So they had gone to his bedroom when his folks were away, and locked the door, and undressed. He had never before seen a live girl naked. She was beautiful, with flaring hips and full breasts. He wished he could do it with her, but his penis remained limp.

"I'll take care of that!" she said confidently. She had fondled it, then put her mouth to it and sucked. He had liked the feeling, and his penis had enlarged a bit, but it didn't come close to an erection.

Finally she had given up. "I guess you really can't," she said frustrated.

"I want to," he said. "But I can't."

"There must be something wrong with you. Maybe a clogged nerve or something, so it won't get hard no matter what. It must be awful!"

"It's awful," he agreed.

She had been nice about it, but before long she had taken up with a boy who could get it hard. That had been Geode's closest approach to sex and to romance. No other girl had bothered to try. Boys had assumed he was queer, but he wasn't; he just couldn't get into sex.

But his animal friends had filled in. Not for sex; that was a lost cause. For companionship. They talked to him. After his time in the crazy house he kept as quiet about that as he did about sex. Not until Œnone had come on to him.

It had taken time to learn her full story, but he had realized right away that she was a lot like him in the matter of being alone. Of wanting companionship. Of wanting sex, and being unable. He could not express himself well, but she could; she just didn't have anyone to listen. She wanted sex, but no one wanted it with her. He wanted to listen, and to have the sex. They were an ideal couple. They should be able to do it together, just as Mad and Nymph had.

But his deep-down heart was slow to believe. It refused to accept what *he* believed. It was a different system, with its own rules. So he had disappointed Œnone as he had the girl. He hated that, but was powerless against it.

Still, Œnone had made progress. He loved her, and he felt that love driving inward, beating at the bastion of his resistance. *If you deny me her love, I'll die!* That was the message his love was sending, and daily it advanced against that hard core of resistance. His lifetime of lonely certainty was under siege by his days of new love, and love was gaining.

Now he supported that love actively. He ran his right hand down along her back, to her buttock. He felt resistance as it approached: the resistance of his core, claiming it was evil to touch a woman. He fought it, forcing his hand down. The resistance increased, taking the strength from his arm, but he put all he had into it and got it there. Her right buttock was cupped by his fingers, and it was the most wonderful thing he could imagine.

Œnone stirred. "You're making it," she whispered into his ear.

Then he knew that she had been awake, or had wakened while he moved his hand down, and been still, letting him do it. She wanted him to make it, and she was letting him try.

He put more force into his arm, willing his fingers to close. Slowly they did, and he had a handful of buttock. But the effort was so great that he was breathing hard.

She lifted her head, moved it over, and kissed him. "Keep going, Geode," she said.

He tried, but his arm would go no further. "I thought I could," he gasped.

"And you can!" she said. "I'll help you!"

She got up and bestrode him. "Nymph is here. You lie there and let her see if she can get it in."

He put his hands behind his head, and she handled his penis. But it did not get hard. She tried licking it and sucking on it, as the girl had done, but to no effect. She moved up, her thighs spread wide, and tried to fit his penis into her, but in its limpness it merely bent and bowed and didn't go in. Determined, she used both hands, and finally did manage to force it in, but even then it had no firmness.

"I thought I could," he said miserably. "I really want to!"

"I know you do," she agreed. "And so do I! But you can't be forced. *You* have to do it; I can't do it for you. I wish I could, but I can't."

Then he felt a small surge of stiffness. She felt it too. "Geode, you

start only when I express true affection and desire. But you are turned
off by any forcing, and by artificiality. You have to want me so much
you are ready to take me."

"I do want you!" he said.

"But there's an inner self that doesn't," she said.

"Yes. I'm trying, but it's resisting. Please don't be angry with me."

"Angry? Oh, Geode, I'm not angry! I love you and want you, and
I'll do anything to help you get there. But I don't know what will help!"

"I think slowly. I'll keep trying, if you have patience."

She smiled. "I don't have a lot of that! But I'll try."

They got up and dressed and had breakfast. Rain was threatening.
"Maybe you should stay in," he said.

"But I want to be with you, Geode!"

"But I want you to be safe and dry."

She started to argue, then reversed course. "Yes, of course. I've
been too pushy. I'll stay in, as you prefer."

He wanted to kiss her, but couldn't move to do it. She stood there,
just waiting, and he knew she wanted him to try.

He did try. He turned toward her, and his body became leaden, but
he forced one step and then another, approaching her. He reached
out, and his fingers caught hold of her sleeve, and he pulled himself
in to her as if grasping at a lifeline. Finally his face was next to hers.

What was this business, where he wanted to, and he knew she
wanted to, but he couldn't do it? He *had* to do it!

He forced his head down until finally his lips grazed hers. As a kiss
it was clumsy, but it *was* a kiss. He had made it!

"Take care of yourself, Geode," she said.

He nodded, and went out without further word. He was relieved
that she understood. Anyone else would have given up in disgust long
since.

He saw a figure a short distance from the drive. It seemed small and
human. He stepped out from the house, toward it, but it was gone.

He went on foot, because he didn't want the water to harm the
bicycle. He set off at a jog through the rain, following the trail that
circled the ranch. The mud squished underfoot, and soon his sneakers
were coated, but there was no help for it. He would wash them and dry
them out when he got back.

There was a small person walking along the trail ahead. He ran to
catch up, but the figure was gone. He continued at a fair pace, and
came to the edge of the main pine plantation.

He looked at the red pump. The rain would fill the tub for the horses; he didn't need to pump it this time. The black biting flies were out in force, forcing him to swat constantly. He glanced over at the pole barn—and saw a figure there, taking shelter from the rain. It was a child, a little girl. She had green eyes and auburn hair.

He approached, cautiously. "Who are you?"

She looked up at him. "I'm Nymph."

Then he knew she wasn't real. "I'm not supposed to talk with you."

"Lie down, take off your clothes. I won't tell."

"It's no good," he said. He turned away, and resumed his jog through the pines.

"You'll be sorry when I'm dead!" she called after him.

He ran on, pretending he hadn't heard. But she had scored. Dead? Why had she said that? He didn't want her dead! But there had been such a ring of conviction in her voice.

He spied a cottontail rabbit nibbling on blades of grass. The rabbit looked at him. "Why didn't you do it?" it asked him.

"I couldn't," he protested. "I wanted to, but I couldn't."

"If my kind ever let such a stupid excuse get in the way, we'd be extinct."

"It's more complicated with my kind. We don't have periods of heat."

"Oh. That must be confusing."

"It is." He ran on.

Near the point where the pine tree lane intersected the paved drive— where Œnone had remarked on it being a triangle—there were clusters of sandspurs. He'd have to chop them out soon, for they accelerated their production when fall came. Several got caught in his socks, and pricked his ankles with every step he took.

He stopped at the gate, pausing to pick them out. Naturally they stuck to his fingers. He cursed under his breath (that was another thing he couldn't do aloud); he needed to get tweezers or something he could carry with him, to pick out the sharp burrs conveniently. As it was, it took him several minutes to get them all out, while the light rain pattered down, wetting his back. Ordinarily the lost time would not have bothered him, but he wanted to get back to Œnone.

He glanced up through the gate, down the other leg of the L turn of the drive—and saw a car approaching. Œnone wouldn't buzz the car in, of course; he had to do that himself. Was it important?

The big gopher tortoise who lived at the corner poked its head out of its burrow. "Of course it's important, dolt! That's May Flowers, with excellent advice for you."

"Oh. Thanks." Geode scrambled over the fence and ran swiftly down the drive, waving, so the car would see him.

It took about two minutes to reach the main gate, as it was about a quarter mile, but the car did wait. He reached the rod with the green button and pushed it, opening the gate. The crank arm took nine seconds to swing the gate all the way open, and after a forty-five-second wait it would crank it closed again. That gave cars plenty of time to get through, but left little chance for intruders.

May Flowers rolled down her window. "How did you know it was me?"

"The tortoise told me."

She paused just a trifle. "Yes, of course. I brought some more groceries."

"You can take them in to Œnone. She'll see you through the window and know it's all right."

"Yes. You are out on your rounds?"

"Yes. But I can wait long enough for your advice."

"My advice?"

"The tortoise said you had excellent advice for me."

She considered briefly. "Then I must have. Come in for a moment, and we'll talk."

"I'm wet."

"The upholstery's water-resistant."

He nodded. He opened the door and got in beside her. "What was the advice?"

"What is your problem?"

"I don't know."

She glanced obliquely at him. "But you are troubled?"

"Yes."

"Do the animals talk to you more freely when you're troubled?"

"Yes. Today I even talked with a person. I've never done that before."

"An imaginary person, you mean?"

"Not exactly. She exists, or did exist, but she's not here now."

"Who is it?"

"Nymph."

"And who is Nymph?" she inquired patiently.

"A five-year-old girl who had sex with a man. He didn't force her;

she wanted it, because her father and brother had molested her, and she wanted to know what it was all about."

"Œnone told you about this?"

"Yes."

"You understand, of course, that this is Œnone's own childhood?"

"Yes."

"There was a trial."

"Yes. The man was found guilty, and he died in prison."

"And she blames herself."

"Yes."

She turned to him, looking squarely into his face. "Geode, it is right for you to be troubled about this. A terrible thing happened to that child. Now she has told you, and she is afraid she will be punished."

"Why?"

"Reason it out, Geode. What happened the last time she told about this?"

"Her lover died."

"Her lover died," she repeated. "And who is her lover now?"

He stared at her, unable to speak.

"Loving is more than sex or potency," she said. "It is possible to have sex without love, and love without sex. Does she love you?"

"Yes, I think so."

"Then what do you suppose she thinks will happen to you, now that she has told you?"

"I'm not going to die!"

"Have you ever known something, yet not believed it deep down?"

"Yes! Right now, because I can't—you mean she—?"

"I think she fears for you, Geode. And you fear for her. That is why you are disturbed. Love is new for you, and you feel inadequate. You are afraid something terrible will happen. And indeed, there is the firefly."

It made such phenomenal sense he was amazed. "Thank you," he said, benumbed. He got out of the car.

She smiled briefly. "Anytime, Geode. Go to her, love her, and do not die."

"I will! After I finish my rounds."

"Of course." She rolled up her window and drove on, while he cut across the field to intersect his normal route.

The tortoise had told him true. May had had excellent advice for him. Now he could love Œnone, even if he couldn't get an erection. It didn't matter! He could love her and not die.

❧ 34 ❧

MAY FLOWERS DROVE on, shaking her head. Playing fairy godmother was a new role to her, but she enjoyed it. The nice irony was that it was coming back to refresh her own life. She had brought Œnone here, and then Œnone had helped her in return, lending her vital support and comfort in the hour of her nadir. She had left Œnone alone with Geode; then the two of them had left May herself alone with Frank. Perhaps the one had not caused the other, but the two relationships were interacting, and the exhilaration of new love was animating each. The abused child and the battered wife—what a common interest they had found!

She rounded the corner, idly noting the passion flower vines bestriding the fence, and continued on south toward the house. She peered into the trees and brush on either side of the drive. She spied a rustling, and screeched to a halt, but in a moment saw that it was just a slender snake, the kind called black racers, that rapidly disappeared. There was no sign of the monster. But of course there wouldn't be; it fed only on the third day, and this was the second. Tomorrow night was the bad one.

Tonight, perhaps, Geode and Œnone would make it. May, having little interest in sex herself, nevertheless found herself excited by this

secondhand prospect. She visualized the two of them together, stripping naked, looking at each other, perhaps for the first time. Œnone
was, of course, long experienced in sex—very long experienced!—
while Geode wasn't. She would have to lead him through it. What
would it be like to do it with a hesitant, normally impotent man? May
somehow found that more intriguing than the other type of sex, and
vastly preferable to what Bull Shauer had visited on her.

She came to the house, letting the brief hill subtract velocity from
her approach. She parked and got out, carrying her groceries. Sure
enough, Œnone spied her and opened the door. "Geode let me in,"
she explained.

"Oh."

"We talked, briefly. He was troubled. I think he didn't quite understand a story you told him, but now he does."

Œnone gazed at her without expression.

"I am a journalist," May said. "I research things. I know something
of your past, just as you know something of mine." She lifted her dark
glasses momentarily to show her black eye.

"Oh. Yes."

"I wish the two of you every happiness, having found some myself."

"Yes, with Frank."

Women weren't good at keeping things from each other! "Yes. The
firefly seems to have brought us all together, in devious ways."

"The firefly," Œnone agreed. Her lips were pale. "Geode is out
there. It is out there. I fear for him."

"It has never to our knowledge taken a man on the move."

"I must love him before I die."

This brought May up short. "Before *you* die? Are you ill?"

"No. But I will die soon. It is the curse of Œnone."

"Oh." May remembered the part of the myth that had not been in
this woman's story. "Because she committed suicide after letting Paris
die."

"Because she could not outlive him for very long. It was fated."

"Paris was a rotten philanderer who deserves no sympathy," May
said. "Either version. You owe him nothing, certainly not your death."

"True. But it is fated."

May realized that the woman's problem was deeper than it had
seemed. Her bad marriage still hung an albatross of guilt around her
neck. She had perhaps cast off the nature of the molested child, who
attempted to seduce every man she encountered because it was the

only way she knew to gain affection, and adopted another, which was not necessarily an improvement. "Your husband was taken by the monster. So was mine. We are both well rid of them. I bear no guilt, only freedom. The same should be true for you. Once we take out the monster, you can remain here with Geode. To hell with fate!"

But the woman would not be persuaded. "Fate cannot be gainsaid, only postponed. It will have its way. Œnone will die."

"Perhaps in the sense that April Shauer died and gave me freedom," May said, nodding in agreement. She saw that argument would get her nowhere with this woman. Only if she could align herself on Œnone's side would she be able to help, and she did want to help. This remained her Good Deed; she wanted it to be perfect, or at any rate, as good as she could make it. "There was no way out for April, but there was for May."

Œnone angled her head prettily. "Yes! A new person. A new name. The only way."

"I planned for months—years, really, before I got the courage to do it. Then I was frightened for years, always looking over my shoulder, always afraid he would find me. And finally he did. But if I had changed my name again in time, maybe he would not have found me. I don't regret the name, only that that man was ever in my life. How did it start for you?" Would the woman respond now?

Œnone turned away, but not in negation. It was as if her confession was too shameful for her to speak directly, so had to be refracted from the wall. "Jade was five when she became Nymph. She had to be Nymph, because Jade would have been punished. Only Nymph could be a real woman and keep the secret. When Mad went to prison, she was just plain dull Jade again, except that now mean George couldn't get her, because she Knew. Knew what it was all about, so much better than he did then. She told him what she would tell their mother if he ever bothered her again, and how their mother would cut off his thing and bake it in the oven, and that scared him. Her father was also scared, and no longer played with her; she didn't care about that, because now she knew what he had wanted, too, and knew what happened to any man who did it with a child. So her life was better in that respect. But it didn't make up for the loss of Mad.

"Then when Jade was ten she learned that Mad was dead. Her mother told her: 'You will be glad to know, dear, that that wicked man who bothered you is dead. The other prisoners got him, finally. You don't need to worry about him ever getting out and bothering you again.' Her mother spoke in an offhand fashion, but there was real satisfaction in it. Her mother hated Mad, just as she hated everything to do with sex. Her mother wished that every man who ever even thought about sex would be castrated. By this time Jade, or perhaps Nymph, understood a bit more about why her father had been so interested in her rather than in her mother: at least the child had been interested *back*. She understood that sexual molestation did not just happen; it was a family situation, and those who seemed most honorable might be the most guilty if the whole picture were understood.

"Mad was dead. Nymph's lingering hope that he would one day get free and come to take her away from her drear Jade-life, and she would put on a dress with no bottom part the way he liked it, and they would go to a castle far away and spend the whole time eating candy and kissing and licking each other and playing with his big thing and making it fountain white fluid, and she would sleep in his arms feeling so safe with his warm thing inside her while it recovered its strength for the next fountaining—all this was gone. She had suspended her grief for five years with the promise that it was temporary, just waiting for Mad's freedom. Gone. Now that accumulated grief descended on her crushingly.

"Her mother was watching her, and she knew the woman wanted to see her suffer for her disgusting crime of *liking sex*, and that this was her mother's private revenge on her. Neither Jade nor Nymph would give her that satisfaction, so Jade said simply, 'Thank you, mother,' and went to her room to do her homework. She showed no emotion, and that was Nymph's little victory.

"But alone in her room, Jade knew that she could not survive the horror. She had indeed loved Mad, or at least the idea of Mad and of freedom from school and of her being the center of his attention and desire. He had represented all the love she lacked at home, and all the mystery and excitement she longed for and could never have as Jade. Without him, she had no life she wanted.

"He was gone because of her. Because she had Told. She had thought she was helping him, but she had instead condemned him. It was her fault. If she had never loved him, he would have been safe. If she had lied and *said* she never loved him, that it was all a big fat mistake, that all they had ever done was play card games he taught her, like strip poker, then he would have been safe. She had learned to lie too late. She had sent him to prison. She had killed him. Forever and ever, she would know she had killed him with her words.

"She wanted to kill herself, but did not know how. She tried to will herself to death, but it didn't work. All evening and all night she struggled to leave life by thinking of fading into nothingness. What she achieved was less than that, but it turned out to be enough. She discovered that the pain was less when she pictured a prison cell being built, brick by brick, bar by bar, around Nymph and her love. The higher the walls went, the more distant the grief seemed. Nymph was slowly closed off, and her pain too.

"The process was not completed that night. It took many days and nights, and often a wall would fall down and the pain would leak out, and it had to be laboriously rebuilt. But as time passed, the enclosure became more comprehensive, and Jade, outside, was able to function in a normal manner. Much of her was missing, so that she was only the shell of a person, but other people were not aware of that. She coped.

"After that, whenever anything evil happened to Jade, she built another enclosure around it, so that it was muted and became a mere memory. She still knew of it, and could feel some of the pain of it, but most of the discomfort was gone. She got better at this as she aged, for there were many things that bothered her. She learned how to construct an almost sealed enclosure in a day, and then in an hour, if the hurt was small. By the time the monster took her husband, she was so well experienced that it hardly required a conscious effort to wall him off; indeed, she was privately glad to be rid of him. For her son it had been more difficult, but a night of denial and a day of concentration had done it.

"Yet that was not enough. Jade remained a mouse, a person of no interest, even to herself. Too much of her was walled away; there was not enough left to operate a full personality. So she compensated by building other enclosures that contained all the things she needed, and often she visited these and became a new and better person for the little time it lasted before the effect ebbed. Deprived of her greatest dream, she fashioned from the fragments lesser dreams, and these sustained her somewhat.

"Until at last she seemed to have the chance to step into one of the worlds of her fancy—for real. With a man unlike any she had imagined, but as good for her as any. One who was like a child in his naiveté about sex, but who wanted love. A man who was like Nymph, with whom she could be Mad. A man she could teach her way."

Œnone turned back to face May. "Thus Œnone, who became the

principal personality, the one you now know. There are many other chambers, each with its woman, but it is Œnone Geode likes, and all of them are intrigued by Geode in their special fashions."

This was much more information than May had hoped for! The dam had burst, and the truth had flowed out. What the woman had told her confirmed May's general notion. Jade had indeed learned to cope, by constructing as well as sealing off multiple personalities. A psychiatrist would have a field day with her! But no psychiatrist was going to get near her. It was time for all the tormented women who occupied this body to have their fulfillment. Time for them to love and be loved. Geode was the perfect complement to Jade, and he did love her in all her forms. If only she could believe that, and believe that the curse was gone.

May had a sudden notion. "You were once a molested child, and once a neglected wife. Now you can be yourself—Jade. Let Œnone die, if she must, but you will remain, in your new aspect. Your old aspect, which has never been fulfilled. That may be your true fate."

The woman's eyes widened. "A new role!" she breathed. "But not Jade! He wouldn't like Jade."

"Yes, he would! He loves you, whatever way you are. You don't need any artifice for him. Just love him, and let him love you."

"But Jade—"

"Jade will do! Ask him! Jade is a new role. Why don't you try it? It may even help you with Geode." For if the woman's nature changed with the role, in the manner of multiple personalities, she could write a whole new slate. She could exclude the prophecy of death.

The woman nodded, then advanced to embrace her. May was touched. She was getting better at the role of fairy godmother.

Later in the day she got in touch with Cyrano. "Tomorrow is Monster Day," she said.

"Tomorrow night I will be in that cabin," he responded. "This time I shall not miss my appointment with the firefly."

"Alone? I don't think that's wise."

"When has it ever taken a person in company? I have to be alone, or it won't come."

"You have a point. But when it attacks a person alone, it seems to have been one hundred percent successful."

"So it may be getting overconfident. This time it will not encounter a person who is sleeping, or who has been dosed with sedative. Or who is blinded by concupiscence. I shall be wearing a gas mask to filter out pheromones."

"How will you kill it when you don't even know what it looks like?"

"I know it depends on chemistry. That means it won't have its lever on me. I will discover what it looks like, and live to tell the tale."

"You already have a notion," she said, reading his reactions.

"A notion. The lab report on the samples was inconclusive, as I expected, but enough to determine that the chemistry is not that of any creature we know. It is reminiscent of the sea. I think it came from the sea, using waterborne pheromones to attract and pacify its prey. Those are not as effective in the air, but at close range they do work. It is able to tune in on the chemistry of potential prey and to formulate variations of its basic formula which incite the prey sexually. That ability could revolutionize a number of aspects of our society."

"You're not planning to kill the monster!" she exclaimed, catching on. "You want to capture it!"

"I've got a cage that should be tight. I figure the thing is gelatinous or like a big snail. Mid should be pleased."

"This is dangerous!"

"Spice of life."

"Have you told Mid?"

"Not yet."

"Tell him before you try it! He has to decide."

"True. I'll set up the cabin tonight, and call him from the ranch on my way in."

"I hope your confidence is justified. I'd prefer to play strip poker with a man-eating tiger."

"That was the nature of your marriage."

She smiled. "Yes. Thank you for that hypo. It made all the difference."

"Mid values you."

"And you. Watch your step with the firefly."

He nodded. She left him. She wondered whether she could arrange another tryst with Frank. She had lost her taste for independence.

✦ 35 ✦

CYRANO WATCHED HER go, then got in his van and set off for the Middle Kingdom Ranch. They had met at a park, as he did not use a hotel or other facilities; all he needed was some water and some privacy. He had slept in the van for years; it was really as good as a room, with all his things right there. The only problem at the moment was the presence of the bones of Bull Shauer; he had them in a tight bag, but even so, some lingering pheromones leaked out, making his dreams continually erotic. It was getting so that even May Flowers looked good, in the manner of an opera Valkyrie, and that Brown woman was as nice a little trick as any man could desire. He was normally satisfied to go his own way, but those pheromones had him so hyped up he'd grab any woman who offered. Well, once he caught the firefly, he'd *see* what offered!

May was right: he had to clear it with Mid, even though he was sure Mid would approve. He wanted that firefly so bad he got an erection just thinking about it. Not really sexual, just that the presence of the firefly brought an erection because of the pheromones, so now an erection made the firefly seem closer. The gas mask should prevent the pheromones from affecting him, but the association remained.

Cyrano was not interested in money as such; Mid gave him all the security and comfort he wanted, which was what money was for. But the discovery and exploitation of a new species—that really turned him on. He had gone from veterinary practice to entomology, but his interest was in all living things.

Insects had a truly phenomenal range of predatory and defensive devices, much greater than the range of mammals or reptiles, and were quicker to adapt chemically as well as physically. In some cases chemical was most of it, as man tried to eradicate them with poison sprays and they developed immunities to his successive efforts. Plants, too, were often effective chemical warriors; they planted the ground around their roots with poisons against competitive plants, and of course their war against predators like caterpillars was continual. Bugs could graze a tree bare two years in succession, but the third year the foliage was poison, and the bugs were done for. Oh, it was a royal battleground, on the chemical level!

But this monster firefly set a new standard of excellence in that regard. Its pacification method tied in to what no species that employed sexual reproduction could resist. Pheromones! Not only that, it adapted its formula for any species it chose to hunt, including man. A single product that affected male and female simultaneously. And did it rapidly—within a period of months, it seemed. First it had tuned in on mammals, then on man. This suggested that its tuning process was not a matter of natural selection, but of conscious intent. What other creature could receive, analyze, and duplicate the sexual signals of its chosen prey?

This did not necessarily imply that the firefly was intelligent. It could simply mean that it had a sophisticated organ of duplication that oriented on what it received and produced a lot more of the same formula. The firefly seemed no longer to feed on animals. That could mean that man was easier or tastier prey. But it could also mean that the firefly oriented on only one type of prey at a time, sticking to that until no more offered, then orienting on another. Its pheromone factory could keep producing the same thing until the market was saturated.

Still, that was impressive enough. Since there were billions of human beings on the planet, there was no reason for the firefly to change to other prey. It could keep feeding and reproducing until no men were left.

That led to diverging lines of speculation. The first related to reproduction: how did the creature who mimicked the reproductive lures of other species reproduce itself? Was it male or female, and did it have a mate? There had been no evidence of two of them; it took its prey every three days now, probably oftener when the victims were smaller. In each case, a rate of travel of three or four hours per mile, plus 50 percent resting time, was sufficient to account for transport. A big snail could probably do that—a snail the mass of a man. That argued for one creature, and for asexual reproduction. That might be appropriate, because it meant that the firefly could not be had the same way it had others. No pheromone would compel it to give up its life.

But if it was asexual, what mode did it employ? Was it like a giant amoeba, growing and dividing in two? Again, that seemed unlikely. If it had divided, there should now be several sites of activity, and there were not. Did it give parthenogenetic birth? Did it lay fertile eggs without requiring fertilization? That seemed more likely. Such eggs could be buried for safety, and incubate for a period, and later hatch and go about their business. The firefly could leave a trail of such eggs, each of which might take weeks, months, or even years to hatch, so that the parent would be far away by the time the young were ready to forage. That was important, because overhunting a given territory was death to predators. There had to be a sufficient population of rabbits to support the wolves, and the balance was mandatory. Nature didn't play games; any creature who violated her rules was dead. That applied to alien predators from the sea as it did to the extinct dinosaurs. The dinosaurs, of course, had a bad rap; they had survived a hundred times as long as man had, dominating their world throughout, before nature changed the rules and brought them down at last.

But a creature from the sea would know about territorial dynamics. Sea resources were not infinite, despite the attitude of commercial fishers. So the concept of extension of foraging range would be honored.

That was the first line of speculation, fascinating and not yet complete. The second was about the firefly's interaction with man. Its mode of predation and reproduction might be adequate for the creatures of the sea, and for most creatures of the land, but this time it was encountering something that had to be new to its experience, and as alien to its understanding as its nature was to those here. That was intelligence.

Man had a brain that was qualitatively as well as quantitatively distinct from that of other animals. That brain had given him dominance over the planet with speed that was lightning, in geological terms. Natural selection no longer applied to man, or applied only fuzzily; instead of adapting to his environment, man adapted the environment to suit himself. The greatest extinction in the history of the planet was not the demise of the dinosaurs, but the demise of all creatures in the Age of Man. Anything that opposed man, or that man hunted, was doomed. Why had the superbly equipped hunter Smilodon, the saber-toothed tiger, become abruptly extinct, while the lesser tiger survived? Because Smilodon had not feared man. Smilodon had preyed boldly on the largest creatures, driving its huge tusks into shoulders, slicing them open, its jaws able to open so wide they were at a 180-degree angle, absolutely irresistible. What had it to fear from puny man? So instead of hiding from man, it had sought to frighten him away. Adios, Smilodon!

Now the firefly was preying on man, and thereby hung its destruction. There was no question about its end; the question was which man would bring it about. Cyrano had the immense good fortune to have the first crack at it. He was sure he could kill it, but what he wanted was to capture it, and study it, and learn everything about it. There was only so much to be had from a corpse, but everything to be had from a living specimen!

He was at the gate. He pushed the buzzer, and in a moment the gate opened. He drove on in. Mid had to agree! Mid would see the commercial ramifications, which were awesome. Cyrano hardly cared about those, but if they justified his action, he would argue their case. Capture the firefly! He could store it in his cage, feed it purchased carcasses, take down its specs. He would come to understand it, divining the mystery of the century. They thought the great fish Coelacanth, supposedly extinct for fifty million years, was a great discovery in present times? Just wait for the firefly!

He stopped at the house. George Demerit came out to meet him. "I have to call Mid, just to be sure my trap for the firefly is okay."

Demerit shrugged, as he tended to do. He was a funny man, repressed.

Cyrano went inside and called his number. He got the answering machine. "I want to trap the firefly," he said, "tomorrow night. Tonight I'll set up at the cabin, and be ready tomorrow. This thing could be a diamond mine, biologically. If you say no, I ask you to give me a chance to argue my case. I'd much rather have the thing alive than dead." He hung up.

The woman was there, watching him, as she had before. "Capture?" she asked.

"Why kill it when it may be unique to science? Fireflies are better if we understand them. Look at snake venom, now used in medicine."

"Yes," she said.

"Come out and tell me what Mid's answer is," Cyrano told Demerit. He went out to his van, hoping there would be no negation from his employer.

✦ 36 ✦

"HE SHOULDN'T DO it," Œnone said. "The firefly will take him."

"How do you know?" Geode asked.

"I just know." Indeed she did, but couldn't say how. It was intuition and fear.

They had been somewhat out of sorts since Geode's return from the rounds. He had taken a shower, and she had hesitated to join him, because he really needed to ask her to do it, and he didn't think of it, or couldn't develop the initiative. She had to encourage him to be more aggressive, establishing the principle, so that he would be able to apply it to sex.

But now, fearful that things were not going right, she risked an initiative. "There is something I should tell you, that perhaps will help."

"That you fear I'll die?"

"That too. I—Œnone must die. That is why I didn't want you to love me, because it would only hurt you. But I am not just Œnone. I am all of them. I can be another. I can be Jade, the way others think of me, but this time truly. Jade doesn't have to die."

"I don't want any of you to die!" he exclaimed. "You are all I ever had!"

"I am me, no matter what my name. If you can accept Jade—"

"Yes!"

"But Jade is mousy, not a child, not lovely, just a thirty-five-year-old housewife nobody notices."

"I don't need a child or a lovely woman. Just one who cares for me."

"Are you sure? Jade has no artifice."

"I saw Nymph by the pole barn. She told me to lie down and take off my clothes, but I wouldn't."

"You wouldn't?"

"She wasn't you. You're here."

"She's here too."

"She said I'd be sorry when she was dead."

"Yes, she betrayed Mad, and she has to die."

"But Jade doesn't. I'll take Jade."

"Then you will have Jade—until you tire of her." She left him, going up to her room. There she changed into the drabbest of the available dresses, tied up her hair somewhat messily, and relaxed her tummy. She had thought she never wanted to assume this role again, but if Geode could accept it, and it allowed her to live—

She went back down. Geode looked at her, and looked again, surprised.

"Are you sure you want this?" she asked.

"I—I don't know you," he said, confused.

"Nor should you want to. I'll change back."

"No! Give me time! I'm not used to this."

"Time we have, this way. The problem is, the time is no fun. Mundane things never are."

"Can you still tell stories?"

"That I can do, yes."

He smiled. "Tonight, in the dark."

"Tonight, in the dark," she agreed. Could it actually work? She hardly dared hope. Jade, after all, was the least of her, of interest to none. How could Jade accomplish what Nymph or Œnone could not?

Then she had another notion. "Maybe I should tell you about Chloe."

"Chloe?"

"Tonight."

Chloe was a rather ordinary woman. She was not beautiful, and she had no wealth, and her talents were mediocre. No man worth his salt had ever given her a second glance. But a circumstance caused her to become the recipient of a single remarkable gift, and that gift changed not only her life but the world.

Acme Korn Pops, a new breakfast cereal by Emptie Calorie Inc., staged a publicity stunt. They selected a woman with a secret, and three leading male artisans of the day. Each would be allowed one date with her, during which he would try to fathom her secret, which she was pledged not to reveal to any. Each would present her with a token of their association. The one who succeeded in learning her secret would win a prize of one million dollars, tax-free. The winner would be announced at a great televised presentation.

Emptie Calorie put on a massive promotional campaign. Any consumer could participate by sending in a Korn Pop star from a package. With the star went a guess: what was the woman's secret? Whoever guessed it correctly would receive a share in a second million-dollar prize, divided evenly among all those who had it right.

There were three key hints for the avid public: televised synopses of the three dates. For concealed cameras recorded each date, especially the dialogue, so that whatever was said could be analyzed for clues. The dates themselves were conducted privately, but both parties knew that they would in due course become public, so they were decorous. It was agreed that nothing would be said off-camera; the two were bound to silence in those moments when recording was not feasible. Thus the full context of the secret was available to all.

The woman was Chloe, and she had agreed to do this in exchange for the realization of her impossible dream: to date the three men she admired most. Each was outstanding in his field, and single: an eligible bachelor. This made for excellent press, which was why the sponsor had agreed to do it. Every ordinary woman could fancy herself on one of the dates with a wonderful man, and every man could think of himself winning a million dollars by truly understanding the woman he dated.

If this stunt succeeded in making Acme Korn Pops a top-selling brand, there could be a sequel contest: an ordinary man with three fantastic dates with starlets, each of whom would exert her utmost wiles in her effort to fathom his secret. That was a notion to conjure with!

But first this more subdued edition, because the primary grocery shoppers were women. Emptie Calorie wanted to attract their specific attention, knowing full well that while males might get excited about potential dates with starlets, they seldom bought cereal on their own, and women were unlikely to buy Korn Pops merely to facilitate their men's interest in other women. Only when the product's identity was established could male-related publicity assist it significantly.

So Chloe went on her date with the first great man. He was Baird, a popular singer whose voice was reckoned by specialty magazines as the most evocative of the day. He could make young girls faint with ecstasy by sustaining a single note. He was not really handsome, but he was young and vibrant and possessed of a compelling personal magnetism. It was not surprising that Chloe had chosen him as one of her great dates; there were tens of thousands of young women who would have done the same.

Baird was extraordinarily attentive. He took her to an extremely "in" restaurant and treated her to a remarkable and expensive meal. He could afford it: Emptie Calorie was picking up the tab. Chloe had little notion of what she was eating; the names were in French, and the dishes were so fancy she was hardly sure where the food began and the accoutrements left off. She fumbled it in places, as when she tasted the vichyssoise and exclaimed "Cold potato soup!" The waiter seemed about to snigger, but Baird cast a steely glance at him. "You have a problem with that, hash-slinger?" The waiter hastily backed away. When that episode was broadcast, there was a rash of orders for "Cold Potato Soup, Hash-Slinger!" with which the waiters had to bear.

They went to a concert by Baird's group, performing without him. Then he stepped out from the audience, took the stage, and sang the most evocative number directly to his date. Chloe flushed, and four hundred attractive young women in the audience turned their envious gaze on her. Who was this seemingly ordinary woman their heartthrob was dating? None of them knew that this was for a publicity stunt, but they were even more jealous when they learned it later.

He danced with her, and young women thronged to cut in, but he shook his head. "She is mine alone, and I am hers alone, tonight," he explained. She did not know the modern dances, but he obliged her with the garden-variety waltz while his group swung into *The Blue Danube* and he held her close but gently. It was an aspect of her dream, come all too true.

He took her to his suite at the local hotel, and here he barred the cameras. "No talking in here, I promise," he promised with a suggestive smile that made Chloe flush again.

Inside he offered her a drink, but she declined. "I want to remember this perfectly," she explained.

"I promised not to talk," he said. "I lied. Chloe, I don't expect you to believe this, but I have fallen in love with you."

She had to smile. "Yes, I don't believe you, but thanks for saying it."

"I am required to give you a token of this occasion," he said. "I will do so, but I would like something in exchange."

"I can't tell you my secret!" she protested, hurt.

"To hell with that!" he exclaimed. "I'm not after your secret. I haven't guessed it, and won't try. One of the others is welcome to the million dollars; I don't need it anyway. I will make you the greatest love song my group can devise: that's my token for you. But in exchange I want your love."

She stared at him, afraid this was some cruel joke.

"Chloe, I want your hand," he insisted, taking it. "You are like no other woman I have met. I'll be frank: I've had a hundred groupies. I'm not pure. But you are. I love you, and I want to marry you. Will you do it?"

"But this—one evening—I am nothing!" she protested.

"Give me leave to do what I want with you, tonight, and I will prove it. Then give me your answer."

Bemused, flattered, barely believing, she could only say, "I give you leave."

He embraced her and kissed her so deeply that her head reeled. He ran his hands over her body. "Tell me no, when," he said. "Otherwise I won't stop."

Dazed, she was silent, for this was the larger part of her dream: to have this heartthrob of millions so taken with her that he could not hold back.

He took her to the bedroom then, and undressed her and himself with an almost unseemly haste, and kissed her on face and neck and shoulder and breast, and then the mouth again, and held it while he penetrated her, and he exploded inside her while holding that kiss, and she was so moved she climaxed with him. He held her, after, and stroked her hair. "That is my true feeling for you," he said. "I never want another woman after you. I beg you, give me your answer."

Now she wept. "Oh, Baird, I wish I could, but I can't."

"Maybe not right now," he said. "You have two other dates. I accept that; it was always part of the deal. But when they are done, and one of them has the money, then I will ask you again. Then will you agree?"

She only wept harder, not answering him.

"Believe me," he said. "I wouldn't lie to any girl about a thing like this, and I'm not lying to you. If you thought I only wanted your body, well, I've had that now, and it is only the beginning. You *are* special, and you are for me. I know it!"

"I believe you," she said, but her tears continued.

Finally she regained her composure, and dressed and cleaned up, and he took her home. They paused at the door. He embraced her again, and kissed her for the camera. "Remember," he told her.

When the edited episode was broadcast, not only did thousands of women envy her, thousands of men envied him. Each had seen how taken with her he was, and each guessed at what he had done with her off-camera, and each was close to the mark. They knew that she had something special, and that Baird had found it. Each man wanted to explore for it himself.

Her second date was with Nahshon, a leading young writer and poet. It was said to be only a matter of time—a short time—before he won an award for excellence in his craft. Like Baird, he was not physically prepossessing, but he had a presence that electrified. When he took her hand, she felt the sensitivity of him, and the insight, and the understanding and the sheer caring, and she melted.

He took her to a subdued, secluded restaurant known only to the elite, where the lights were dim and privacy was rampant. While they ate he quoted bits of his work to her, and it was so feeling and beautiful that it transported her. Then he took her to a play, where color and action and the awareness of the living nature of the players lent heightened effect; television could not match the immediacy of this. He took her for a walk in a safe section of the park, and the night breeze caressed her, fluffing out her hair, making her feel lovely and wanton. Then they sat on a park bench, and instead of having her sit beside him, he asked her to sit on his lap. He kissed her, and she became warm all over.

Then he gazed into her face in the dim light from a distant street lantern, and his eyes asked a question, and she felt his urgency beneath her thighs. She knew they were in the public view of the camera, but it couldn't see under their clothing. "Yes, yes, I will, yes!" she whispered, quoting from James Joyce, and of course he recognized and understood the reference instantly. She adjusted herself and managed to slide her panties down, and he adjusted himself and got his fly open, and there under the cover of her spreading skirt they established a connection. He entered her, not deeply, for that was impossible while she sat sidewise on him, but enough. Then he repeated a love poem of such subtlety and significance and relevance to their situation that her whole body shivered and warmed to it, and her internal muscles clenched, and she felt him spurt into her, the camera all-unknowing. The thought of getting away with this, so near to discovery, heightened her feeling, and in a moment she shuddered into her own finale. They kissed again, letting it linger as they cooled. She had made it with another of the men she most admired, and that was the true fulfillment of her dream. Kisses were for the camera; the hidden connection was for herself, because she knew a man could not make a pretense of that desire; it had to be real.

In due course she worked a tissue into place to take up the remnant, and they stood. They walked slowly out of the park. "You are like no woman I have encountered," Nahshon said. "I would like you to be with me always."

Stricken, she had to deny him. "There is only tonight," she said. "I wish it could be forever, but that is impossible."

"I will write you a love poem," he said. "That will be my token for you. It will express my feeling as closely as is possible. Then, perhaps, you will reconsider."

She felt the tears coming. How she wished it were possible!

Her third date was with Standish, one of the brightest of sculptors. He was older than the others, and handsome, and remarkably suave. Everything in his vicinity seemed to be appropriately molded, even in its occasional dishevelment.

He took her directly to his studio, where his sculptures finished and in progress abounded. "I will sculpt you," he said, "and that sculpture will be my token for you. Will you pose for me *au naturel*?"

"But we are on camera!" she protested, not really affronted.

He fetched a screen and set it around her so that she could pose on a stool without being seen by other than himself. "The camera can see only what I do, not what you do," he said. "But it will be mirrored in my art."

"But I have no body!" she said. "I mean, you can get spectacular models. You don't have to settle for—"

"Your body is only the beginning. Just as I see the potential in the stone or clay, I see the potential in you. I will sculpt you as I see you, and you shall not be ashamed."

So she stripped away her clothing and perched somewhat nervously on a high stool, and he made a shape in clay. It was tiny, but exquisite; she wished she really looked like that!

Meanwhile, posing nude did something to her. She felt both prim and wanton, as if in a cold pool where the water immediately adjacent to her skin was warmed by her body to a tolerable level; if she moved even a fraction the cold would strike through. So she was frozen in place, and therefore warm. She was also unreal, to a degree; it was as if her body were not hers, but merely an affectation, something she was using for the moment, like a pencil, and therefore no source of embarrassment.

Despite this seeming detachment, she found herself becoming aroused. This man she so much admired was looking at her, transcribing her every physical nuance to his living clay. It was as though he were stroking her body instead of the clay; she felt the moving touch. Her genital region was open to his view; she wanted it similarly open to his body.

"Is it finished?" she asked, wanting him to come and mold her body instead, as if he could shape it to the impossible ideal of the clay form.

"This is only my interim model," he said. "The art itself will be in stone, and life-size."

"But I can't return for other sessions!" she exclaimed.

"Once I have my model, I have you. This is the only sitting you need do."

"Oh." She was perversely disappointed.

"But if you care to stay after—"

"I can't. I must go home."

He left his clay and came to her in the enclosure. He put his arms about her, and the touch of them was phenomenal. "I must have you," he whispered in her ear.

Those were the words she had longed for. She didn't speak; she only spread her knees a bit farther, in a silent invitation.

Shielded by the screen, he loosened his belt and let down his trousers and shorts. Above the screen only her head and his head showed, and the top of his shoulders, which remained clothed. Below he was as bare as she, and his sexual interest in her was manifest. With greater daring than she had ever thought possible, she took his divine member in her hand and brought it to her.

"But of course I would like for you to pose for me again," he said, as his tip touched her cleft.

"I wish I could," she said, urging that tip on in. She was hot and moist, eager to make the connection. "But it is in the rules: one date per man, no more."

"I am aware of that," he said, letting his torso move forward, in the process penetrating her. He was not a tall man, and his crotch was just the elevation of hers as she sat on the high stool. "But after this contest is done, then, perhaps."

Her tears came again. "I wish so! But I cannot." She put her hands on his hips, hauling him in, and as he came in all the way, she circled his torso and caught hold of his hard little buttocks. She found that she needed no other stimulation; her sexual being was proceeding on its own course to fulfillment. She was in control, and it was as if *she* were penetrating *him* and working toward her completion. Their heads and shoulders remained apart, but their centers were now tightly connected. She had never done anything like this before, except perhaps when she had sat on the poet's lap, and it was exciting as much because of its naughtiness as because of its nature.

"But can you not tell me why?" he asked with evident disappointment as their member swelled and jetted deep within them, pumping its exquisite elixir into their being.

"I cannot," she said tearfully, as their body shuddered in the climax.

"Then I can only kiss you and hope that you will change your mind another day," he said. For the first time their two heads came together, as their bodies ebbed, in a passionate kiss. The thrill was electric, as the genital contact had been.

"I wish I could," she repeated, as he withdrew.

"I seem to have dropped something," he remarked, stooping to pick up his shorts and trousers. Then, as they continued their nonessential dialogue, he dressed, and stepped out of the enclosure, seemingly unchanged from the way he had entered it.

She cleaned herself and donned her own clothing. She was amazed at the aplomb with which they had carried it off, holding a dull conversation for the camera while interacting in a far more intimate manner below. What an exciting realm this was!

Then Standish brought her to his kitchen, where he cooked her a wonderful meal, for his artistic hands could mold a banquet as readily as clay. They ate and talked, and she loved him too, as she had the others, and it was the culmination of the whole of her dream.

He took her home. "I don't know how to thank you," she said. "You have made me feel so—so much like what I never was. Even if it is just for the prize, you were wonderful to me."

"It started for the prize," he said. "Now you *are* the prize. I did not know before why I never married; now I know I was waiting for you."

She smiled at him, but again her tears were coursing down her cheeks. "Thank you for the most wonderful date," she said.

"Whatever pleasure you have had in it, I have shared," he said. "This matter is not ended."

How much she wished that were true!

The three dates were broadcast, and the audience thrilled to these rather decorous episodes as if something much more interesting were happening. Folk wondered what the two had done, in their silence of visitation in Baird's suite, and they discovered something mysteriously suggestive about the way Chloe sat on Nahshon's lap in the park, and in the way Standish approached her when she was nude behind the screen. Everything was innocent, of course, yet spectators found themselves excited. What strange quality was there in these dates?

The response was tremendous, and Acme Korn Pops became a major contender in the supermarkets as people sent in their stars. Then came the day of decision: the presentation of the three tokens, and the speaking of Chloe's secret, for a million dollars. The meters showed a tremendous viewership for that live program.

Baird was first. His group was there, and it struck up the music. Then he sang the song he had made: "Chloe." It was a love song so true that it excited passionate emotion in every person hearing it. All knew that it would top the charts for a long time; indeed, it was to become one of the all-time favorites of the current generation. For it was not just a love song, it was a proposal, and such was its power that in the ensuing weeks it triggered more engagements than had been

known in any similar period before. It was truly the ultimate work of
musical love. No one needed to inquire; all knew that it was Baird's
proposal to Chloe, and girlish tears flowed even as the young women
echoed the melody, for they knew that Baird was off the market.

Then Nahshon read his poem, "Chloe," and it was a work of such
feeling and sensitivity that all who heard it in the studio audience and
the television audience and the endlessly expanding rebroadcast audience were transported. It became an instant classic, and Nahshon won
the Nobel prize for literature on the strength of it, by acclamation;
there were no other contenders. He, too, loved Chloe, and meant to
marry her. This did not seem incongruous, in this situation; half the
men in the audience, including many who had never seen her in the
broadcasts, wanted to marry her too.

Finally Standish unveiled his sculpture, "Chloe." There was a gasp
of awe as all beheld what was to become known as Venus II: the
definitive representation of contemporary woman, and the statue of the
age. It evoked joy and tears at once, and folk could not gaze steadily at
it because their passions overwhelmed them. Copies of it were soon to
grace parks all over the world, and each would gather its separate daily
audience, as people simply stood and gazed as long as they were able
before the tears of intensifying emotion clouded their vision. He, too,
loved Chloe; no one could doubt.

Now came the moment for which all had been waiting: who had
fathomed Chloe's secret, to win the prize? What *was* that secret?

All three men shook their heads. After a moment Nahshon stepped
forward, as tacit spokesman. "I believe I speak for us all," he said. "We
do not know what secret you intended, but we have found the secret
meaningful to us. Chloe is the woman each of us can truly love in
every way, from the divine to the erotic, and we want to marry her and
be with her forever. Nothing else matters. Do with your prize what you
wish. Only let Chloe come forward now and choose between us."

The others nodded; it was the way they felt. Indeed, the three men
had come to a deep mutual respect, each appreciating both the art and
the taste in women of the others. There was no rivalry between them,
only a shared longing.

There was a pause. The program moderator was handed an enve-
lope. He had not been advised of the secret; now he would read it out.
Then Chloe herself would appear, to confirm it and to make her
choice of men.

But he didn't read it. He stood there, frowning.

The studio audience became impatient. A chant started and gained volume. "Chloe! Chloe! Chloe! Chloe!"

Finally the moderator shook his head and took the mike. The chant stilled.

"I want to say that I did not know this," the moderator said. "It comes as much of a surprise to me as it will to you. Frankly, I think someone has shown abysmal judgment, but it is my job to read this to you, and I shall do so."

What was going on? The audience was absolutely quiet.

"Chloe's secret was that she had a terminal ailment," he read. "A tumor on the brain stem, inoperable, and extremely painful. Only a nerve block enabled her to function normally. At the time of the dates she had only ten days left to function as a human being; thereafter she would be confined to the hospital, in intensive care, and would die within weeks. Instead of that, she elected to expend her last physical resources having the time of her life, and then to undertake euthanasia, making her death quick and clean."

The members of the studio audience maintained horrified silence.

After a moment he returned to the paper. "She left her regrets for the three fine men she dated. She loved each, and each made her happier than she had ever been in her life. She felt terrible guilt for the secret she could not tell them. Had she known that they were going to take the dates seriously, she would not have gone through with it. She had thought they would only pretend, and she would have been happy with that. Instead they gave her far more than she expected or deserved, and she leaves her most abject apology to them for the horror she inadvertently brought them into."

He looked up. "Chloe died yesterday."

There was a kind of low moan from the studio audience. The three men stared at each other, the shock of utter loss making masks of their faces.

"Her secret was death," Baird said, stunned.

"We fell in love with death," Standish agreed.

"We are all depressives, as truly creative people tend to be," Nahshon said. "We recognized that essential quality in her, and it transcended all else. She was the essence of what we all most deeply fear yet crave."

Then they left the stage, and the program was over. No one was interested in the money anymore. Sales of Acme Korn Pops plummeted, for now they reminded buyers of death.

The three great men did not die, but neither did they do any more significant creation. Their tokens for Chloe represented the pinnacles of their careers, and the terminations of them. They had no further interest in worldly things. They remained fast and melancholy friends for the rest of their lives, and faded into obscurity.

❖ 37 ❖

GEODE THOUGHT ABOUT the story of Chloe as he lay beside Jade in the dark. It was a story of love and sex and death. All her stories seemed to be of that nature. Œnone, who had lost her false husband and sought death. The Little Mermaid, who had never had a fair chance at her beloved. Teensa and the Bad Noble—that one hadn't had the main characters die, but it had flirted with it. Eve, who hadn't died unnaturally, but who had revolutionized human sexuality and was long dead. Nymph, whose childhood lover had died. Now Chloe, the epitome of those themes.

Jade was obsessed with sex and death, and she defined love in those terms. Those who loved most truly died. It didn't matter what she called herself, her obsession remained. That might be why she was convinced she would die.

But she was the only woman who had ever taken more than a brief interest in him. He did love her, and he believed she loved him. He thought he could be potent with her. He felt the stirrings in his groin. But if he was, and consummated their relationship, what would remain between her and death?

He wasn't sure, and for that reason he wasn't eager to try sex again.

Success might be worse than failure—if it meant she would no longer be with him.

"What are you thinking, Geode?" she asked.

Was he going to lie to her? No, he couldn't do that. "I think you think that any man with whom you share love is doomed to die, or if he isn't, you are. If I share love with you, you may die."

"Yes," she breathed, and he felt a hot tear drop on him.

"I don't want you to die. I'd rather not have sex, if that keeps you with me."

"That's sweet, Geode."

He caught her arm, and brought her down with him. She came down gladly; she liked it when he was able to assert himself with her, however innocently. Embraced, they slept.

In the morning, not waiting for routine matters, they set out on the rounds. It was more fun to see the dawn, Jade pointed out, and he was satisfied to do it. So by seven o'clock they started out. Geode ran, with Jade on the bicycle.

It was overcast, after the rains. Hundreds of nighthawks were flying low over the trees, going east, evidently questing through a layer of flying bugs. Then, above them, a ragged V formation of about twenty gooselike birds flew north.

"Oh, what are those?" she asked.

"Cattle egrets. Usually I see them moving one at a time, going to their day's assignments."

"Assignments?"

"They land near horses or cows, and eat the flies that cluster around them. They are good friends to cattle. They came here from Europe a generation or two ago, so some bird books don't list them, but no one wants them to go home."

"How nice," she said, swerving as a rabbit dashed across the road in front of her. It didn't hop, it ran somewhat in the fashion of a horse galloping: the two front feet, then the two hind feet together.

They moved off the paved road to the trail, going north. "Do you think the firefly is out?" she asked.

"The monster? Tonight."

"Yes, it's its time. But it must travel before it feeds. I wonder if it carries its smell along with it."

"Some, maybe. But it must save it for when it gets close to its prey."

"I think I smelled a whiff."

He paused, and she stopped the bicycle and stood beside him. "Here?" he asked, concerned.

"I'm not sure. Maybe I just wanted to."

"Wanted to? But the firefly kills people!"

"But what a way to go!"

He shook his head, horrified by the notion. "Cyrano will get it. We'll check in on him soon."

She laid down the bike. "I am afraid of what will happen. Geode, can you do it now?"

"Do what?"

For answer, she clutched him to her and kissed him ardently. Her body pressed tightly against him. "No one knows what will happen," she said. "Tomorrow may be too late."

She wanted sex, now. "I—don't want you to die," he protested.

"I think I will die if you don't."

That disturbed him. She would die if he didn't die—or if he didn't succeed in having sex with her? He didn't care to get that clarified.

"Jade, I want to. But you know I have to do it myself."

"Yes, and I shouldn't push, I know it! But I am like Chloe, I don't have a lot of time. Please, Geode, love me now!"

Geode had always known that he was not like other men; it was the major reason for his isolation. Now he knew that Jade was not like other women. Her change of names had not abated her preoccupation with death, it had accelerated it. What was he to do?

"Tell me a story," he said. "When it ends—"

"Yes, you're right!" she agreed eagerly.

"But not about death."

"Oh." She seemed out of sorts, but did not object.

They resumed their travel, and she spoke as she rode. "There was an old maid who lived in a house on a large, bedraggled lot. When she was younger, she kept it up, but now she just let it slide.

"One day some neighbor's children wandered through. They spied an old shed at the back of the old maid's house, and went in. They did not realize that the main house was occupied; they were too young to know how long the old maid had lived there. Finding themselves in this fairly comfortable and private mini-house, they proceeded to 'play house.'

"But as it happened, that shed had once been used for a dog, long since dead, and because the old maid had worried about the welfare of the dog, she had installed a one-way mirror that enabled her to see into the shed from a darkened back room of the main house. In that manner she had been able to check on her pet without disturbing him. Both the mirror and the room had long been unused, but when the old maid heard the children in the shed, she went quietly to check. She cleaned the cobwebs off the mirror, and found that it still worked as well as ever; she could see clearly into the shed, without its occupants seeing into her darkened room. In fact, she had an excellent view.

"What she saw surprised her. The two children were male and female, about ten and nine years old, and, it seemed, of different families. Naturally curious about each other and the opposite sex, they had decided to investigate. Thus the routine 'this is the stove, this is the chair, this is the food' (a pile of sand) had progressed to 'this is the bedroom, it is time to go to bed.' The boy had been getting bored with imagined furniture, but his interest was oddly restored when it came to the bedroom activity.

"The old maid watched as the little girl removed her clothes and lay down on the ancient straw mattress that was the play bed. The little boy took off his clothes and lay down beside her. 'No, you have to lie on top,' the girl said. So he lay on top of her, but it wasn't very comfortable for either of them. They compared notes, discussing what each had seen at one time or another, and concluded that he was supposed to put his thing into her, but first it had to be hard.

"He didn't know how to get it hard, but she had an idea. She stroked it with her hands, then licked it with her tongue. That worked; soon it was standing up. Then she spread her legs wide and he tried to put it in. It didn't work very well, and finally they gave it up as a bad job. They put their clothing back on and left the shed.

"The old maid sat in the dark room for some time, pondering. Then she fetched a small tube of lubricant intended for rectal thermometers and took it out to the shed. She left it on the straw bed. If the children returned on another day, she would be watching. For she realized that her dull life could become somewhat more interesting if she simply waited and watched and kept her mouth shut.

"And so it came to pass that on other days the children were more successful in their efforts to play house, and the old maid shared their secret without their knowing. Each had made the life of the other more interesting."

Geode, listening, realized that there was another theme which came into many of the stories: youth. Young girls having sex, or even children having sex with each other. Now that he had learned about Nymph, he understood why. But the notion of child sex didn't turn him on. Also, all her stories were from the viewpoint of the girl. "Do you have a story about a man?"

"A man?" She considered that, as if it were an odd notion.

"And not about children."

Again she seemed a bit disgruntled, but didn't object. "I suppose I can try, but I don't know how it will turn out."

He jogged on, satisfied to find out.

"There was a man whose neighbor's house was sold. When the new family arrived, it turned out to be a woman and her two daughters, one about sixteen, the other about twelve. The woman was unloading things from their rented truck, and fussing, so the man went over to inquire whether he could offer any assistance. 'Yes,' she said. 'If you would be so kind as to carry my daughter to her room, that would be a big help.'

"He was taken aback. 'Carry your daughter? Can't she walk?'

" 'Not well. She has an illness of the nerves, and cannot walk well, especially when tired from a long trip like this. When she has had suitable rest, she will be able to move around her room without falling, and of course outside she can use crutches.'

"Now he understood. 'Of course I will carry her,' he agreed.

" 'Thank you. She is sitting on the front seat.'

"He walked around the truck to the cab, and there was the older daughter. She had fine brown-black hair and blue eyes and delicate features; she was a fair-looking girl in her adolescence. 'May I carry you to your room?' he inquired.

"She put her hands down on the seat and shifted her body somewhat so that she was able to turn her legs toward him. She wore some kind of a hospital robe, which fell open to reveal her rather shapely legs to the thighs. She reached out and put her hands on his shoulders and leaned forward into him.

" 'I don't know if this is the best way to—' he said. He had supposed he would get an arm around her shoulders and the other under her knees and carry her that way, but instead she was coming down on him vertically. He had no choice but to put his arms around her quickly, so that she would not fall to the ground. As she slid off the seat he caught her under the bottom, but he could not quite get around her to link his hands. She continued to slide down, and he had to grab her any way he could. This turned out to be on the buttocks, one hand on each; he couldn't let go for fear of dropping her. The mounds he grasped were surprisingly full and soft; the girl had seemed not to be full-bosomed, but she was filling out below. To make it worse, her gown was falling open in the manner typical of its kind, and her back was bare. His fingers, groping for a better hold, closed on bare flesh.

"She circled her arms around his neck and clung tightly to him, her head beside his head, her breasts pressing against his chest. He had been mistaken about her upper development; she was braless, so that her bosom was not standing out, but it was definitely there. She was the softest thing he had handled in a long time! He found himself reacting, for though his mind knew that he was merely carrying her to her room, his body only knew that a very fine and shapely body was plastered to his own.

"He turned, leaning back to get her full weight on him, keeping his balance, and stumbled forward toward the house. But with each step he took, her body slid down a touch, and he couldn't prevent it. 'Maybe if you grip me with your knees, you won't slide down so much,' he gasped. 'Can you do that?'

"Her knees tightened against his sides; she was doing it. But still she slid, and he realized with distress that her slowly descending body was now carrying with it his trousers. He wore no belt, preferring elastic around the waist, and this elastic gave way readily to the pressure. He was in the process of being depanted!

"But he couldn't let her go. As he entered the house, he tried a desperate device. 'I will heave you up, and catch you higher,' he told her. 'Are you ready? Heave!' And he heaved, and she rose several inches—but his trousers didn't. He staggered several steps farther, then heaved again, and again it worked, but not for his trousers. He was in desperate straits.

" 'Where is your room?' he gasped.

"She indicated a room to the right. He carried her in there—and discovered that there was no bed as yet, or other furniture in it. Unwilling to dump her on the floor, but needing to put her somewhere so that he could pull up his trailing trousers, he lumbered across the room to the window. He set her posterior on the sill just as his trousers and shorts lost their last purchase and dropped to the floor, about his ankles.

"He looked past her head and her cloud of hair, out the window. This was a rear chamber, opening on a small yard limited by a big wooden wall that screened it from his own house beyond. But the oddest thing was that to the side there seemed to be a bit of forest and a body of water, perhaps a lake, when he knew there was nothing like that in this neighborhood. He stared, but could not get a sufficient view of it past her head. He drew back his head—and she drew back hers, and met his gaze directly. Her eyes seemed as deep as the sky.

"Now he realized that somehow not only had his trousers dropped, but her robe had ridden up or been drawn aside, so that his crotch was against hers. His member had shrunk in the effort of carrying her, but now it was resurging—and it was right at her cleft. If he didn't move away quickly, it would grow right into her!

"He knew that he should disengage immediately. But her eyes held him, and her grip on his shoulders did not relent. Only her knees relaxed, letting his body nudge more firmly against hers as her legs spread wide. She was a lovely girl, and seemed so willing, that somehow he just remained in place and let his erection find its way.

"Then he heard a sound outside the house. The girl's mother was coming in! In a moment they would be discovered! Yet such was the passion of the moment, he did not draw away. Instead he began to thrust, hoping that somehow he could complete the job and disengage before her mother—"

They were coming into the vicinity of the cabin. Geode discovered that he had an erection himself. He stopped and turned to her. Jade literally jumped off the bike and hiked up her skirt; she had nothing on beneath now, though he was sure she had when they started out. He loosened his belt and dropped his jeans and shorts, and she leaped into his arms, wrapping her legs around him. "In! In!" she exclaimed.

He was trying to hold her up, catching her in the same grip as described in the story, his hands on her buttocks. But he wasn't in her. What would the man in the story have done?

"He let go with one hand for a moment," Jade gasped, as if continuing the story. "And reached around and between her spread thighs, finding his member and pushing it into place."

Gratefully, he suited her word to his action. But not with perfect skill. He was standing, barely maintaining his balance, with her clinging to him, and somehow it just wasn't aligned. Things were jamming instead of juxtaposing.

"It snagged," she said. "But then she wiggled, and abruptly it went in." Her skill was greater than his, making her words accurate.

Just like that, he penetrated her. She clung to him, and bounced, and then pulled her face around to meet his, and kissed him. The muscles of her cleft clenched, and then he was thrusting, and the spasm of it took him.

He was so awe-stricken by the accomplishment that it muted much of the pleasure. *He had achieved sex with a woman!* He stood there, holding her, as his orgasm passed. What an accomplishment!

She broke the kiss at last, and smiled at him. "I knew you could do it, Geode. I love you."

"I love you," he echoed.

Then the position became awkward. Actually, it had been awkward from the start, but their mutual eagerness to get the job done had overridden all else. She put down her feet, touched the ground as he bent his knees to bring her down, and let him slide out of her. Quickly, efficiently, she mopped herself with a tissue, and put on her panties (which magically reappeared) and skirt. He put on his own clothing.

Then they resumed their travel, without speaking a further word. None was necessary.

Yet even as they came in sight of the cabin, Geode had his erection back. It struggled for straightness within his jeans, embarrassing him. He managed to get it vertical, relieving some of the discomfort, but the desire for renewed sex remained.

"It's the firefly!" Jade exclaimed, noticing. "I feel it too!"

That was it, of course. She had thought she smelled it before, and had begged him for sex; now they were closer to the source, and were both affected.

"We can't let Cyrano see us like this!" she said. Indeed, her bosom was heaving, her eyes were staring, and her mouth fell to slackness when she wasn't talking.

"But I have to check on him, and tell him Mid didn't call back."

"Yes. So take the edge off, now." She got off the bike again and grabbed his arm, drawing him behind a large live oak.

It made sense. If they did it now, they would be relaxed in Cyrano's presence, and not embarrass themselves. He dropped his jeans again, as she scrambled out of her skirt and panties.

There was no art to it. He spread his legs and bent his knees so as to lower his torso, and she stepped in and set herself on his member. She was so well lubricated that penetration was immediate and complete. It was just like one of her stories! Then she closed her legs tightly, sealing him into her, and clasped his body to hers. Spread-legged, he thrust, so hard it actually lifted her from the ground, and burst. The orgasm was more powerful than before, radiating out from his groin and spreading through his thighs and belly. The entire center of his torso was a nexus of ultimate pleasure.

"The wine of the gods," she gasped, shuddering against him. Her climax provided pleasure to the waning stages of his, extending its delight. "I've never had one like this! You're some lover, Geode!"

"It's the firefly," he reminded her. That was the one flaw in this bliss. He knew he hadn't done it himself, he had borrowed the pheromones provided by the firefly. It signaled not his conquest of impotence, but the power of the creature they hunted. The power to give even an impotent man a violent erection, and to make a woman climax almost as fast as he did, just from that penetration. No sex was like that, in ordinary life, he was sure.

"We'll do it again at the house!" she exclaimed as she relaxed. "We'll do it on our own! We don't need the firefly!"

Geode nodded agreement, though he wasn't sure. The sniff of the monster's victims had given him erections, yet his impotence had remained. Now the firefly was close, and performing its magic.

"Now we've done it, we can do it again!" she said as she got hastily back into her clothing, and he got into his.

He hoped so! This had been an experience like no other, and he didn't want to give it up.

But now they had to see Cyrano. They checked each other, making sure that their sudden savage bout of sex did not show, and cut across the field toward the cabin.

Yet even as he reached the door, Geode felt his erection returning. Those pheromones would not let go!

Cyrano let them in. His trousers were bulging, and the man did not bother to conceal it. "The thing is close, and getting closer," he said. "How many times did you folk have to have it off before you made it here?"

Secrecy was impossible! "Twice," Geode said.

"And more coming up," Jade agreed.

"I figure the thing never went far, after the last one," Cyrano said. "It stayed near, so its ambience built up, and now it's closing for the kill, turning it on. It doesn't even care if I know it's coming; it figures it can take me."

"You shouldn't wait for it alone," Jade said.

"You folk don't dare wait here! You'd be so busy fucking you wouldn't be any help anyway, no offense."

"No offense," she agreed. "It's true."

"Mid never called back," Geode said.

"Good! After sitting through this, damned if I want to give it up. I can't eat or relax; I just sit here watching and thinking of sex orgies. Gimme a hundred women, any age, or a hundred men even—it wouldn't be enough. I'm saving the mask for nightfall; that's when the firefly'll come all the way in. That's when I've got to have my mind on my business instead of my pecker. Now get out of here before I attack the two of you. Come back in the morning, and I'll have the thing caged."

They nodded, and made a hasty retreat. Such was their renewed urgency that they couldn't even get clear of the house; they stepped into each other against the outer wall, tearing fly open and panties aside, and pounded into mergence. They didn't care if Cyrano overheard; he understood the situation well enough. They didn't bother with kissing; that only slowed things.

This time Geode wasn't sure he actually ejaculated, but he did have the orgasm. It seemed to reach down to his knees and up to his chest. Jade seemed to feel the same; every part of her body touching him was hot and slick with sweat.

Then she pulled back, not waiting for his erection to subside, and yanked her clothing into place. Geode crammed his member back into his jeans. As an afterthought, she hauled her panties off and tucked them into a pocket, so that she was bare-bottomed. He didn't need to ask why. They resumed their tour, he afoot, she on the bike.

But instead of going limp, his penis only softened somewhat. Already it was girding for further action. Jade, glancing sidelong at him, licked her lips. How far through the forest would they make it before they had to pause again?

"Maybe next time you can stay on the bike," he said. "I'll come up behind. You can support yourself better, using the handlebars."

"Yes," she said. "That will be faster. I'll just lean forward." Because, as they both knew now, love was not the object here; there was only sex, as fast and often as feasible. Until they got out of the ambience of the firefly.

✦ 38 ✦

CYRANO HEARD THEM going at it just outside the door. God, what he wouldn't do for a woman right now! But that would be no good for the same reason that their company was no good: you couldn't keep good watch while you were fucking.

He walked to the window and watched them go. She was riding the red bicycle, with a short skirt, and her bare bottom showed in flashes as her legs pumped. Damn, he envied Demerit right now! That little bitch might be in her thirties, but in the ambience of the firefly she had become the sexiest creature on two legs.

But the lure of the monster was greater. Sex was a sometime thing, but the capture of the firefly would be the accomplishment of the century. After that he could have all the sex he wanted, simply by bringing a woman near it. Mid would make a fortune—the man knew how to exploit a thing like this!—and he would reward Cyrano suitably. Success, notoriety, and wealth: everything offered, after this night. So what was a little sexual frustration?

He turned from the window and walked back to his central chair. His trousers pulled tight in the crotch, and he felt his member throbbing again, going into a familiar spasm.

He waited for it to subside, then opened his fly. He unwrapped the handkerchief from his penis, wiped around himself, and brought out a new handkerchief. He wound this carefully around the member and tucked the mass in, closing his fly. He had lost count of the number of spasms he had had; there was a pile of soggy handkerchiefs in the sink. He was trying to avoid climaxing, because it wasn't good to push the body too far; after a time the semen would be exhausted and a bloodlike fluid would spurt instead. To the pheromones it made no difference; they whipped the horse onward though it died in the effort. But he wanted to preserve his health. So he mostly sat, unmoving, and watched, though there were hours yet before the firefly came.

Came—now there was a nice entendre. The firefly came, and the victim came. But the firefly was feeding, and the victim was dying. Dying in ecstasy, but nevertheless done for. That wasn't what he wanted.

Had the firefly ever before encountered a victim who was ready for it? Cyrano doubted it. Down in the depths of the sea, there was no human intelligence. Oh, there were some pretty smart creatures, all right. The whale had a brain bigger than man's—but when figured as a proportion of total body mass, it was smaller. The giant squids were smart; they had to be, to control their prehensile tentacles. But only man had gone beyond the constraints of his environment and into art and technology and philosophy. Only man was aware of his own mortality—and guarded against it with a foresight unmatchable by any other creature.

Even if the thing had human intelligence, it didn't have technology, and that would spell the difference. A native from an uncivilized tribe would have complete human intelligence, but would be helpless against the marvels of civilization. The Europeans had destroyed the primitives of America not because they were better men, or smarter, but because they had technology. The simple facet of it known as the gun had made all the difference.

Well, Cyrano had a gun here, but he didn't expect to use it. He had a cattle prod too, and assorted other gimmicks. The prod he expected to use; with it he would prod the firefly into the cage. He still didn't know what the firefly looked like, but he judged it was small, really no larger than a man, and defenseless, other than its chemical factory. Otherwise it wouldn't be sneaking in at night; it would be charging in by day, in the manner of a tiger.

Mainly, he would be alert, as the victims usually weren't, and using the gas mask, as none had before. Instead of a passive victim, the firefly would find an active one. That should be an entirely different matter.

The firefly. That was certainly a good name for it. To human beings, the flashing of fireflies in the dusk was pretty and quaint, but to the fireflies themselves it was a matter of reproduction and death. The flashes were sexual signals, and the males would fly around for days in the hope of a connection that would be over in seconds. Sometimes a female of a related, predator species would signal a male in, and he would come down with ardent expectations. But when he tried to mate, his light would flash in desperation, for instead of cop- ulation he found death. The female caught him and consumed him. Sex had lured him to his doom. Cyrano had speculated more than once on the irony of that. That might have been a reason he had never married.

His erection was painful again. It required only minutes for the urge to recharge. Those pheromones were amazingly potent! They were the firefly lights that signaled human beings in, and they were every bit as compelling.

But a firefly who knew the signals were false would not fly in. In every species, survival was stronger than the sexual urge. Even among the praying mantises, maligned as cannibals. It was true that in some species the female consumed the male, and indeed even decapitated him before he completed copulation, but he survived long enough to impregnate her, and in most cases he completed his mission and moved away unscathed. If he knew she was going to eat him, he would stay clear. There was the key: *if he knew*.

Cyrano knew the monster was coming to consume him. No amount of sexual incentive could override that awareness. The firefly did not know that this victim was aware and ready, so the tables would be turned. If the firefly knew, it would avoid him—but it couldn't know. It was coming in for the kill; that was the proof it didn't know.

Where was the monster hiding? The more Cyrano dwelt on this, the more he realized that it had to be close, very close. The prior victims had not been aware of such tremendous sexual imperative; they had slept, or in the case of Bull Shauer, had been stunned. So they had been unconscious or unable to move, and the monster had crept up on them and taken them. Had they wakened when it touched them? Maybe, but then it was too late. The pheromones in the air had been replaced by the pheromones in direct contact. Or by paralyzing drugs, more likely. Contact was too late, whether the victim was an amorous male firefly or a human being.

So the monster had homed in on sleeping victims, and the pheromones had been less evident. But this time it had remained in the vicinity, and its cloud of pheromones had intensified. It might even be snoozing under this house. Cyrano had checked the place carefully, inside and out, and found nothing, but since he did not know what he was looking for, that didn't mean much. Maybe the firefly had watched him, then moved close when he finished checking. That would not take more intelligence than was available to any predator. Certainly the presence was strong, and had been all day. Last night too; Cyrano had slept, and had had violently sexy dreams, but had been secure in the knowledge that it was too soon for the firefly to feed.

He pondered again its likely mode of reproduction. Parthenogenic egg-laying, using the substance culled from the victims as the substance of the eggs, there to feed the developing embryo. All the elements of a good diet were present, except perhaps those locked in the bones. The firefly might not have bones. So it laid an egg every three days, and went in search of more protein.

Where were those eggs? They must be buried somewhere. Surely they weren't out in the open, where any animal could chew on them! They had to be under the earth, or perhaps in the water of the river or lake. A creature from the sea surely returned to the water for that; it would be thousands of years before it adapted to the land. So under the muck of the lake was where the eggs had to be. When would they hatch? After he captured the firefly, maybe he would be able to track down the eggs and learn their cycle. Maybe the firefly would lay an egg in captivity, and he could study it that way. The possibilities were exciting.

So Cyrano pondered, as he waited for the firefly, all afternoon. The waiting was dull, and he began to get sleepy, but he knew that was death. He roused himself, took a drink of water, and sat back in his chair. He could sleep after he had captured the firefly!

At last dusk came. The ambience of sex was even more intense. His erection was painful, and didn't subside even when there was another emission. In fact, he seemed to be approaching a state of continuous low-grade orgasm, his groin hot and pleasant. It was time for the mask.

He donned it. Soon his body relaxed; the pheromones were being filtered out. It was a relief!

Now he heard something. It was a high keening, as of a tuning fork, faint but definite. Was that the hunting melody of the firefly? No one now alive knew for sure! Maybe its metabolism was such that it had to make that noise when traveling, the way the wings of wood doves whistled as they flew up from the ground. But the sound was so faint that it wouldn't wake a sleeping person.

He gripped his cattle prod in one hand and a knife in the other. The thing was flesh, so the knife would cut it, but he hoped he wouldn't have to do that. He intended to trap it in the cabin and then prod it into the cage and seal it in. Then he would feed it chunks of meat or whatever it would consume; soon enough he would find out how to maintain it. But first he had to catch his rabbit.

The keening grew louder. Where was its origin? He couldn't tell; it seemed directionless. But it meant the monster was close, very close. He felt excitement, and some fear; this was dangerous, he knew. Before, the concupiscence had blotted out fear, which might also account for prior victims' failure to flee. In a moment it should show itself.

He was sweating. Nervous energy—and a long time seated. His trousers were clammy against his buttocks; he felt almost as if he were sitting on a cushion of water. But he was not about to move until he spied the firefly. He didn't want to scare it off. It had to think he was asleep or helpless. Once it discovered otherwise, the battle would be on.

His posterior was turning numb. He ought to stand up, get some circulation in his legs, but not right at this moment. The keening was loud now, seeming to be all around him. The firefly was close, close! In a moment he would see it slide in that door. For he suspected it was snakelike; only a python could account for its lack of footprints. Or a slug. Something low and quiet, with the ability to move across the ground without leaving a trace. A snake was the most likely. But maybe more like a ribbonfish, flat, so it could squeeze under a door. He didn't dare move until it committed itself, and actually entered the chamber.

He must be sweating something fierce! Now he felt a trickle sliding down between his buttocks, across his anus. He wanted to scratch, but his hands were full of prod and knife. Where was that monster? He was about to slide out of his chair on a tide of nervous sweat!

Something seemed to probe his anus; it was an almost physical sensation, distracting him from his watch on the doorway. Wouldn't it be ironic if he broke his concentration to shift about and scratch at his ass, and right then the firefly came in and caught him with his guard down! He held his gaze where it belonged; to hell with his sweaty seat!

The probe centered, and infiltrated. It was like grease sliding into his rectum, setting up for the enema hose. As it got inside, it felt good, very good. It was as though the enema were starting, warm and smooth, distending his chamber, no real pressure yet, just nice and relaxing. With a pretty nurse operating it, her touch delicate, almost caressing. It was on the verge of sexual, the way it spread into the tissue, the lining, turning it on. In fact, it was as if he were starting another orgasm, this one centered on the anus instead of the penis.

An orgasm? He touched his mask. Was it leaking? Were the pheromones getting through? No, it seemed tight. But he was definitely feeling a sexual thrill down there.

Then, slowly, he realized. The firefly—it had somehow come up behind him! It had extended a pseudopod into his pants and gotten into his ass! It was cornholing him!

He should jump up, rip it out, turn, and bash it! Everything depended on immediate action. He knew that.

But he knew also that what he was feeling was the most exquisite sensation ever in his life. His entire colon was radiating pleasure. Forget about orgasms; this was beyond them! It was so great, he just had to savor it a moment more, just a moment more, before he gave it up. He knew what he had to do, but it could wait that one second. Two seconds.

Cyrano sat there, and he didn't move. The rapture spread upward and outward, through his body.

The firefly was feeding.

❖ 39 ❖

"**D**AMN IT!" FRANK Tishner gazed at
the clothed skeleton sitting in the chair. Even the gas mask remained in
place, hanging on the front of the skull. Cyrano had so eagerly sought
the monster, and had underestimated it. One more victim claimed.

What was he going to do? Cyrano had taken away the last body, but
that couldn't happen now. There seemed to be no alternative; he had
to do it himself.

He went out and checked Cyrano's van. Sure enough, there was a
shovel there, in an assortment of useful tools. He walked to the verge
of the forest, where leaves covered the floor. He donned gloves and
carefully brushed the leaves to one side, making a pile. Then, picking
a section without roots, he went to work with the shovel.

He dug a deep, narrow hole, setting the dirt on the piled leaves.
Then he went to the cabin and gingerly picked up the chair with the
bones. This close contact gave him a whiff of it; he wished he could
hold his breath, but he couldn't. In consequence, he got an erection.
He hated this business of handling a gruesome corpse and reacting as
if it gave him a sexual thrill. Understanding about pheromones helped
some, but not enough; he knew that what was coming off those bones
was entering his system and putting it through hoops.

303

He balanced the chair so that nothing slid off, and carried it out to his hole. There he tilted it, letting the bones slide off, into the hole. They hung up at the rim; he did what he didn't like, and used his gloves to pack them together so that they would go down. When they were all in, he shoveled in the dirt, packing it down firmly. There was too much, so he carried several shovelfuls to the river and tossed them in. Then he spread the leaves back across, so that the site looked undisturbed. Only if someone knew exactly where to look would this be discovered—and who would be looking?

It was well hidden; his erection was subsiding. What a way to verify a thing like that!

He took the chair back to the cabin and set it where it had been. He took Cyrano's knife and cattle prod back to the van and added them and the shovel to the pile of tools. He checked to make sure there was no other evidence of Cyrano's presence. Fortunately, the man had been all business, not even eating during his vigil; there were no traces.

Now, what about the van? Where could he take it, where it wouldn't be found?

The question prompted others. How could he drive it somewhere distant—without leaving his own car here? And in order to drive it, he needed the keys. The keys! He had forgotten to take them from the body! Was he going to have to dig it up again to get them?

But when he checked, he found them in the ignition. He could drive it! Had that been carelessness? Cyrano had not struck him as a careless man. More likely he hadn't wanted them to clink on his person, possibly alerting the monster, so had left them here. There seemed to have been no coins among the bones, either. So it was care rather than careless.

Yet the firefly had won the game. It had taken an alert, prepared victim—indeed, one who had expected to capture or kill it. That was chilling in its own special way.

Where was the firefly now? Surely it hadn't gone far, bloated with the flesh of another man, yet it was hidden at least as well as the buried bones.

He stood beside the van, pondering. He would have to get help; that was the only way. Geode, most likely.

Well, so be it. Geode had as big a stake in this as anyone.

He returned to his car, removed the gloves, and got in. This was his own car, not the marked sheriff's department vehicle. He started it and drove down the trail.

Somewhere in this forest was the firefly. They could probably kill it readily, if only they could find it! How could the thing hide so well, and strike so well, even when they knew the time and place of its next feeding? They had assumed it was an animal, but this was cunning beyond animal level.

Cyrano had obviously been sitting there, waiting for the firefly—yet had not moved when it came. He would not have been sleeping—unless the monster had the ability to put its prey to sleep. Had the gas mask malfunctioned? Frank didn't know how effective it would be against pheromones, yet presumably Cyrano had been assured that it was. In any event, an erection wouldn't have put him to sleep, it would have alerted him.

About all Frank could conclude was that it wasn't smart to await the firefly alone. It had never taken two people together, or taken one in the alert presence of another. So far.

He came to the house and stopped. Geode emerged, and after a moment, the woman. She was calling herself Jade now, instead of Œnone; May had explained about that. She did look duller, not nearly as pretty as she had two days ago.

"It got him," he said simply. "I buried the bones. Need help to hide the truck."

Geode nodded. "I'll go."

"Wait," Jade said. "You will have to take it a long way, so that when it is found it won't be associated with this region where people have already disappeared. If anybody sees you, that's trouble. Someone else should do it, and come back with Frank."

Was she trying to be difficult? "We don't have much choice or time," Frank pointed out. "Or personnel. Who were you thinking of?"

"May."

Frank paused, surprised. Of course May could do it! "Yeah, I suppose so, if she's willing."

The woman merely looked at him, and abruptly he knew that she knew everything about him and May Flowers. That was why she had suggested it. She was giving him an excuse for time alone with May.

He turned back to his car. "Thanks."

Jade only smiled faintly. She seemed self-satisfied about more than that, despite her duller appearance, and he could figure only one reason why: she must finally have landed her man. Odd that she had done it while looking worse instead of better.

As he drove on, he pieced that minor mystery together. The firefly

had fed again, and they all knew about its use of pheromones. Geode
and Jade were touring the Middle Kingdom Ranch together now; the
woman had fastened on him with rare tenacity. They had checked on
Cyrano; he knew that, because they had advised him, so he could be
on the scene to solve the riddle of the firefly, according to the deal he
had made at the outset with May. The fact that he had found Cyrano's
body instead didn't matter in this connection; it only confirmed that
they had been right, and that the firefly had come to the cabin that
night. The ambience of sex, as it came in to feed, must have been
horrendous. If the little bit left on the corpse was enough to give him
a continuous erection, what of the firefly itself? So they had passed that
region, and smelled the approaching monster, and—you bet they'd
made a night of it! Now they were happy but worn out. Mystery solved.

Which reminded him of May. Damn, he wanted that woman again!
Maybe it was a thinning cloud of pheromones in this region, causing
sexual reactions all over. But mostly it was May. She was no sexy
young beauty, but that really wasn't his type anyway. Sure, he'd watch
the pert figures on TV, but that was the stuff of fantasy. Reality was a
woman he could relate to, and that had turned out to be May Flowers.
He never would have predicted it, but it was so. Maybe it was that he
knew she didn't give any part of herself to any man lightly. He could
hardly blame her, after the marriage she'd had with that thug. But she
was competent and knew her own mind, and if she saw something in
him, he sure as hell saw something in her. He had never figured
himself for a two-timer, considering that his wife had never given him
cause, but there it was.

So he would ask May to help him with that van, because he wanted
to be with her again. She would accept, for much the same reason.
Jade Brown had understood that much perfectly.

He stopped at a pay phone and called her. Quickly he explained the
need, and as quickly she agreed, no questions asked. He arranged to
pick her up around the corner from the hotel, so as not to be obvious;
neither one of them wanted that sort of publicity, and small towns had
big eyes.

He drove her out to the cabin, updating her on what he had done.
Then she got out and took over the van. They had decided to leave it
in a large parking lot in another county, near a train station; with luck,
it would be weeks before anyone realized it was deserted. Some pas-

senger trains still ran, but often late, so there were always cars parked in the vicinity. What he didn't say was that he was hot for her again, for whatever reason; they did have work to do, so it wasn't the time.

She drove the van up to Ocala. Then, a few minutes behind her, he drove to the station and through the lot, pausing only long enough at a deserted corner for her to appear and get in. He doubted that anyone had seen them. He moved by another route back down to Citrus County, not wanting to attract any possible attention from anyone who might know him.

Then he glanced at her. "This may be way out of line, but—"

"Of course, Frank," she said, understanding perfectly. No cutesy games about her; she was all business, even in pleasure, and right now he really appreciated that.

"You know you don't have to," he said, though his erection was there, as it had been intermittently the whole time.

"With you, I want to." She laughed. "That is a compliment, because I never wanted to before. In all my years with Bull, it was never voluntary on my part. It was obligation, and then fear. I did anything to keep him from getting angry. I thought I'd never have any use for sex, other than as self-defense. But now, knowing you want me, I want you. I was thinking about you the whole time I drove that van, foolish as that may have been."

He pulled into a side road, and drove until they came to a lonely turnaround. "This sort of thing isn't much, in a car."

"It's enough." She pulled down her panties, lifted her skirt, and hauled herself up off the seat, giving him room to slide into the passenger seat beneath her as he got his trousers down to the knees. Then she sat on him, much as before—and as before, he climaxed almost as he completed entry. There was something about her fleshy thighs and soft posterior against his legs and belly, and the audacity of doing it like teenagers in a car, with their clothing not even off, just pushed aside enough, that triggered him instantly. Even the damned discomfort of the jammed situation contributed, making it seem forbidden and therefore more exciting.

"Oh, no!" he groaned, chagrined again.

But she was laughing. "I never thought I was sexy, but you certainly make me feel that way!"

"Must be the position," he muttered.

"Or the pheromones," she said cheerfully.

"Look, I'm spent, but there are ways to—if you want me to—"

She squirmed around so that she could bring her mouth to his, kissing him. "It's enough," she repeated. "I wanted to make you happy, and I think I have done so in the most efficient manner."

"You really don't mind?" he asked incredulously.

"I really don't mind. Just hold me."

That he could do. So, awkwardly and not yet disconnected, they embraced, and kissed again, more deeply. Then, oddly, he felt her reaction.

"I sure see something in you," he said squeezing her, "but I'm damned if I see what you see in me."

"What you have in me cannot be seen at the moment," she remarked. "As for the other—you're a gentle man."

"I'm not a gentle man! I run people in all the time, in my business."

"Yes, you are gentle—where it counts."

"If you mean I'm not like that wife-beating husband you had—"

"Exactly."

"But he was a freak! Only criminals are like that. The average man condemns that sort of thing just as I do."

"But you're the one I encountered."

"It's thin, very thin," he said. "Just because I don't beat up on women is no reason to—"

But she cut him off with another kiss. He decided not to argue further. She had to have more reason than that—he hoped. Perhaps she did, for again he felt her reaction around his member, which had not diminished far yet. She was, after all, getting something out of it, in her way. He was glad.

In due course they straightened out and he started back toward town. They had succeeded in hiding yet another depredation of the firefly—but it would be impossible to keep the lid on much longer if they didn't get rid of the monster. Inevitably it would take a regular townsman, and then all hell would break loose. They both knew that.

He dropped her off near her hotel, then went to swap his car for the deputy car. He had his regular job to do too, and it was getting harder to answer questions about his time.

❖ 40 ❖

May RETURNED TO her room, more satisfied than she felt she had a right to be. It remained a new experience for her to turn on a man to such a degree that he lost control—and to have him be apologetic for that. Never in all her years with Bull had that been the case, and it was exhilarating now. Who would have thought that it could happen when she was a too-solid forty! It was the stuff of dreams. But apart from that she did like him, and it did please her to please him, so she had not deceived him. She was in love late, but in love. The future was at best murky, but the moment was wonderful.

Actually, she had gotten a kind of satisfaction from the act itself. It could not have been an orgasm in that little time, yet she had thrilled physically as she felt him spurting up into her, and their continued contact had allowed her pleasure to last, perhaps even to increase. Maybe the sheer audacity of it, of pulling up her skirt like a whore in a car, in daylight, and jamming down on his member, had excited her to the point of a reaction. She had wanted that sex, and had reveled in it, though this was completely unlike her. In a private room, in darkness, she could have been properly receptive, but in that car—that was amazing. Now she felt warm there, satiated. Had she realized, she would have told Frank that, and pleased him even more.

But the larger situation was dubious indeed. Frank was right: it had been only sheer luck and grit that this thing hadn't blown wide open yet. Now the firefly had taken Cyrano, and their best chance to destroy it without notoriety was gone. What were they to do? If this thing blew open, Mid would fire her and Geode, and Frank would lose his job, and they would all be in dire straits.

Well, there was no help for it: she would have to call Mid and let him know. She should have called him in the morning, but had wanted to get the bases covered first. She did not relish this at all. Therefore she did it immediately. With luck, she would get the answering machine.

Mid answered directly. "You hid the body?" he asked.

May was taken aback. Then she realized that Geode would have called; he was an employee too. She was off the hook!

"Frank Tishner did," she said. "Then we took the van to another town and—"

"Your husband's body," he snapped.

"What?" She had never heard Mid angry before.

"In Cyrano's van. You hid those bones?"

"OhmyGod!" she gasped, appalled. "They must have been still in there, in his body bag!"

"Did you not smell them?"

The sex—they had both been so eager for it! Frank might be understandable, being male, but she—she should have realized that something more was goosing her along! She had been glad to oblige him, true—but she had had no reticence at all. She had *wanted* it. There in the car, where they might have been discovered at any moment, jammed in uncomfortably—of course those lingering pheromones had acted! She had driven that van all those miles, soaking them up, thinking of Frank with increasing ardor. Those pheromones, clinging to her, setting him off too!

"I think my husband had vengeance on me even in death," she said.

"Your fingerprints—you wiped them off?"

May's heart sank. "I—didn't think of it," she said leadenly. So obvious, to wipe the wheel and gearshift and door handle clean, to remove the last vestige of her association with it. She had been so eager to get away from the van, and back with Frank, that she had bungled badly.

"Get those bones!" Mid hung up.

May got up, left the room, went down to her car, and started driving. She drove toward Ocala, depressed. At least Mid hadn't fired her outright. But she had let him down seriously.

There was something on the road. She could not swerve far enough to avoid it; there was opposing traffic. She ran over it—and felt the bump, and heard a horrendous hiss.

She had run over a badly twisted fragment of metal and punctured a tire.

She pulled over to the side, getting out of the way of other traffic. It could have been worse; she could have gone out of control and had a serious accident. As it was, all she would lose was time.

She unlocked and opened the trunk. She started to take out the spare tire—and discovered it was flat.

There was a cut in it. The tire had been deliberately punctured.

But why, and how? The trunk had been locked, and she had the only key!

Then she remembered Bull. He had taken her car. He must have done this as a special surprise for her, for such time as she got her car back. It was his way.

Twice now, in death, he had scored on her. How she hated that man!

There was no salvaging either tire. She was stuck.

She turned on the blinker lights and waited for help to come. The need galled her, but she knew that fretting was pointless. So she fretted.

Before long a car from the sheriff's department stopped. If she had had the flat in Citrus County it might have been Frank who stopped, but this was Marion County. She explained her predicament.

"May I see your registration, please?"

"Of course." She kept it with the car. She opened the dash compartment—and discovered Bull's third mean-spirited gift. The registration was gone.

Was it somewhere in the hotel room, as her purse with her own identification had been? Or had he hidden it in his own car, which had disappeared? With sick certainty she knew it was the latter. He had taken it so as to hold her car hostage to his will. He might even have planned to make her drive her own car while he drove his, knowing that the moment she strayed he could report her car as stolen. He had died before he could put the whole of this mischief into practice, but this piece of it was bad enough.

Before it was done, she had to go to the station and make a call to Geode. Soon Mid called the station and established the ownership of the car. "Don't go to the van," he told her tersely. She knew why: she was now known, and any contact with the van on her part would be mischief enough. She was lucky the deputy hadn't checked her purse and found its keys. They would have to let the van take its chances. With luck it wouldn't be checked soon, and when it was, someone else might be assigned to drive it away, and her prints would be obscured. She hated having to depend on luck, but it was now her best chance.

In due course she was on her way back to Inverness, tires repaired, chastened. She had messed up, and though Mid understood what her husband had done, it remained her failing. If anything else happened, her employment would be in trouble. Mid would not fire her with prejudice, because he knew that she had done her best, but she knew that sentiment went only so far with him. Her job was now as tenuous as Frank's job, for similar reasons. What damage Bull had done, even after his death!

She shopped for groceries again and went out to the ranch. She explained in more detail what had happened. "So it is a gamble; when that van is checked, the bones will be discovered. If they are identified as Bull's, they will know that he had a connection with Cyrano, who is mysteriously missing. It will land here at the Middle Kingdom Ranch soon enough, because Cyrano was Mid's employee, and Bull was my husband, and I am Mid's employee. I will be under suspicion, especially if they find my fingerprints there. It will not be possible to hide the firefly much longer."

"You have been so kind to me," Jade said. She was calling herself that now, as the result of their conversation, but May was uncertain whether it truly helped. "I am sorry to be the cause of such distress."

"You are not the cause!" May protested. "It's my husband, and the firefly, working in unwitting tandem. We have to get rid of the firefly! Then perhaps we can stifle the rest of it."

"Yes, of course," Jade agreed, subdued.

But privately May was doubtful that it could be done. The monster was such an ugly thing, its revelation would attract wide attention. In order to explain the bones they would have to reveal the firefly, and there would not be any quick end to the matter.

Still, if they killed the firefly soon, so that the depredations ceased, then they might go quietly out to the van before it was discovered and move it elsewhere, or at least remove the bones and prints. Then things might remain quiet. They could tide through—if they were able to wrap it up quickly.

Moderately heartened, May drove away from the house. Maybe she could find a pretext for another liaison with Frank; that notion cheered her.

❖ 41 ❖

GEODE WATCHED HER go, then turned to Jade. "The next time it feeds, we have to get it," he said.

"Geode, I am afraid."

"The firefly can't get in here."

"I think it can."

"Even if it could, there are two of us. We can stop it. That's the best way—to let it try."

She looked doubtful. "Still, I don't know. Geode, I love you. Come to bed with me now."

They had had sex several times yesterday, in the ambience of the firefly, and again at the house, to prove that they could do it without the firefly. That was important to them both. The barrier of his impotence had been broken. This morning they had done it again, before getting up. And yet again, in the forest, near the cabin, when the remaining ambience of the firefly hit them. He was sexually tired, yet the excitement of being able to perform was such that it was a pleasure to prove himself each time.

They went to his room and stripped. This time they made more of a production of it. He kissed her, and stroked her breasts, and kissed them. She reacted as if electrified, her body getting hot. She ran her hands over his body, and caressed his member, and finally urged it into her. She had a hunger that was independent of the pheromones. What joy to do this, knowing that he could finish it!

"I love you, Geode," she repeated. "I want you to know that."

"I do know it. And I love you. I could not do this otherwise."

"I want you to understand how completely I do," she insisted. "Because I may ask you to do something strange, and I want you never to doubt."

"Nothing is stranger than our love." But how odd to hear himself talking this way, and meaning it! How readily the words of love came to him now, with her.

"I never really loved my husband. He was just—there. I thought I loved my son, but I have to confess that we really were not close. Only now have I approached anything like—"

She did not finish, but he understood. She had loved a man as a child. Now she was recapturing that feeling. He could only be glad that it was him she had fixed on, for she had brought to him the whole of the life he had never had.

Embraced, they slept.

"Tell me a story," he said, waking.

She stirred. "After what I have given you, you want a story?" She stroked his chest, her fingers sliding downward teasingly.

"You have given me everything, but it is your stories I love the best."

She seemed to smile in the darkness. "How can I refuse? I will tell you the story of 'Once Upon a Time.' "

There existed two university professors who were discussing when it would be the most appropriate time to interchange their respective spouses. As the child of one of them came into the principal's office:

"What am I holding?" he asked them.

"A gory skull," replied Andy, the anthropologist.

"Wrong. This is a ladybug. What you perceive to be cavities are instead spots."

"What is its use?" Brandy, the lawyer, inquired, meddling in.

"It is a probability machine. Whoever follows it would be following it out into alternate developments of reality."

As that was said, all of them got into their compact shuttle, and took off after the blood-red ladybug. She, on the run, avoided them by shoving, elbowing, and jumping over possibilities, so creating her own "reality track." Meanwhile the ship, point-blank, did not cease from its pursuit behind her.

"I'm reaching my utmost!" groaned the engine.

"We have to hasten, pet," grumbled back the driver, Candi, the historian. "We are in a hurry." Assuming that she made that claim because their own time and place were visible, away off but reachable. But only if they approached such a location at breakneck speed. And indeed, in the nick of time, now, here they were.

"Whether I am not behind the times," Candi then outcried, "we are, in a sketchy way, toward the end of the first century before the shift."

"The 'in' things nowadays," Andy said as he thought it over, "are lies, pollution, and child abuse."

"You are wearing a uniform! So you are becoming a private!"

"No way, boy. I would have to fight either in the Vietnam War or in the universal invasion. Each of you have to do the same, to his own taste. Methinks it is better to vanish away into the 'doubt area.' "

Then he did.

The kid turned toward Brandy. "Now you lack an eye, a hand, and a leg."

"Odd," Candi commented. "Privateers should be over, ever since two centuries ago, at least."

"Not at all. There are some left who work for the planetary gods. For instance, in Atlantis, northward, some of them just seized a pigpen."

"Well," Brandy decided, "I realize this is a Dutch treat. Andy has told 'Uncle' and myself. I, instead, am going to say 'Cain'—I love it, to go a buccaneer, and therefore at all hazards, I am proceeding to go into the Atlantis mess." Next he was gone.

As for Sandy, the geologist, she had turned into a dryad.

"I advise you," Candi said, "to prove to be planted in a park, rather than amid the woods, where carelessness and avidity would quickly slay you. In a park the worst to happen to you would be a gay couple engraving a heart on your skin in a tattoolike fashion."

Sandy obeyed. The lagoon behind her appeared, and so Candi found out from her reflection that she was now a bogeyman. She burst into tears. The lad went to comfort her/him.

"Chin up! Because an adage goes like this: 'Don't count your chickens before you join 'em' . . . no, it is not like that. I think that I've got it now: 'If you can't lick 'em, they are hatched' . . . no, it is not so either . . . well, the idea is something of the sort. What I wanted was to let you know that this is the Flower State, and here, just midway between the spaceport and the cartoon-comic city, an ogre dwells. He is a teacher. You could learn from him how to become a *good* bogeyman, one to whom the tots would expect to go with eagerness and in safety. Let's go: I shall show you the way."

Then they started.

Geode woke. Beside him, Œnone slept. He realized two things: that despite her changes of identity, she would always be Œnone to him, his fantasy woman; and that though he had dreamed of her telling him a story, it was no match for her real stories.

He stroked her bare back. "How do I love thee," he murmured. "Let me count the ways."

She stirred, this time in life, not the dream. "Yes, Geode?"

"Sorry; I didn't mean to wake you."

"I am happy with you, waking or sleeping. What do you wish of me?"

So he told her. "You are Œnone; I don't think you have to give that up to live."

"Maybe not, since this is my dream realm."

"I dreamed you were telling me a story, but it didn't match the type you usually tell, and I woke. I can't dream you; I have to have the real you."

"I'm glad." She crawled across him, her breasts sliding from his left side to his right ribs as her face zeroed in on his, and kissed him.

"Will you tell me a story?"

"Always, Geode."

He held her, thrilling to the sound of her voice as she told it, and he knew she felt his reaction and understood how he loved her and loved listening. She had first truly warmed to him when she learned that he liked listening to her, and it was deeper now.

There came the time when she had to broach a difficult matter to her husband. She had been patient, and understanding, but it simply could be put off no longer. "Donald, we have been married for fifteen years and I have borne you three fine offspring, yet you have not taken a mistress."

"Well, I'm going to, Yvonne," he said defensively.

"But you know it is standard after three children or ten years, whichever comes first. You have far exceeded the guidelines! Do you want folk to think you are impotent?"

He gave up pretense. "I desire only you, Yvonne. No other woman appeals to me."

"So you admit it!" she said severely. "You aren't even looking!"

Abashed, he could not deny it.

"Then you leave me no choice," she said with tearful determination. "I shall have to do what any woman threatened with dishonor would, and find you one myself."

"Couldn't we just pretend it's one of the maids?" he asked desperately. "That upstairs maid is pretty sexy."

"No, we can't pretend! We have never lied before, and we won't start now. Unless you are prepared to take her to your bed tonight."

"She's a cow, while you are a gazelle!" he protested.

"So your true sentiments are coming out! Well, if you won't take advantage of the help, we shall have to import a decent mistress— another gazelle, perhaps."

"Whatever you say, Yvonne," he agreed meekly. "But until then, why don't you come to my bed yourself?"

"Definitely not! Would you ever take an interest in another woman if I were freely available to you?"

He grimaced. She had him dead to rights. She marched out, determined to do the proper thing no matter how much he resisted it. There were, after all, standards that a woman of merit did not suffer to be abridged.

But as she searched for a suitable woman, she knew that none would do. She understood her husband's tastes in the manner that only perspicacious wives do, and realized that the more beautiful the woman was, the less he would be inclined toward her, because he would feel she was competitive with Yvonne herself. Yet she could not abide his having a homely one; what would people think!

Finally she hit upon a scheme. It was risky, but if it worked, all would be well. She set about implementing it with the dispatch and subtlety expected of a woman of quality.

Meanwhile, Donald went about his business, nominally looking for a mistress, but actually having little if any urgency in the matter. No woman appealed, compared with his lovely and sensible wife. But it would become difficult if she withheld her favors from him for long, so he did wish he could somehow resolve the matter.

Aware of the situation, a number of women presented themselves to him. They were universally lovely and well connected, for he was considered a leading eligible married man. They arranged to bump into him so that their assets impinged upon his awareness, or to drop jewelry by seeming accident, which they then stooped to pick up, in this manner presenting both their well-formed legs under short skirts and their robust breasts beneath low décolletages. When he chanced to pass a lake where bathing was in progress, one especially shapely damsel managed to lose her suit in the water, so that when she emerged in seeming innocence the whole of her endowments was revealed. But he was unmoved; he had no use for designing women.

Yet well he knew that he could not dally long, for Yvonne was searching for a suitable prospect for him, and any woman his wife presented would have to be most seriously considered, lest his offense be compounded. Then he would be forced to pretend attraction to a woman who had all the right qualities, yet who could never be but a poor substitute for his wife. Suppose the situation led him to impotence, and the word got out? Yvonne's shame would be doubled.

Then one day he passed a hedged house, and was startled by an outcry. Without intending to pry, he glanced in that direction, and through the hedge perceived a man with a young woman. The man was holding the woman by one slender arm, and drawing his belt out with his free hand. "Despicable girl!" he raged. "Not only did you have the audacity to be born female, when all knew I wanted a son, but you are too homely to command a decent bride price! Now you refuse even to be sold as a slave, thus denying me any return at all on my investment in clothing and feeding you these sixteen years. Well, I have had my fill of you, and shall beat you until I bend you to my will!"

"Father, I beg of you, no!" she cried. "I will try to win a good husband. Only give me another chance!"

"Bah! Everyone knows how willful you are, demanding to learn to read, instead of whoring with the boys. What need has a woman of an education? It was sex you needed to learn—yet you remain a virgin! My patience is at an end. Now you will feel the belt at your back until you agree to be sold!"

"But slaves are horribly abused!" she protested.

"You should have considered that before you buried your nose in books, you ungrateful vixen. Now get down on your knees, that I may more readily beat you."

"I beg you, have mercy!" she pleaded. "I am the way I am, and cannot change, though you beat me senseless."

"We shall see about that," he said grimly. "Down, girl!"

Tearfully, she sank to her knees, her hair falling disheveled across her face in the aspect of the fallen woman who is ashamed to face the light. He walked around her and raised his belt.

Donald could maintain silence no more, for he was a compassionate man. "My apology, sir, for interrupting," he called through the hedge.

"What nuisance is this?" the man demanded, peering around. "Can't a man beat his own daughter without some pervert snooping on private matters?"

"I apologize for snooping," Donald said. "I was only passing by, and happened to come upon you at this inopportune moment. But perhaps I can assist you. I have need of a woman. What is the bride price on this child?"

The man named an outrageous sum. No wonder he had not been able to place her! Even the loveliest of women would hardly go for such a price, and this one, on her knees, hunched forward, faceless and prideless and hopeless, was a far cry from that. Yet Donald could not suffer her to be beaten. "I will pay it."

"You seek a bride?" the man asked, amazed.

"No, I am married. But I do seek a mistress."

"No way! Mistresses command only half the bride price!"

"I will pay the full bride price regardless! Give her to me now, and I will arrange for the payment before the day is out."

"Well, now," the man said, considering. "Are you sure this isn't some trick? It is obvious the girl isn't worth the payment."

Donald did not want to agree, or to admit that it was only compassion for the plight of the girl that motivated him. So he told another aspect of the truth. "I am without a mistress, and my wife is restive. It is necessary that I remedy the matter promptly, and it happens that your daughter is convenient."

"That she is," the man agreed. "But if you mean to use her only briefly and discard her, I will have none of it. A man's got some pride, you know."

"I understand. I will not discard her." There went a loophole; now that he had committed, he would be stuck with her for a prolonged period. But there was no help for it.

So they went together to the money changer, and the price was duly paid and the transaction notarized, and Donald took the wretched girl home with him. She followed meekly, barely speaking. She was aware that he had saved her from a beating, but she did not seem eager for the denouement.

Yvonne met them at the door. "What is this?"

Abashed, Donald mumbled something about a mistress.

"What's that? I didn't hear you."

"Mistress," he said with more force. "I found this girl, she was about to be beaten—"

"Mistress!" Yvonne exclaimed disapprovingly. "That wretched child? Have you no pride at all? What will the neighbors think?"

Donald finally got up some gumption. "Let them think what they choose! I paid a hefty price for her, and I shall use her for the purpose intended."

"You just didn't want her to be beaten!" Yvonne accused him, accurately enough. "You are so softhearted, sometimes it's sickening. Look at her—she's a waif! Probably a virgin too! What pleasure could she possibly give you?"

"She's educated," he said miserably. "I can dress her up, and she may appear passable, and no doubt she can hold her own in conversation, as educated folk normally can. I'm sure she will give a good account of herself, with a little application."

"I doubt it. But it's your decision; I can't dictate something as personal as your sex life. But if she becomes an embarrassment to the family, then it will become my business. Take her and wash her and dress her—she looks about the size of the downstairs maid, so you can preempt some of her clothes for now—and take her to your bed tonight. I will ask you in the morning, and you know you cannot lie to me."

"I know," he said despondently. "I will do everything, I assure you." He only hoped he could!

"See that you do. There must be no scandal in this house!"

So he took the girl to his master bathroom and put her in the tub and had a maid scrub her down. He was surprised at how clean she was already, under her common clothing, and at how well developed. Her hunched posture had concealed the extent of her attributes. Then he saw, as the maid brushed back her hair, that her face was actually quite comely. "Why, you are not plain at all!" he exclaimed.

"You are just saying that," the girl demurred, embarrassed.

"I am not! I would venture to say that you are as lovely a girl as any I've seen, potentially. We shall fix you up and see how you are in appropriate dress."

She cast her eyes down to the bubbly water below her nicely formed breasts, not believing him. Yet there was a slight flush on her delicate ears and slender neck, suggesting that she really desired to believe him. Donald departed, not wanting to betray his own skepticism about the matter.

In due course the girl was washed, dried, powdered, painted, and suitably garbed. The dress they had found for her fitted amazingly well. She stood before Donald demurely, for inspection. Her lips were pursed and full, her eyes great and dark, and overall she much resembled an angel, except for the most womanly contours of her body.

"My dear, you are ravishing!" he exclaimed, genuinely surprised to find himself speaking truly. "How can anyone ever have thought you plain!"

"You took me only from pity," she said. "You do not need to pretend I am more than I am."

"Oh, my dear—what is your name?"

"Kim," she murmured apologetically.

"My dear Kim, I did take you from pity. I could not stand by and watch an innocent girl be beaten! But you have surprised me with your loveliness. I would like to hold you."

"It is your duty," she said. "You bought me to be your mistress."

"It is my duty that threatens to become my pleasure," he said gallantly, taking her in his arms. She was remarkably supple and soft.

"You are cruelly teasing me." Her long eyelashes flickered.

He realized that the lack of confidence of a lifetime could not be banished by a few kind words. "My dear, I will demonstrate."

Forthwith he stripped away her clothes and his own, threw her on the bed, and proceeded to the most thorough bout of lovemaking. At first she seemed duly reticent, but then she became interested, and finally she screamed with passion and fulfillment.

"Have you any remaining doubt?" he inquired as they lay panting, side by side.

"None, sir!" she responded. "You have thrust me from hell to heaven."

Thrust—was that a conscious pun? He had certainly done enough of it, in the course of putting his seed into her twice within the half hour. She had been so delectable and cooperative in her naiveté, and so in need of reassurance, that he had been unable to stop after the first event, and had kissed her all over and spoken words of passion and love to her as he built up to the second. If his first spending had been in a virgin, his second had been in an experienced lover. How quickly she had learned!

"So it will continue," he assured her. "Now we must dress you again, and show you off to my wife and the town, for in my effort to spare a waif pain, I discovered a woman to love." Oh, it was true she was young, barely half Yvonne's age, but somehow the words did not seem to be exaggerated.

"It is all your doing," she said gratefully. "I was nothing before you rescued me and made me yours."

Pleased, he had the maids dress her again and put fine jewelry on her, so that she sparkled like a princess. Then he brought her to his wife, and there was no need to say anything, as it was obvious that Kim was, if anything, more lovely even than Yvonne, if youth was considered, and every inch a woman a man could call a mistress.

Yvonne watched them depart. Then she put in a call to the man who had claimed to be Kim's father. "It worked perfectly," she said. "The girl is now firmly entrenched. I thank you most sincerely for your device."

"Anytime, lovely woman," he replied. "I'm always glad to render good service for a friend, especially when I can benefit myself in the process. When will I see you again?"

"You may come over now," she said. "My husband will not be home for some hours, while he shows off the lovely wench."

"No sooner said than done! Make yourself ready, woman, for you are about to receive the plumbing of your life!"

Yvonne smiled in anticipation. Now that her husband had his mistress, she was free to disport herself as she might, and she expected to enjoy the affair. Extramarital sex was always so much more pleasurable than marital sex, she understood. She was doubly fortunate in the fact that the man she had hankered for was clever enough to play the required part, so that the girl Yvonne had chosen for the sake of appearances, the most beautiful and accomplished of her generation, was able to win Donald's interest. Kim, of course, would never tell; she knew what was what. She was, after all, a woman.

❧ 42 ❧

ŒNONE COMPLETED THE story. It was still dark, but soon dawn would come, and the chores of the day. She feared the day because she knew she had to tell Geode what she had concluded. "Are you satisfied?" she inquired.

"I am satisfied that I can not dream of you half as well as the reality of you," he said. "My dream was just not you; it was disjointed and different. I must have the real you."

"I fear I must tell you something you will not like," she said, inwardly trembling. "I would like to love you ultimately before I do."

He was suddenly alert. "Œnone, you haven't tired of me?"

"No, Geode, no! I love you! I will love you till I die, and beyond. You are my dream man. But I fear you will not want me after I tell you my secret."

"Tell it to me, and I will prove I love you still!"

But she was not reassured. "Let me love you first."

"Yes! Love me and tell me, and love me again!"

"I want to love you as Nymph."

"Any way you want."

She wished she could believe that he would feel that way after she

324

told him. But first she would play out her dream. "Will you speak what needs to be spoken?"

"Yes!"

So they played it out. She bent her knees and spread her legs, bestriding him, as he told her how a real man made love to a real woman. She took his erect member and wedged it slowly in her, clenching her muscles so that it could not penetrate far, squeezing it until it jetted at the verge. Then she sat down all the way, holding the softening member, and kept it in her as she rubbed her finger near her clitoris, bringing herself slowly to a climax. She felt his erection returning, and moved herself on him so that his member went in and out, in and out, and finally spouted again as she had her own orgasm. Then she lay on him, still connected, and kissed him passionately. Nymph had loved again, her way.

"My life is now complete," she said.

"So is mine—when I am with you."

"I must tell you what I fear. Then you must do what you must do."

"Tell me."

"Have you noticed how I am always near when the firefly strikes?"

"I won't let it get you!"

In the dark she put her finger against his lips. "No one has seen it, but it took a hunter who was alone. Then it took my son. Then it took my husband. Then May's cruel husband. Then Cyrano. I have always been close."

"You're lucky it didn't get you, before. But now you are safe here. The alarm system—"

"And a few small animals, and my dog, as if practicing—and I was near those too. Because of the firefly, I am free of my dreary family, and here in love with you."

"Yes. The firefly did us a favor."

"Doesn't it seem like a great coincidence, the firefly appearing right where I am, and making it possible for me to live my dream?"

He shrugged. "Everything is coincidence. I'm just glad it happened."

She nerved herself, then said it. "Geode, I am afraid I am the firefly."

He laughed. "No way! It's a monster!"

"Can you prove I'm not?"

"It sucks all the flesh out! How could you do that?"

"With a big needle, maybe. Inject something that dissolves flesh, the way fireflies do, then suck it all out as liquid, leaving only what won't dissolve in a few hours. The bones."

"But you don't have anything like that! Nobody does! It's impossible!"

"The firefly does."

He shook his head; she saw the motion in the first wan light of dawn. "How could you have it when nobody else does?"

"Maybe I found it—some chemical that does it. And instead of telling the world, I kept it secret, and tried it out on animals, and then on a hunter alone in the forest. Just snuck up and injected him before he knew, and he fell down and dissolved. Then used a big needle to suck it all out, and took it somewhere, and dumped it, maybe in the river. And it worked so well I knew I could get away with it, and used it on my son when he slept, and then on my husband. When that awful Bull Shauer beat up May, and came for her, and was lying there unable to move, I came and used it on him. Then Cyrano was going to find me out, so I got him too."

"But even if you had something like that, you wouldn't use it!" Geode protested. "You're way too nice."

"Am I, Geode? Here I am living my fantasy. You know I have different personalities. Nymph, the child seductress who killed her lover. Œnone, who killed her husband. Why not also the firefly?"

"But none of yours are mean!"

"None of the ones I show to you, Geode. Because I love you. But what of those I hate, or who get in my way? What of you, my love, when something changes? Do you see what frightens me? *I kill those I am with*, sooner or later."

He didn't answer for a moment, and she knew he was starting to consider it seriously.

"No. You forgot one thing. The pheromones. They show when the firefly is near. You don't have those."

"Suppose I found them too? Some acid that dissolves flesh but not skin, and a vial of pheromones? I could sneak close and let out some of the vial, then when the victim is thinking of sex, sneak up and inject him."

"But he'd see you!"

"He'd see mousy little Jade Brown. No need to fear her! He might even want her to get close, because he's alone and those pheromones are driving him crazy with sexual desire, so he wants to take her and screw her even if she isn't much, because at least she's a woman. And while he's trying to do that, intent only on sex, she injects him. How will anyone else know? He's dead, and no one else sees her."

Geode retrenched. "If you had those things, why didn't you do it to me? I've been with you all the time!"

"Because I love you, and it wasn't finished with you. You weren't reacting sexually, so I couldn't take you. But now that you have learned to do it, and I have had you—"

"And if you were with me all night, how could you go out to do it to anyone else?"

"I could start the night with you, and give you something to make you sleep, then go out, and come back before you wake."

"No! I woke last night, after my dream, and you were right there sleeping."

"But that wasn't a firefly night. Can you say the same for the nights the victims have been taken?"

He paused again. "I just don't believe it," he said at last. "Everything I know about you—you're not like that!"

"And there is a perfect alibi," she continued. "You will swear I was with you, and you think I was—but maybe I wasn't. So the firefly keeps striking. It will take anyone who is any kind of a threat to it—or to me. So it won't take you, or May, and maybe not Frank Tishner. Not yet. Not while we cover for it. But it will be out there, catching anyone who may be snooping around."

He shook his head determinedly. "That's crazy!"

"Multiple personalities is a form of insanity. Maybe I lost my sanity when I lost my lover as a child. Maybe I had to, to survive in that family, where I was the sexual target of those who I thought loved me, and society and the law were blind to the truth. I may be crazy—but that doesn't absolve me, that indicates my guilt."

"No," he said, holding on to that.

"Let's assume that this is true. That I am a crazy killer, every third night. Now can you love me?"

"I love you no matter what!" he said without hesitation. "But I don't believe you are the firefly!"

"But if I am, I should be killed."

"No!"

"Yes. The firefly is a killer. It can't be allowed to go on sucking human beings dry. I suck out your water of love, through your dear warm penis, but it doesn't stop there, it sucks out the whole of you.

The firefly has to be stopped. And if you can stop it by stopping me—"

"I'll stay up with you, the next victim night! Then I'll prove it isn't you!"

"But if it *is* me, what will happen to you?"

"You love me! You won't hurt me!"

"Yes. But if my firefly-alternate has the urge to kill again, and you stand in its way, will it be bound? Geode, I'm not sure it would. I fear the greatness of its hunger."

"I'll be awake! Watching! So it couldn't do anything to me anyway!"

"Would you? Suppose I do this to you?" She lifted herself and reached for his penis, kneading it gently between her fingers. It began to harden. She put her mouth on it, stroking it with her tongue. It hardened further.

"You see?" she asked after a moment. "You didn't try to stop me. I could have stabbed you with a concealed needle. That may be why none of those men resisted. What man would, when offered this?" She put her mouth down again, sliding it far onto the shaft, massaging him moistly. "Or this?" She got up and set her slick open cleft on him, absorbing his member. "Twice you gave me your dear elixir, as we reenacted Nymph, and this is not long after, but you remain ready for love and for sex. Even without the pheromones, you react and you hold still. Would you be any different then?"

Geode didn't answer.

She had made her point, but in the process had gotten herself interested again. So she spread herself down on him, and kissed him, and clenched her internal muscles in a peristaltic sequence, milking him for all he had left, until he erupted once more.

"Geode, we must tell the others. May and Frank. We don't want anything to happen to them."

"They'll think you're crazy! They already think I'm crazy!"

He was starting to believe; she could tell by the way he was reacting. "Then maybe we can find some other way; it's not till tomorrow night."

"Yes."

They treated the day as routine, going out on the rounds, this time carrying carrots and making the acquaintance of the three half-wild burros, Burrito, Frito, and Dorito. Burrito got very friendly, but the other two remained wary. They went on, pausing to make love near the cabin where a trace of the scent of pheromones lingered. Œnone told a story along the way, because if there was one thing Geode liked better than sex with her, it was listening to her stories. She loved him for that too! They did not talk of the firefly again, but it was on her mind, and she knew it was on his mind. They returned, and ate, and talked, and kissed, but the consciousness of the firefly remained with them.

May Flowers came by again, and Frank Tishner showed up before she left. The two no longer bothered to try to conceal their interest in each other.

"We have to stop the firefly," May said. "Without Cyrano, we'll have to do it ourselves. That will be clumsy, but if we can catch it tomorrow night, we can still get through. It has never taken a person in company."

"Which means we have to lay another trap at the cabin," Frank said. "One person as decoy, another to nab the firefly when it comes."

"You and I will do it," May said. She looked drawn but determined.

"But if the two of us wait there, you know what we'll be doing," Frank said. "Those pheromones—"

"They are strong," Œnone said. "When we went there, we were affected similarly." In this manner she let them know that it had come to love between herself and Geode; there seemed no reason to conceal it.

May reconsidered. "Yes. That's no way to stand guard. We'd better have a third person." She glanced at Geode and Œnone.

"Geode can do it!" Œnone said immediately. "I'll stay here at the house." For she had just thought of a way.

"But that would leave you alone," May protested. "We don't want anyone left alone."

"If I came too, you know what Geode and I would be doing," Œnone said, and the others had to nod in agreement. "That would be no good either. You need someone who isn't—otherwise occupied. The house here is secure; we can have the alarm system on, so nothing can get in without setting it off."

Frank nodded. "That does make sense. You safe, us ready for the firefly. With luck we'll wrap it up, and the threat will be over."

"Tomorrow night," Œnone agreed.

So it was decided. The others left. Geode turned to her. "But if you think you're—"

"I suddenly realized that the security system is the key!" she said. "If nothing can get in, nothing can get out! When you go, you leave me inside, and if I try to leave, the alarm will go off and everyone will know. So if I'm the firefly, I'll be caught, as I deserve to be."

"I don't like this!"

"Geode, it's the only way to be sure. If I'm not the firefly, this will prove it, because it will come to the cabin and you will kill it and I'll still be here. But if I am, you must either confine me or kill me. I'll be safe here, either way, and you'll know."

"I can't believe you are the firefly. I love you!"

"And if this proves me innocent, I'll be yours forever," she concluded. "Geode, you've got to do it!"

He remained doubtful. But she told him another story, and made love to him again, and wheedled him winsomely, and slept naked in his arms, and he agreed to go along with it. Any man would have, with such persuasion. The daughters of Eve knew their business.

The following afternoon they set it up. Frank and May drove out to the cabin together, and Geode agreed to join them within the hour. May was going to be the decoy again, with Frank armed with knife and pistol in the cabin and Geode in the pickup truck. They would all be in contact with each other, the two men watching May from their respective positions. If the pheromones increased, they would know the firefly was coming, and would be especially alert. If Geode saw the other two having sex, he would know the firefly was near, and would try to intercept it. There was no prudery here, no false modesty; they all knew what they faced and what they had to do. One way or another, they intended to get the job done. Pride no longer mattered; they were in a conspiracy of sorts, and none of them would make any issue of sex, just of survival. There was the distinct possibility that the firefly would try to take two oblivious people together, as they copulated uncontrollably. But then the third one would get it.

All this they agreed on. What Œnone feared did not affect it. She intended to see that she hurt none of them.

"Now put me in the special room and tie me up," Œnone told him.

"But—"

"Do it, Geode. It's the only way. You know I know the layout here; I could avoid the seeing-eye and break out a window without opening it, and I'd be out without setting off the alarm. You need to put me where I can't escape."

Reluctantly, he took her to the special room. This was a large windowless closet off the room above the one Geode slept in. The alarms were normally off in the rest of the house except for the night or when it was empty, but the alarm was always on in this room. It could be disabled only with the use of a special key, and Geode carried that key on his person. When he put her in there and "locked" her in with the security system, she would be unable to leave without setting it off.

The room had its own air conditioning vent and fluorescent light. They brought in cushions so she could lie down. "I can bring in a book for you to read," he said.

"No. Tie me up. Get rope from the garage and tie my wrists and ankles so I can't escape."

"But—"

"Suppose I found a way to make a hole in the door without opening it? I could climb through it. Then the alarm wouldn't go off. This has to be sure. Tie me."

"Oh, Œnone, I hate this!"

"If you truly believe me innocent, this will prove it. Nothing can get in or out. In the morning you can disable the alarm and come in and untie me. Then we will be together."

Obviously loath, he fetched cord and tied her hands and feet. "Tighter," she said. "Make sure I can't escape."

Finally he had it done to her satisfaction. She had circulation in hands and feet, but no leeway to struggle. She was securely bound.

"Kiss me, turn out the light, lock me in, and don't come back until morning," she said.

He kissed her, trussed on the cushions; then he went to the switch, and hesitated. "You aren't afraid of the dark?"

She reconsidered. "I *am* afraid of the dark now! When I'm without you beside me. Very well, leave the light on; it won't make any difference."

He went out the door. "I love you, Geode," she said. "Never doubt that, no matter what happens."

"I love you, Œnone," he replied, a catch in his voice. Then he closed the door. She heard the faint click of his key in the security lock, and then his footsteps going away. He would arm the main alarm system, then drive to the cabin to help watch for the firefly.

She was alone.

She was afraid.

← 43 →

I⊤ WAS QUIET. Unable to do any-
thing else, Œnone drifted to sleep, woke, and slept again. It was
timeless here, because she couldn't see her watch, and because the
closed room with the constant light made it impossible for her to judge
the progress of day or night outside.

Had she done the right thing? Now that she was so thoroughly
committed, she was uncertain. Where would she, a dull housewife,
have found such things as a flesh dissolver or pheromones unknown to
science? Why would she use them to go on a rampage of killing? Why
every three days? It really didn't seem to make much sense now. Oh,
maybe she had hated her husband for his faithlessness, when she had
offered him several times as much sex as any man could use, but
killing him certainly hadn't brought him back. She would have done
better to use those pheromones to go on a rampage of sex herself,
uncorking the vial under the nose of any man she might hanker for,
causing him to fornicate with her uncontrollably. She could have used
it on Paris himself, keeping him so worn out sexually that he had none
left over for Helen. That would have been a truly suitable ploy! "Have
you been having at your wife again, you poor excuse for a philan-

derer?!" Helen would have demanded angrily, gazing at his limp member. "What will everyone think?"

Œnone's fantasies were like that; why not make them reality, if she had the means? Most women had fantasies, but few actually wanted them to come true. They dreamed of being raped, and loving it, being freed from any responsibility of the sin of sexual appetite, so they could enjoy it without guilt. But real rape was violent and painful, and carried formidable risks. Fantasy rape was merely a mechanism, a token act without its ugly aspects. Fantasy rape was the only kind that was worthwhile. Much the same was true of being the object of unbridled passion by many men. A dream of facing a crowd of naked, virile men who were all desperate for her sexual favor was a turn-on, because it meant she was infinitely desirable and had control of the situation; she could have anything she wanted. But a similar reality was apt to be disgusting. Men orgasming simultaneously in her vagina, her anus, her mouth, on her breasts, in her hands as she squeezed their stiff members, their semen fountaining—what a mess that would be! Who would clean the sheets, the bed, the floor, the walls, after? More was not better in real sex; love was better. As for the fantasies of monstrous penises, animal penises, huge amounts of semen jetting as from firehoses—those would be painful at best. No, none of it made sense in real terms.

But with the vial of pheromones to compel the ultimate attention of any man she chose—there was a fantasy whose realization was practical! What delight it had been, passing near the cabin with Geode, he become potent at last, having at her twice before the cabin, once at it, and twice more after it before his sexual exhaustion and their removal from the cloud of pheromones had allowed them to complete their travel in peace. That had been her dream of bliss!

Then, having proved his potency, she had made love to him again in the evening, and in the night, and in the morning, arousing him whenever she chose. He was so glad to be able to perform, and he loved her—the two were certainly linked, once the two of them were free of the pheromones, but it had been the pheromones that forced the breakthrough—so he had done his best. There was the realization of yet another aspect of her fantasy: to cause an impotent man to make love to her repeatedly. What did that say for a woman's desirability?

So even if she had an evil facet of her personality, hidden from the others, she shouldn't have used the discoveries to harm others instead of benefiting herself. To be evil was not to be stupid. So now she questioned her hypothesis on two grounds: she was unlikely to have gotten those vials of acid and pheromones, and she wouldn't have used them to kill.

Still, she wasn't only proving her innocence to herself, she was also proving it to Geode. If the firefly struck tonight, she would be exonerated even if they didn't manage to kill it, because there was no way she could be responsible. Then she could be free of her doom of death, free to love Geode forever. She had never really believed in that, being sure that anyone she truly loved would die, or that she would die if truly loved by anyone. Yet now she had reenacted the love of her childhood, and in the process expiated the geis that had burdened her for thirty years. The spell had been dissipated, and she could now love normally. Geode had to know beyond any question that she was innocent of any harm to others, and this would be the proof.

There was a faint sound. At first she wasn't sure whether she imagined it, but it was getting louder. A keening, as of the edge of a radio station. Maybe the security system was adjusting itself.

Yet she felt déjà vu. Hadn't she heard that sound before, maybe in her sleep? She had forgotten, but now it seemed she had.

Then she realized that if she were not the firefly, something else must be. Those deaths had certainly occurred, and those pheromones certainly existed. There *was* a monster. That being the case, whom would it attack next? The three who were ready for it—or the one who wasn't?

Œnone struggled in her bonds, but only chafed her wrists. Geode had done his work too well; she could not escape.

But if some other person had found those vials and was using them to kill, how could he get in here? If he drove in by car, the gate would not admit him. If he climbed the fence and walked in, and forced open a door, the alarm would go off, dialing the security folk and summoning the authorities. If he broke in a window without opening it, he would still be caught by the infra-red eye, and the alarm would sound. If he was smart enough to bypass that, and came up here and opened the door, the alarm would go off. There really was not much way a man could do it—and if he were an expert in breaking in without activating the alarm, and knew exactly what to do, why should he waste his time coming after her, instead of robbing the house? How would he even know she was here? If he did, why should he take the risk of dispatching her, when the others could return at any moment?

For if he were here, he would not be there at the cabin, and they would give up their stakeout and return here. So it made little sense to take that risk for so little.

The sound intensified. Now she started feeling sexy.

The pheromones! There was no mistaking that eroticism. That was the hallmark of the firefly. She thought of Geode, of his poor flaccid penis, and how she had made it stand tall. She thought of touching it, kneading it, kissing it, climbing on it, absorbing it, flinging her legs around his waist, kissing him, clenching her internal muscles, drawing from him the most avid spurts of passion. Of falling down with him, and riding him, his member still in place, and forcing him to a second climax, and a third. She felt her vagina wet with eagerness for him. "Oh, Geode, come into me!" she breathed clenching her legs together in an effort to hold him there.

But at the same time, on another level, she thought of the firefly. The pheromones were its flashes, its signals to its prey. Once the prey saw those flashes, it was helpless; it had to come in and try to mate, though it died of the effort. If the prey did not come to the firefly, the firefly came to the prey, and took it anyway.

A man might find vials of acid and pheromones, but how could he find a vial of that keening sound?

But suppose it wasn't a man, but a creature, as the others had conjectured? Something like a monstrous slug that slid along the ground without leaving a trace? That made no sound, other than its faint keening as it traveled? Suddenly that interpretation was making sense!

Yet how could it get past the security system? It had to come in a door or a window or something, and that should set off the alarms. If it were an animal, it wouldn't know about such alarm systems; Œnone herself hadn't known much about them until she had come here and Geode had told her. It would just come on in, any way it could, maybe down the chimney into the fireplace, and then the infra-red eye would catch it and hell would break loose in the house.

Yet it had never broken anything before, or left any other evidence of its presence. Just the bones of its victims. It didn't seem to use doors or windows—yet it had enough mass to be able to consume a full human body in the course of a night. How did it do that? By squeezing flat under the door?

Suddenly she knew it did. That it was completely malleable, like a gelatin dessert that hadn't quite firmed up. A jellyfish that could go on land. That was why it was so quiet and left no footprints. It might have no hard parts at all, no claws or teeth. That was why it needed the acid, to dissolve the victim's flesh and turn it liquid so it didn't have to be chewed, it could be sucked up through a straw. And the pheromones, so the victim wouldn't try to flee. Did a dog flee from a bitch in heat? Did a man flee from a woman with her legs spread? These pheromones were multipurpose; they made women get just as eager as the men usually were. How well she knew! If the victim didn't know that it was more than sex which offered, that it was death—

The keening seemed loud now, and close. Actually it wasn't loud, it was faint to the verge of inaudibility, but things were relative; she was tuning in on it all too well. It was directionless, yet seemed to come from the direction of the stairs. What could come up those stairs without alerting the infra-red eye? Well, the sensor actually tuned in on heat and motion. If something seemed not to be distinct from its background, if it seemed like no more than a wrinkle in the carpet, it might slowly flow up stair by stair without making enough of a stir to trigger the sensor. A human body was big and hot and clumsy, but something shaped like a rug, perhaps even looking like a rug, maybe even coming up *under* the rug—

She struggled again, but again her bonds were tight. She could not free her hands or her feet. But maybe she could save herself. If she rolled over, got on her feet somehow, and hopped to the door, she could crash it open and set off the alarm herself.

She struggled with more direction now, not trying to free her extremities but to achieve a position. But her hands were tied behind her. Had they been tied in front of her, she could have moved like an inchworm and humped her way to the door. It wasn't physically locked, just latched; any thief who yanked it open would bring the authorities down on his head in short order. With her hands behind her, she couldn't inchworm, unless she did it on her face. The moment she squirmed off the cushions, she was uncomfortable, with her arms jamming into her back.

She rolled over, and found herself prone, her face on the rug. She couldn't go anywhere this way! She tried to lift herself up to her knees, and couldn't. And if she could, what then? Now that she was closer to the position, it seemed to her that to inch along she would have to put more of the weight on her head than on her feet, and how would she do that? There must be a better way!

She rolled onto her side. The repeated efforts flexed her legs and buttocks against each other, and the effect was unfortunately suggestive. She was on the verge of sexual spasming, though she knew that was not smart right now. God, she wanted a man in her! She could not afford to let sex distract her from her effort to escape.

The keening changed quality. It seemed to be right in the room with her.

Then her gaze fell on the door. She gulped in horror. *Something was flowing under it!* Something brownish, like dilute chocolate syrup, squeezing under, forming a bubble inside. As she watched, the bubble swelled, sucking more of itself through.

It was the firefly. She had no doubt of that. And it was between her and the door.

She rolled onto her back. She pressed her head down, and her feet, arching her back so as to lift her midsection off the floor. She could inch along this way. But where could she go? The monster had her trapped!

Could she try to plow through it to the door? But then she would butt her head against the door, and not be able to escape, with the muck of the monster all around her. It would surely trap her before she could get away.

How could she open the door, anyway? The handle had to be turned. It was a handle, not a knob, so if she could get any part of her body against it, she could shove it up, and then the door would open and the alarm would go off. Then she could heave herself outside, and keep flopping around so as to win clear of the firefly, until help came.

The bubble of liquid flesh continued to expand. Now its total mass was approaching that of a human being, if a person could be melted down into liquid. And of course that was possible; this was the thing that did it. She was about to join Cyrano and Bull Shauer and her husband.

Join that trio? No way!

What she had to do was scoot herself down to the door feet first, then lift her feet to shove up the handle and push open the door. After that she could just flop around as long as she could, not giving the thing any purchase on her, basking in the sound of the alarm. Even if she died, she would take the firefly with her. She felt no fear—or if she did, it had been locked into some other personality. She knew she could not afford to be hampered by that. She had one chance to save herself, and she meant to make it count.

Now the thing seemed to be all inside. It extended a slow pseudopod toward her.

She stared at that swelling thing, and thought of a penis. The urge to mate took her with gale-like force. Why not let that sexy thing go up into her, the world's most potent member? If it wasn't hard yet—well, neither had Nymph's lover's thing been hard after it jetted, but she had gotten it into her and then it had solidified inside her. All she had to do now was spread her knees, open her legs where it counted despite the tied ankles, get her cleft wide—

No! Once that thing got into her, it would never get out again! Not while she lived! She had to fight it, no matter how horribly sexy it seemed.

Œnone started her motion. She was not in a position to roll; the available floor space was too narrow for her to roll sidewise, and she needed her hands free to manage somersaults. So she lifted her back and shoved with her head and bucked herself down toward the monster.

In a moment she landed on the pseudopod. She gritted her teeth, expecting it to squish, but could feel nothing; it must have flattened so readily that it offered no resistance. She continued to hump as well as she could, substituting vigor for skill. The firefly was gelatinous; it had no bones. It couldn't jam into her, it had to insinuate. External contact wouldn't hurt, as long as she gave it no chance to get internal.

Her posterior began to feel good. This was surprising since she was bumping fairly hard on the floor and might be abrading her skin under the clothing. Maybe the banging was making it numb. She paused, wondering. It was almost as if she had found a new cushion, a water-cushion, warm and medicinal.

The good feeling spread around her buttocks and into the cleft between them. It reached her genital area, and intensified. It was as if the most wonderful man in all the world were stroking her and seeking to enter.

She spread her legs to the extent possible, to facilitate that entry. Something slid into her vagina, bringing rapture. Never in her life had she experienced as gentle, steady yet intense pleasure; it was like an interminably sustained orgasm.

Then she realized what was happening. She had planted her bottom on the firefly, and it was reaching up past her clothing to have its kind of sex with her. This was how it had taken the others; it had brought them such genital delight that they simply hadn't *wanted* to move.

But though she lived for good sexual experience, she also knew that this was death. She had seen the bones! So her mind overrode the joy of her vulva, and she tried to struggle free.

And could not. For with the pleasure came anesthesia. She willed her legs to move, her back to arch, but the response was partial; only the upper portion of her body moved. The lower portion substituted joy for action.

She was, after all, caught. She had paused for that critical moment, savoring the pleasure, and that had been her undoing.

What could she do? Her body was no longer hers. Only the upper part of it. Even her hands were going numb and happy, for they were now in the region of the firefly. All she had, really, was her head.

"Help!" she called. But there was no answer, and could be none, for she was alone in the house and no one else could enter. Geode was miles away, staking out the cabin. The firefly had outsmarted them all, coming for the lone bound person instead of the three ready ones. What a fool she had been, to set herself up for it!

The rapture was radiating from her vagina to her womb. She wanted to give herself up wholly to the pleasure, but fought it. The moment she stopped fighting, she would be truly lost. It was ironic: all her life she had sought the pleasure of the penetration of that region; now she had it in greater measure than ever before, and she was trying to escape it.

If she couldn't call for help, maybe she could defend herself. With her mind, and her mouth. She would talk to the firefly.

"Oh Firefly," she said. "Listen to me, for I am not one to be taken lightly. Hear me, for I have better for you than my flesh."

The burgeoning orgasm was spreading out through her abdomen, into her intestines and organs.

"I have information for you, I have entertainment, I have insight into the human condition, which you hardly understand. You will surely be caught and killed if you do not learn more about our species and how it thinks. Listen to me, or feel me think, oh Firefly, or you will die as surely as I."

The rapture continued. It was as if her colon were illuminating, becoming a convoluted channel of pleasure. Her bladder was a container of joy, and her kidneys were beginning to tingle. If there were wastes in those parts, they were being dissolved into the glow.

"Our bodies may be familiar to you, but it is our minds that set us apart," she continued. "Other species have preyed on us for a time, but they have inevitably been hunted to extinction, because man is a social animal, and he avenges his own. You, alone, cannot hope to prevail, unless you first come to understand us. Listen, Firefly, and feel our spirit."

The rapture seemed to dim for a moment. Was the firefly listening? Could Scheherazade charm even an alien creature bent on sexual consumption?

"There was a man and his daughter. His marriage had broken up, and such was the situation that the almost automatic propensity of the courts to give children to mothers was reversed; he had fought for his beloved child and won her. They loved each other truly, and agreed never to be separated. Of course, he knew that in time she would grow up and become another person, and then would go her own way, as was proper, but while she was a child he would always be with her.

"Then there was an accident. A drunken driver crossed the center-line and collided head-on with their car. The crash was horrendous. Both were seriously injured. But even as they were extricated from the mangled car, he called to her and held her hand. 'It's okay, honey, I won't leave you,' he said, and she was reassured. She knew her daddy always told the truth.

"They tried to separate them in the hospital, but both reacted so strongly that the doctors realized that both could die unless they were allowed to remain together. So they were given a room between the adult ward and the pediatric ward, with adjacent beds, where they could reach out and touch each other's hands. Both were swathed in splints and bandages, so that they could not even see each other, and it was hard for them to talk, because her larynx had been torn and his chest was paralyzed; he had spoken no more after calling to her at the site of the accident. Both had extensive internal injuries, but his right arm and her left arm remained mobile, and they touched hands often, reassuring each other.

"They were taken to surgery together, and while the adult doctors operated on him, the pediatric doctors operated on her. Both were in critical condition now, because of loss of blood and the stress of the surgery. But now he was on a respirator, and was able to talk with the help of a mike, while she had her larynx repaired to some extent. The monitors showed that her heart and respiration improved when she heard his voice and felt the gentle squeeze of his fingers, and his vital signs stabilized when he received her response.

"But she had lost her liver, and was declining. A search was on for a possible transplant, but her tissue type as rare and hope was faint. She was dying. It was impossible to hide this from her; she *knew*, as the dying generally do. But her father reassured her. 'Don't worry, honey,' he gasped, 'I'm going with you. I will not let you go alone to that place.' And she smiled through her pain, knowing he always told her true.

"They wound down together, and it was evident that they would die within hours or even minutes of each other. He really was going with her. The doctors shook their heads; they had never seen such a bond between two people. He might have survived, but he didn't want to; he wanted to be with his daughter, to help see her through the valley of the shadow of death. She went into coma, and when he felt that, so did he.

"Then a miracle happened. A baby died, and its liver matched the girl's almost perfectly. They rushed the comatose child into surgery and did the transplant. It was touch and go at this late stage, but they worked heroically, and saved her. The new liver functioned, and her vital signs began to improve. She would live after all.

"But her father had not known. He somehow felt her absence; they found his hand outstretched in air, where hers had been. He had thought her absence was because of her death—and he had died himself.

"When she recovered she discovered that her father had honored his commitment to go with her—but she had reneged. He had gone alone to death. 'Oh, Daddy!' she cried, grief-stricken, torn by guilt. She tried to die, to rejoin him, but was too young to know how. The doctors maintained her in life—but to what point? She was alone."

The rapture seemed to have paused, as long as Œnone spoke. Now it resumed.

"I have told you of the tragedy of a little girl," she said. "This is one aspect of the way our kind feels about death. We do not take it lightly, and neither should you. But there are other aspects to our nature. We are a species of two sexes, and men have interests too. I will tell you of a man, because I think the man I love would like that. He understands about conversing with animals."

The joy was extending down her thighs toward her knees, and up toward her chest. If it did not reverse soon, it would be too late. She had to get through to the firefly!

"A man once took a walk in the country. He was an ordinary man, living alone, and no one paid any special attention to him, but he was a decent sort who would always do a good deed if he had the chance.

"A dog approached him. This was a mongrel cur of no account, hungry and ill-kempt, but of good character. 'I see that you are alone,' the dog said to the man. 'I would like to be your dog, and do for you all the things a dog does for a man, and have you do for me all the things a man does for a dog.' The man, seeing that the dog was sincere, agreed, and adopted it, and took it home. He fed the dog, and groomed it, and gave it pills to abolish internal vermin, and the dog grew healthy and robust and became a fine specimen of its breed. In return, the dog served as the man's companion and guard, so that the man walked safely through even the worst of neighborhoods, and had no concern about being mugged.

"One day as the two walked forth, a horse approached. This was a swaybacked gelding with scars on his hide and stones stuck in his hooves and a tangled mane. 'I see you are a good person,' the horse said. 'But you are without transportation. I would like to be your horse, and do for you the things a horse does for a man, and have you do for me the things a man does for a horse.' The man considered, and consulted with the dog, and agreed. He adopted the horse, and led it home, and gave it feed and hay, and pried the stones out of its hooves, and washed and brushed its hide. The horse prospered, and its back lost its sway, and its mane became lustrous, and the muscles formed and stood out on its body. In return, the horse became a fine steed for the man, taking him wherever he wished to go with dispatch and style, while the dog ran along beside and guarded them both.

"The neighbors marveled to see this. 'How is it that this nondescript man has obtained such a fine dog and horse?' they asked. 'Indeed, he is not nondescript anymore; he has become a fine figure of a man, surely through no fault of his own.'

"Then a woman approached the trio. She was bowed and lean, and her hair hung limply across her face, and she had little or no pride. 'I see you are a solid citizen,' she said. 'You have fine animals, and you look fine yourself. I would like to be your woman, and do for you all the things that a woman does for a man. In return, I would like to have you do for me the things a man does for a woman.' The man considered, and consulted with his companions, and they concluded that the house and kennel and barn were somewhat uncomfortable, and the food could be improved, and that a woman might indeed be a suitable addition to the family. So the man married the woman, and turned over his estate to her, and she lost her stoop and stood up straight, and her body filled out and became attractive, and her hair turned lovely and her face beautiful. In return, she cooked for the man, and fed the dog and horse better than before, and came to his bed at night and introduced him to delights of the flesh that he had not before imagined.

"The neighbors were amazed. 'How is it that he has now won the loveliest woman in the area, and is so happy,' they asked, 'while we plod on with our mangy dogs, decrepit horses, and sag-breasted wives?' But they never were able to figure it out, for they were not decent folk, and had no proper understanding of the type."

The rapture had paused again. Now it resumed, extending past her knees and up into her chest. Her breasts began to glow with the delight, the nipples turning rigid. It was like experiencing the sexual embrace of God.

"But I have more to tell you!" she gasped, for now her breathing was suffering. "Like Scheherazade of the Arabian Nights, I have more tales to tell than you can listen to in years! You must hear them, for in them is the nature of my kind."

The rapture paused again. Something, perhaps, was interested. But it did not slow all the way to a halt.

Œnone struggled to speak, and when that became impractical, she stopped speaking and simply thought through the stories as if she were speaking them. She continued this until the rapture finally reached her brain, and then, with a mixture of sacrifice and joy unknown to any remaining human being, she became one with the firefly.

❖ 44 ❖

THE FIREFLY COMPLETED the melt-
down of the prey and disengaged itself from the bones and material that
remained. It collected its mass, now swollen to double by the addition
of the proteins of the prey, and began its retreat. It extended a pseudopod under the door and squeezed it through the crevice there. Then it
funneled its mass through, until the whole of it was on the other side.
It proceeded on back the way it had come.

Now it needed to find a suitable spot to bury its egg. But as it moved,
it would assimilate the new substance, so that it could be formed into
the egg. The meltdown was only the first step; the proteins had to be
adapted so as to serve as proper nourishment for the developing embryo.

*There was a fierce female griffin ensorcelled to the form of a human
woman, as the result of some more complicated story that need not be
explored here. It is enough to say that she was a bit player in a scene
soon forgotten by the major players. Alone and naked, she wandered to
the house of a farmer. She realized that she was virtually helpless in this
strange, weak, wingless, beakless, ugly body, balanced awkwardly on
its hind legs, so had to suppress her fighting instincts and accept what
came, lest she be quickly slain.*

So when the farmer came out and spied her, she acted as submissive as she could, merely standing there as if stupid. He spoke to her in the grating human tongue, which naturally she did not understand, so she did not reply. He seemed quite interested in her body, though it was entirely typical of the females of his species: not even any feathers to cover its puniness, and laughably tiny claws on its fleshy fat feet, and distressingly soft mammalian dugs hanging on its front. He took her by an appendage and led her into his den, and she went. He put cloth on her, and she tolerated this unnatural thing because she realized it was the way of this gross species. He put gruel before her, and a flat curved stick in her hand, and indicated that she should shove the stuff in her mouth. She realized that this was his idea of eating; men did not tear living flesh apart and gulp the gobbets raw, as was natural. So she clumsily dumped stickfuls of tne stuff in her mouth and swallowed it. Then he took the cloth from her body and also removed his own cloth, and caused her to lie flat on a soft mat, with her legs separated somewhat, and he lay on top of her and poked something into an orifice she had, and she realized that this was the human notion of mating. It was clumsy and dull compared to griffin breeding, but in keeping with the clumsy and dull species.

Over the course of the next days he began making her repeat the crude noises of his language, and she learned the sounds for particular things. As the season passed she learned more, until she was able to understand and speak with him. By that time she was gravid with the cub he had labored so inefficiently to plant in her; it had taken him scores of attempts to do it, and even after it was there he continued to stick his puny instrument in her torso every evening, as if not believing it had finally worked. What a waste of energy! Men were strange indeed. A griffin male would have done it only once, in grand and violent style, when she was in heat, and it would have set the cub immediately. But what was to be expected of the human kind, so inferior in every respect?

Winter passed, and she grew thick in the torso, and then the man finally understood, and ceased his continual poking inside her. That was a relief. She continued to eat and to do the dull things he demanded, such as cleaning off the wooden bowl and spoon after each use, and wearing the cloth covering when going about in the daytime. It was better than being killed and eaten.

Spring came, and she birthed the cub. It was a perfect little griffin. When the man saw it he was discomfited. "What is that?" he demanded in his crude tongue.

"That is my offspring, a griffin," she replied.

"But how can that be?"

"I am a griffin," she explained. "Our genes are dominant, so my cub is a griffin."

"Why didn't you tell me you were a griffiness?"

"You did not ask."

Somehow that didn't satisfy him. *"I can't have a griffin for a son!"*

"Then change me back to my natural form, and I will take him into the sky with me, where we belong."

But he didn't seem satisfied with that either. Finally he decided to keep her and the cub, but to pretend that it was a foundling.

Then, amazingly, he started in again, trying in his inefficient way to impregnate her a second time. And indeed, after the second was birthed and explained as a foundling, he tried for a third. So it went for many years, until she began to put on weight, gaining a nice rondure, and then his mating efforts slackened. So at last he allowed her to return to her kind, along with her offspring, and when she did, the transformation finally abated and she was a griffiness again. There was just no understanding the ways of man!

The firefly absorbed the narration. It had not encountered anything like this before. It realized, without understanding how it had come by the realization, that it should learn more about the nature of its prey, or the prey would turn on it and destroy it, as soft flabby men might turn on a fierce griffin. So it accepted the narration, and tried to fit it into its way of existence.

Meanwhile, it proceeded out of the structure by squeezing through another crevice. It knew the importance of maintaining a low profile, for it lacked the natural weapons of attack and defense employed by others. Its strategy was to hide, and use the mating odors when suitable prey was near and isolated, and lay as many eggs as it could before its inevitable destruction. The eggs had to be laid in waterlogged sand, hidden, and forgotten. That was all.

Here's one you might appreciate, Firefly. There was a maiden who was exceedingly sexy. A kobold desired her, but he was so ugly that clocks went awry in his vicinity, and she refused to have anything to do with him. Angered, he put a hex on her. "You want to be sexy?" he raged. "Then be ultimately sexy!" And he made his spell, and cast it on her, and it enclosed her like an invisible cloud.

She feared that his magic would make her as ugly as he, but it did not; in fact, her mirror informed her that she was if anything even more luscious than before. She feared it would prevent her from enjoying herself with handsome men, but she found that her parts were all in order. Indeed, while before she had amplified her sexiness in order to lure men in and toy with them, now she longed to have them complete the act. She had indeed become more sexy, because what had been pretense had intensified into reality. In fact, she pictured many men coming to enjoy her offerings, one after the other without end. In her mind, she was a nymphomaniac. If that was the worst the kobold could do, it wasn't all that bad; she expected to enjoy herself!

Soon she espied a suitable young man, one who was tall and muscular and handsome, and whom she had tormented before by her teasing. "Come to me, stud," she called to him, exposing her center of gravity. "I am through with teasing; I want you inside me." Indeed, under her skirt were no panties; she was ready for business.

"Oh-ho!" he exclaimed, and ripped open his trousers as he approached her. His member sprang out, as tall and firm and handsome as he.

But as he came nigh her, something embarrassing happened. His proud member became too excited, and jetted its contents prematurely. The valuable seed fell upon the ground a yard from her, and his member promptly gave up its ghost and became insignificant.

So it was with every man she approached. No one could get close enough to her to complete the act in the manner she desired.

She was doomed to hunger for sex, but to be eternally teased by near-misses.

She pondered. She was not completely stupid, as pretty girls went. She realized that if the kobold could put this hex on her, he could take it off again. She would have to go and beg him to release her from this torture. But she had a fair notion what price he would ask. Well, at this point appearances didn't matter; she just wanted hot flesh in hers.

So she sought out the kobold. "You have made your point," she told him. "What must I do to lift this sex-hex from me?"

"It is a permanent spell," he replied. "It can be abated only by being fornicated away. With each successful fornication, it will fade a trifle, until at last it becomes too weak to force ejaculation outside your orifice. Then it will be indistinguishable from the ordinary magic of women, who force men to yield their seed inside their cavities."

"But no one can get into me!" she protested.

"No one except the one who placed the hex," he replied. "That one will be able to hold off the magic until actually inside; then the force of the spell can have its way without spoiling the occasion."

She had rather suspected it would be that way. "How many times will it take to wear off the hex?"

He shrugged. "Perhaps no more than a thousand or so."

"A thousand!" she exclaimed, appalled.

"It is a potent hex."

Literally true, she realized. She sighed. "Very well. Proceed to work it off."

The kobold was glad to oblige. But he had forgotten one detail. Though the hex could not cause him to jettison prematurely, it did excite him sexually, as long as he was close to the maiden. He entered her and squirted his seed, and she was finally satisfied. But the potency of her proximity was such that before he could withdraw, the urge returned, and seconds after the first time, he gushed again. She was similarly affected, her satiation lasting only seconds, so she was glad for the repetition. Seconds later came a third eruption, and then a fourth, fifth, and sixth.

The kobold was tired, and tried to withdraw, but another detonation caught him and he had to remain. His seed was getting very thin, and indeed the orgasms were becoming uncomfortable, but he could not escape. He was not immune to the magic, just to its application outside her body.

The maiden, catching on, clasped her arms around him and hugged him close, and clenched her muscles about his laboring member so that it was trapped. Thus, as the power of the sex-hex gradually faded, the kobold remained, spasming uncontrollably. Ten, twenty, fifty, a hundred, it continued. The kobold's flesh melted down to provide substance for the geysering member, and he shrank.

Finally, when the thousandth effort occurred, there was nothing left of the kobold except his penis. It spluttered out its final driblet of fluid and dissolved into smoke.

The maiden had been freed of the hex. She was sore but still sexy, and soon would be back at her business. It had taken only three hours in all.

Now, isn't that a tale for your edification, Firefly? This is what you do, placing a spell of sexual desire and performance on your victims, and in the process humiliating them. But there is a catch to it, for you are being swallowed by that very passion you have used. Now it is in you, and will govern you.

The firefly continued its slow motion. It was assimilating the new flesh—but in the process was also assimilating the mind of that flesh. The details of the concepts were confusing, but the underlying feeling was strong. The firefly was faced with intellect and feeling far greater than its own. Because it was equipped to assimilate whatever it consumed, and did so automatically, it had no defense against this, and indeed did not understand the need for any defense. The new mind was taking over from the old, and the new feeling was registering where there had been little or none before.

By the time the night had passed, the firefly understood human intellect and felt human passion. Like the kobold, it was doomed just when it achieved its desire.

For as it sought to hide under the brush and leaves of the forest floor, a man approached it—and instead of lying low, it rose up and made itself known to that man.

❖ 45 ❖

GEODE FACED THE firefly, seeing it for the first time. It was a brownish lump of protoplasm, amoeba-like in its ability to extend pseudopods and flow into them. It humped up before him, not even trying to hide. Yet it was not generating pheromones, either, for he was having no reaction. It was as though the thing were trying to meet him.

The situation was unreal. No monster had come to the cabin, and there had been no imperative sexual performance; their stakeout had fallen flat. Frank and May had returned to town to catch up on sleep in the wee hours, while Geode had gone back to the house, turned off the alarm during its thirty-second warning period, and come upstairs to release Œnone from her confinement in the security closet.

Now he remembered every detail with stark clarity, and he reviewed the sequence, hoping to find some hint for understanding of the present situation.

There had been no alarm, and no doors had been opened. The security closet remained secure, with just a sliver of light showing under its door. He turned the key in the special lock, deactivating the alarm, and opened the door. He suffered an erection as he did so, he presumed from eagerness to be with her again.

There he found the clothes and bones of Œnone. The lovely gold and gem dragonfly Mid had given her remained pinned to her blouse. *The firefly had come and taken her.* It had been the lingering pheromones, not his own desire, that had prompted his excitement.

Numbed, he found his way to his room and picked up the knife he had set down. With this he could deal with just about anything. Then he set out on the trail of the firefly. It was in his mind that he would kill it first, and then himself. He knew he should have called Mid, or May Flowers, but he could tolerate no delay; the monster might be just ahead.

In the cool predawn dimness he saw a shape above the house, outlined against the pale sky. He oriented on it: was it the firefly? No, it was only the great horned owl, perched on the top of the television antenna.

"Did you see the firefly?" he asked it.

"I don't eat fireflies," the owl replied.

"This isn't that kind. It's a—thing maybe the size of a man, that maybe crawls along the ground like a big slug."

"Oh, *that* firefly," the owl said. "Does it make a keening noise as it travels?"

Geode was taken aback. "Does it?"

"It does. It went toward the pond."

"Thank you." Geode walked toward the pond that bounded the southwest section of the ranch. There was no direct access, so he cut through the jungle, his boots and body brushing past the thickly growing palmettos.

His nose and penis guided him: if he got an erection when he sniffed, he was on the right trail. He tracked the firefly through the thick of the jungle toward the verge of the pond. Progress was slow because it was still dark in here and he didn't want to lose the scent. He had to backtrack constantly, sniffing again and again, getting down on his belly to put his nose to the ground like a bloodhound, squirming all around, heedless of the briars and roots until he felt the tug of the pheromones.

Even so it was chancy. He found himself near the lake. Fortunately, he encountered a rabbit nibbling on shoots. "Did you see the firefly?"

"Two nights ago I saw one flashing," the rabbit replied.

"I mean the monster."

"Oh, that. It oozed down toward the pond."

That put him back on the track. He reoriented, and caught the sexual smell again. He made his way through the hardwood hammock of laurel oaks, down toward the marshy fringe of the pond.

Now the dawn came with a thin layer of cloud to the east, and island-clouds scattered across the welkin, their bases in shades of gray and their tops in shades of orange, and the huge blazing red ball of the sun striking through the massed foliage. In that glory of the new day, near the overgrown shore of the pond that inlet from the lake west of the house, beside a large leaning hickory tree, he found it. There was the firefly, a sluglike glob of substance without eyes, ears, arms, legs, or anything else familiar, just a globular mass.

He had the knife ready. He knew the thing would die readily if he just cut it open and sliced up the pieces. It looked like a bag of dirty water. But he hesitated. There was something about it.

"You know I have come to kill you," he said to it. "Why aren't you fleeing me?"

"I cannot flee you," it replied. "I love you."

Geode was numb, and he knew that others, even May Flowers, would think him crazy. Œnone was the only one who had truly understood about the way he talked to animals; May did not challenge it, but didn't accept it either. But even Œnone might have looked askance if she heard him talking to the firefly, and to hear it say it loved him—!

Was this a dream? It seemed unreal enough to be one.

Hope flared. If this were a dream—maybe Œnone wasn't dead! He could wake, and she would be there beside him, to love and be loved by him. Or he would wake and find himself still on stakeout by the cabin; he could go and find her in the security closet, and untie her, and she would have proved she was not the firefly, and they could be together forever.

But he seemed awake. That wasn't good.

He tried again. "If you love me, you should not have taken the woman I love. Now you must die."

"I took the woman who loves you, and now I love you. If you kill me, you destroy her too."

"I saw her bones! She is dead!"

"She left her bones behind. She changed her form, but not her nature. I am her."

Geode felt a cold shiver. Œnone had thought she was the firefly; now the firefly said this was true!

"You cannot be her. I saw her bones! She was human, and she died, and I shall too—and you."

"How may I convince you?" the firefly asked.

"Not by using my own crazy imagination!" he snapped. "I know animals don't really talk; it's just the way I relate to them. Anything you tell me is my own imagination. I won't let you fool me that way."

"I will tell you your name: Geode," it said. "I will tell you hers: Œnone, also known as Jade, as Nymph, as Teensa, as Chloe, as anything she chooses, and now as Firefly. I will tell you anything about her."

"All from my mind, not yours!" he protested. "I tell you, I'm not crazy enough to fool myself about the death of my beloved! You shall not escape my vengeance that way!"

"Suppose I tell you about the plain young woman and the lost child?" it asked.

"I don't care about anyone else, only about Œnone!"

"The young woman had little or no social life because she was neither robustly endowed nor beautiful of face. She was brown-skinned, which meant her family didn't have much money. She was a decent person, but men took no note of that, seeing no further than the superficial. This is all too often the way of men."

"I know it is!" Geode exclaimed. "And Œnone was plain until she came to me, and then she was beautiful. But I don't care about any other woman, plain or beautiful."

"One day she was walking to the store in a tough neighborhood, and she saw a lost child. It was a little brown boy about two years old, bawling, and the other people were ignoring him. The cars were whizzing by, dangerously close; he could wander into them at any time, as he wasn't looking where he was going."

"I don't care about someone's lost child!" Geode said. "This has nothing to do with Œnone!"

"So the young woman, Enid, hurriedly crossed the street, dodging the cars, and caught up the little boy. 'What is your name?' she asked him, but he just kept on crying.

"Enid didn't know what to do with him, but she couldn't set him loose again on the street. 'Do you live near here?' she asked, but he just kept crying. So she carried him to a store and bought him a cookie with some of the money she had for her own groceries, and he chewed on that and stopped crying. But still he didn't tell his name or where he lived.

"Then some idle teenagers spied her. They were white, and that was likely to mean trouble, because the white folk tended to think that brown folk weren't really people, and had no rights. They were boys, and that meant more trouble, because boys were always out for thrills, and sometimes thought it was a thrill to rape a black girl.

" 'Whatcha doing, baby?' one of the boys called, and she couldn't tell whether he was addressing her or the little boy or both. She carried the child quickly away from there.

"But the boys followed, taunting her. She couldn't get away from them on the busy street, and no one else seemed to care. But if she went into an alley, not only would that be taking the child away from the place she had found him, so that his mother would not know where he was when she came looking for him, she would be exposing herself to whatever the white boys might choose to do to her when unrestrained by public view. That was no good.

"So she crossed the street, in an effort to avoid them, the child in her arms. But she didn't see a car coming at her. Suddenly there was the blaring of a horn and the squealing of tires. She threw herself to the side and managed to avoid the vehicle, but in the process fell into the gutter. She only had time to clasp the child tightly and hunch her body, so that she took the brunt of the fall instead of him. Her shoulder hit the curb and she heard something snap; then the pain started.

"She sat in the filthy water, her dress ruined, holding the little boy as well as she could. He was crying again, his face burrowing into her other shoulder. She was crying too, now, hurt and humiliated. How had she ever gotten into this?

"The gang of white boys closed in for the kill, hooting and jeering. 'Brown bitch's where she likes it!' 'Taking a bath!' 'Polluting the water!' One of them bent to scoop a splash of water at her face. 'Hey, bitch, wanna drink?'

"Then a pair of feet stopped at the curb, beside her. Enid cowered, fearing a blow. 'What's this?' a gruff masculine voice growled.

"Enid clasped the child more tightly, turning away from the man, so that the kick would score on her rather than on the little boy. But it was a great brown hand that came down instead, touching the boy. 'No!' Enid cried. 'Don't hurt him! Please don't hurt him! Hurt me instead!'

"The white boys, seeing the involvement of the newcomer, abruptly scattered. Enid, glancing fearfully up, saw a massive, muscular, brute-faced hulk of a man scowling down at her. This was even worse! The white boys had meant cruel mischief; they would have let her be after humiliating her enough. This man was all business, a virtual ogre.

" 'You don't even know this kid!' the man said. 'What's he to you?'

" 'He was lost!' she cried. 'Please, he's just a little child, let him go! I'll do anything you want!'

" 'Okay,' the man said. 'Hand him up to me.'

"Enid stared at him. 'You'll let him go?'

" 'No way,' the man said, reaching with both hands to take the boy from her grasp. She tried to cling to the child, but pain racked her right shoulder and she could not. She had been betrayed even in this. She bowed her head and wept into the flowing gutter water.

" 'Daddy!'

"Then hands were coming down to touch her. 'You're hurt,' the man said. 'Come on, gal, let me heave you up.'

"Enid was beyond all resistance. His hands slid around her body and his mighty arms heaved. She came up like a feather, dripping. Then the man was carrying her to his car, the little boy running along beside.

"At last it penetrated. 'He called you "Daddy"!' she said.

"He set her in the car, and pulled the seat belt across. 'Now you hold tight while I get you to a doctor.' He lifted the little boy and strapped him in the back. 'You married?'

"Enid had to laugh through her pain. 'Me? Of course not!' She did not need to point out that plain girls like her did not get snapped up quickly; that was obvious.

"He got into the driver's seat. 'See, it's hard to know the bitches from the real women when you're going for the light-heavy championship. I never had much judgment. I thought my woman was real, but she hardly had my baby out of her before she split with half my money. I swore I'd never be fooled by a gold-digger again, but I don't know how to find the other kind. The sluts, they can look good for one-night stands, but I wouldn't want any of them near my boy. I love my boy! But with training, I don't have much time anyway, and what I know about taking care of a kid isn't much. I turn around and he's gone, and pretty soon he'll get killed if I don't do something. I need a woman bad—and I think I just found one.'

"Enid rode beside him, hardly believing that her life had so quickly and radically changed. But it had."

Geode had stopped protesting as the story proceeded. Increasingly it had become apparent that this was the kind of story Œnone told. He could not imagine such stories for himself; his fouled-up dream had shown him that.

How could the firefly tell such a story if Œnone were not there? Yet how could he be sure her mind had survived, when he doubted his own sanity? If he guessed wrong, he could kill all that remained of his love—or be fooled into letting the monster escape. Neither was tolerable.

"What are you?" he asked.

"I am what you call the firefly. I feed on living flesh, and dissolve it without killing it, so that it becomes my substance. When I have enough, I form a sac and fill it with the excess. I bury that, and my egg slowly assimilates it and becomes a new firefly. This is the life cycle of my kind."

"Where did you come from?"

"I hatched beside water. My kind may have lived in water, but I came out on land and survived. That is all I know."

It seemed to make sense. This wasn't really a monster, just a different kind of animal. "Are you intelligent?"

"I do not know the meaning of the term. I assume the characteristics of those I feed on, and pass those characteristics on to the egg I lay, for they are inherent in the living substance. In this manner I adapt to new conditions. If intelligence is a characteristic of the one I have imbibed, then I have it, until I give it to the egg."

"If you are not intelligent by yourself, how can you talk to me like this?"

"I do only what the new substance enables me to do while it is with me. I can talk to you, I can tell you stories, I can love you. I know you will do me harm if you do not realize this, so I am telling you."

Again Geode was in doubt. He loved Œnone; he didn't want her dead. That could cause him to invent ways to see her as alive, even though he had seen her bones. He could not afford a mistake. But how could he be sure?

"How can I be sure of you?" he asked.

"You can never be sure of me, nor I of you. But I could tell you a tale you have heard before, so that you know there is no other source for it. The story of Œnone, for example."

"My memory is another source for it."

"Then I can tell you a story you have not heard."

"You just did. Someone else could have made that up."

"Then I can tell you a tale derived from elements you request, in the way only Œnone could do."

That seemed possible to him. Œnone had been able to do that, and still surprise him with the outcome. If the firefly had picked up only what was in Œnone's memory, it would not be able to integrate his input with her storytelling ability. "Tell me a tale of telepathy and childhood." For it had seemed to him that his own situation might have been explained by that: if he could read the minds of animals, he could communicate with them, and it might seem as if they were talking with him. Instead of being crazy, then and now, he might be telepathic. Animals, monsters—it would not matter whether their mouths could form human words, they would still be able to speak in this manner.

"There was a child, a little girl named Sela, who was telepathic," the firefly said. Œnone always had a female viewpoint unless he requested otherwise, and she oriented a great deal on children. "She picked up the thoughts of all who were near her, and their feelings. When someone in the house was happy, Sela was happy, and when someone was angry, she was angry, even as a baby. When someone was ill, she felt the discomfort, and when the person nearest her slept, Sela was apt to sleep too.

"The other members of the family were not telepathic. Sela could read their minds, but they could not read hers. Thus they thought her strange. Even as a baby, she reacted oddly. Once her parents made love in the next room, and Sela felt the sexual thrills of both and writhed in her crib and moaned with desire. When her father climaxed, Sela cried out with fulfillment. Then her mother, who had not climaxed, came to the crib, and Sela scowled with unfulfillment.

"Sela's behavior could not be explained by others, and indeed, the feelings constantly coming in to her mind overrode the normal feelings of a baby. As a result, Sela was not able to learn the way normal babies did, and—"

"No!" Geode exclaimed. He knew where this was leading: the girl would be thought crazy, and would be institutionalized, and perhaps find secret love with an aide at the sanitarium, who would then be fired for his abuse of his position. He didn't want to hear it.

"If the story is wrong, it can be changed," the firefly said.

"No, I want a different story, not like that. No telepathy, no young child. Male viewpoint—older male. Make it a king." That was as far away from telepathy and insanity as he could think of at the moment.

The firefly paused. "This is difficult," it said.

Which was exactly what Œnone would have said. She had little affinity with older men, unless they related to young girls, especially sexually.

The firefly began to speak.

Once there was a King of a small distant kingdom. He was a good and honest man, and a capable ruler, but his kingdom was not prosperous, and his palace was really no more than an adapted castle. His Queen was a frivolous woman, and his son the Prince was all right but somewhat irresponsible. The King was trying to impress on his son the supreme importance of honor; if he could do that, he believed, the rest would fall into place and the Prince would in time become a good King after him.

One day the Prince, riding on a hunt alone (for the kingdom was too poor to support a royal retinue), chanced to fall from his horse. The horse bolted, and he was stranded in the countryside. He limped to the nearest house and identified himself. "I need a horse to carry me back to the palace," he said. "Have you one I may borrow?"

"I need my horse for plowing," the farmer said. "If it is taken to the castle, it may be days before I get it back, and it will be tired, and my plowing will suffer, and my crop will be late."

"I can pay you for the animal," the Prince said impatiently. But he discovered that his purse had been lost with his horse, and he was for the moment penniless. "Will you take an IOU?"

"With all due respect, sir, I will not," the farmer said. "From the King I would, for he is a man of honor and will always make good on his debts, but you are unproven. I can not risk my horse, which represents much of my livelihood, so cavalierly."

The Prince, annoyed, nevertheless had to bargain, for this was an enlightened kingdom and farmers had rights. "If I cannot pay you immediately in money, is there some other way I may satisfy you, so that you will agree to take this risk?"

The farmer considered. "Actually, there is a way, but it might not appeal to you."

"At this point, anything that will get me a good horse appeals to me!"

"My daughter is a homely girl," the farmer said. "She might have been beautiful, for her form is good, but she was scalded on the face in a childhood accident, and now no man will sleep with her, let alone marry her."

"Now just a minute!" the Prince protested. "A Prince does not marry a commoner; that's fairy-tale stuff! A beautiful one he might take for a concubine, but that's about the limit."

"Just so. If my daughter bore the child of a Prince, she would have honor, and thereafter be able to attract a husband. It is known that your father the King has a policy of recognizing royal bastards, and often they receive a stipend. That can be a big help to a common family."

The Prince nodded, now that he got the farmer's drift. He had sown certain wild oats himself, and the babies had been duly stipended. This policy made it easier for him to have casual affairs with pretty commoners, and there was no swell of outrage in the populace. "Let me see your daughter."

The farmer brought out his daughter. He had described her accurately: she was a buxom lass, but her face was a mass of scar tissue, making it most unattractive. The thought of kissing her turned the Prince's stomach, and the notion of making love to her did not have much appeal.

Still, he needed the horse. "Very well. Put a sack over her head and bring her to the royal guest cottage when she is in season, and I will join her that night and impregnate her and will recognize the offspring. She shall have a royal bastard."

"Thank you, Prince," the farmer said, gratified. He then saddled his horse and turned it over to the Prince.

The Prince mounted the horse and rode swiftly to the palace. Once there, he turned it over to the chief squire. "Feed this horse well, groom it, and return it to the farmer who owns it with my thanks," he said. "Ask him when he expects his daughter to be in season."

"I hear and obey, Prince," the loyal squire said.

The Prince then went inside and reported the matter to his father the King. The King nodded. "This was a sensible way out of your dilemma," he said. "The farmer shall have value for his service to the crown."

The Prince then forgot the matter. He had his abrasions from the fall salved, and he bathed, and took a luscious and perfect-faced maid to his bed for the evening. Soon it was as if the episode during the hunt had never occurred.

In due course the message came: the girl was in season, and would be at the cottage this night. It happened that the Prince had scheduled a night of gaming in a distant town; it was to be one great carouse.

Disgusted that the appointment with the ugly peasant girl should fall
on this of all nights, he decided on a stratagem: he would send a
substitute. The girl, in the dark with a sack over her head, would never
know the difference, and the Prince would be relieved of a chore he
hadn't much appreciated anyway. So he assigned the task to the loyal
chief squire, then headed off for the distant town.

Now it happened that the King noted the departure of the Prince
and of the squire in opposite directions. He was no fool. He made
inquiries, and quickly ascertained the nature of the deception. He was
enraged: the Prince had given his Royal Word, and it had to be
honored. But it was probably too late to catch the Prince and reverse
his course; dusk was approaching, and by the time that could be
straightened out, it would be too late. The King paced the palace halls,
muttering. How was the royal honor to be salvaged? He sent horsemen
out to apprehend both Prince and squire, but the chances of getting
them exchanged in time were remote.

Meanwhile, suspicion of the Prince's perfidy had developed in the
local population. It was generally known that the Prince had intended
to attend the gaming extravaganza, and the word about the assignation
with the peasant girl had also spread. When her season turned out to
be the very night of the bash, they wondered which event the Prince
would choose to honor with his presence. Royalty-watching was a
prime pursuit in the kingdom; it was the source of all the most worthwhile gossip. So they knew the moment the Prince's charger rode out
in the wrong direction, and they guessed the mission of the squire.
Actually, the squire didn't go directly to the cottage; he went to the
local tavern for a drink or two, to brace himself for the ordeal he faced
that night. He was loyal, and he would do what he had been told to do,
but there was more than one aspect of it he didn't really like.

Now, the kingdom was enlightened for its day, but there were
limits. The Royal Word was supposed to be sacrosanct, and its abridg-
ment was cause for general unrest. Righteous folk saw an opportunity
to embarrass the crown in the name of defending it, which was of
course much too good a thing to let pass. The fact was that when it
came right down to it, peasants didn't really like being lowly, and
valued the chance to bring royalty down to their level, however peripherally.

So they organized a posse of men, and went privately to the royal
guest cottage. They laid quiet siege to it a couple of hours after dark.
Their lookout assured them that the squire's horse had approached the

cottage shortly after dusk, and had been turned loose to graze for the night; its rider had gone inside and not emerged.

"So he's had time to futter her," the posse leader said, and the others agreed. It was important that the act actually occur, because otherwise the Prince could claim that he had merely sent the squire to advise the girl that the Prince would be arriving late, and the trap would not be tight.

They sneaked up and peered in the window. Inside, by the sputtering glow of a stubby candle, lay two naked figures embraced. "Amazing!" the leader whispered. "He dehooded her as well as devirginating her. What a glutton for punishment." For though the light was wan, the girl's lustrous black hair was spread out on the pillow.

Now was the time. The men gathered by the door, then abruptly bashed it in. The sleeping figures within came awake and sat up, blinking. The girl screamed.

"So, miscreant!" the posse leader declaimed. "You sought to deceive this innocent maiden. You are no Prince!"

"Indeed I am not," the man said, standing. He fetched the candle and held it by his face.

The posse of men stared, appalled. For there before them was the visage of the King.

"The seed within this maiden is mine," the King said. "I had heard a tale that she was ugly, but she seems beautiful to me. Do any disagree?"

The men gazed at the scar-crusted face of the girl. No one disagreed. Indeed, in her fulfillment, she did seem to possess a quality of appeal not before fathomed. Scars were, after all, superficial things.

"Now I charge you, loyal henchmen, to fetch me my horse, and do not tell the Queen, who might not understand."

Chagrined, they fetched the horse and departed. No one spread the news to the Queen. But in due course the farmer's ugly daughter bore a fine son, who was stipended as a royal bastard, and she was able to attract a husband. The King's reputation for honor was unsullied, and his personal popularity increased, though often there was a sly wink when this was spoken of among peasants.

Geode shook his head. This was certainly the kind of story Œnone would have told. It had all the elements she favored, and that he related to, because they were hers.

Œnone was in the monster. He could not kill it.

He turned and cut across to the drive, then up it to the house. What was he to do?

But already he knew. He went to the security closet with a bag and packed the bones into it. He would bury these where they would not be found. No one would know that the firefly had come here. The secret would be kept, protecting the estate—and the firefly.

The house phone rang. He set down the bag and answered it; he didn't want anything to seem to be out of the ordinary.

It was Frank Tishner. "Listen, Demerit, hell's about to break loose. They found the bones in the van."

Geode froze. How was he going to cover up the existence of the firefly now?

❖ 46 ❖

Frank set down the phone, disgusted. It had been so close! If the firefly had shown up last night, when they were ready for it, and they had killed it, then maybe they could have finessed the bones. But with it still loose, and probably more bones somewhere else, waiting to be discovered, things were falling apart.

What were the dangers, and how could they be avoided? He would be in trouble soon, for sure, because his department knew he had been investigating just such bones before. May, too, because she had driven that van up there, and her fingerprints were on the wheel. If only they had been able to return to it and clean everything up!

He had to call her and get their stories straight. He reached for the phone again, then hesitated. He was at home, for it was still early; he didn't want to call her from here.

"Go ahead and call her," Trudy said, making him jump.

He looked at her. He hadn't realized she was up yet. But of course the same call that had notified him of the bones in Ocala would have awakened her. How much did she know or suspect?

"You were out all night on that project," she said. "That was no deputy business."

"Not exactly," he agreed guardedly.

"You were with that woman."

So that was it! "Her and George Demerit," he agreed.

"Doing what?"

"Staking out a cabin, trying to catch a monster. Without success." He took a breath and plowed on. "Now two of the victims of that monster have been discovered, and I'm implicated, and May Flowers. That's why I have to call her."

"You're having an affair with her."

He could not deny it.

"And you're implicated in a murder?"

Better tell her now. "Her estranged husband, Bull Shauer, went after her again. She was hiding at a cabin on the Middle Kingdom Ranch. That's where I took her, after he beat her up. The monster got him instead of her. But officially there is no monster, so it would have looked like murder. So we—it's complicated, but the essence is we left his body in a van in Ocala. And the body of a prior victim. We forgot those bodies were in that vehicle. I helped her hide the van, or she helped me. Now it will all come out, and I think you know what that means."

"Your job."

"My job."

"Then I'm going home."

There was no point in arguing with her; they had finished their dialogue on that matter long ago. His recent affair with May hardly helped. "I'm sorry to see it end this way. But I think my job was doomed the moment the monster came on the scene. The woman was incidental to that."

She nodded. "I don't blame you for the woman, Frank. I saw what that man did to her. She needed someone, and you were there. You and I really never were right for each other. So call her."

He looked at her. "You have been fair about this, Trudy. I regret I wasn't able to do better by you. You're a good woman."

She almost smiled. "Thank you, Frank." She returned to the bedroom.

He dialed May's number. She answered immediately. "They found the bones in the van," he said. "Both sets; we forgot about Paris Brown. They'll be after you in hours because of the prints. What are you going to tell them?"

"There's no way to keep it quiet now?"

"I'm afraid not."

"But your office won't want national headlines about a monster!"

"Right. So someone's head will roll. Mine. But maybe yours too, if they think you had something to do with Bull's death."

"He was here, he beat me up, he turns up dead with my prints on the vehicle," she said. "I see the problem."

"So I think we had better tell the truth and take our medicine," he said.

"Which is?"

"You work for Mid, I work for Citrus County. Neither wanted any commotion about a monster. Your employer allowed you to hide at his cabin, Bull came after you, you stabbed him with an anesthetic dart intended for the firefly and fled—and the firefly got him instead. It had already gotten Paris Brown. In the morning you and I collaborated to dispose of the bodies quietly, serving our mutual interest. That may have been a mistake, but we were rattled at the time."

"Um," she said. "I have two questions. What does your wife think of this?"

"She's packing now, to return to her folks. Because she knows this is it for my job. And—she knows about us."

"What of Cyrano?"

Frank grimaced at the phone. "Ouch! That's his van! Where is he?"

"He was going to dispose of the bodies," she said. "Then he got taken by the monster himself. We haven't found his remains. So we used his vehicle to hide the bodies, and to mask the fact of his death."

"Got it," he said. "Maybe you had better go out and explain to Demerit and Jade."

"Immediately," she agreed.

"This will still be hairy," he reminded her. "Especially if the firefly keeps killing. You know they'll burn the whole ranch if they think the firefly's using it as a base to roam out and kill people."

"The firefly must die," she said grimly. "You tell them what you have to. I'll tell Geode."

"Who?"

"Demerit. If the thing hasn't fed yet, it will be out again tonight, and we'll have to get it. Not privately; publicly, so it is clear it is dead. How is that best done, assuming we can find it?"

"Gasoline," he said. "Dump it on, light it, stand back. I'll see to it."

"Agreed. I'm sorry about your wife. I had no intention to—"

"It was coming anyway," he said. "Not your fault." That was true, but what he didn't say was that he would like to take up with May now. How could he, jobless? So the monster had done him in that way too.

"I will see you in due course," she said.

"Sure thing." He hesitated a moment, then hung up.

He braced himself to drive to the office and say his piece. If only that van hadn't been discovered so soon!

❖ 47 ❖

MAY SET DOWN the receiver. She
had spoken in a businesslike manner to him, uncertain whether his
wife was listening to his conversation. She would have preferred to be
more personal. He was in trouble and probably would lose his job
because of her foul-up. Also, she liked him, perhaps loved him, and
for the first time in her life was interested in having sex with a man, he
being the man. She wished she could help him. But he was independent and honest; she knew he disliked this business of telling partial
truth, covering up for their foul-ups. If he didn't have a job, he would
not take help from a woman.

But maybe if Mid offered him a job . . .

She organized herself, then drove out to the ranch. Geode buzzed
her in, and came out to meet her. "I didn't bring groceries this time,"
she said. "Things are breaking loose, and we have to work out what to
do. Better let me talk to Œnone, too."

"Can't," he said.

"She's in this too! If they come here and find her, it will be complicated to explain."

"When we staked out the cabin, the firefly—"

She glanced sharply at him. "Are you saying it came here?"

367

"Œnone—she thought maybe she was doing it, so she made me tie her up—"

May stared at him with downing horror. "She was bound—and the firefly came?"

He nodded. "I just—buried the—"

"Oh, Geode!" she said, seeing him break down. She more or less grabbed him and hauled him in to her, and he sobbed against her shoulder. "Oh, Geode, I didn't know!"

The firefly *had* struck, outwitting them all. It was the most devastating loss yet. Œnone, little Œnone, with her fantastic storytelling ability—suddenly gone! And Geode—obviously he loved her. They had been intimate, and were well matched. Now—

She sat the man down and questioned him, getting the story. Œnone had foolishly thought she might be a killer, in an alternate personality. It was apparent, now, that the woman had suffered from a syndrome of some sort, assuming multiple personalities, of which the fabled nymphly wife of Paris was only one. So she had inadvertently rendered herself helpless against the firefly, and disaster had struck. If she, May, had thought she had a problem, or that Frank Tishner had, what of this one for Geode?

This certainly solved the problem of Œnone being discovered here—but in what a grisly fashion!

"Geode, let me think about this," she said. "I realize how important Œnone was to you. Will you be all right for now?"

He nodded, looking miserable.

She left him, not able to do anything else. Œnone dead! She had never thought this would happen!

The firefly had to be destroyed, and quickly! But how could they do it when the thing had struck at will, taking even the exterminator?

Well, probably a mass search by thousands of men would do it, setting fire to the brush of the ranch to kill the monster or drive it out. The thing seemed to be gelatinous, with no bones; Geode had shown her where Œnone had been taken, in a secure closed room, without the set alarm going off. Either it was ghostly, which she refused to accept, or it could squeeze under the door. So they had learned more about it, in a most unfortunate way. That might explain how it had caught Cyrano: he had been on guard against a solid or at least a visible creature, but it could have slid under the floorboards and squeezed quietly up through a crack and gotten him from behind. That explained, too, its lack of footprints and its silence; it didn't walk, it flowed or oozed. The clothing on victims had never been disturbed, except sometimes in the genital region, which they might have done themselves in response to the sexual urgency of the pheromones. A gelatinous creature would have no concern for clothing; it would simply squeeze around it or through its various apertures.

It would also relate to the apertures of human beings, especially the genital or excretory ones. If it had no hard parts, no claws or teeth, it might have trouble gaining entry. Animal or human skin might be a barrier. But if it could get inside, to the soft mucous tissues, then it could use its acids to dissolve them away. So anus, vagina, or penis— or ear, nose, or mouth, except that the use of the pheromones suggested that sexual tissue was more likely. Once it was inside, the rest would proceed, with the skin itself serving as the container for the solution. Perhaps the firefly itself entered the body, digesting as it went, and leaving when all available flesh had been absorbed.

Such a creature should be virtually defenseless against an alert man or woman. As Frank had said, gasoline would destroy it, but a knife would too. Destroying it would be no problem—if they could find it. And there was the rub: how to find it. Before hell broke loose.

Because, she realized, all was not yet lost. Œnone was dead, and she would grieve for her in due course. But the Middle Kingdom Ranch remained, and if they could catch and kill the firefly before it struck again, they could avoid the separate horror of a slash-and-burn search across the ranch. That would satisfy Mid and save May's job, and Geode's. It would also preserve a lovely piece of real estate, with all the innocent plants and animals on it.

So the firefly had to go. All else had failed. Now it was up to her. The thing had proved marvelously elusive, and horrendously dangerous, but she was coming to know it. It did not seem intelligent or particularly malignant; it merely sought isolated human beings for its meals, every three days. Had she realized that Œnone was tied as well as being alone—

So the bait had worked. It was just that the firefly had gone for the better bait, the single person instead of the grouped people. Another single person could lure it in again. But this time that person would have a can of gasoline, and a match.

May was prepared to do this herself, but she knew Frank would not allow it. He would insist on doing it himself, or on having Geode do it. Geode had the strongest motive now.

Yes, she believed she had the answer. The day after tomorrow, they would be ready. They would kill it, and show the authorities the ashes. Then they could quietly pick up the pieces.

She drove on, satisfied. Now she could weep for Œnone.

The next two days developed predictably. Frank told the sheriff the story, and the sheriff himself drove out to look at the cabin and to talk to Geode. Geode agreed to destroy the firefly. He said he thought he could locate it by the smell. May knew he could; they had not told the sheriff about the particular effect of that odor!

Frank's wife shipped her things and caught a plane north. He was left alone in the rented house. He still had his job, but it was hanging by a thread, and both he and May knew that the moment the firefly was gone, that shoe would drop. He was despondent, but such was the attention on them both now that she could not go to console him.

The news remained sequestered. The sheriff was keeping the lid on while the investigation continued. It was understood that the nature of Frank's departure from his department depended on how tightly that lid remained on. He might even go with a decent reference if things remained quiet and the firefly was taken out as scheduled.

She made a call to Mid, who agreed with her plan. Things were falling grimly into place, even as they seemed to be falling apart.

On the assigned day, she went to the ranch. Frank joined her there. Geode was ready: he had his matches and can of gasoline. The two of them would wait at the main house while Geode went out and found the firefly. They would be together, but there would be no relaxation; if they found the notion of sex intruding, they would know the firefly was near, and if it came close enough, Frank would be able to dispatch it himself.

Geode headed out an hour before dusk. He would walk to the cabin, or wherever the firefly seemed to be. He was quite sure he could find it. May hoped his optimism was justified.

✦ 48 ✦

GEODE WALKED AWAY from the
house. He hoped he had succeeded in fooling May; she was pretty
sharp, but right now she was so tied up with her own worries that she
wasn't really watching him. She thought him stupid, as most people
did, except for Mid. She was nice enough about it, and he didn't
mind. She had seen only the outside of the rock, not the inside. In this
case it had been helpful, because she had not fathomed what was in his
mind. She did not realize that he had actually found the firefly, and
talked to it.

He had thought deeply about the matter, and come to a terrible
decision. They were right: the firefly had to die. But not for quite the
reason they thought. Geode didn't care whether the firefly fed on other
people; there were too many people in the world anyway, people like
the poaching hunters and Bull Shauer, who were no good. If there
were a hundred fireflies, a thousand, feeding on people, it would do
the world good. People were breeding too fast, crowding out all the
other species, destroying the trees, polluting the ground and water and
air, ruining the planet. The public was a slob, leaving litter, dumping
garbage wherever it went. Mid had the right idea: buy a tract, preserve

it, keep everyone off. It would be great to do that with the whole world!

But the firefly would attract a lot of attention. People would barge in, hunting it. They might, as May said, burn the ranch, to drive out the firefly so they could kill it. So the firefly was doomed; sooner or later it would die. The question was whether the ranch could be saved, and all the other creatures on it. If he killed the firefly now, the ranch would be spared, and Mid would be pleased, and Geode would retain his job. If he didn't, much worse would happen. So he had to do it. He and May and Frank agreed on that.

But there was more that the others didn't know. He had talked with the firefly several times now, as it proceeded to assimilate Œnone and make ready to lay its next egg. He now knew how it operated. It would lay its egg near the pond, down below the water table so that it would not dry out. That egg would rest quiescent for a time, perhaps months or years. Then it would hatch, though that wasn't the proper term. It would mature into a new firefly, with its own personality. It was really a form of fissioning, with the original firefly dividing into rough halves, one active, the other passive. The active one would eventually get killed; it always happened, because it was defenseless and its prey wasn't. But the chain of eggs left behind would survive, and would emerge later to feed and fission themselves. Thus the species would survive, though the original individual did not.

And it was the original. It did not know where it had come from, but Geode had figured it out. It derived from the deep sea, but the hunting there was becoming more limited, so it had spread to the shallows and finally to the rivers. But recently river pollution had gotten worse, so to escape that one had laid an egg not below the riverbed, but to the side. That egg had hatched upward onto dry land, and managed to survive the strange environment.

The firefly assimilated some of the qualities of each animal it fed on, for it took in only living flesh, without killing it. When it took a raccoon, or a rabbit, it learned better how to manage on land, and how to hide. When it took a man, it became aware of the power of intelligence, and learned to be far more cunning about its activity. This awareness lasted only until it fissioned, for the new substance went almost wholly to the egg. When the egg hatched, it would be more intelligent than the original firefly.

When it took Œnone, it had assumed much of her personality. That personality would be permanent in the egg. The mobile portion of the firefly would lose it.

That egg had been laid on the second day. The firefly had delved down into the moist earth, infiltrating in an almost liquid manner, and then separated itself from the mass below. The fissioning was complete. Œnone-Firefly had entered the quiescent stage, hidden from the knowledge of others.

If a posse of men went through the ranch, slashing and burning and bulldozing, the buried eggs might be damaged and perhaps would die. The one that was Œnone would perish with them. Geode could not tolerate that.

So he would kill the active firefly so that the other people would be satisfied, and there would be no invasion of the Middle Kingdom Ranch. Œnone would be saved. That was the secret he had kept, for he knew that neither May nor Frank would have agreed to allow the eggs to remain. Cyrano might have, for he had wanted to study the creature, but Cyrano would have to continue his studies in another manner when his egg hatched.

It should be interesting when the several new fireflies emerged, each with the personality of a different human being.

But Geode could not stay for that. He alone knew the truth. If they questioned him, it might come out. So he needed to disappear as soon as he killed the firefly. He had called Mid and asked to be reassigned, and Mid had agreed. A car would come for him in the night, and he would get in it, and disappear. Until Œnone hatched. Then he would return quietly to take her with him, and she would go, because she loved him, just as he loved her. If she got too hungry, and consumed him, that was all right too; they would be together.

He knew where to find the firefly because he knew everything about it now. Œnone had made it tell him. He knew where the egg had been buried, and where it would hunt next. It would be crossing the driveway at the lowest point, just north of the house. From there it would turn north, heading for new territory. It probably would not feed tonight, because it traveled at only a third of a mile an hour, and would have to get all the way off the ranch to find suitable people to take. Only the continued availability of solitary people on the ranch had held it here this long; it normally kept moving, because the prey became more wary in any region where the bones were found.

He heard the sound of it, that faint keening. He felt an erection starting. The firefly was near, and it was coming toward him, supposing him to be suitable prey. It had never attacked him while Œnone was part of it, both because she loved him and because it could not feed again until it set its egg. But now it had done so, and was hungry.

He stopped in the middle of the drive. He removed the cap from the can of gasoline and got out two matches. He set the matches between his teeth. He shone his flashlight around. The firefly was indifferent to light, having no eyes; it foraged by night because it had learned that this was safer, and that the prey was more likely to be quiescent. Most of its victims were caught sleeping.

The mound of brown appeared at the edge. Geode remained standing. His erection was now pulsing, as the pheromones made him mad for sex. He thought of Œnone and her wonderful body, drawing ecstasy from him again and again.

The mound sent out a pseudopod. This slid up toward Geode, then swelled. In short order the firefly was beside him, ready to send a new pseudopod up his leg to his genital region, where there were apertures for entry. Prey normally did not flee or resist at this stage; it was too sexually excited.

But Geode knew the firefly, and what he had to do. He lifted the can and poured gasoline on the mound, holding the flashlight awkwardly while he did so. It splashed across the shape, seemingly harmlessly. The firefly did not know this fluid's purpose. The pseudopod continued to extend toward Geode's leg.

Geode set down the can. He turned off the flashlight and put it in his pocket. He took the two matches from between his teeth. He set their heads together, ready to strike them against each other.

"I am going to kill you," he told it.

The firefly hesitated. Now it realized that he knew its nature, and that meant danger for it. "Why do you wish to do that?" it asked. Meanwhile its pseudopod was at his shoe, beginning to climb.

"It is nothing personal," Geode replied. "It is to protect your eggs from discovery, so that they will survive. Especially the one I love." Then he struck the matches.

They flared, just as the pseudopod touched the bare flesh of his leg above the shoe and sock. He hesitated; that touch was wonderfully conducive! How easy it would be to let it proceed, providing him with rapture unknown elsewhere! But he knew what he had to do. He dropped the two burning matches onto the firefly and stepped quickly back.

The gasoline caught. It did not explode, for it was not confined; it merely burned brilliantly, outlining the mound of the firefly.

The thin skin of the firefly burst. Its fluid body spread out across the asphalt, but the fire followed it. The odor changed from sexually provocative to sickening. The firefly was dying horribly.

Goede watched it, tears flowing down his cheeks. He hated it for taking Œnone, but he loved it too, for preserving Œnone. He knew it was just another creature, a unique predator, trying to survive. He would have let it be, had he had any choice.

He heard footsteps behind him. Frank and May had spied the fire and were coming down.

"That's it," he told them. "It's just a bag of fluid. If you think it's getting away, put more gas on it." Then he turned and walked back toward the house.

He felt dead inside.

❖ **49** ❖

T HEY WATCHED THE fire as it fol-
lowed the sinking substance. Geode was right: the monster was just a
bag of fluid, in the end. The fire was cooking it like so much egg white.
There was no doubt it was the firefly; they had felt the strength of its
pheromones. It was oddly insubstantial now, spread out on the pavement, burning down.

"Not with a bang, but a whimper," May murmured.

"Just a carnivorous jellyfish," Frank said. "I guess it hunted by night
because it didn't have any fur or weapons. Just its smell."

"Like a succubus," she said. "Coming to make men dream of sex,
though it killed them. And women too. I'm almost sad for it."

"Me too. I thought I was crazy, but—" He shrugged.

"Speaking of crazy," she said, "I hope I am not being unkind, but
I suspect that both Geode and Œnone were some of that. He seems to
have had a deprived life, and compensated by developing his inner
resources, perhaps too far. He believes he can talk to animals. He was
hospitalized for a time, so now he isn't open about the matter, but he
does still believe it."

"But he did a good enough job here," Frank said. "He has been a
good man, as far as my dealings with him are concerned. Let's face it,

376

we're all a little crazy about something. My wife thought I was crazy to blow the whistle on my employer and get myself blacklisted, and maybe she was right."

"Yes, I agree," she said. "I respect Geode for coping as he has. I like him personally, and I think he was very good for Œnone—and she for him. But I have to say that she was farther gone than he. She had multiple personalities, which I think stemmed from the abuse she suffered as a child."

"Abuse? She seemed like one winsome little lady to me, once I got to know her."

"*Too* winsome! Some little girls are taught to be that way, cajoling men, proceeding on into sexual precocity. Some grown women act childish in order to wheedle favors from men too. Œnone had what appears to have been voluntary sex with an adult man when she was only five years old."

He stared at her. "*Five?*"

"Five. Her father and her brother had been at her sexually, so she thought that that was the only way to gain love. She seems to have closed off much of the bad memories by separating that personality from her adopted one, but she remained sexually biased. Yet I think she really loved Geode, and I'm sure he loved her. Society might call her crazy, but I have suffered enough myself to understand the pressure she was under. I mean, what is a child warped by sexual abuse that can not be escaped supposed to do? How does she adjust, once she is grown, with those terrible scars remaining internally? Our society has barely addressed the problem, and it is unfortunately widespread. So if Œnone was crazy, I don't blame her, I blame our callous society."

"If there was evidence of abuse, why didn't they take it to court?"

"They did. They convicted, perhaps, the wrong man—and sent her back to her family. So much for justice, for her. No wonder she retreated to fantasy!"

"So much for justice," he echoed glumly, remembering his own experience with it. "The world is one hell of a place."

"We can't all choose our estate in life. Often we have to make compromises, sometimes serious ones, just to get through."

He glanced at her. "What are you getting at?"

"You know that they are only waiting for confirmation of the monster's death before they fire you," she said.

"But they'll give me a decent reference, because in the end I pulled it out, and there won't be much bad publicity."

"But your reputation will precede you, wherever you go. I fear you are finished in law enforcement, Frank."

He sighed. He knew she was right, and that it meant he would have to start again in some other line. It would be years before he was sufficiently established to be able to think of marrying. He had done what he had to do, here, but there was no joy in it.

"Then I guess this is good-bye," he said. "I can't say I didn't wish for some other way out. It's been great knowing you, May."

"If you had a good job, you could marry again," she said. "But are you too proud to take what offers?"

He laughed bitterly. "I *am* a proud cuss, and I can't afford it! If I had a good, secure job right now, I'd—" But he cut it off; what was the point?

"In the process of saving the county's reputation, you have also saved Mid's ranch," she said. "Mid has a better set of values than politically conscious county administrators do. Two days ago I called him, and today he called me back. He is reassigning Geode to another estate; only he knows where. This ranch needs a new caretaker. The work is simple and not demanding. I realize it would be no challenge for a man like you, far beneath your competence, but it has compensations."

Frank was surprised. "Me? Mid wants to hire me?"

"I mentioned sometime back that Mid takes care of his own, and you have become one of his own—if you want to be. He is impressed by your résumé; you have always been competent and honest, and have gotten in trouble for it. He might soon have more challenging uses for your expertise. But at the moment what he needs is a caretaker. The pay is good, and you get free board, and occasional gifts, and—"

He turned to her, aware that she was holding back something. "And what?"

"And me," she finished. "If you want me, Frank. Of course I'll be traveling a lot, on his assignments, but when I'm not, I'll be glad to stay here at this lovely ranch with—"

He cut her off with his kiss. She did, after all, want him as much as he wanted her, and she had arranged it so that he could not refuse, regardless of his pride.

The fire guttered down, but they were heedless of it.

✦ 50 ✦

IN THE GROUND, nearby, the egg reposed, motionless, quiescent. Only its mind was active, as it shaped its future nature according to its past nature.

On the battlefield a soldier lay grievously wounded, dying. As night closed, hope faded, for his unit had not found him amid the carnage and assumed he was already dead.

A child from a ruined farmstead wandered out. Her house had been destroyed and her family was dead; only she survived, and she did not know what to do. "Mommy!" she called, unable to believe what had happened. "Daddy! Where are you?"

The dying soldier groaned. Attracted to the sound, she went to him. "Daddy?"

His awareness shrouded by loss of blood and the beginning of hallucination, he thought she said "Daryl," which was his name. "Gina?" he rasped, dreaming he was back home with his true love.

She thought he said "Gisela," which was her name. "Yes!" she cried, and plumped down beside him, and cradled his head in her arms. "Are you all right?"

"I am now," he said, delighting in her loving embrace.

So they endured through the night, each giving the other comfort, and by morning, when the truth became evident, they had new reasons to endure. She helped him drag himself up, and he took her with him, and they were a family.

The mind shifted, perhaps sleeping. The entity was as yet imperfectly formed, for though flesh could be readily dissolved, it took time to shape it into a cohesive, fully functioning firefly. That was why the quiescent stage was necessary. Then the mind resumed, in its fashion dreaming.

Any number of matchings were possible, but few were perfect. Physically there was no problem; any man could match with any woman. But emotionally it was more difficult. The quest was for perfect love. This could be judged by the glow.

When one person was attracted to another, he/she glowed. When a person was truly committed, the glow was stronger. Complete love made him glow so brightly as to shine. The trick was to match up the glows, so that they enhanced each other and generated a greater mutual brilliance.

However, sexual interest also caused a glow, of a different hue. Sometimes the object of the sex-glow did not match the object of the love-glow. Then it could get complicated.

One day an ardent couple discovered that . . .

The egg continued the story, warming into it. One day these stories will be told to one who would listen, one who loved. For now, they were only being rehearsed.

A man found a beautiful woman. But she was like a zombie; she lacked self-assertion. She did anything he asked, no matter what it was, but never initiated anything, even a thought. At first he was delighted, for what he wanted of her had little to do with intellect. It had to do with her lying down naked and spreading her legs every hour or two, which she did without question or emotion. What delight!

But in time even this grew stale; he discovered that a woman with no will of her own was scarcely better than a mannequin. She was no good as a companion, because she never said anything except "yes." She could not be trusted with chores on her own, because she needed specific instructions for every detail. He could tell her to "pick up that bucket" and she would do so, but then he would have to tell her what to do with it. He couldn't tell her to wash the dishes, only to pick up a dish, pass the sponge over it, put it under the tap, turn on the water, let it rinse off the dish, turn off the water, and set the dish down. Then the same series for the next dish. It was easier to do it himself. She really was good only for one thing, and as it turned out, not awfully good at that. Because after he had sated himself upon her, she just lay there, not even cleaning herself up, until he instructed her to do it, step by step. That diminished the effect somewhat.

Finally he realized what the problem was. She had no personality! Perhaps she had no soul. She was just the body of a woman, not the whole of her. For the first time he appreciated the fact that a woman needed to be more than an attractive body, and it was a considerable revelation.

So he decided to do something about it. Obviously she had had a personality once; she must have lost it. He went on a quest to find that lost personality. When he found it, he would restore it to her, and then he would have a whole woman—and be ready to appreciate her that way.

He set out with her, and had many adventures along the way, and . . .

The tale continued. The author had lost her essence, but surely would recover it in due course. That had to be believed. It had to be!

My love set out on his quest through the wilds of the wilderness, running, running indefatigably. He ran along the hard pavement of the road, and it pounded against his feet, but he did not yield. He ran through the blackberry bushes, and the fierce thorns caught at his legs, but he did not pause. He ran through a horrendous patch of sandspur grass, and the cruel little barbed balls stuck in his socks. Now he paused to take them out, but then a great swarm of black biting flies descended on him. He swatted them away and went on, and the sugary sand gave way beneath his feet, sapping his speed and balance, but he kept on. He ran past rabbits and tortoises, past toads and rattlesnakes, even a beautiful little coral snake. Above him a great pileated woodpecker pecked in its tree, marveling at his persistence in the oppressive heat. He came to the verge of the lake, where alligators lurked. He would not be stopped!

But at last he came to me, down by the edge of the pond. Oh my love, my darling, you have reached me at last! Now our love can be complete, and we shall forage together, because for the first time our kind will have human intelligence and knowledge. We will know how to handle human prey. . . .

Author's Note

This is, as you may have gathered, a special novel, the first of several unrelated projects I have had in mind for some time that are of more consequence than my fantasy. From inception to completion was about seven years, because I did not pursue it until I was satisfied about its nature. It is technically a monster story, concluding with a suggestion of the horror to come when alien fireflies who understand man are loosed on the world. If one ignorant monster could cause such mischief, what of the knowledgeable ones? I have no sequel in mind; the reader may imagine that aspect for himself. The essence of this novel is in the characters, especially Œnone. I am of course in love with her, as I am with all my leading ladies, and I hope you are too, if you are male, and that you understand her if you are female. She represents the triumph of imagination over dull reality or quiet desperation, and I think there are many women like her to some degree. This can be an ugly world.

This novel addresses more than peripherally the problem of abuse. It occurs in many forms, physical and emotional, and is exacerbated by the insensitivity, ignorance, or downright malice of others. It does happen in "nice" families, and much of it is not of the screaming rape type. It may be subtle and persistent, yet it can be hellish. The games five-year-old Nymph played with Mad were a joy to her at the time, but it was nevertheless abuse by our society's definition (not necessarily by that of other societies), and her life was significantly colored by the experience thirty years later. What happened to May is unfortunately also not that rare. I don't know what to do about such problems, but surely there will be no genuine solutions until there is a proper recognition of the situation.

The setting for this novel is my home; Œnone used our guest bedroom. The house, cabin, landscape, roads, trees, and wildlife are as described, except for location; my avocation is tree farming. I believe that the salvation of the world well may lie in trees, and not just the commercial varieties. The community of wild creatures resides in the noncommercial wilderness.

One of the included stories was written by Santiago Hernandez, in prison for pedophilia. This is one of the few nonsexual, nonromantic entries: the one about two professors pondering exchanging their spouses, concluding with a reference to me: the ogre in the Flower State near the cartoon-comic city. This is the story Œnone did not tell; Geode dreamed she was telling it, so it was a product of his own imagination, and came out completely different from any she would have told. The point is that later, when the monster starts telling him stories, he knows it really is Œnone, because he can not invent anything similar himself. I know this one is not the kind I would devise, because I did not; to me it is mostly incomprehensible, as a wild dream might be.

But this is another bit of evidence of the problem in our society: as far as I know, Santiago Hernandez did not hurt anyone. He just happens to be sexually attracted to small boys. We assume that the only normal state is adult heterosexuality, and certainly this is my own preference, but I am in doubt whether other types of interest are not also natural to our species. Homosexual men, for example, are not likely to produce many offspring, yet around the world the percentage of homosexuals remains fairly constant at about ten percent. I suspect there is a similarly constant percentage of bisexuals, and of other supposedly deviant preferences. There seems to be a broad spectrum of human desire, and what we call normal is only the central component. May's sadistic husband was sexually normal by the standard definition. It may be that the problem is not with what is deviant, but with our definitions. I suggest in the novel that little Nymph was abused not by the man with whom she had sex, but by members of her family who warped her taste, and by the society that preferred to condemn her lover rather than address the source of the problem in her family.

Those who feel that Œnone's stories represent abnormal taste should read *My Secret Garden* by Nancy Friday, which details some of the sexual fantasies of women. Neither is Nymph an invention; similar cases are all too frequent. These aspects were from my research rather than my imagination. I don't know what is right and what is wrong; I merely hope to raise some social questions along with the entertainment provided in the novel. I suspect our priorities are confused. We have problems enough with world hunger and injustice, without making more by punishing people for deviant but perhaps harmless behavior.